D1132174

THE HUNT FOR RED OCTOBER

TOM CLANCY

BERKLEY BOOKS, NEW YORK

All the characters in this book, with the exception of Sergey Gorshkov, Yuri Padorin, Oleg Penkovskiy, Valery Sablin, Hans Tofte, and Greville Wynne, are fictitious, and any resemblance to actual persons, living or dead, is purely coincidental. The names, incidents, dialogue, and opinions expressed are products of the author's imagination and are not to be construed as real. Nothing is intended or should be interpreted as expressing or representing the views of the U.S. Navy or any other department or agency of any governmental body.

This Berkley book contains the complete
text of the original hardcover edition.
It has been completely reset in a typeface
designed for easy reading, and was printed
from new film.

THE HUNT FOR RED OCTOBER

A Berkley Book / published by arrangement with
Naval Institute Press

PRINTING HISTORY
Naval Institute Press edition published 1984
Berkley international edition / October 1985

ISBN: 0-425-08760-3

A BERKLEY BOOK ® TM 757,375
Berkley Books are published by The Berkley Publishing Group,
200 Madison Avenue, New York, New York 10016.
The name "BERKLEY" and the stylized "B" with design
are trademarks belonging to Berkley Publishing Corporation.
PRINTED IN THE UNITED STATES OF AMERICA

Acknowledgments

For technical information and advice I am especially indebted to Michael Shelton, former naval aviator; Larry Bond, whose naval wargame, "Harpoon," was adopted for the training of NROTC cadets; Drs. Gerry Sterner and Craig Jeschke; and Lieutenant Commander Gregory Young, USN.

For Ralph Chatham,
a sub driver who spoke the truth,
and for all the men who wear dolphins

THE FIRST DAY

FRIDAY, 3 DECEMBER

The Red October

Captain First Rank Marko Ramius of the Soviet Navy was dressed for the Arctic conditions normal to the Northern Fleet submarine base at Polyarnyy. Five layers of wool and oilskin enclosed him. A dirty harbor tug pushed his submarine's bow around to the north, facing down the channel. The dock that had held his *Red October* for two interminable months was now a water-filled concrete box, one of the many specially built to shelter strategic missile submarines from the harsh elements. On its edge a collection of sailors and dockyard workers watched his ship sail in stolid Russian fashion, without a wave or a cheer.

"Engines ahead slow, Kamarov," he ordered. The tug slid out of the way, and Ramius glanced aft to see the water stirring from the force of the twin bronze propellers. The tug's commander waved. Ramius returned the gesture. The tug had done a simple job, but done it quickly and well. The *Red October,* a *Typhoon*-class sub, moved under her own power towards the main ship channel of the Kola Fjord.

"There's *Purga*, Captain." Gregoriy Kamarov pointed to the icebreaker that would escort them to sea. Ramius nodded. The two hours required to transit the channel would tax not his seamanship but his endurance. There was a cold north wind blowing, the only sort of north wind in this part of the world. Late autumn had been surprisingly mild, and scarcely any snow had fallen in an area that measures it in meters; then a week before a major winter storm had savaged the Murmansk coast, breaking pieces off the Arctic icepack. The icebreaker was no formality. The *Purga* would butt aside any ice that might have drifted overnight into the channel. It would not do at all for the Soviet Navy's newest missile submarine to be damaged by an errant chunk of frozen water.

The water in the fjord was choppy, driven by the brisk wind. It began to lap over the *October*'s spherical bow, rolling back down the flat missile deck which lay before the towering black sail. The water was coated with the bilge oil of numberless ships, filth that would not evaporate in the low temperatures and that left a black ring on the rocky walls of the fjord as though from the bath of a slovenly giant. An altogether apt simile, Ramius thought. The Soviet giant cared little for the dirt it left on the face of the earth, he grumbled to himself. He had learned his seamanship as a boy on inshore fishing boats, and knew what it was to be in harmony with nature.

"Increase speed to one-third," he said. Kamarov repeated his captain's order over the bridge telephone. The water stirred more as the *October* moved astern of the *Purga*. Captain Lieutenant Kamarov was the ship's navigator, his last duty station having been harbor pilot for the large combatant vessels based on both sides of the wide inlet. The two officers kept a weather eye on the armed icebreaker three hundred meters ahead. The *Purga*'s after deck had a handful of crewmen stomping about in the cold, one wearing the white apron of a ship's cook. They wanted to witness the *Red October*'s first operational cruise, and besides, sailors will do almost anything to break the monotony of their duties.

Ordinarily it would have irritated Ramius to have his ship escorted out—the channel here was wide and deep—but not today. The ice was something to worry about. And so, for Ramius, was a great deal else.

"So, my Captain, again we go to sea to serve and protect the *Rodina!*" Captain Second Rank Ivan Yurievich Putin poked his head through the hatch—without permission, as usual—and clambered up the ladder with the awkwardness of a landsman. The tiny control station was already crowded enough with the captain, the navigator, and a mute lookout. Putin was the ship's *zampolit* (political officer). Everything he did was to serve the *Rodina* (Motherland), a word that had mystical connotations to a Russian and, along with V. I. Lenin, was the Communist party's substitute for a godhead.

"Indeed, Ivan," Ramius replied with more good cheer than he felt. "Two weeks at sea. It is good to leave the dock. A seaman belongs at sea, not tied alongside, overrun with bureaucrats and workmen with dirty boots. And we will be warm."

"You find this cold?" Putin asked incredulously.

For the hundredth time Ramius told himself that Putin was the perfect political officer. His voice was always too loud, his humor too affected. He never allowed a person to forget what he was. The perfect political officer, Putin was an easy man to fear.

"I have been in submarines too long, my friend. I grow accustomed to moderate temperatures and a stable deck under my feet." Putin did not notice the veiled insult. He'd been assigned to submarines after his first tour on destroyers had been cut short by chronic seasickness—and perhaps because he did not resent the close confinement aboard submarines, something that many men cannot tolerate.

"Ah, Marko Aleksandrovich, in Gorkiy on a day like this, flowers bloom!"

"And what sort of flowers might those be, Comrade Political Officer?" Ramius surveyed the fjord through his binoculars. At noon the sun was barely over the southeast horizon, casting orange light and purple shadows along the rocky walls.

"Why, snow flowers, of course," Putin said, laughing loudly. "On a day like this the faces of the children and the women glow pink, your breath trails behind you like a cloud, and the vodka tastes especially fine. Ah, to be in Gorkiy on a day like this!"

The bastard ought to work for Intourist, Ramius told himself, except that Gorkiy is a city closed to foreigners. He had been there twice. It had struck him as a typical Soviet city, full of ramshackle buildings, dirty streets, and ill-clad citizens. As it was in most Russian cities, winter was Gorkiy's best season. The snow hid all the dirt. Ramius, half Lithuanian, had childhood memories of a better place, a coastal village whose Hanseatic origin had left rows of presentable buildings.

It was unusual for anyone other than a Great Russian to be aboard—much less command—a Soviet naval vessel. Marko's father, Aleksandr Ramius, had been a hero of the Party, a dedicated, believing Communist who had served Stalin faithfully and well. When the Soviets first occupied Lithuania in 1940, the elder Ramius was instrumental in rounding up political dissidents, shop owners, priests, and anyone else who might have been troublesome to the new regime. All were shipped off to fates that now even Moscow could only guess at. When the Germans invaded a year later, Aleksandr fought heroically as a political commissar, and was later to distinguish himself in the Battle of Leningrad. In 1944 he returned to his native land with the spearhead of the Eleventh Guards Army to wreak bloody vengeance on those who had collaborated with the Germans or been suspected of such. Marko's father had been a true Soviet hero—and Marko was deeply ashamed to be his son. His mother's health had been broken during the endless siege of Leningrad. She died giving birth to him, and he was raised by his paternal grandmother in Lithuania while his father strutted through the Party Central Committee in Vilnius, awaiting his promotion to Moscow. He got that, too, and was a candidate member of the Politburo when his life was cut short by a heart attack.

Marko's shame was not total. His father's prominence had made his current goal a possibility, and Marko planned to wreak his own vengeance on the Soviet Union, enough, perhaps, to satisfy the thousands of his countrymen who had died before he was even born.

"Where we are going, Ivan Yurievich, it will be colder still."

Putin clapped his captain's shoulder. Was his affection feigned or real? Marko wondered. Probably real. Ramius was an honest man, and he recognized that this short, loud oaf did have some human feelings.

"Why is it, Comrade Captain, that you always seem glad to leave the *Rodina* and go to sea?"

Ramius smiled behind his binoculars. "A seaman has one country, Ivan Yurievich, but two wives. You never understand that. Now I go to my other wife, the cold, heartless one that owns my soul." Ramius paused. The smile vanished. "My only wife, now."

Putin was quiet for once, Marko noted. The political officer had been there, had cried real tears as the coffin of polished pine rolled into the cremation chamber. For Putin the death of Natalia Bogdanova Ramius had been a cause of grief, but beyond that the act of an uncaring God whose existence he regularly denied. For Ramius it had been a crime committed not by God but the State. An unnecessary, monstrous crime, one that demanded punishment.

"Ice." The lookout pointed.

"Loose-pack ice, starboard side of the channel, or perhaps something calved off the east-side glacier. We'll pass well clear," Kamarov said.

"Captain!" The bridge speaker had a metallic voice. "Message from fleet headquarters."

"Read it."

"'Exercise area clear. No enemy vessels in vicinity. Proceed as per orders. Signed, Korov, Fleet Commander.'"

"Acknowledged," Ramius said. The speaker clicked off. "So, no *Amerikantsi* about?"

"You doubt the fleet commander?" Putin inquired.

"I hope he is correct," Ramius replied, more sincerely than his political officer would appreciate. "But you remember our briefings."

Putin shifted on his feet. Perhaps he was feeling the cold.

"Those American 688-class submarines, Ivan, the *Los Angeles*es. Remember what one of their officers told our spy? That they could sneak up on a whale and bugger it before it knew they were there? I wonder how the KGB got that bit of information. A beautiful Soviet agent, trained in the ways of the decadent West, too skinny, the way the imperialists like their women, blond hair . . ." The captain grunted amusement. "Probably the American officer was a boastful boy, trying to find a way to do something similar to our agent, no? And feeling his liquor, like most sailors. Still. The American *Los*

Angeles class, and the new British *Trafalgar*s, those we must guard against. They are a threat to us."

"The Americans are good technicians, Comrade Captain," Putin said, "but they are not giants. Their technology is not so awesome. *Nasha lutcha,"* he concluded. Ours is better.

Ramius nodded thoughtfully, thinking to himself that *zampoliti* really ought to know something about the ships they supervised, as mandated by Party doctrine.

"Ivan, didn't the farmers around Gorkiy tell you it is the wolf you do not see that you must fear? But don't be overly concerned. With this ship we will teach them a lesson, I think."

"As I told the Main Political Administration," Putin clapped Ramius' shoulder again, *"Red October* is in the best of hands!"

Ramius and Kamarov both smiled at that. You son of a bitch! the captain thought, saying in front of my men that *you* must pass on my fitness to command! A man who could not command a rubber raft on a calm day! A pity you will not live to eat those words, Comrade Political Officer, and spend the rest of your life in the gulag for that misjudgment. It would almost be worth leaving you alive.

A few minutes later the chop began to pick up, making the submarine roll. The movement was accentuated by their height above the deck, and Putin made excuses to go below. Still a weak-legged sailor. Ramius shared the observation silently with Kamarov, who smiled agreement. Their unspoken contempt for the *zampolit* was a most un-Soviet thought.

The next hour passed quickly. The water grew rougher as they approached the open sea, and their icebreaker escort began to wallow on the swells. Ramius watched her with interest. He had never been on an icebreaker, his entire career having been in submarines. They were more comfortable, but also more dangerous. He was accustomed to the danger, though, and the years of experience would stand him in good stead now.

"Sea buoy in sight, Captain." Kamarov pointed. The red lighted buoy was riding actively on the waves.

"Control room, what is the sounding?" Ramius asked over the bridge telephone.

"One hundred meters below the keel, Comrade Captain."

"Increase speed to two-thirds, come left ten degrees." Ramius looked at Kamarov. "Signal our course change to *Purga,* and hope he doesn't turn the wrong way."

Kamarov reached for the small blinker light stowed under the bridge coaming. The *Red October* began to accelerate slowly, her 30,000-ton bulk resisting the power of her engines. Presently the bow wave grew to a three-meter standing arc of water; man-made combers rolled down the missile deck, splitting against the front of the sail. The *Purga* altered course to starboard, allowing the submarine to pass well clear.

Ramius looked aft at the bluffs of the Kola Fjord. They had been carved to this shape millennia before by the remorseless pressure of towering glaciers. How many times in his twenty years of service with the Red Banner Northern Fleet had he looked at the wide, flat U-shape? This would be the last. One way or another, he'd never go back. Which way would it turn out? Ramius admitted to himself that he didn't much care. Perhaps the stories his grandmother had taught him were true, about God and the reward for a good life. He hoped so—it would be good if Natalia were not truly dead. In any case, there was no turning back. He had left a letter in the last mailbag taken off before sailing. There was no going back after that.

"Kamarov, signal to *Purga*: 'Diving at—,'" he checked his watch, "'—1320 hours. Exercise OCTOBER FROST begins as scheduled. You are released to other assigned duties. We will return as scheduled.'"

Kamarov worked the trigger on the blinker light to transmit the message. The *Purga* responded at once, and Ramius read the flashing signal unaided: "IF THE WHALES DON'T EAT YOU. GOOD LUCK TO *RED OCTOBER!*"

Ramius lifted the phone again, pushing the button for the sub's radio room. He had the same message transmitted to fleet headquarters, Severomorsk. Next he addressed the control room.

"Depth under the keel?"

"One hundred forty meters, Comrade Captain."

"Prepare to dive." He turned to the lookout and ordered him below. The boy moved towards the hatch. He was probably glad to return to the warmth below, but took the time for one last look at the cloudy sky and receding cliffs. Going to sea on a submarine was always exciting, and always a little sad.

"Clear the bridge. Take the conn when you get below, Gregoriy." Kamarov nodded and dropped down the hatch, leaving the captain alone.

Ramius made one last careful scan of the horizon. The sun

was barely visible aft, the sky leaden, the sea black except for the splash of whitecaps. He wondered if he were saying goodbye to the world. If so, he would have preferred a more cheerful view of it.

Before sliding down he inspected the hatch seat, pulling it shut with a chain and making sure the automatic mechanism functioned properly. Next he dropped eight meters down the inside of the sail to the pressure hull, then two more into the control room. A *michman* (warrant officer) shut the second hatch and with a powerful spin turned the locking wheel as far as it would go.

"Gregoriy?" Ramius asked.

"Straight board shut," the navigator said crisply, pointing to the diving board. All hull-opening indicator lights showed green, safe. "All systems aligned and checked for dive. The compensation is entered. We are rigged for dive."

The captain made his own visual inspection of mechanical, electrical, and hydraulic indicators. He nodded, and the *michman* of the watch unlocked the vent controls.

"Dive," Ramius ordered, moving to the periscope to relieve Vasily Borodin, his *starpom* (executive officer). Kamarov pulled the diving alarm, and the hull reverberated with the racket of a loud buzzer.

"Flood the main ballast tanks. Rig out the diving planes. Ten degrees down-angle on the planes," Kamarov ordered, his eyes alert to see that every crewman did his job exactly. Ramius listened carefully but did not look. Kamarov was the best young seaman he had ever commanded, and had long since earned his captain's trust.

The *Red October*'s hull was filled with the noise of rushing air as vents at the top of the ballast tanks were opened and water entering from the tank floods at the bottom chased the buoying air out. It was a lengthy process, for the submarine had many such tanks, each carefully subdivided by numerous cellular baffles. Ramius adjusted the periscope lens to look down and saw the black water change briefly to foam.

The *Red October* was the largest and finest command Ramius had ever had, but the sub had one major flaw. She had plenty of engine power and a new drive system that he hoped would befuddle American and Soviet submarines alike, but she was so big that she changed depth like a crippled whale. Slow going up, even slower going down.

"Scope under." Ramius stepped away from the instrument after what seemed a long wait. "Down periscope."

"Passing forty meters," Kamarov said.

"Level off at one hundred meters." Ramius watched his crewmen now. The first dive could make experienced men shudder, and half his crew were farmboys straight from training camp. The hull popped and creaked under the pressure of the surrounding water, something that took getting used to. A few of the younger men went pale but stood rigidly upright.

Kamarov began the procedure for leveling off at the proper depth. Ramius watched with a pride he might have felt for his own son as the lieutenant gave the necessary orders with precision. He was the first officer Ramius had recruited. The control room crew snapped to his command. Five minutes later the submarine slowed her descent at ninety meters and settled the next ten to a perfect stop at one hundred.

"Well done, Comrade Lieutenant. You have the conn. Slow to one-third speed. Have the sonarmen listen on all passive systems." Ramius turned to leave the control room, motioning Putin to follow him.

And so it began.

Ramius and Putin went aft to the submarine's wardroom. The captain held the door open for the political officer, then closed and locked it behind himself. The *Red October*'s wardroom was a spacious affair for a submarine, located immediately forward of the galley, aft of the officer accommodations. Its walls were soundproofed, and the door had a lock because her designers had known that not everything the officers had to say was necessarily for the ears of the enlisted men. It was large enough for all of the *October*'s officers to eat as a group— though at least three of them would always be on duty. The safe containing the ship's orders was here, not in the captain's stateroom where a man might use his solitude to try opening it by himself. It had two dials. Ramius had one combination, Putin the other. Which was hardly necessary, since Putin undoubtedly knew their mission orders already. So did Ramius, but not all the particulars.

Putin poured tea as the captain checked his watch against

the chronometer mounted on the bulkhead. Fifteen minutes until he could open the safe. Putin's courtesy made him uneasy.

"Two more weeks of confinement," the *zampolit* said, stirring his tea.

"The Americans do this for two *months,* Ivan. Of course, their submarines are far more comfortable." Despite her huge bulk, the *October*'s crew accommodations would have shamed a gulag jailer. The crew consisted of fifteen officers, housed in fairly decent cabins aft, and a hundred enlisted men whose bunks were stuffed into corners and racks throughout the bow, forward of the missile room. The *October*'s size was deceptive. The interior of her double hull was crammed with missiles, torpedoes, a nuclear reactor and its support equipment, a huge backup diesel power plant, and bank of nickle-cadmium batteries outside the pressure hull, which was ten times the size of its American counterparts. Running and maintaining the ship was a huge job for so small a crew, even though extensive use of automation made her the most modern of Soviet naval vessels. Perhaps the men didn't need proper bunks. They would only have four or six hours a day to make use of them. This would work to Ramius' advantage. Half of his crew were draftees on their first operational cruise, and even the more experienced men knew little enough. The strength of his enlisted crew, unlike that of Western crews, resided much more in his eleven *michmanyy* (warrant officers) than in his *glavnyy starshini* (senior petty officers). All of them were men who would do—were specifically trained to do—exactly what their officers told them. And Ramius had picked the officers.

"You want to cruise for two months?" Putin asked.

"I have done it on diesel submarines. A submarine belongs at sea, Ivan. Our mission is to strike fear into the hearts of the imperialists. We do not accomplish this tied up in our barn at Polyarnyy most of the time, but we cannot stay at sea any longer because any period over two weeks and the crew loses efficiency. In two weeks this collection of children will be a mob of numbed robots." Ramius was counting on that.

"And we could solve this by having capitalist luxuries?" Putin sneered.

"A true Marxist is objective, Comrade Political Officer," Ramius chided, savoring this last argument with Putin. "Objectively, that which aids us in carrying out our mission is good,

that which hinders us is bad. Adversity is supposed to hone
one's spirit and skill, not dull them. Just being aboard a submarine is hardship enough, is it not?"

"Not for you, Marko." Putin grinned over his tea.

"I am a seaman. Our crewmen are not, most never will be.
They are a mob of farmers' sons and boys who yearn to be
factory workers. We must adjust to the times, Ivan. These
youngsters are not the same as we were."

"That is true enough," Putin agreed. "You are never satisfied, Comrade Captain. I suppose it is men like you who force
progress upon us all."

Both men knew exactly why Soviet missile submarines spent
so little of their time—barely fifteen percent of it—at sea, and
it had nothing to do with creature comforts. The *Red October*
carried twenty-six SS-N-20 Seahawk missiles, each with eight
500-kiloton multiple independently targetable reentry vehicles—MIRVs—enough to destroy two hundred cities. Land-
based bombers could only fly a few hours at a time, then had
to return to their bases. Land-based missiles arrayed along the
main East-West Soviet rail network were always where par-
amilitary troops of the KGB could get at them lest some missile
regiment commander suddenly came to realize the power at
his fingertips. But missile submarines were by definition beyond any control from land. Their entire mission was to disappear.

Given that fact, Marko was surprised that his government
had them at all. The crew of such vessels had to be trusted.
And so they sailed less often than their Western counterparts,
and when they did it was with a political officer aboard to stand
next to the commanding officer, a second captain always ready
to pass approval on every action.

"Do you think you could do it, Marko, cruise for two months
with these farmboys?"

"I prefer half-trained boys, as you know. They have less to
unlearn. Then I can train them to be seamen the right way, my
way. My personality cult?"

Putin laughed as he lit a cigarette. "That observation has
been made in the past, Marko. But you are our best teacher
and your reliability is well known." This was very true. Ramius
had sent hundreds of officers and seamen on to other submarines whose commanders were glad to have them. It was an-

other paradox that a man could engender trust within a society that scarcely recognized the concept. Of course, Ramius was a loyal Party member, the son of a Party hero who had been carried to his grave by three Politburo members. Putin waggled his finger. "You should be commanding one of our higher naval schools, Comrade Captain. Your talents would better serve the state there."

"It is a seaman I am, Ivan Yurievich. Only a seaman, not a schoolmaster—despite what they say about me. A wise man knows his limitations." And a bold one seizes opportunities. Every officer aboard had served with Ramius before, except for three junior lieutenants, who would obey their orders as readily as any wet-nosed *matros* (seaman), and the doctor, who was useless.

The chronometer chimed four bells.

Ramius stood and dialed in his three-element combination. Putin did the same, and the captain flipped the lever to open the safe's circular door. Inside was a manila envelope plus four books of cipher keys and missile-targeting coordinates. Ramius removed the envelope, then closed the door, spinning both dials before sitting down again."

"So, Ivan, what do you suppose our orders tell us to do?" Ramius asked theatrically.

"Our duty, Comrade Captain." Putin smiled.

"Indeed." Ramius broke the wax seal on the envelope and extracted the four-page operation order. He read it quickly. It was not complicated.

"So, we are to proceed to grid square 54-90 and rendezvous with our attack submarine *V. K. Konovalov*—that's Captain Tupolev's new command. You know Viktor Tupolev? No? Viktor will guard us from imperialist intruders, and we will conduct a four-day acquisition and tracking drill, with him hunting us— if he can." Ramius chuckled. "The boys in the attack submarine directorate still have not figured how to track our new drive system. Well, neither will the Americans. We are to confine our operations to grid square 54-90 and the immediately surrounding squares. That ought to make Viktor's task a bit easier."

"But you will not let him find us?"

"Certainly not," Ramius snorted. "Let? Viktor was once my pupil. You give nothing to an enemy, Ivan, even in a drill. The imperialists certainly won't! In trying to find us, he also practices finding their missile submarines. He will have a fair chance of locating us, I think. The exercise is confined to nine squares, forty thousand square kilometers. We shall see what he has learned since he served with us—oh, that's right, you weren't with me then. That's when I had the *Suslov*."

"Do I see disappointment?"

"No, not really. The four-day drill with *Konovalov* will be interesting diversion." Bastard, he said to himself, you knew beforehand exactly what our orders were—and you do know Viktor Tupolev, liar. It was time.

Putin finished his cigarette and his tea before standing. "So, again I am permitted to watch the master captain at work—befuddling a poor boy." He turned towards the door. "I think—"

Ramius kicked Putin's feet out from under him just as he was stepping away from the table. Putin fell backwards while Ramius sprang to his feet and grasped the political officer's head in his strong fisherman's hands. The captain drove his neck downward to the sharp, metal-edged corner of the ward-room table. It struck the point. In the same instant Ramius pushed down on the man's chest. An unnecessary gesture—with the sickening crackle of bones Ivan Putin's neck broke, his spine severed at the level of the second cervical vertebra, a perfect hangman's fracture.

The political officer had no time to react. The nerves to his body below the neck were instantly cut off from the organs and muscles they controlled. Putin tried to shout, to say something, but his mouth flapped open and shut without a sound except for the exhalation of his last lungful of air. He tried to gulp air down like a landed fish, and this did not work. Then his eyes went up to Ramius, wide in shock—there was no pain, and no emotion but surprise. The captain laid him gently on the tile deck.

Ramius saw the face flash with recognition, then darken. He reached down to take Putin's pulse. It was nearly two minutes before the heart stopped completely. When Ramius was sure that his political officer was dead, he took the teapot from the table and poured two cups' worth on the deck, careful to drip some on the man's shoes. Next he lifted the body to the wardroom table and threw open the door.

"Dr. Petrov to the wardroom at once!"

The ship's medical office was only a few steps aft. Petrov was there in seconds, along with Vasily Borodin, who had hurried aft from the control room.

"He slipped on the deck where I spilled my tea," Ramius gasped, performing closed heart massage on Putin's chest. "I tried to keep him from falling, but he hit his head on the table.

Petrov shoved the captain aside, moved the body around, and leapt on the table to kneel astride it. He tore the shirt open, then checked Putin's eyes. Both pupils were wide and fixed. The doctor felt around the man's head, his hands working downward to the neck. They stopped there, probing. The doctor shook his head slowly.

"Comrade Putin is dead. His neck is broken." The doctor's hands came loose, and he closed the *zampolit*'s eyes.

"No!" Ramius shouted. "He was alive only a minute ago!" The commanding officer was sobbing. "It's my fault. I tried to catch him, but I failed. My fault!" He collapsed into a chair and buried his face in his hands. "My fault," he cried, shaking his head in rage, struggling visibly to regain his composure. An altogether excellent performance.

Petrov placed his hand on the captain's shoulder. "It was an accident, Comrade Captain. These things happen, even to experienced men. It was not your fault. Truly, Comrade."

Ramius swore under his breath, regaining control of himself. "There is nothing you can do?"

Petrov shook his head. "Even in the finest clinic in the Soviet Union nothing could be done. Once the spinal cord is severed, there is no hope. Death is virtually instantaneous—but also it is quite painless," the doctor added consolingly.

Ramius drew himself up as he took a long breath, his face set. "Comrade Putin was a good shipmate, a loyal Party member, and a fine officer." Out the corner of his eye he noticed Borodin's mouth twitch. "Comrades, we will continue our mission! Dr. Petrov, you will carry our comrade's body to the freezer. This is—gruesome, I know, but he deserves and will get an honorable military funeral, with his shipmates in attendance, as it should be, when we return to port."

"Will this be reported to fleet headquarters?" Petrov asked.

"We cannot. Our orders are to maintain strict radio silence." Ramius handed the doctor a set of operations orders from his pocket. Not those taken from the safe. "Page three, Comrade Doctor."

Petrov's eyes went wide reading the operational directive. "I would prefer to report this, but our orders are explicit: Once we dive, no transmissions of any kind, for any reason."

Petrov handed the papers back. "Too bad, our comrade would have looked forward to this. But orders are orders."

"And we shall carry them out."

"Putin would have it no other way," Petrov agreed.

"Borodin, observe: I take the comrade political officer's missile control key from his neck, as per regulations," Ramius said, pocketing the key and chain.

"I note this, and will so enter it in the log," the executive officer said gravely.

Petrov brought in his medical corpsman. Together they took the body aft to the medical office, where it was zippered into a body bag. The corpsman and a pair of sailors then took it forward, through the control room, into the missile compartment. The entrance to the freezer was on the lower missile deck, and the men carried the body through the door. While two cooks removed food to make room for it, the body was set reverently down in the corner. Aft, the doctor and the executive officer made the necessary inventory of personal effects, one copy for the ship's medical file, another for the ship's log, and a third for a box that was sealed and locked up in the medical office.

Forward, Ramius took the conn in a subdued control room. He ordered the submarine to a course of two-nine-zero degrees, west-northwest. Grid square 54-90 was to the east.

THE SECOND DAY

SATURDAY, 4 DECEMBER

The Red October

It was the custom in the Soviet Navy for the commanding officer to announce his ship's operational orders and to exhort the crew to carry them out in true Soviet fashion. The orders were then posted for all to see—and be inspired by—outside the ship's Lenin Room. In large surface ships this was a classroom where political awareness classes were held. In *Red October* it was a closet-sized library near the wardroom where Party books and other ideological material were kept for the men to read. Ramius disclosed their orders the day after sailing to give his men the chance to settle into the ship's routine. At the same time he gave a pep talk. Ramius always gave a good one. He'd had a lot of practice. At 0800 hours, when the forenoon watch was set, he entered the control room and took some file cards from an inside jacket pocket.

"Comrades!" he began, talking into the microphone, "this is the captain speaking. You all know that our beloved friend and comrade, Captain Ivan Yurievich Putin, died yesterday in a tragic accident. Our orders do not permit us to inform fleet

17

headquarters of this. Comrades, we will dedicate our efforts and our work to the memory of our comrade, Ivan Yurievich Putin—a fine shipmate, an honorable Party member, and a courageous officer.

"Comrades! Officer and men of *Red October!* We have orders from the Red Banner Northern Fleet High Command, and they are orders worthy of this ship and this crew!

"Comrades! Our orders are to make the ultimate test of our new silent propulsion system. We are to head *west,* past the North Cape of America's imperialist puppet state, Norway, then to turn southwest towards the Atlantic Ocean. We will pass all of the imperialist sonar nets, and we will *not* be detected! This will be a true test of our submarine and his capabilities. Our own ships will engage in a major exercise too locate us and at the same time to befuddle the arrogant imperialist navies. Our mission, first of all, is to evade detection by anyone. We will teach the Americans a lesson about Soviet technology that they will not soon forget! Our orders are to continue southwest, skirting the American coast to challenge and defeat their newest and best hunter submarines. We will proceed all the way to our socialist brothers in Cuba, and we will be the *first ship* to make use of a new and supersecret nuclear submarine base that we have been building for two years right under their imperialist noses on the south coast of Cuba. A fleet replenishment vessel is already en route to rendezvous with us there.

"Comrades! If we succeed in reaching Cuba undetected by the imperialists—and we will!—the officers and men of *Red October* will have a week—*a week*—of shore leave to visit our fraternal socialist comrades on the beautiful island of Cuba. I have been there, comrades, and you will find it to be exactly what you have read, a paradise of warm breezes, palm trees, and comradely good fellowship." By which Ramius meant women. "After this we will return to the Motherland by the same route. By this time, of course, the imperialists will know who and what we are, from their slinking spies and cowardly reconnaissance aircraft. It is intended that they should know this, because we will again evade detection on the trip home. This will let the imperialists know that they may not trifle with the men of the Soviet Navy, that we can approach their coast at the time of our choosing, and that they must respect the Soviet Union!

"Comrades! We will make the first cruise of *Red October* a memorable one!"

Ramius looked up from his prepared speech. The men on watch in the control room were exchanging grins. It was not often that a Soviet sailor was allowed to visit another country, and a visit by a nuclear submarine to a foreign country, even an ally, was nearly unprecedented. Moreover, for Russians the island of Cuba was as exotic as Tahiti, a promised land of white sand beaches and dusky girls. Ramius knew differently. He had read articles in *Red Star* and other state journals about the joys of duty in Cuba. He had also been there.

Ramius changed cards in his hands. He had given them the good news.

"Comrades! Officers and men of *Red October!*" Now for the bad news that everyone was waiting for. "This mission will not be an easy one. It demands our best efforts. We must maintain absolute radio silence, and our operating routines must be *perfect!* Rewards only come to those who truly earn them. Every officer and every man aboard, from your commanding officer to the newest *matros,* must do his socialist duty and do it well! If we work together as comrades, as the New Soviet Men we are, we shall succeed. You young comrades new to the sea: Listen to your officers, to your *michmanyy,* and to your *starshini.* Learn your duties well, and carry them out exactly. There are no small jobs on this ship, no small responsibilities. Every comrade depends for his life upon every other. Do your duty, follow your orders, and when we have completed this voyage, you will be true Soviet sailors! That is all." Ramius released his thumb from the mike switch and set it back in the cradle. Not a bad speech, he decided—a large carrot and a small stick.

In the galley aft a petty officer was standing still, holding a warm loaf of bread and looking curiously at the bulkhead-mounted speaker. That wasn't what their orders were supposed to be, was it? Had there been a change in plans? The *michman* pointed him back to his duties, grinning and chuckling at the prospect of a week in Cuba. He had heard a lot of stories about Cuba and Cuban women and was looking forward to seeing if they were true.

In the control room Ramius mused. "I wonder if any American submarines are about?"

"Indeed, Comrade Captain," nodded Captain Second Rank Borodin, who had the watch. "Shall we engage the caterpillar?"

"Proceed, Comrade."

"Engines all stop," Borodin ordered.

"All stop." The quartermaster, a *starshina* (petty officer), dialed the annunciator to the STOP position. An instant later the order was confirmed by the inner dial, and a few seconds after that the dull rumble of the engines died away.

Borodin picked up the phone and punched the button for engineering. "Comrade Chief Engineer, prepare to engage the caterpillar."

It wasn't the official name for the new drive system. It had no name as such, just a project number. The nickname *caterpillar* had been given it by a young engineer who had been involved in the sub's development. Neither Ramius nor Borodin knew why, but as often happens with such names, it had stuck.

"Ready, Comrade Borodin," the chief engineer reported back in a moment.

"Open doors fore and aft," Borodin ordered next.

The *michman* of the watch reached up the control board and threw four switches. The status light over each changed from red to green. "Doors show open, Comrade."

"Engage caterpillar. Build speed slowly to thirteen knots."

"Build slowly to one-three knots, Comrade," the engineer acknowledged.

The hull, which had gone momentarily silent, now had a new sound. The engine noises were lower and very different from what they had been. The reactor plant noises, mainly from pumps that circulated the cooling water, were almost imperceptible. The caterpillar did not use a great deal of power for what it did. At the *michman*'s station the speed gauge, which had dropped to five knots, began to creep upward again. Forward of the missile room, in a space shoehorned into the crew's accommodations, the handful of sleeping men stirred briefly in their bunks as they noted an intermittent rumble aft and the hum of electric motors a few feet away, separated from them by the pressure hull. They were tired enough even on their first day at sea to ignore the noise, fighting back to their precious allotment of sleep.

"Caterpillar functioning normally, Comrade Captain," Borodin reported.

"Excellent. Steer two-six-zero, helm," Ramius ordered.

"Two-six-zero, Comrade." The helmsman turned his wheel to the left.

The USS Bremerton

Thirty miles to the northeast, the USS *Bremerton* was on a heading of two-two-five, just emerging from under the icepack. A 688-class attack submarine, she had been on an ELINT—electronic intelligence gathering—mission in the Kara Sea when she was ordered west to the Kola Peninsula. The Russian missile boat wasn't supposed to have sailed for another week, and the *Bremerton*'s skipper was annoyed at this latest intelligence screw-up. He would have been in place to track the *Red October* if she had sailed as scheduled. Even so, the American sonarmen had picked up on the Soviet sub a few minutes earlier, despite the fact that they were traveling at fourteen knots.

"Conn, sonar."

Commander Wilson lifted the phone. "Conn, aye."

"Contact lost, sir. His screws stopped a few minutes ago and have not restarted. There's some other activity to the east, but the missile sub has gone dead."

"Very well. He's probably settling down to a slow drift. We'll be creeping up on him. Stay awake, Chief." Commander Wilson thought this over as he took two steps to the chart table. The two officers of the fire control tracking party who had just been establishing the track for the contact looked up to learn their commander's opinion.

"If it was me, I'd go down near the bottom and circle slowly right about here." Wilson traced a rough circle on the chart that enclosed the *Red October*'s position. "So let's creep up on him. We'll reduce speed to five knots and see if we can move in and reacquire him from his reactor plant noise." Wilson turned to the officer of the deck. "Reduce speed to five knots."

"Aye, Skipper."

Severomorsk, USSR

In the Central Post Office building in Severomorsk a mail sorter watched sourly as a truck driver dumped a large canvas sack on his work table and went back out the door. He was late—well, not really late, the clerk corrected himself, since the idiot had not been on time once in five years. It was a Saturday,

and he resented being at work. Only a few years before, the
forty-hour week had been started in the Soviet Union. Unfortunately this change had never affected such vital public services as mail delivery. So, here he was, still working a six-day
week—and without extra pay! A disgrace, he thought, and
had said often enough in his apartment, playing cards with his
workmates over vodka and cucumbers.

He untied the drawstring and turned the sack over. Several
smaller bags tumbled out. There was no sense in hurrying. It
was only the beginning of the month, and they still had weeks
to move their quota of letters and parcels from one side of the
building to the other. In the Soviet Union every worker is a
government worker, and they have a saying: As long as the
bosses pretend to pay us, we will pretend to work.

Opening a small mailbag, he pulled out an official-looking
envelope addressed to the Main Political Administration of the
Navy in Moscow. The clerk paused, fingering the envelope. It
probably came from one of the submarines based at Polyarnyy,
on the other side of the fjord. What did the letter say? the sorter
wondered, playing the mental game that amused mailmen all
over the world. Was it an announcement that all was ready for
the final attack on the imperialist West? A list of Party members
who were late paying their dues, or a requisition for more toilet
paper? There was no telling. Submariners! They were all prima
donnas—even the farmboy conscripts still picking shit from
between their toes paraded around like members of the Party
elite.

The clerk was sixty-two. In the Great Patriotic War he had
been a tankrider serving in a guards tank corps attached to
Konev's First Ukrainian Front. That, he told himself, was a
man's job, riding into action on the back of the great battle
tanks, leaping off to hunt for the German infantrymen as they
cowered in their holes. When something needed doing against
those slugs, it was *done!* Now what had become of Soviet
fighting men? Living aboard luxury liners with plenty of good
food and warm beds. The only warm bed he had ever known
was over the exhaust vent of his tank's diesel—and he'd had
to fight for that! It was crazy what the world had become. Now
sailors acted like czarist princes and wrote tons of letters back
and forth and called it work. These pampered boys didn't know
what hardship was. And their privileges! Every word they com-

mitted to paper was priority mail. Whimpering letters to their sweethearts, most of it, and here he was sorting through it all on a Saturday to see that it got to their womenfolk—even though they couldn't possibly have a reply for two weeks. It just wasn't like the old days.

The sorter tossed the envelope with a negligent flick of the wrist towards the surface mailbag for Moscow on the far side of his work table. It missed, dropping to the concrete floor. The letter would be placed aboard the train a day late. The sorter didn't care. There was a hockey game that night, the biggest game of the young season, Central Army against Wings. He had a liter of vodka bet on Wings.

Morrow, England

"Halsey's greatest popular success was his greatest error. In establishing himself as a popular hero with legendary aggressiveness, the admiral would blind later generations to his impressive intellectual abilities and a shrewd gambler's instinct to—" Jack Ryan frowned at his computer. It sounded too much like a doctoral dissertation, and he had already done one of those. He thought of dumping the whole passage from the memory disk but decided against it. He had to follow this line of reasoning for his introduction. Bad as it was, it did serve as a guide for what he wanted to say. Why was it that introductions always seemed to be the hardest part of a history book? For three years now he had been working on *Fighting Sailor*, an authorized biography of Fleet Admiral William Halsey. Nearly all of it was contained on a half-dozen floppy disks lying next to his Apple computer.

"Daddy?" Ryan's daughter was staring up at him.

"And how's my little Sally today?"

"Fine."

Ryan picked her up and set her on his lap, careful to slide his chair away from the keyboard. Sally was all checked out on games and educational programs, and occasionally thought that this meant she was able to handle Wordstar also. Once that had resulted in the loss of twenty thousand words of electronically recorded manuscript. And a spanking.

She leaned her head against her father's shoulder.

"You don't look fine. What's bothering my little girl?"

"Well, Daddy, y'see, it's almost Chris'mas, an . . . I'm not sure that Santa knows where we are. We're not where we were last year."

"Oh, I see. And you're afraid he doesn't come here?"

"Uh huh."

"Why didn't you ask me before? Of course he comes here. Promise."

"Promise?"

"Promise."

"Okay." She kissed her father and ran out of the room, back to watching cartoons on the telly, as they called it in England. Ryan was glad she had interrupted him. He didn't want to forget to pick up a few things when he flew over to Washington. Where was—oh, yeah. He pulled a disk from his desk drawer and inserted it in the spare disk drive. After clearing the screen, he scrolled up the Christmas list, things he still had to get. With a simple command a copy of the list was made on the adjacent printer. Ryan tore the page off and tucked it in his wallet. Work didn't appeal to him this Saturday morning. He decided to play with his kids. After all, he'd be stuck in Washington for much of the coming week.

The V. K. Konovalov

The Soviet submarine *V. K. Konovalov* crept above the hard sand bottom of the Barents Sea at three knots. She was at the southwest corner of grid square 54-90 and for the past ten hours had been drifting back and forth on a north-south line, waiting for the *Red October* to arrive for the beginning of Exercise OCTOBER FROST. Captain Second Rank Viktor Alexievich Tupolev paced slowly around the periscope pedestal in the control room of his small, fast attack sub. He was waiting for his old mentor to show up, hoping to play a few tricks on him. He had served with the Schoolmaster for two years. They had been good years, and while he found his former commander to be something of a cynic, especially about the Party, he would unhesitatingly testify to Ramius' skill and craftiness.

And his own. Tupolev, now in his third year of command, had been one of the Schoolmaster's star pupils. His current vessel was a brand-new *Alfa,* the fastest submarine ever made. A month earlier, while Ramius had been fitting out the *Red*

October after her initial shakedown, Tupolev and three of his officers had flown down to see the model sub that had been the test-bed for the prototype drive system. Thirty-two meters long and diesel-electric powered, it was based in the Caspian Sea, far from the eyes of imperialist spies, and kept in a covered dock, hidden from their photographic satellites. Ramius had had a hand in the development of the caterpillar, and Tupolev recognized the mark of the master. It would be a bastard to detect. Not quite impossible, though. After a week of following the model around the north end of the Caspian Sea in an electrically powered launch, trailing the best passive sonar array his country had yet made, he thought he had found a flaw. Not a big one, just big enough to exploit.

Of course there was no guarantee of success. He was not only in competition with a machine, but also with the captain commanding her. Tupolev knew this area intimately. The water was almost perfectly isothermal; there was no thermal layer for a submarine to hide under. They were far enough from the freshwater rivers on the north coast of Russia not to have to worry about pools and walls of variable salinity interfering with their sonar searches. The *Konovalov* had been built with the best sonar systems the Soviet Union had yet produced, copied closely from the French DUUV-23 and a bit improved, the factory technicians said.

Tupolev planned to mimic the American tactic of drifting slowly, with just enough speed to maintain steerage, perfectly quiet and waiting for the *Red October* to cross his path. He would then trail his quarry closely and log each change in course and speed, so that when they compared logs in a few weeks the Schoolmaster would see that his erstwhile student had played his own winning game. It was about time someone did.

"Anything new on sonar?" Tupolev was getting tense. Patience came hard to him.

"Nothing new, Comrade Captain." The *starpom* tapped the X on the chart that marked the position of the *Rokossovskiy,* a *Delta*-class missile sub they had ben tracking for several hours in the same exercise area. "Our friend is still cruising in a slow circle. Do you think that *Rokossovskiy* might be trying to confuse us? Would Captain Ramius have arranged for him to be here, to complicate our task?"

The thought had occurred to Tupolev. "Perhaps, but prob-

ably not. This exercise was arranged by Korov himself. Our
mission orders were sealed, and Marko's orders should have
been also. But then, Admiral Korov is an old friend of our
Marko." Tupolev paused for a moment and shook his head.
"No. Korov is an honorable man. I think Ramius is proceeding
this way as slowly as he can. To make us nervous, to make us
question ourselves. He will know we are to hunt him and will
adjust his plans accordingly. He might try to enter the square
from an unexpected direction—or to make us think that he is.
You have never served under Ramius, Comrade Lieutenant.
He is a fox, that one, an old gray-whiskered fox. I think we
will continue to patrol as we are for another four hours. If we
have not yet acquired him then, we will cross over to the
southeast corner of the square and work our way in to the
center. Yes."

Tupolev had never expected that this would be easy. No
attack submarine commander had ever embarrassed Ramius.
He was determined to be the first, and the difficulty of the task
would only confirm his own prowess. In one or two more years,
Tupolev planned to be the new master.

THE THIRD DAY

SUNDAY, 5 DECEMBER

The Red October

The *Red October* had no time of her own. For her the sun neither rose nor set, and the days of the week had little significance. Unlike surface ships, which changed their clocks to conform with the local time wherever they were, submarines generally adhered to a single time reference. For American subs this was Zulu, or Greenwich mean time. For the *Red October* it was Moscow standard time, which by normal reckoning was actually one hour ahead of standard time to save on utility expenses.

Ramius entered the control room in mid-morning. Their course was now two-five-zero, speed thirteen knots, and the submarine was running thirty meters above the bottom at the west edge of the Barents Sea. In a few more hours the bottom would drop away to an abyssal plain, allowing them to go much deeper. Ramius examined the chart first, then the numerous banks of instruments covering both side bulkheads in the compartment. Last he made some notations in the order book.

"Lieutenant Ivanov!" he said sharply to the junior officer of the watch.

"Yes, Comrade Captain!" Ivanov was the greenest officer aboard, fresh from Lenin's Komsomol School in Leningrad, pale, skinny, and eager.

"I will be calling a meeting of the senior officers in the wardroom. You will now be the officer of the watch. This is your first cruise, Ivanov. How do you like it?"

"It is better than I had hoped, Comrade Captain," Ivanov replied with greater confidence than he could possibly have felt.

"That is good, Comrade Lieutenant. It is my practice to give junior officers as much responsibility as they can handle. While we senior officers are having our weekly political discussion, *you* are in command of this vessel! The safety of this ship and all his crew is *your* responsibility! You have been taught all you need to know, and my instructions are in the order book. If we detect another submarine or surface ship you will inform me at once and instantly initiate evasion drill. Any questions?"

"No, Comrade Captain." Ivanov was standing at rigid attention.

"Good." Ramius smiled. "Pavel Ilych, you will forever remember this as one of the great moments of your life. I know, I can still remember my first watch. Do not forget your orders or your responsibilities!"

Pride sparkled in the boy's eyes. It was too bad what would happen to him, Ramius thought, still the teacher. On first inspection, Ivanov looked to have the makings of a good officer.

Ramius walked briskly aft to the ship's medical office.

"Good morning, Doctor."

"Good morning to you, Comrade Captain. It is time for our political meeting?" Petrov had been reading the manual for the sub's new X-ray machine.

"Yes, it is, Comrade Doctor, but I do not wish you to attend. There is something else I want you to do. While the senior officers are at the meeting, I have the three youngsters standing watch in control and the engineering spaces."

"Oh?" Petrov's eyes went wide. It was his first time on a submarine in several years.

Ramius smiled. "Be at ease, Comrade. I can get from the wardroom to control in twenty seconds, as you know, and Comrade Melekhin can get to his precious reactor just as fast. Sooner or later our young officers must learn to function on their own. I prefer that they learn sooner. I want you to keep an eye on them. I know that they all have the knowledge to do their duties. I want to know if they have the temperament. If Borodin or I watch over them, they will not act normally. And in any case, this is a medical judgment, no?"

"Ah, you wish me to observe how they react to their responsibilities."

"Without the pressure of being observed by a senior line officer," Ramius confirmed. "One must give young officers room to grow—but not too much. If you observe something that you question, you will inform me at once. There should be no problems. We are in open sea, there is no traffic about, and the reactor is running at a fraction of its total power. The first test for young officers ought to be an easy one. Find some excuse for traveling back and forth, and keep an eye on the children. Ask questions about what they are doing."

Petrov laughed at that. "Ah, and also you would have me learn a few things, Comrade Captain? They told me about you at Severomorsk. Fine, it will be as you say. But this will be the first political meeting I have missed in years."

"From what your file says, you could teach Party doctrine to the Politburo, Yevgeni Konstantinovich." Which said little about his medical ability, Ramius thought.

The captain moved forward to the wardroom to join his brother officers, who were waiting for him. A steward had left several pots of tea along with black bread and butter to snack on. Ramius looked at the corner of the table. The bloodstains had long since been wiped away, but he could remember exactly what it looked like. This, he reflected, was one difference between himself and the man he had murdered. Ramius had a conscience. Before taking his seat, he turned to lock the door behind him. His officers were all sitting at attention, since the compartment was not large enough for them to stand once the bench seats were folded down.

Sunday was the normal day for the political awareness session at sea. Ordinarily Putin would have officiated, reading some *Pravda* editorials, followed by selected quotations from the works of Lenin and a discussion of the lessons to be learned from the readings. It was very much like a church service.

With the demise of the *zampolit* this duty developed upon the commanding officer, but Ramius doubted that regulations anticipated the sort of discussion on today's agenda. Each officer in this room was a member of his conspiracy. Ramius outlined their plans—there had been some minor changes which he had not mentioned to anyone. Then he told them about the letter.

"So, there is no going back," Borodin observed.

"We have all agreed upon our course of action. Now we are committed to it." Their reactions to his words were just what he expected them to be—sober. As well they might be. All were single; no one left behind a wife or children. All were Party members in good standing, their dues paid up to the end of the year, their Party cards right where they were supposed to be, "next to their hearts." And each one shared with his comrades a deep-seated dissatisfaction with, in some cases a hatred of, the Soviet government.

The planning had begun soon after the death of his Natalia. The rage he had almost unknowingly suppressed throughout his life had burst forth with a violence and passion that he had struggled to contain. A lifetime of self-control had enabled him to conceal it, and a lifetime of naval training had enabled him to choose a purpose worthy of it.

Ramius had not yet begun school when he first heard tales from other children about what his father Aleksandr had done in Lithuania in 1940 and after that country's dubious liberation from the Germans in 1944. These were the repeated whisperings of their parents. One little girl told Marko a story that he recounted to Aleksandr, and to the boy's uncomprehending horror her father vanished. For his unwitting mistake Marko was branded an informer. Stung by the name he was given for committing a crime—which the State taught was not a crime at all—whose enormity never stopped pulling at his conscience, he never informed again.

In the formative years of his life, while the elder Ramius ruled the Lithuanian Party Central Committee in Vilnius, the motherless boy was raised by his paternal grandmother, common practice in a country savaged by four years of brutal war. Her only son left home at an early age to join Lenin's Red Guards, and while he was away she kept to the old ways, going to mass every day until 1940 and never forgetting the religious education that had been passed on to her. Ramius remembered her as a silver-haired old woman who told wonderful bedtime stories. Religious stories. It would have been far too dangerous for her to bring Marko to the religious ceremonies that had never been entirely stamped out, but she did manage to have him baptized a Roman Catholic soon after his father had deposited him with her. She never told Marko about this. The risk would have been too great. Roman Catholicism had been brutally suppressed in the Baltic states. It was a religion, and as he grew older Marko learned that Marxism-Leninism was a jealous god, tolerating no competing loyalties.

Grandmother Hilda told him nighttime stories from the Bible, each with a lesson of right and wrong, virtue and reward. As a child he found them merely entertaining, but he never told his father about them because even then he knew that Aleksandr would object. After the elder Ramius again resumed control of his son's life, this religious education faded into Marko's memory, neither fully remembered nor fully forgotten.

As a boy, Ramius sensed more than thought that Soviet Communism ignored a basic human need. In his teens, his misgivings began to take a coherent shape. The Good of the People was a laudable enough goal, but in denying a man's soul, an enduring part of his being, Marxism stripped away the foundation of human dignity and individual value. It also cast aside the objective measure of justice and ethics which, he decided, was the principal legacy of religion to civilized life. From earliest adulthood on, Marko had his own idea about right and wrong, an idea he did not share with the State. It gave him a means of gauging his actions and those of others. It was something he was careful to conceal. It served as an anchor for his soul and, like an anchor, it was hidden far below the visible surface.

Even as the boy was grappling with his first doubts about his country, no one could have suspected it. Like all Soviet children, Ramius joined the Little Octobrists, then the Young Pioneers. He paraded at the requisite battle shrines in polished boots and blood-red scarf, and gravely stood watch over the remains of some unknown soldier while clasping to his chest a deactivated PPSh submachinegun, his back ramrod straight before the eternal flame. The solemnity of such duty was no accident. As a boy Marko was certain that the brave men whose graves he guarded so intensely had met their fates with the same sort of selfless heroism that he saw portrayed in endless war movies at the local cinema. They had fought the hated Germans to protect the women and children and old people behind the lines. And like a nobleman's son of an earlier Russia, he took special pride in being the son of a Party chieftain. The Party, he heard a hundred times before he was five, was the Soul of the People; the unity of Party, People, and Nation was the holy trinity of the Soviet Union, albeit with one segment more important than the others. His father fit easily into the cinematic image of a Party apparatchik. Stern but fair, to Marko he was a frequently absent, gruffly kind man who brought his son what presents he could and saw to it that he had all the advantages the son of a Party secretary was entitled to.

Although outwardly he was the model Soviet child, inwardly he wondered why what he learned from his father and in school conflicted with the other lessons of his youth. Why did some parents refuse to let their children play with him? Why when he passed them did his classmates whisper *"stukach,"* the cruel and bitter epithet of informer? His father and the Party taught that informing was an act of patriotism, but for having done it once he was shunned. He resented the taunts of his boyhood peers, but he never once complained to his father, knowing that this would be an evil thing to do.

Something was very wrong—but what? He decided that he had to find the answers for himself. By choice Marko became individual in his thinking, and so unknowingly committed the gravest sin in the Communist pantheon. Outwardly the model of a Party member's son, he played the game carefully and according to all the rules. He did his duty for all Party organizations, and was always the first to volunteer for the menial tasks allotted to children aspiring to Party membership, which he knew was the only path to success or even comfort in the Soviet Union. He became good at sports. Not team sports— he worked at track and field events in which he could compete as an individual and measure the performance of others. Over the years he learned to do the same in all of his endeavors, to watch and judge the actions of his fellow citizens and officers with cool detachment, behind a blank face that concealed his conclusions.

In the summer of his eighth year the course of his life was forever changed. When no one would play with "the little *stukach*," he would wander down to the fishing docks of the small village where his grandmother had made her home. A ragtag collection of old wooden boats sailed each morning, always behind a screen of patrol boats manned by MGB—as the KGB was then known—border guards, to reap a modest harvest from the Gulf of Finland. Their catch supplemented the local diet with needed protein and provided a minuscule income for the fishermen. One boat captain was old Sasha. An officer in the czar's navy, he had revolted with the crew of the cruiser *Avrora*, helping to spark the chain of events that changed the face of the world. Marko did not learn until many years later that the crewmen of the *Avrora* had broken with Lenin— and been savagely put down by Red Guards. Sasha had spent twenty years in labor camps for his part in that collective indiscretion and only been released at the beginning of the Great Patriotic War. The *Rodina* had found herself in need of experienced seamen to pilot ships into the ports of Murmansk and Archangel, to which the Allies were bringing weapons, food, and the sundries that allow a modern army to function. Sasha had learned his lesson in the gulag: he did his duty efficiently and well, asking for nothing in return. After the war he'd been given a kind of freedom for his services, the right to perform back-breaking work under perpetual suspicion.

By the time Marko met him, Sasha was over sixty, a nearly bald man with ropy old muscles, a seaman's eye, and a talent for stories that left the youngster wide-eyed. He'd been a midshipman under the famous Admiral Marakov at Port Arthur in 1906. Probably the finest seaman in Russian history, Marakov's reputation as a patriot and an innovative fighting sailor was sufficiently unblemished that a Communist government would eventually see fit to name a missile cruiser in his memory. At first wary of the boy's reputation, Sasha saw something in him that others missed. The boy without friends and the sailor without a family became comrades. Sasha spent hours telling and retelling the tale of how he had been on the admiral's flagship, the *Petropavlovsk,* and participated in the one Russian victory over the hated Japanese—only to have his battleship sunk and his admiral killed by a mine while returning to port. After this Sasha had led his seamen as naval infantry, winning three decorations for courage under fire. This experience—he waggled his finger seriously at the boy—taught him of the mindless corruption of the czarist regime and convinced him to join one of the first naval soviets when such action meant certain death at the hands of the czar's secret police, the *okhrana.* He told his own version of the October Revolution from the thrilling perspective of an eyewitness. But Sasha was very careful to leave the later parts out.

He allowed Marko to sail with him and taught him the fundamentals of seamanship that decided a boy not yet nine that his destiny lay on the sea. There was a freedom at sea he could never have on land. There was a romance about it that touched the man growing within the boy. There were also dangers, but in a summer-long series of simple, effective lessons, Sasha taught the boy that preparation, knowledge, and discipline can deal with any form of danger; that danger confronted properly is not something a man must fear. In later years Marko would reflect often on the value this summer had held for him, and wonder just how far Sasha's career might have led if other events had not cut it short.

Marko told his father about Sasha towards the end of that long Baltic summer and even took him to meet the old seadog. The elder Ramius was sufficiently impressed with him and what he had done for his son that he arranged for Sasha to have command of a newer, larger boat and moved him up on the list for a new apartment. Marko almost believed that the Party could do a good deed—that he himself had done his first manly good deed. But old Sasha died the following winter, and the good deed came to nothing. Many years later Marko realized that he hadn't known his friend's last name. Even after years of faithful service to the *Rodina,* Sasha had been an unperson.

At thirteen Marko traveled to Leningrad to attend the Nakhimov School. There he decided that he, too, would become a professional naval officer. Marko would follow the quest for adventure that had for centuries called young men to the sea. The Nakhimov School was a special three-year prep school for youngsters aspiring to a career at sea. The Soviet Navy at that time was little more than a coastal defense force, but Marko wanted very much to be a part of it. His father urged him to a life of Party work, promising rapid promotion, a life of comfort and privilege. But Marko wanted to earn whatever he received on his own merits, not to be remembered as an appendage of the "liberator" of Lithuania. And a life at sea offered romance and excitement that even made serving the State something he could tolerate. The navy had little tradition to build on. Marko sensed that in it there was room to grow, and saw that many aspiring naval cadets were like himself, if not mavericks then as close to mavericks as was possible in a society so closely controlled as his own. The teenager thrived with his first experience of fellowship.

Nearing graduation, his class was exposed to the various components of the Russian fleet. Ramius at once fell in love with submarines. The boats at that time were small, dirty, and smelled from the open bilges that the crews used as a convenient latrine. At the same time submarines were the only offensive arm that the navy had, and from the first Marko wanted to be on the cutting edge. He'd had enough lectures on naval history to know that submarines had twice nearly strangled England's maritime empire and had successfully emasculated the economy of Japan. This had greatly pleased him; he was glad the Americans had crushed the Japanese navy that had so nearly killed his mentor.

He graduated from the Nakhimov School first in his class, winner of the gold-plated sextant for his mastery of theoretical navigation. As leader of his class, Marko was allowed the school of his choice. He selected the Higher Naval School for Underwater Navigation, named for Lenin's Komsomol, VVMUPP, still the principal submarine school of the Soviet Union.

His five years at VVMUPP were the most demanding of his life, the more so since he was determined not to succeed but to excel. He was first in his class in every subject, in every year. His essay on the political significance of Soviet naval power was forwarded to Sergey Georgiyevich Gorshkov, then commander in chief of the Baltic Fleet and clearly the coming man in the Soviet Navy. Gorshkov had seen the essay published in *Morskoi Sbornik (Naval Collections)*, the leading Soviet naval journal. It was a model of progressive Party thought, quoting Lenin six different times.

By this time Marko's father was a candidate member of the Presidium, as the Politburo was then called, and very proud of his son. The elder Ramius was no one's fool. He finally recognized that the Red Fleet was a growing flower and that his son would someday have a position of importance in it. His influence moved his son's career rapidly along.

By thirty, Marko had his first command and a new wife. Natalia Bogdanova was the daughter of another Presidium member whose diplomatic duties had taken him and his family all over the world. Natalia had never been a healthy girl. They had no children, their three attempts each ending in miscarriage, the last of which had nearly killed her. She was a pretty, delicate woman, sophisticated by Russian standards, who polished her husband's passable English with American and British books—politically approved ones to be sure, mainly the thoughts of Western leftists, but also a smattering of genuine literature, including Hemingway, Twain, and Upton Sinclair. Along with his naval career, Natalia had been the center of his life. Their marriage, punctuated by prolonged absences and joyous returns, made their love even more precious than it might have been.

When construction began on the first class of Soviet nuclear-powered submarines, Marko found himself in the yards learning how the steel sharks were designed and built. He was soon known as a very hard man to please as a junior quality control inspector. His own life, he was aware, would ride on the workmanship of these often drunk welders and fitters. He became an expert in nuclear engineering, spent two years as a *starpom*, and then received his first nuclear command. She was a *November*-class attack submarine, the first crude attempt by the Soviets to make a battleworthy long-range attack boat to threaten Western navies and lines of communication. Not a month later a sister ship suffered a major reactor casualty off the Norwegian coast, and Marko was first to arrive on the scene. As ordered, he successfully rescued the crew, then sank the disabled sub lest Western navies learn her secrets. Both tasks he performed expertly and well, a noteworthy tour de force for a young commander. Good performance was something he had always felt it was important to reward in his subordinates, and the fleet commander at that time felt the same way. Marko soon moved on to a new *Charlie I*–class sub.

It was men like Ramius who went out to challenge the Americans and the British. Marko took few illusions with him. The Americans, he knew, had long experience in naval warfare—their own greatest fighter, Jones, had once served the Russian navy for the Czaritza Catherine. Their submariners were legendary for their craftiness, and Ramius found himself pitted against the last of the war-trained Americans, men who had endured the sweaty fear of underwater combat and utterly defeated a modern navy. The deadly serious game of hide-and-seek he played with them was not an easy one, the less so because they had submarines years ahead of Soviet design. But it was not a time without a few victories.

Ramius gradually learned to play the game by American rules, training his officers and men with care. His crews were rarely as prepared as he wished—still the Soviet Navy's greatest problem—but where other commanders cursed their men for their failings, Marko corrected the failings of his men. His first *Charlie*-class submarine was called the Vilnius Academy. This was partially a slur against his half-Lithuanian blood—though since he had been born in Leningrad of a Great Russian, his internal passport designated him as that—but mainly recognition that officers came to him half-trained and left him ready for advancement and eventual command. The same was true of his conscripted crewmen. Ramius did not permit the hazing and low-level terrorism normal throughout the Soviet military. He saw his task as the building of seamen, and he produced a greater percentage of reenlistments than any other submarine commander. A full ninth of the *michmanyy* in the Northern Fleet submarine force were Ramius-trained professionals. His brother submarine commanders were delighted to take aboard his *starshini*, and more than one advanced to officer's school.

After eighteen months of hard work and diligent training, Marko and his Vilnius Academy were ready to play their game of fox and hounds. He happened upon the USS *Triton* in the Norwegian Sea and hounded her mercilessly for twelve hours. Later he would note with no small satisfaction that the *Triton* was soon thereafter retired, because, it was said, the oversized vessel had proven unable to deal with the newer Soviet designs. The diesel-powered submarines of the British and the Norwegians that he occasionally happened across while snorkling he dogged ruthlessly, often subjecting them to vicious sonar lashing. Once he even acquired an American missile submarine, managing to maintain contact with her for nearly two hours before she vanished like a ghost into the black waters.

The rapid growth of the Soviet Navy and the need for qualified officers during his early career prevented Ramius from attending the Frunze Academy. This was normally a *sine qua non* of career advancement in all of the Soviet armed services. Frunze, in Moscow near the old Novodevichiy Monastery, was named for a hero of the Revolution. It was the premiere school for those who aspired to high command, and though Ramius had not attended it as a student, his prowess as an operational commander won him an appointment as an instructor. It was something earned solely on merit, for which his highly placed father was not responsible. That was important to Ramius.

The head of the naval section at Frunze liked to introduce Marko as "our test pilot of submarines." His classes became a prime attraction not only for the naval officers in the academy but also for the many others who came to hear his lectures on naval history and maritime strategy. On weekends spent at his father's official dacha in the village of Zhukova-1, he wrote manuals for submarine operations and the training of crews, and specifications for the ideal attack submarine. Some of his ideas had been controversial enough to upset his erstwhile sponsor, Gorshkov, by this time commander in chief of the entire Soviet Navy—but the old admiral was not entirely displeased.

Ramius proposed that officers in the submarine service should work in a single class of ship—better yet, the same ship—for years, the better to learn their profession and the capabilities of their vessels. Skilled captains, he suggested, should not be forced to leave their commands for desk-bound promotions. Here he lauded the Red Army's practice of leaving a field commander in his post so long as the man wanted it, and deliberately contrasted his view on this matter with the practice of imperialist navies. He stressed the need for extended training in the fleet, for longer-service enlisted men, and for better living conditions on submarines. For some of his ideas he found a sympathetic ear in the high command. For others he did not, and thus Ramius found himself destined never to have his own admiral's flag. By this time he did not care. He loved his submarines too much ever to leave them for a squadron or even a fleet command.

After finishing at Frunze, he did indeed become a test pilot of submarines. Marko Ramius, now a captain first rank, would take out the first ship of every submarine class to "write the book" on its strengths and weaknesses, to develop operational routines and training guidelines. The first of the *Alfa*s was his, the first of the *Delta*s and *Typhoon*s. Aside from one extraordinary mishap on an *Alfa*, his career had been one uninterrupted story of achievement.

Along the way he became the mentor of many young officers. He often wondered what Sasha would have thought as he taught the demanding art of submarine operations to scores of eager young men. Many of them had already become commanding officers themselves; more had failed. Ramius was a commander who took good care of those who pleased him—and took good care of those who did not. Another reason why he had never made admiral was his unwillingness to promote officers whose fathers were as powerful as his own but whose abilities were unsatisfactory. He never played favorites where duty was concerned, and the sons of a half-dozen high Party officials received unsatisfactory fitness reports despite their active performance in weekly Party discussions. Most had become *zampoliti*. It was this sort of integrity that earned him trust in fleet command. When a really tough job was at hand, Ramius' name was usually the first to be considered for it.

Also along the way he had gathered to himself a number of young officers whom he and Natalia virtually adopted. They were surrogates for the family Marko and his wife never had. Ramius found himself shepherding men much like himself, with long-suppressed doubts about their country's leadership. He was an easy man to talk to, once a man had proven himself. To those with political doubts, those with just grievances, he gave the same advice: "Join the Party." Nearly all were already Komsomol members, of course, and Marko urged them to take the next step. This was the price of a career at sea, and guided by their own craving for adventure most officers paid that price. Ramius himself had been allowed to join the Party at eighteen, the earliest possible age, because of his father's influence. His occasional talks at weekly Party meetings were perfect recitations of the Party line. It wasn't hard, he'd tell his officers patiently. All you had to do was repeat what the Party said— just change the words around slightly. This was much easier than navigation—one had only to look at the political officer to see that! Ramius became known as a captain whose officers were both proficient and models of political conformity. He was one of the best Party recruiters in the navy.

Then his wife died. Ramius was in port at the time, not unusual for a missile sub commander. He had his own dacha in the woods west of Polyarnyy, his own Zhiguli automobile, the official car and driver those which his command station enjoyed, and numerous other creature comforts that came with his rank and his parentage. He was a member of the Party elite, so when Natalie had complained of abdominal pain, going to the Fourth Department clinic which served only the privileged had been a natural mistake—there was a saying in the Soviet Union: Floors parquet, docs okay. He'd last seen his wife alive lying on a gurney, smiling as she was wheeled towards the operating room.

The surgeon on call had arrived at the hospital late, and drunk, and allowed himself too much time breathing pure oxygen to sober up before starting the simple procedure of removing an inflamed appendix. The swollen organ burst just as he was retracting tissue to get at it. A case of peritonitis immediately followed, complicated by the perforated bowel the surgeon caused by his clumsy haste to repair the damage.

Natalia was placed on antibiotic therapy, but there was a shortage of medicine. The foreign—usually French—pharmaceuticals used in Fourth Department clinics had run out. Soviet antibiotics, "plan" medications, were substituted. It was a common practice in Soviet industry for workers to earn bonuses by manufacturing goods over the usual quota, goods that bypassed what quality control existed in Soviet industry. This particular batch of medication had never been inspected or tested. *And the vials had probably been filled with distilled water instead of antibiotics,* Marko learned the next day. Natalia had lapsed into deep shock and coma, dying before the series of errors could be corrected.

The funeral was appropriately solemn, Ramius remembered

bitterly. Brother officers from his own command and over a hundred other navy men whom he had befriended over the years were there, along with members of Natalia's family and representatives of the Local Party Central Committee. Marko had been at sea when his father died, and because he had known the extent of Aleksandr's crimes, the loss had had little effect. His wife's death, however, was nothing less than a personal catastrophe. Soon after they had married Natalia had joked that every sailor needs someone to return to, that every woman needs someone to wait for. It had been as simple as that—and infinitely more complex, the marriage of two intelligent people who had over fifteen years learned each other's foibles and strengths and grown ever closer.

Marko Ramius watched the coffin roll into the cremation chamber to the somber strain of a classical requiem, wishing that he could pray for Natalia's soul, hoping that Grandmother Hilda had been right, that there was something beyond the steel door and mass of flame. Only then did the full weight of the event strike him: *the State had robbed him of more than his wife, it had robbed him of a means to assuage his grief with prayer, it had robbed him of the hope—if only an illusion— of ever seeing her again.* Natalia, gentle and kind, had been his only happiness since that Baltic summer long ago. Now that happiness was gone forever. As the weeks and months wore on he was tormented by her memory; a certain hairstyle, a certain walk, a certain laugh encountered on the streets or in the shops of Murmansk was all it took to thrust Natalia back to the forefront of his consciousness, and when he was thinking of his loss, he was not a professional naval officer.

The life of Natalia Bogdanova Ramius had been lost at the hands of a surgeon who had been drinking while on call—a court-martial offense in the Soviet Navy—but Marko could not have the doctor punished. The surgeon was himself the son of a Party chieftain, his status secured by his own sponsors. Her life might have been saved by proper medication, but there had not been enough foreign drugs, and Soviet pharmaceuticals were untrustworthy. The doctor could not be made to pay, the pharmaceutical workers could not be made to pay—the thought echoed back and forth across his mind, feeding his fury until he decided that the State would be made to pay.

The idea had taken weeks to form and was the product of

a career of training and contingency planning. When the construction of the *Red October* was restarted after a two-year hiatus, Ramius knew that he would command her. He had helped with the designing of her revolutionary drive system and had inspected the model, which had been running on the Caspian Sea for some years in absolute secrecy. He asked for relief from his command so that he could concentrate on the construction and outfitting of the *October* and select and train his officers beforehand, the earlier to get the missile sub into full operation. The request was granted by the commander of the Red Banner Northern Fleet, a sentimental man who had also wept at Natalia's funeral.

Ramius had already known who his officers would be. All graduates of the Vilnius Academy, many the "sons" of Marko and Natalia, they were men who owed their place and their rank to Ramius; men who cursed the inability of their country to build submarines worthy of their skills; men who had joined the Party as told and then become even more dissatisfied with the Motherland as they learned that the price of advancement was to prostitute one's mind and soul, to become a highly paid parrot in a blue jacket whose every Party recitation was a grating exercise in self-control. For the most part they were men for whom this degrading step had not borne fruit. In the Soviet Navy there were three routes to advancement. A man could become a *zampolit* and be a pariah among his peers. Or he could be a navigation officer and advance to his own command. Or he could be shunted into a specialty in which he would gain rank and pay—but never command. Thus a chief engineer on a Soviet naval vessel could outrank his commanding officer and still be his subordinate.

Ramius looked around the table at his officers. Most had not been allowed to pursue their own career goals despite their proficiency and despite their party membership. The minor infractions of youth—in one case an act committed at age eight—prevented two from ever being trusted again. With the missile officer, it was because he was a Jew; though his parents had always been committed, believing Communists, neither they nor their son was ever trusted. Another officer's elder brother had demonstrated against the invasion of Czechoslovakia in 1968 and disgraced his whole family. Melekhin, the chief engineer and Ramius' equal in rank, had never been allowed the route to command simply because his superiors wanted him to be an engineer. Borodin, who was ready for his own command, had once accused a *zampolit* of homosexuality; the man he had informed on was the son of the chief *zampolit* of the Northern Fleet. There are many paths to treason.

"And what if they locate us?" Kamarov speculated.

"I doubt that even the Americans can find us when the caterpillar is operating. I am certain that our own submarines cannot. Comrades, I helped design this ship," Ramius said.

"What will become of us?" the missile officer muttered.

"First we must accomplish the task at hand. An officer who looks too far ahead stumbles over his own boots."

"They will be looking for us," Borodin said.

"Of course," Ramius smiled, "but they will not know where to look until it is too late. Our mission, comrades, is to avoid detection. And so we shall."

THE FOURTH DAY

MONDAY, 6 DECEMBER

CIA Headquarters

Ryan walked down the corridor on the top floor of the Langley, Virginia, headquarters of the Central Intelligence Agency. He had already passed through three separate security checks, none of which had required him to open his locked briefcase, now draped under the folds of his buff-colored toggle coat, a gift from an officer in the Royal Navy.

What he had on was mostly his wife's fault, an expensive suit bought on Savile Row. It was English cut, neither conservative nor on the leading edge of contemporary fashion. He had a number of suits like this arranged neatly in his closet by colors, which he wore with white shirts and striped ties. His only jewelry was a wedding band and a university ring, plus an expensive but accurate digital watch on a more expensive gold band. Ryan was not a man who placed a great deal of value in appearances. Indeed, his job was to see through these in the search for hard truth.

He was physically unremarkable, an inch over six feet, and his average build suffered a little at the waist from a lack of exercise enforced by the miserable English weather. His blue eyes had a deceptively vacant look; he was often lost in thought, his face on autopilot as his mind puzzled through data or research material for his current book. The only people Ryan needed to impress were those who knew him; he cared little for the rest. He had no ambition to celebrity. His life, he judged, was already as complicated as it needed to be—quite a bit more complicated than most would guess. It included a wife he loved and two children he doted on, a job that tested his intellect, and sufficient financial independence to choose his own path. The path Jack Ryan had chosen was in the CIA. The agency's official motto was, The truth shall make you free. The trick, he told himself at least once a day, was finding that truth, and while he doubted that he would ever reach this sublime state of grace, he took quiet pride in his ability to pick at it, one small fragment at a time.

The office of the deputy director for intelligence occupied a whole corner of the top floor, overlooking the tree-covered Potomac Valley. Ryan had one more security check to pass.

"Good morning, Dr. Ryan."

"Hi, Nancy." Ryan smiled at her. Nancy Cummings had held her secretarial job for twenty years, had served eight DDIs, and if the truth were known she probably had as good a feel for the intelligence business as the political appointees in the adjacent office. It was the same as with any large business—the bosses came and went, but the good executive secretaries lasted forever.

"How's the family, Doctor? Looking forward to Christmas?"

"You bet—except my Sally's a little worried. She's not sure Santa knows that we've moved, and she's afraid he won't make it to England for her. He will," Ryan confided.

"It's so nice when they're that little." She pressed a hidden button. "You can go right in, Dr. Ryan."

"Thanks, Nancy." Ryan twisted the electronically protected knob and walked into the DDI's office.

Vice Admiral James Greer was reclining in his high-backed judge's chair reading through a folder. His oversized mahogany desk was covered with neat piles of folders whose edges were bordered with red tape and whose covers bore various code words.

"Hiya, Jack!" he called across the room. "Coffee?"

"Yes, thank you, sir."

James Greer was sixty-six, a naval officer past retirement age who kept working through brute competence, much as Hyman Rickover had, though Greer was a far easier man to work for. He was a "mustang," a man who had entered the naval service as an enlisted man, earned his way into the Naval Academy, and spent forty years working his way to a three-star flag, first commanding submarines, then as a full-time intelligence specialist. Greer was a demanding boss, but one who took care of those who pleased him. Ryan was one of these.

Somewhat to Nancy's chagrin, Greer liked to make his own coffee with a West Bend drip machine on the credenza behind his desk, where he could just turn around to reach it. Ryan poured himself a cup—actually a navy-style handleless mug. It was traditional navy coffee, brewed strong, with a pinch of salt.

"You hungry, Jack?" Greer pulled a pastry box from a desk drawer. "I got some sticky buns here."

"Why, thanks, sir. I didn't eat much on the plane." Ryan took one, along with a paper napkin.

"Still don't like to fly?" Greer was amused.

Ryan sat down in the chair opposite his boss. "I suppose I ought to be getting used to it. I like the Concorde better than the wide-bodies. You only have to be terrified half as long."

"How's the family?"

"Fine, thank you, sir. Sally's in first grade—loves it. And little Jack is toddling around the house. These buns are pretty good."

"New bakery just opened up a few blocks from my place. I pass it on the way in every morning." The admiral sat upright in his chair. "So, what brings you over today?"

"Photographs of the new Soviet missile boat, *Red October*," Ryan said casually between sips.

"Oh, and what do our British cousins want in return?" Greer asked suspiciously.

"They want a peek at Barry Somers' new enhancement gadgets. Not the machines themselves—at first—just the finished product. I think it's a fair bargain, sir." Ryan knew the CIA didn't have any shots of the new sub. The operations directorate did not have a man at the building yard at

Severodvinsk or a reliable man at the Polyarnyy submarine base. Worse, the rows of "boat barns" built to shelter the missile submarines, modeled on World War II German submarine pens, made satellite photography impossible. "We have ten frames, low obliques, five each bow and stern, and one from each perspective is undeveloped so that Somers can work on them fresh. We are not committed, sir, but I told Sir Basil that you'd think it over."

The admiral grunted. Sir Basil Charleston, chief of the British Secret Intelligence Service, was a master of the quid pro quo, occasionally offering to share sources with his wealthier cousins and a month later asking for something in return. The intelligence game was often like a primitive marketplace. "To use the new system, Jack, we need the camera used to take the shots."

"I know." Ryan pulled the camera from his coat pocket. "It's a modified Kodak disk camera. Sir Basil says it's the coming thing in spy cameras, nice and flat. This one, he says, was hidden in a tobacco pouch."

"How did you know that—that we need the camera?"

"You mean how Somers uses lasers to—"

"Ryan!" Greer snapped. "How much do you know?"

"Relax, sir. Remember back in February, I was over to discuss those new SS-20 sites on the Chinese border? Somers was here, and you asked me to drive him out to the airport. On the way out he started babbling about this great new idea he was heading west to work on. He talked about it all the way to Dulles. From what little I understood, I gather that he shoots laser beams through the camera lenses to make a mathematical model of the lens. From that, I suppose, he can take the exposed negative, break down the image into the—original incoming light beams, I guess, then use a computer to run *that* through a computer-generated theoretical lens to make a perfect picture. I probably have it wrong." Ryan could tell from Greer's face that he didn't.

"Somers talks too goddamned much."

"I told him that, sir. But once the guy gets started, how the hell do you shut him up?"

"And what do the Brits know?" Greer asked.

"Your guess is as good as mine, sir. Sir Basil asked me about it, and I told him that he was asking the wrong guy—I mean, my degrees are in economics and history, not physics. I told him we needed the camera—but he already knew that. Took it right out of his desk and tossed it to me. I did not reveal a thing about this, sir."

"I wonder how many other people he spilled to. Geniuses! They operate in their own crazy little worlds. Somers is like a little kid sometimes. And you know the First Rule of Security: The likelihood of a secret's being blown is proportional to the *square* of the number of people who're in on it." It was Greer's favorite dictum.

His phone buzzed. "Greer . . . Right." He hung up. "Charlie Davenport's on the way up, per your suggestion, Jack. Supposed to be here half an hour ago. Must be the snow." The admiral jerked a hand towards the window. There were two inches on the ground, with another inch expected by nightfall. "One flake hits this town and everything goes to hell."

Ryan laughed. That was something Greer, a down-easter from Maine, never could seem to understand.

"So, Jack, you say this is worth the price?"

"Sir, we've wanted these pictures for some time, what with all the contradictory data we've been getting on the sub. It's your decision and the judge's but, yes, I think they're worth the price. These shots are very interesting."

"We ought to have our own men in that damned yard," Greer grumped. Ryan didn't know how Operations had screwed that one up. He had little interest in field operations. Ryan was an analyst. How the data came to his desk was not his concern, and he was careful to avoid finding out. "I don't suppose Basil told you anything about their man?"

Ryan smiled, shaking his head. "No, sir, and I did not ask." Greer nodded his approval.

"Morning, James!"

Ryan turned to see Rear Admiral Charles Davenport, director of naval intelligence, with a captain trailing in his wake.

"Hi, Charlie. You know Jack Ryan, don't you?"

"Hello, Ryan."

"We've met," Ryan said.

"This is Captain Casimir."

Ryan shook hands with both men. He'd met Davenport a few years before while delivering a paper at the Naval War College in Newport, Rhode Island. Davenport had given him a hard time in the question-and-answer session. He was supposed to be a bastard to work for, a former aviator who had lost flight status after a barrier crash and, some said, still bore a grudge. Against whom? Nobody really knew.

"Weather in England must be as bad as here, Ryan." Davenport dropped his bridge coat on top of Ryan's. "I see you stole a Royal Navy overcoat."

Ryan was fond of his toggle coat. "A gift, sir, and quite warm."

"Christ, you even talk like a Brit. James, we gotta bring this boy home."

"Be nice to him, Charlie. He's got a present for you. Grab yourself some coffee."

Casimir scurried over to fill a mug for his boss, then sat down at his right hand. Ryan let them wait a moment before opening his briefcase. He took out four folders, keeping one and handing the others around.

"They say you've been doing some fairly good work, Ryan," Davenport said. Jack knew him to be a mercurial man, affable one moment, brittle the next. Probably to keep his subordinates off balance. "And—Jesus Christ!" Davenport had opened his folder.

"Gentlemen, I give you *Red October*, courtesy of the British Secret Intelligence Service," Ryan said formally.

The folders had the photographs arranged in pairs, four each of four-by-four prints. In the back were ten-by-ten blowups of each. The photos had been taken from a low-oblique angle, probably from the rim of the graving dock that had held the boat during her post-shakedown refit. The shots were paired, fore and aft, fore and aft.

"Gentlemen, as you can see, the lighting wasn't all that great. Nothing fancy here. It was a pocket camera loaded with 400-speed color film. The first pair was processed normally to establish high levels. The second was pushed for greater brightness using normal procedures. The third pair was digitally enhanced for color resolution, and the fourth was digitally enhanced for line resolution. I have undeveloped frames of each view for Barry Somers to play with."

"Oh?" Davenport looked up briefly. "That's right neighborly of the Brits. What's the price?" Greer told him. "Pay up. It's worth it."

"That's what Jack says."

"Figures," Davenport chuckled. "You know he really is working for them."

Ryan bristled at that. He liked the English, liked working with their intelligence community, but he knew what country he came from. Jack took a deep breath. Davenport liked to goad people, and if he reacted Davenport would win.

"I gather that Sir John Ryan is still well connected on the other side of the ocean?" Davenport said, extending the prod.

Ryan's knighthood was an honorary one. It was his reward for having broken up a terrorist incident that had erupted around him in St. James's Park, London. He'd been a tourist at the time, the innocent American abroad, long before he'd been asked to join the CIA. The fact that he had unknowingly prevented the assassination of two very prominent figures had gotten him more publicity than he'd ever wanted, but it had also brought him in contact with a lot of people in England, most of them worth the time. Those connections had made him valuable enough that the CIA asked him to be part of a joint American-British liaison group. That was how he had established a good working relationship with Sir Basil Charleston.

"We'd have lots of friends over there, sir, and some of them were kind enough to give you these," Ryan said coolly.

Davenport softened. "Okay, Jack, then you do me a favor. You see whoever gave us these gets something nice in his stocking. They're worth plenty. So, exactly what do we have here?"

To the unschooled observer, the photographs showed the standard nuclear missile submarine. The steel hull was blunt at one end, tapered at the other. The workmen standing on the floor of the dock provided scale—she was huge. There were twin bronze propellers at the stern, on either side of a flat appendage which the Russians called a beaver tail, or so the intelligence reports said. With the twin screws the stern was unremarkable except in one detail.

"What are these doors for?" Casimir asked.

"Hmm. She's a big bastard." Davenport evidently hadn't heard. "Forty feet longer than we expected, by the look of her."

"Forty-four, roughly." Ryan didn't much like Davenport, but the man did know his stuff. "Somers can calibrate that for us. And more beam, two meters more than the other *Typhoon*s.

She's an obvious development of the *Typhoon* class, but—"

"You're right, Captain," Davenport interrupted. "What are those doors?"

"That's why I came over." Ryan had wondered how long this would take. He'd caught onto them in the first five seconds. "I don't know, and neither do the Brits."

The *Red October* had two doors at the bow and stern, each about two meters in diameter, though they were not quite circular. They had been closed when the photos were shot and only showed up well on the number four pair.

"Torpedo tubes? No—four of them are inboard." Greer reached into his drawer and came out with a magnifying glass. In an age of computer-enhanced imagery it struck Ryan as charmingly anachronistic.

"You're the sub driver, James," Davenport observed.

"Twenty years ago, Charlie." He'd made the switch from line officer to professional spook in the early sixties. Captain Casimir, Ryan noted, wore the wings of a naval aviator and had the good sense to remain quiet. He wasn't a "nuc."

"Well, they can't be torpedo tubes. They have the normal four of them at the bow, inboard of these openings . . . must be six or seven feet across. How about launch tubes for the new cruise missile they're developing?"

"That's what the Royal Navy thinks. I had a chance to talk it over with their intelligence chaps. But I don't buy it. Why put an anti-surface-ship weapon on a strategic platform? We don't, and we deploy our boomers a lot further forward than they do. The doors are symmetrical through the boat's axis. You can't launch a missile out of the stern, sir. The openings barely clear the screws."

"Toward sonar array," Davenport said.

"Granted they could do that, if they trail one screw. But why two of them?" Ryan asked.

Davenport gave him a nasty look. "They love redundancies."

"Two doors forward, to aft. I can buy cruise missile tubes. I can buy a towed array. But both sets of doors exactly the same size?" Ryan shook his head. "Too much of a coincidence. I think it's something new. That's what interrupted her construction for so long. They figured something new for her and spent the last two years rebuilding the *Typhoon* configuration to accommodate it. Note also that they added six more missiles for good measure."

"Opinion," Davenport observed.

"That's what I'm paid for."

"Okay, Jack, what do you think it is?" Greer asked.

"Beats me, sir. I'm no engineer."

Admiral Greer looked his guests over for a few seconds. He smiled and leaned back in his chair. "Gentlemen, we have what? Ninety years of naval experience in this room, plus this young amateur." He gestured at Ryan. "Okay, Jack, you've set us up for something. Why did you bring this over personally?"

"I want to show these to somebody."

"Who?" Greer's head cocked suspiciously to one side.

"Skip Tyler. Any of you fellows know him?"

"I do," Casimir nodded. "He was a year behind me at Annapolis. Didn't he get hurt or something?"

"Yeah," Ryan said. "Lost his leg in an auto accident four years ago. He was up for command of the *Los Angeles* and a drunk driver clipped him. Now he teached engineering at the Academy and does a lot of consulting work with Sea Systems Command—technical analysis, looking at their ship designs. He has a doctorate in engineering from MIT, and he knows how to think unconventionally."

"How about his security clearance?" Greer asked.

"Top secret or better, sir, because of his Crystal City work."

"Objections, Charlie?"

Davenport frowned. Tyler was not part of the intelligence community. "Is this the guy who did the evaluation of the new *Kirov?*"

Yes, sir, now that I think about it," Casimir said. "Him and Saunders over at Sea Systems."

"That was a nice piece of work. It's okay with me."

"When do you want to see him?" Greer asked Ryan.

"Today, if it's all right with you, sir. I have to run over to Annapolis anyway, to get something from the house, and— well, do some quick Christmas shopping."

"Oh? A few dolls?" Davenport asked.

Ryan turned to look the admiral in the eye. "Yes, sir, as a matter of fact. My little girl wants a Skiing Barbie doll and some Jordache doll outfits. Didn't you ever play Santa, Admiral?"

Davenport saw that Ryan wasn't going to back off anymore. He wasn't a subordinate to be browbeaten. Ryan could always walk away. He tried a new tack. "Did they tell you over there that *October* sailed last Friday?"

"Oh?" They hadn't. Ryan was caught off guard. "I thought she wasn't scheduled to sail until this Friday."

"So did we. Her skipper is Marko Ramius. You heard about him?"

"Only secondhand stuff. The Brits say he's pretty good."

"Better than that," Greer noted. "He's about the best sub driver they have, a real charger. We had a considerable file on him when I was at DIA. Who's bird-diggin' him for you, Charlie?"

"*Bremerton* was assigned to it. She was out of position doing some ELINT work when Ramius sailed, but she was ordered over. Her skipper's Bud Wilson. Remember his dad?"

Greer laughed out loud. "Red Wilson? Now there was one spirited submarine driver! His boy any good?"

"So they say. Ramius is about the best the Soviets have, but Wilson's got a 688 boat. By the end of the week, we'll be able to start a new book on *Red October*." Davenport stood. "We gotta head back, James." Casimir hurried to get the coats. "I can keep these?"

"I suppose, Charlie. Just don't go hanging them on the wall, even to throw darts at. And I guess you want to get moving, too, Jack?"

"Yes, sir."

Greer lifted his phone. "Nancy, Dr. Ryan will need a car and a driver in fifteen minutes. Right." He set the receiver down and waited for Davenport to leave. "No sense getting you killed out there in the snow. Besides, you'd probably drive on the wrong side of the road after a year in England. Skiing Barbie, Jack?"

"You had all boys, didn't you, sir? Girls are different." Ryan grinned. "You've never met my little Sally."

"Daddy's girl?"

"Yep. God help whoever marries her. Can I leave these photographs with Tyler?"

"I hope you're right about him, son. Yes, he can hold onto them—if and only if he has a good place to keep them."

"Understood, sir."

"When you get back—probably be late, the way the roads are. You're staying at the Marriott?"

"Yes, sir."

Greer thought that over. "I'll probably be working late. Stop by here before you bed down. I may want to go over a few things with you."

"Will do, sir. Thanks for the car." Ryan stood.

"Go buy your dolls, son."

Greer watched him leave. He liked Ryan. The boy was not afraid to speak his mind. Part of that came from having money and being married to more money. It was a sort of independence that had advantages. Ryan could not be bought, bribed, or bullied. He could always go back to writing history books full time. Ryan had made money on his own in four years as a stockbroker, betting his own money on high-risk issues and scoring big before leaving it all behind—because, he said, he hadn't wanted to press his luck. Greer didn't believe that. He thought Jack had been bored—bored with making money. He shook his head. The talent that had enabled him to pick winning stocks Ryan now applied to the CIA. He was rapidly becoming one of Greer's star analysts, and his British connections made him doubly valuable. Ryan had the ability to sort through a pile of data and come out with the three or four facts that meant something. This was too rare a thing at the CIA. The agency still spent too much of its money collecting data, Greer thought, and not enough collating it. Analysts had none of the supposed glamour—a Hollywood-generated illusion—of a secret agent in a foreign land. But Jack knew how to analyze reports from such men and data from technical sources. He knew how to make a decision and was not afraid to say what he thought, whether his bosses liked it or not. This sometimes grated the old admiral, but on the whole he liked having subordinates whom he could respect. The CIA had too many people whose only skill was kissing ass.

The U.S. Naval Academy

The loss of his left leg above the knee had not taken away Oliver Wendell Tyler's roguish good looks or his zest for life. His wife could testify to this. Since leaving the active service four years before, they had added three children to the two they already had and were working on a sixth. Ryan found him sitting at a desk in an empty classroom in Rickover Hall, the U.S. Naval Academy's science and engineering building. He was grading papers.

"How's it goin', Skip?" Ryan leaned against the door frame. His CIA driver was in the hall.

"Hey, Jack! I thought you were in England." Tyler jumped to his foot—his own phrase—and hobbled over to grab Ryan's hand. His prosthetic leg ended in a square, rubber-coated band instead of a pseudo-foot. It flexed at the knee, but not by much. Tyler had been a second-squad All American offensive tackle sixteen years before, and the rest of his body was as hard as the aluminum and fiberglass in his left leg. His handshake could make a gorilla wince. "So, what are you doing here?"

"I had to fly over to get some work done and do a little shopping. How's Jean and your . . . five?"

"Five and two-thirds."

"Again? Jean ought to have you fixed."

"That's what she said, but I've had enough things disconnected." Tyler laughed. "I guess I'm making up for all those monastic years as a nuc. Come on over and grab a chair."

Ryan sat on the corner of the desk and opened his briefcase. He handed Tyler a folder.

"Got some pictures I want you to look at."

"Okay." Tyler flipped it open. "Whose—a Russian! Big bastard. That's the basic *Typhoon* configuration. Lots of modifications, though. Twenty-six missiles instead of twenty. Looks longer. Hull's flattened out some, too. More beam?"

"Two or three meters' worth."

"I heard you were working with the CIA. Can't talk about that, right?"

"Something like that. And you never saw these pictures, Skip. Understood?"

"Right." Tyler's eyes twinkled. "What do you want me not to look at them for?"

Ryan pulled the blowups from the back of the folder. "These doors, bow and stern."

"Uh-huh." Tyler set them down side by side. "Pretty big. They're two meters or so, paired fore and aft. They look symmetrical through the long axis. Not cruise missile tubes, eh?"

"On a boomer? You put something like that on a strategic missile sub?"

"The Russkies are a funny bunch, Jack, and they design things their own way. This is the same bunch that built the *Kirov* class with a nuclear reactor *and* an oil-fired steam plant. Hmm . . . twin screws. The aft doors can't be for a sonar array. They'd foul the screws."

"How 'bout if they trail one screw?"

"They do that with surface ships to conserve fuel, and sometimes with their attack boats. Operating a twin-screw missile boat on one wheel would probably be tricky on this baby. The *Typhoon*'s supposed to have handling problems, and boats that handle funny tend to be sensitive to power settings. You end up jinking around so much that you have trouble holding course. You notice how the doors converge at the stern?"

"No, I didn't."

Tyler looked up. "Damn! I should have realized it right off the bat. It's a propulsion system. You shouldn't have caught me marking papers, Jack. It turns your brain to Jell-O."

"Propulsion system?"

"We looked at this—oh, must have been twenty some years ago—when I was going to school here. We didn't do anything with it, though. It's too inefficient."

"Okay, tell me about it."

"They called it a tunnel drive. You know how out West they have lots of hydroelectric power plants? Mostly dams. The water spills onto wheels that turn generators. Now there's a few new ones that kind of turn that around. They tap into underground rivers, and the water turns impellers, and they turn the generators instead of a modified mill wheel. An impeller is like a propeller, except the water drives it instead of the other way around. There's some minor technical differences, too, but nothing major. Okay so far?

"With this design, you turn that around. You suck water in the bow and your impellers eject it out the stern, and that moves the ship." Tyler paused, frowning. "As I recall you have to have more than one tunnel. They looked at this back in the early sixties and got to the model stage before dropping it. One of the things they discovered is that one impeller doesn't work as well as several. Some sort of back pressure thing. It was a new principle, something unexpected that cropped up. They ended up using four, I think, and it was supposed to look something like the compressor sets in a jet engine."

"Why did we drop it?" Ryan was taking rapid notes.

"Mostly efficiency. You can only get so much water down the pipes no matter how powerfully your motors are. And the drive system took up a lot of room. They partially beat that with a new kind of electric induction motor, I think, but even then you'd end up with a lot of extraneous machinery inside the hull. Subs don't have that much room to spare, even this monster. The top speed limit was supposed to be about ten knots, and that just wasn't good enough, even though it did virtually eliminate cavitation sounds."

"Cavitation?"

"When you have a propeller turning in the water at high speed, you develop an area of low pressure behind the trailing edge of the blade. This can cause water to vaporize. That creates a bunch of little bubbles. They can't last long under the water pressure, and when they collapse the water rushes forward to pound against the blades. That does three things. First, it makes noise, and us sub drivers hate noise. Second, it can cause vibration, something else we don't like. The old passenger liners, for example, used to flutter several inches at the stern, all from cavitation and slippage. It takes a hell of a lot of force to vibrate a 50,000-ton ship; that kind of force breaks things. Third, it tears up the screws. The big wheels only used to last a few years. That's why back in the old days the blades were bolted onto the hub instead of being cast in one piece. The vibration is mainly a surface ship problem, and the screw degradation was eventually conquered by improved metallurgical technology.

"Now, this tunnel drive system avoids the cavitation problem. You still have cavitation, but the noise from it is mainly lost in the tunnels. That makes good sense. The problem is that you can't generate much speed without making the tunnels too wide to be practical. While one team was working on this, another was working on improved screw designs. Your typical sub screw today is pretty large, so it can turn more slowly for a given speed. The slower the turning speed, the less cavitation you get. The problem is also mitigated by depth. A few hundred feet down, the higher water pressure retards bubble formation."

"Then why don't the Soviets copy our screw designs?"

"Several reasons, probably. You design a screw for a specific hull and engine combination, so copying ours wouldn't automatically work for them. A lot of this work is still empirical, too. There's a lot of trial and error in this. It's a lot harder, say, then designing an airfoil, because the blade cross-section changes radically from one point to another. I suppose another reason is that their metallurgical technology isn't as good as ours—same reason that their jet and rocket engines are less efficient. These new designs place great value on high-strength alloys. It's a narrow specialty, and I only know the generalities."

"Okay, you say that this is a silent propulsion system, and it has a top speed limit of ten knots?" Ryan wanted to be clear on this.

"Ballpark figure. I'd have to do some computer modeling to tighten that up. We probably still have the data laying around at the Taylor Laboratory." Tyler referred to the Sea Systems Command design facility on the north side of the Severn River. "Probably still classified, and I'd have to take it with a big grain of salt."

"How come?"

"All this work was done twenty years ago. They only got up to fifteen-foot models—pretty small for this sort of thing. Remember that they had already stumbled across one new principle, that back-pressure thing. There might have been more out there. I expect they tried some computer models, but even if they did, mathematical modeling techniques back then were dirt-simple. To duplicate this today I'd have to have the old data and programs from Taylor, check it all over, then draft a new program based on this configuration." He tapped the photographs. "Once that was done, I'd need access to a big league mainframe computer to run it."

"But you could do it?"

"Sure. I'd need exact dimensions on this baby, but I've done this before for the bunch over at Crystal City. The hard part's getting the computer time. I need a big machine."

"I can probably arrange access to ours."

Tyler laughed. "Probably not good enough, Jack. This is specialized stuff. I'm talking about a Cray-2, one of the biggies. To do this you have to mathematically simulate the behavior of millions of little parcels of water, the water flow over—and through, in this case—the whole hull. Same sort of thing NASA has to do with the Space Shuttle. The actual work is easy enough—it's the *scale* that's tough. They're simple calculations, but you have to make millions of them per second. That means a big Cray, and there's only a few of them around. NASA has one in Houston, I think. The navy has a few in Norfolk for ASW work—you can forget about those. The air force has one in the Pentagon, I think, and all the rest are in California."

"But you could do it?"

"Sure."

"Okay, get to work on it, Skip, and I'll see if we can get you the computer time. How long?"

"Depending on how good the stuff at Taylor is, maybe a week. Maybe less."

"How much do you want for it?"

"Aw, come on, Jack!" Tyler waved him off.

"Skip, it's Monday. You get us this data by Friday and there's twenty thousand dollars in it. You're worth it, and we want this data. Agreed?"

"Sold." They shook hands. "Can I keep the pictures?"

"I can leave them if you have a secure place to keep them. Nobody gets to see them, Skip. Nobody."

"There's a nice safe in the superintendent's office."

"Fine, but he doesn't see them." The superintendent was a former submariner.

"He won't like it," Tyler said. "But okay."

"Have him call Admiral Greer if he objects. This number." Ryan handed him a card. "You can reach me here if you need me. If I'm not in, ask for the admiral."

"Just how important is this?"

"Important enough. You're the first guy who's come up with a sensible explanation for these hatches. That's why I came here. If you can model this for us, it'll be damned useful. Skip, one more time: This is highly sensitive. If you let anybody see these, it's my ass."

"Aye aye, Jack. Well, you've laid a deadline on me, I better get down to it. See you." After shaking hands, Tyler took out a lined pad and started listing the things he had to do. Ryan left the building with his driver. He remembered a Toys-R-Us right up Route 2 from Annapolis, and he wanted to get that doll for Sally.

CIA Headquarters

Ryan was back at the CIA by eight that evening. It was a quick trip past the security guards to Greer's office.

"Well, did you get your Surfing Barbie?" Greer looked up.

"Skiing Barbie," Ryan corrected. "Yes, sir. Come on, didn't you ever play Santa?"

"They grew up too fast, Jack. Even my grandchildren are all past that stage." He turned to get some coffee. Ryan wondered if he ever slept. "We have something more on *Red October*. The Russians seem to have a major ASW exercise running in the northeast Barents Sea. Half a dozen ASW search aircraft, a bunch of frigates, and an *Alfa*-class attack boat, all running around in circles."

"Probably an acquisition exercise. Skip Tyler says those doors are for a new drive system."

"Indeed." Greer sat back. "Tell me about it."

Ryan took out his notes and summarized his education in submarine technology. "Skip says he can generate a computer simulation of its effectiveness," he concluded.

Greer's eyebrows went up. "How soon?"

"End of week, maybe. I told him if he had it done by Friday we'd pay him for it. Twenty thousand sound reasonable?"

"Will it mean anything?"

"If he gets the background data he needs, it ought to, sir. Skip's a very sharp cookie. I mean, they don't give doctorates away at MIT, and he was in the top five of his Academy class."

"Worth twenty thousand dollars of our money?" Greer was notoriously tight with a buck.

Ryan knew how to answer this. "Sir, if we followed normal procedure on this, we'd contract one of the Beltway Bandits—," Ryan referred to the consulting firms that dotted the beltway around Washington, D.C., "—they'd charge us five or ten times as much, and we'd be lucky to have the data by Easter. This way we might just have it while the boat's still at sea. If worse comes to worst, sir, I'll foot the bill. I figured you'd want this data fast, and it's right up his alley."

"You're right." It wasn't the first time Ryan had short-

circuited normal procedure. The other times had worked out
fairly well. Greer was a man who looked for results. "Okay,
the Soviets have a new missile boat with a silent drive system.
What does it all mean?"

"Nothing good. We depend on our ability to track their
boomers with our attack boats. Hell, that's why they agreed a
few years back to our proposal about keeping them five hundred
miles from each other's coasts, and why they keep their missile
subs in port most of the time. This could change the game a
bit. By the way, *October*'s hull, I haven't seen what it's made
of."

"Steel. She's too big for a titanium hull, at least for what
it would cost. You know what they have to spend on their
*Alfa*s."

"Too much for what they got. You spend that much money
for a superstrong hull, then put a noisy power plant in it.
Dumb."

"Maybe. I wouldn't mind having that speed, though. Anyway, if this silent drive system really works, they might be able
to creep up onto the continental shelf."

"Depressed-trajectory shot," Ryan said. This was one of the
nastier nuclear war scenarios in which a sea-based missile was
fired within a few hundred miles of its target. Washington is
a bare hundred air miles from the Atlantic Ocean. Though a
missile on a low, fast flight path loses much of its accuracy, a
few of them can be launched to explode over Washington in
less than a few minutes' time, too little for a president to react.
If the Soviets were able to kill the president that quickly, the
resulting disruption of the chain of command would give them
ample time to take out the land-based missiles—there would
be no one with authority to fire. This scenario is a grand-
strategic version of a simple mugging, Ryan thought. A mugger
doesn't attack his victim's arms—he goes for the head. "You
think *October* was built with that in mind?"

"I'm sure the thought occurred to them," Greer observed.
"It would have occurred to us. Well, we have *Bremerton* up
there to keep an eye on her, and if this data turns out to be
useful we'll see if we can come up with an answer. How are
you feeling?"

"I've been on the go since five-thirty London time. Long
day, sir."

"I expect so. Okay, we'll go over the Afghanistan business tomorrow morning. Get some sleep, son."

"Aye, aye, sir." Ryan got his coat. "Good night."

It was a fifteen-minute drive to the Marriott. Ryan made the mistake of turning the TV on to the beginning of Monday Night Football. Cincinnati was playing San Francisco, the two best quarterbacks in the league pitted against one another. Football was something he missed living in England, and he managed to stay awake nearly three hours before fading out with the television on.

SOSUS Control

Except for the fact that everyone was in uniform, a visitor might easily have mistaken the room for a NASA control center. There were six wide rows of consoles, each with its own TV screen and typewriter keyboard supplemented by lighted plastic buttons, dials, headphone jacks, and analog and digital controls. Senior Chief Oceanographic Technician Deke Franklin was seated at console fifteen.

The room was SOSUS (sonar surveillance system) Atlantic Control. It was in a fairly nondescript building, uninspired government layer cake, with windowless concrete walls, a large air-conditioning system on a flat roof, and an acronym-coded blue sign on a well-tended but now yellowed lawn. There were armed marines inconspicuously on guard inside the three entrances. In the basement were a pair of Cray-2 supercomputers tended by twenty acolytes, and behind the building was a trio of satellite ground stations, all up- and down-links. The men at the consoles and the computers were linked electronically by satellite and landline to the SOSUS system.

Throughout the oceans of the world, and especially astride the passages that Soviet submarines had to cross to reach the open sea, the United States and other NATO countries had deployed gangs of highly sensitive sonar receptors. The hundreds of SOSUS sensors received and forwarded an unimaginably vast amount of information, and to help the system operators classify and analyze it a whole new family of computers had to be designed, the supercomputers. SOSUS served its purpose admirably well. Very little could cross a barrier without being detected. Even the ultraquiet American and British attack sub-

marines were generally picked up. The sensors, lying on the
bottom of the sea, were periodically updated; many now had
their own signal processors to presort the data they forwarded,
lightening the load on the central computers and enabling more
rapid and accurate classification of targets.

Chief Franklin's console received data from a string of sensors planted off the coast of Iceland. He was responsible for
an area forty nautical miles across, and his sector overlapped
the ones east and west so that, theoretically, three operators
were constantly monitoring any segment of the barrier. If he
got a contact, he would first notify his brother operators, then
type a contact report into his computer terminal, which would
in turn be displayed on the master control board in the control
room at the back of the floor. The senior duty officer had the
frequently exercised authority to prosecute a contact with a
wide range of assets, from surface ships to antisubmarine aircraft. Two world wars had taught American and British officers
the necessity of keeping their sea lines of communication—
SLOCs—open.

Although this quiet, tomblike facility had never been shown
to the public, and though it had none of the drama associated
with military life, the men on duty here were among the most
important in the service of their country. In a war, without
them, whole nations might starve.

Franklin was leaning back in his swivel chair, puffing con-
templatively on an old briar pipe. Around him the room was
dead quiet. Even had it not been, his five-hundred-dollar headphones would have effectively sealed him off from the outside
world. A twenty-six year chief, Franklin had served his entire
career on destroyers and frigates. To him, submarines and submariners were the enemy, regardless of what flag they might
fly or what uniform they might wear.

An eyebrow went up, and his nearly bald head cocked to
one side. The pulls on the pipe grew irregular. His right hand
reached forward to the control panel and switched off the signal
processors so that he could get the sound without computerized
interference. But it was no good. There was too much background noise. He switched the filters back on. Next he tried
some changes in his azimuth controls. The SOSUS sensors
were designed to give bearing checks through the selective use
of individual receptors, which he could manipulate electroni-

cally, first getting one bearing, then using a neighboring gang to triangulate for a fix. The contract was very faint, but not too far from the line, he judged. Franklin queried his computer terminal. The USS *Dallas* was up there. *Gotcha!* he said with a thin smile. Another noise came through, a low-frequency rumble that only lasted a few seconds before fading out. Not all that quiet, though. Why hadn't he heard it before switching the reception azimuth? He set his pipe down and began making adjustments on his control board.

"Chief?" A voice came over his headphones. It was the senior duty officer.

"Yes, Commander?"

"Can you come back to control? I have something I want you to hear."

"On the way, sir." Franklin rose quietly. Commander Quentin was a former destroyer skipper on a limited duty after a winning battle with cancer. Almost a winning battle, Franklin corrected himself. Chemotherapy had killed the cancer—at the cost of nearly all his hair, and turning his skin into a sort of transparent parchment. Too bad, he thought, Quentin was a pretty good man.

The control room was elevated a few feet from the rest of the floor so that its occupants could see over the whole crew of duty operators and the main tactical display on the far wall. It was separated from the floor by glass, which allowed them to speak to one another without disturbing the operators. Franklin found Quentin at his command station, where he could tap into any console on the floor.

"Howdy, Commander." Franklin noted that the officer was gaining some weight back. It was about time. "What do you have for me, sir?"

"On the Barents Sea net." Quentin handed him a pair of phones. Franklin listened for several minutes, but he didn't sit down. Like many people he had a gut suspicion that cancer was contagious.

"Damned if they ain't pretty busy up there. I read a pair of *Alfa*s, a *Charlie*, a *Tango*, and a few surface ships. What gives, sir?"

"There's a *Delta* there, too, but she just surfaced and killed her engines."

"Surfaced, Skipper?"

"Yep. They were lashing her pretty hard with active sonar, then a 'can queried her on a gertrude."

"Uh-huh. Acquisition game, and the sub lost."

"Maybe. Quentin rubbed his eyes. The man looked tired. He was pushing himself too hard, and his stamina wasn't half what it should have been. "But the *Alfa*s are still pinging, and now they're headed west, as you heard."

"Oh." Franklin pondered that for a moment. "They're looking for another boat, then. The *Typhoon* that was supposed to have sailed the other day, maybe?"

"That's what I thought—except she headed west, and the exercise area is northeast of the fjord. We lost her the other day on SOSUS. *Bremerton*'s up sniffing around for her now."

"Cagey skipper," Franklin decided. "Cut his plant all the way back and just drifting."

"Yeah," Quentin agreed. "I want you to move down to the North Cape barrier supervisory board and see if you can find her, Chief. She'll still have her reactor working, and she'll be making some noise. The operators we have on that sector are a little young. I'll take one and switch him to your board for a while."

"Right, Skipper," Franklin nodded. That part of the team was still green, used to working on ships. SOSUS required more finesse. Quentin didn't have to say that he expected Franklin to check in on the whole North Cape team's boards and maybe drop a few small lessons as he listened in on their channels.

"Did you pick up on *Dallas?*"

"Yes, sir. Real faint, but I think I got her crossing my sector, headed northwest for Toll Booth. If we get an Orion down there, we might just get her locked in. Can we rattle their cage a little?"

Quentin chuckled. He didn't much care for submarines either. "No, NIFTY DOLPHIN is over. Chief. We'll just log it and let the skipper know when he comes back home. Nice work, though. You know her reputation. We're not supposed to hear her at all."

"That'll be the day!" Franklin snorted.

"Let me know what you find, Deke."

"Aye aye, Skipper. You take care of yourself, hear?"

THE FIFTH DAY

TUESDAY, 7 DECEMBER

Moscow

It was not the grandest office in the Kremlin, but it suited his needs. Admiral Yuri Ilych Padorin showed up for work at his customary seven o'clock after the drive from his six-room apartment in the Kutuzovskiy Prospekt. The large office windows overlooked the Kremlin walls; except for those he would have had a view of the Mosow River, now frozen solid. Padorin did not miss the view, though he had won his spurs commanding river gunboats forty years before, running supplies across the Volga into Stalingrad. Padorin was now the chief political officer of the Soviet Navy. His job was men, not ships.

On the way in he nodded curtly to his secretary, a man of forty. The yeoman leaped to his feet and allowed his admiral into the inner office to help him off with his greatcoat. Padorin's navy-blue jacket was ablaze with ribbons and the gold star medal of the most coveted award in the Soviet Military, Hero of the Soviet Union. He had won that in combat as a freckled boy of twenty, shuttling back and forth on the Volga. Those were good days, he told himself, dodging bombs from the

German Stukas and the more random artillery fire with which the Fascists had tried to interdict his squadron . . . Like most men he was unable to remember the stark terror of combat.

It was a Tuesday morning, and Padorin had a pile of mail waiting on his desk. His yeoman got him a pot of tea and a cup—the usual Russian glass cup set in a metal holder, sterling silver in this case. Padorin had worked long and hard for the perqs that came with this office. He settled in his chair and read first through the intelligence dispatches, information copies of data sent each morning and evening to the operational commands of the Soviet Navy. A political officer had to keep current, to know what the imperialists were up to so that he could brief his men on the threat.

Next came the official mail from within the People's Commissariat of the Navy and the Ministry of Defense. He had access to all of the correspondence from the former, while that from the latter had been carefully vetted since the Soviet armed services share as little information as possible. There wasn't too much mail from either place today. The usual Monday afternoon meeting had covered most of what had to be done that week, and nearly everything Padorin was concerned with was now in the hands of his staff for disposition. He poured a second cup of tea and opened a new pack of unfiltered cigarettes, a habit he'd been unable to break despite a mild heart attack three years earlier. He checked his desk calendar—good, no appointments until ten.

Near the bottom of the pile was an official-looking envelope from the Northern Fleet. The code number at the upper left corner showed that it came from the *Red October*. Hadn't he just read something about that?

Padorin rechecked his ops dispatches. So, Ramius hadn't turned up in his exercise area? He shrugged. Missile submarines were supposed to be elusive, and it would not have surprised the old admiral at all if Ramius were twisting a few tails. The son of Aleksandr Ramius was a prima donna who had the troubling habit of seeming to build his own personality cult: he kept some of the men he trained and discarded others. Padorin reflected that those rejected for line service had made excellent *zampoliti,* and appeared to have more line knowledge than was the norm. Even so, Ramius was a captain who needed watching. Sometimes Padorin suspected that he was too much a sailor and not enough a Communist. On the other hand, his father had been a model Party member and a hero of the Great Patriotic War. Certainly he had been well thought of, Lithuanian or not. And the son? Years of letter-perfect performance, as many years of stalwart Party membership. He was known for his spirited participation at meetings and occasionally brilliant essays. The people in the naval branch of the GRU, the Soviet military intelligence agency, reported that the imperialists regarded him as a dangerous and skilled enemy. Good, Padorin thought, the bastards ought to fear our men. He turned his attention back to the envelope.

Red October, now there was a fitting name for a Soviet warship! Named not only for the revolution that had forever changed the history of the world but also for the Red October Tractor Plant. Many was the dawn when Padorin had looked west to Stalingrad to see if the factory still stood, a symbol of the Soviet fighting men struggling against the Hitlerite bandits. The envelope was marked Confidential, and his yeomen had not opened it as he had the other routine mail. The admiral took his letter opener from the desk drawer. It was a sentimental object, having been his service knife years before. When his first gunboat had been sunk under him, one hot August night in 1942, he had swum to shore and been pounced on by a German infantryman who hadn't expected resistance from a half-drowned sailor. Padorin had surprised him, sinking the knife in his chest and braking off half the blade as he stole his enemy's life. Later a machinist had trimmed the blade down. It was no longer a proper knife, but Padorin wasn't about to throw this sort of souvenir away.

"Comrade Admiral," the letter began—but the type had been scratched out and replaced with a hand-written "Uncle Yuri." Ramius had jokingly called him that years back when Padorin was chief political officer of the Northern Fleet. "Thank you for your confidence, and for the opportunity you have given me with command of this magnificent ship!" Ramius ought to be grateful, Padorin thought. Performance or not, you don't give this sort of command to—

What? Padorin stopped reading and started over. He forgot the cigarette smoldering in his ashtray as he reached the bottom

of the first page. A joke. Ramius was known for his jokes—
but he'd pay for this one. This was going too fucking far! He
turned the page.

"This is no joke, Uncle Yuri—Marko."

Padorin stopped and looked out the window. The Kremlin
wall at this point was a beehive of niches for the ashes of the
Party faithful. He couldn't have read the letter correctly. He
started to read it again. His hands began to shake.

He had a direct line to Admiral Gorshkov, with no yeomen
or secretaries to bar the way.

"Comrade Admiral, this is Padorin."

"Good morning, Yuri," Gorshkov said pleasantly.

"I must see you immediately. I have a situation here."

"What sort of situation?" Gorshkov asked warily.

"We must discuss it in person. I am coming over now."
There was no way he'd discuss this over the phone; he knew
it was tapped.

The USS Dallas

Sonarman Second Class Ronald Jones, his division officer noted,
was in his usual trance. The young college dropout was hunched
over his instrument table, body limp, eyes closed, face locked
into the same neutral expression he wore when listening to one
of the many Bach tapes on his expensive personal cassette player.
Jones was the sort who categorized his tapes by their flaws, a
ragged piano tempo, a botched flute, a wavering French horn.
He listened to sea sounds with the same discriminating intensity. In all the navies of the world, submariners were regarded
as a curious breed, and submariners themselves looked upon
sonar operators as odd. Their eccentricities, however, were
among the most tolerated in the military service. The executive
officer liked to tell a story about a sonar chief he'd served with
for two years, a man who had patrolled the same areas in missile submarines for virtually his whole career. He became so
familiar with the humpback whales that summered in the area
that he took to calling them by name. On retiring, he went to
work for the Woods Hole Oceanographic Institute, where his
talent was regarded not so much with amusement as awe.

Three years earlier, Jones had been asked to leave the
California Institute of Technology in the middle of his junior

year. He had pulled one of the ingenious pranks for which Cal Tech students were justly famous, only it hadn't worked. Now he was serving his time in the navy to finance his return. It was his announced intention to get a doctorate in cybernetics and signal processing. In return for an early out, after receiving his degree he would go to work for the Naval Research Laboratory. Lieutenant Thompson believed it. On joined the *Dallas* six months earlier, he had read the files of all his men. Jones' IQ was 158, the highest on the boat by a fair margin. He had a placid face and sad brown eyes that women found irresistible. On the beach Jones had enough action to wear down a squad of marines. It didn't make much sense to the lieutenant. He'd been the football hero at Annapolis. Jones was a skinny kid who listened to Bach. It didn't figure.

The USS *Dallas*, a 688-class attack submarine, was forty miles from the coast of Iceland, approaching her patrol station, code-named Toll Booth. She was two days late getting there. A week earlier, she had participated in the NATO war game NIFTY DOLPHIN, which had been postponed several days because the worst North Atlantic weather in twenty years had delayed other ships detailed to it. In that exercise the *Dallas*, teamed with HMS *Swiftsure*, had used the foul weather to penetrate and ravage the simulated enemy formation. It was yet another four-oh performance for the *Dallas* and her skipper, Commander Bart Mancuso, one of the youngest submarine commanders in the U.S. Navy. The mission had been followed by a courtesy call at the *Swiftsure*'s Royal Navy base in Scotland, and the American sailors were still shaking off hangovers from the celebration ... Now they had a different mission, a new development in the Atlantic submarine game. For three weeks, the *Dallas* was to report on traffic in and out of Red Route One.

Over the past fourteen months, newer Soviet submarines had been using a strange, effective tactic for shedding their American and British shadowers. Southwest of Iceland the Russian boats would race down the Reykjanes Ridge, a finger of underwater highlands pointing to the deep Atlantic basin. Spaced at intervals from five miles to half a mile, these mountains with their knife-edged ridges of brittle igneous rock rivaled the Alps in size. Their peaks were about a thousand feet beneath the stormy surface of the North Atlantic. Before the late sixties

submarines could barely approach the peaks, much less probe
their myriad valleys. Throughout the seventies Soviet naval
survey vessels had been seen patrolling the ridge—in all sea-
sons, in all weather, quartering and requartering the area in
thousands of cruises. Then, fourteen months before the *Dallas'*
present patrol, the USS *Los Angeles* had been tracking a Soviet
Victor II–class attack submarine. The *Victor* had skirted the
Icelandic coast and gone deep as she approached the ridge. The
Los Angeles had followed. The *Victor* proceeded at eight knots
until she passed between the first pair of seamounts, informally
known as Thor's Twins. All at once she went to full speed and
moved southwest. The skipper of the *Los Angeles* made a
determined effort to track the *Victor* and came away from it
badly shaken. Although the 688-class submarines were faster
than the older *Victors,* the Russian submarine had simply not
slowed down—for fifteen hours, it was later determined.

At first it had not been all that dangerous. Submarines had
highly accurate inertial navigation systems able to fix their
positions to within a few hundred yards from one second to
another. But the *Victor* was skirting cliffs as though her skipper
could see them, like a fighter dodging down a canyon to avoid
surface-to-air missile fire. The *Los Angeles* could not keep track
of the cliffs. At any speed over twenty knots both her passive
and active sonar, including the echofathometer, became almost
useless. The *Los Angeles* thus found herself navigating completely blind. It was, the skipper later reported, like driving a
car with the windows painted over, steering with a map and a
stopwatch. This was theoretically possible, but the captain
quickly realized that the inertial navigation system had a built-
in error factor of several hundred yards; this was aggravated
by gravitational disturbances, which affected the "local vertical," which in turn affected the inertial fix. Worst of all, his
charts were made for surface ships. Objects below a few hundred
feet had been known to be misplaced by miles—something
that mattered to no one until recently. The interval between
mountains had quickly become less than his cumulative navigational error—sooner or later his submarine would drive into
a mountainside at over thirty knots. The captain backed off.
The *Victor* got away.

Initially it was theorized that the Soviets had somehow staked
out one particular route, that their submarines were able to

follow it at high speed. Russian skippers were known to pull some crazy stunts, and perhaps they were trusting to a combination of inertial systems, magnetic and gyro compasses attuned to a specific track. This theory had never developed much of a following, and in a few weeks it was known for certain that the Soviet submarines speeding through the ridge were following a multiplicity of tracks. The only thing American and British subs could do was stop periodically to get a sonar fix of their positions, then race to catch up. But the Soviet subs never slowed, and the 688s and *Trafalgar*s kept falling behind.

The *Dallas* was on Toll Booth station to monitor passing Russian subs, to watch the entrance to the passage the U.S. Navy was now calling Red Route One, and to listen for any external evidence of a new gadget that might enable the Soviets to run the ridge so boldly. Until the Americans could copy it, there were three unsavory alternatives: they could continue losing contact with the Russians; they could station valuable attack subs at the known exits from the route; or they could set up a whole new SOSUS line.

Jones' trance lasted ten minutes—longer than usual. He ordinarily had a contact figured out in far less time. The sailor leaned back and lit a cigarette.

"Got something, Mr. Thompson."

"What is it?" Thompson leaned against the bulkhead.

"I don't know." Jones picked up a spare set of phones and handed them to his officer. "Listen up, sir."

Thompson himself was a masters candidate in electrical engineering, an expert in sonar system design. His eyes screwed shut as he concentrated on the sound. It was a very faint low-frequency rumble—or swish. He couldn't decide. He listened for several minutes before setting the headphones down, then shook his head.

"I got it a half hour ago on the lateral array," Jones said. He referred to a subsystem of the BQQ-5 multifunction submarine sonar. Its main component was an eighteen-foot-diameter dome located in the bow. The dome was used for both active and passive operations. A new part of the system was a gang of passive sensors which extended two hundred feet down both sides of the hull. This was a mechanical analog to the sensory organs on the body of a shark. "Lost it, got it back, lost it, got it back," Jones went on. "It's now screw sounds, not whales

or fish. More like water going through a pipe, except for that
funny rumble that comes and goes. Anyway, the bearing is
about two-five-zero. That puts it between us and Iceland, so
it can't be too far away."

"Let's see what it looks like. Maybe that'll tell us something."

Jones took a double-plugged wire from a hook. One plug
went into a socket on his sonar panel, the other into the jack
on a nearby oscilloscope. The two men spent several minutes
working with the sonar controls to isolate the signal. They
ended up with an irregular sine wave which they were only
able to hold a few seconds at a time.

"Irregular," Thompson said.

"Yeah, it's funny. It sounds regular, but it doesn't look
regular. Know what I mean, Mr. Thompson?"

"No, you've got better ears."

"That's cause I listen to better music, sir. That rock stuff'll
kill your ears."

Thompson knew he was right, but an Annapolis graduate
doesn't need to hear that from an enlisted man. His vintage
Janis Joplin tapes were his own business. "Next step."

"Yessir." Jones took the plug from the oscilloscope and
moved it into a panel to the left of the sonar board, next to a
computer terminal.

During her last overhaul, the *Dallas* had received a very
special toy to go along with her BQQ-5 sonar system. Called
the BC-10, it was the most powerful computer yet installed
aboard a submarine. Though only about the size of a business
desk, it cost over five million dollars and ran at eighty million
operations per second. It used newly developed sixty-four-bit
chips and made use of the latest processing architecture. Its
bubble memory could easily accommodate the computing needs
of a whole squadron of submarines. In five years every attack
sub in the fleet would have one. Its purpose, much like that of
the far larger SOSUS system, was to process and analyze sonar
signals; the BC-10 stripped away ambient noise and other naturally produced sea sounds to classify and identify man-made
noise. It could identify ships by name from their individual
acoustical signatures, much as one could identify the finger or
voice prints of a human.

As important as the computer was its programming software. Four years before, a PhD candidate in geophysics who was working at Cal Tech's geophysical laboratory had completed a program of six hundred thousand steps designed to predict earthquakes. The problem the program addressed was one of signal versus noise. It overcame the difficulty seismologists and genuinely unusual signals that foretell a seismic event.

The first Defense Department use of the program was in the Air Force Technical Applications Command (AFTAC), which found it entirely satisfactory for its mission of monitoring nuclear events throughout the world in accordance with arms control treaties. The Navy Research Laboratory also redrafted it for its own purposes. Though inadequate for seismic predictions, it worked very well indeed in analyzing sonar signals. The program was known in the navy as the signal algorythmic processing system (SAPS).

"SAPS SIGNAL INPUT," Jones typed into the video display terminal (VDT).

"READY," the BC-10 responded at once.

"RUN."

"WORKING."

For all the fantastic speed of the BC-10, the six hundred thousand steps of the program, punctuated by numerous GOTO loops, took time to run as the machine eliminated natural sounds with its random profile criteria and then locked into the anomalous signal. It took twenty seconds, an eternity in computer time. The answer came up on the VDT. Jones pressed a key to generate a copy on the adjacent matrix printer.

"Hmph." Jones tore off the page. "'ANOMALOUS SIGNAL EVALUATED AS MAGMA DISPLACEMENT.' That's SAPS' way of saying take two aspirin and call me at end of the watch."

Thompson chuckled. For all the ballyhoo that had accompanied the new system, it was not all that popular in the fleet. "Remember what the papers said when we were in England? Something about seismic activity around Iceland, like when that island poked up back in the sixties."

Jones lit another cigarette. He knew the student who had originally drafted this abortion they called SAPS. One problem

was that it had a nasty habit of analyzing the wrong signal—
and you couldn't tell it was wrong from the results. Besides,
since it had been originally designed to look for seismic events,
Jones suspected it of a tendency to interpret anomalies as seismic events. He didn't like the built-in bias, which he felt the
research laboratory had not entirely removed. It was one thing
to use computers as a tool, quite another to let them do your
thinking for you. Besides, they were always discovering new
sea sounds that nobody had ever heard before, much less classified.

"Sir, the frequency is all wrong for one thing—nowhere
near low enough. How 'bout I try an' track in on this signal
with the R-15?" Jones referred to the towed array of passive
sensors the *Dallas* was trailing behind her at low speed.

Commander Mancuso came in just then, the usual mug of
coffee in his hand. If there was one frightening thing about the
captain, Thompson thought, it was his talent for showing up
when something was going on. Did he have the whole boat
wired?

"Just wandering by," he said casually. "What's happening
this fine day?" The captain leaned against the bulkhead. He
was a small man, only five eight, who had fought a battle
against his waistline all his life and was now losing because
of the good food and lack of exercise on a submarine. His dark
eyes were surrounded by laugh lines that were always deeper
when he was playing a trick on another ship.

Was it day, Thompson wondered? The six-hour one-in-three
rotating watch cycle made for a convenient work schedule, but
after a few changes you had to press the button on your watch
to figure out what day it was, else you couldn't make the proper
entry in the log.

"Skipper, Jones picked up a funny signal on the lateral. The
computer says it's magma displacement."

"And Jonesy doesn't agree with that." Mancuso didn't have
to make it a question.

"No, sir, Captain, I don't. I don't know what it is, but for
sure it ain't that."

"You against the machine again?"

"Skipper, SAPS works pretty well most of the time, but
sometimes it's a real *kludge*." Jones' epithet was the most

perjorative curse of electronics people. "For one thing the frequency is all wrong."

"Okay, what do you think?"

"I don't know, Captain. It isn't screw sounds, and it isn't any naturally produced sound that I've heard. Beyond that..." Jones was struck by the informality of the discussion with his commanding officer, even after three years on nuclear subs. The crew of the *Dallas* was like one big family, albeit one of the old frontier families, since everybody worked pretty damned hard. The captain was the father. The executive officer, everyone would readily agree, was the mother. The officers were the older kids, and the enlisted men were the younger kids. The important thing was, if you had something to say, the captain would listen to you. To Jones, this counted for a lot.

Mancuso nodded thoughtfully. "Well, keep at it. No sense letting all this expensive gear go to waste."

Jones grinned. Once he had told the captain in precise detail how he could convert this equipment into the world's finest stereo rig. Mancuso had pointed out that it would not be a major feat, since the sonar gear in this room alone cost over twenty million dollars.

"Christ!" The junior technician bolted upright in his chair. "Somebody just stomped on the gas."

Jones was the sonar watch supervisor. The other two watchstanders noted the new signal, and Jones switched his phones to the towed array jack while the two officers kept out of the way. He took a scratch pad and noted the time before working on his individual controls. The BQR-15 was the most sensitive sonar rig on the boat, but its sensitivity was not needed for this contact.

"Damn," Jones muttered quietly.

"Charlie," said the junior technician.

Jones shook his head. *"Victor. Victor* class for sure. Doing turns for thirty knots—big burst of cavitation noise, he's digging big holes in the water, and he doesn't care who knows it. Bearing zero-five-zero. Skipper, we got good water around us, and the signal is real faint. He's not close." It was the closest thing to a range estimate Jones could come up with. Not close meant anything over ten miles. He went back to working his controls. "I think we know this guy. This is the one with a bent blade on his screw, sounds like he's got a chain wrapped around it."

"Put it on speaker," Mancuso told Thompson. He didn't want to disturb the operators. The lieutenant was already keying the signal into the BC-10.

The bulkhead-mounted speaker would have commanded a four-figure price in any stereo shop for its clarity and dynamic perfection; like everything else on the 688-class sub, it was the very best that money could buy. As Jones worked on the sound controls they heard the whining chirp of propeller cavitation, the thin screech associated with a bent propeller blade, and the deeper rumble of a *Victor*'s reactor plant at full power. The next thing Mancuso heard was the printer.

"Victor I–class, number six," Thompson announced.

"Right," Jones nodded. *"Vic*-six, bearing still zero-five-zero." He plugged the mouthpiece into his headphones. "Conn, sonar, we have a contact. A *Victor* class, bearing zero-five-zero, estimated target speed thirty knots."

Mancuso leaned out into the passageway to address Lieutenant Pat Mannion, office of the deck. "Pat, man the fire-control tracking party."

"Aye, Cap'n."

"Wait a minute!" Jones' hand went up. "Got another one!" He twiddled some knobs. "This one's a *Charlie* class. Damned if he ain't digging holes, too. More easterly, bearing zero-seven-three, doing turns for about twenty-eight knots. We know this guy, too. Yeah, *Charlie II,* number eleven." Jones slipped a phone off one ear and looked at Mancuso. "Skipper, the Russkies have sub races scheduled for today?"

"Not that they told me about. Of course, we don't get the sports page out here," Mancuso chuckled, swirling the coffee around in his cup and hiding his real thoughts. What the hell was going on? "I suppose I'll go forward and take a look at this. Good work, guys."

He went a few steps forward into the attack center. The normal steaming watch was set. Mannion had the conn, with a junior officer of the deck and seven enlisted men. A first-class firecontrolman was entering data from the target motion analyzer into the Mark 117 fire control computer. Another officer was entering control to take charge of the tracking exercise. There was nothing unusual about this. The whole watch went about its work alertly but with the relaxed demeanor that came with years of training and experience. While the other armed services routinely had their components run exercises against allies or themselves in emulation of Eastern Bloc tactics, the navy had its attack submarines play their games against the real thing—and constantly. Submariners typically operated on what was effectively an at-war footing.

"So we have company," Mannion observed.

"Not that close," Lieutenant Charles Goodman noted. "These bearings haven't changed a whisker."

"Conn, sonar." It was Jones' voice. Mancuso took it.

"Conn, aye. What is it, Jonesy?"

"We got another one, sir. *Alfa 3*, bearing zero-five-five. Running flat out. Sounds like an earthquake, but faint, sir."

"*Alfa 3?* Our old friend, the *Politovskiy*. Haven't run across her in a while. Anything else you can tell me?"

"A guess, sir. The sound on this one warbled, then settled down, like she was making a turn. I think she's heading this way—that's a little shaky. And we have some more noise to the northeast. Too confused to make any sense of just now. We're working on it."

"Okay, nice work, Jonesy. Keep at it."

"Sure thing, Captain."

Mancuso smiled as he set the phone down, looking over at Mannion. "You know, Pat, sometimes I wonder if Jonesy isn't part witch."

Mannion looked at the paper tracks that Goodman was drawing to back up the computerized targeting process. "He's pretty good. Problem is, he thinks we work for him."

"Right now we are working for him." Jones was their eyes and ears, and Mancuso was damned glad to have him.

"Chuck?" Mancuso asked Lieutenant Goodman.

"Bearing still constant on all three contacts, sir." Which probably meant they were heading for the *Dallas*. It also meant that they could not develop the range data necessary for a fire control solution. Not that anyone wanted to shoot, but this was the point of the exercise.

"Pat, let's get some sea room. Move us about ten miles east," Mancuso ordered casually. There were two reasons for this. First, it would establish a base line from which to compute probable target range. Second, the deeper water would make for better acoustical conditions, opening up to them the distant sonar convergence zone. The captain studied the chart as his navigator gave the necessary orders, evaluating the tactical situation.

Bartolomeo Mancuso was the son of a barber who closed his shop in Cicero, Illinois, every fall to hunt deer on Michigan's Upper Peninsula. Bart had accompanied his father on these hunts, shot his first deer at the age of twelve and every year thereafter until entering the Naval Academy. He had never bothered about that. Since becoming an officer on nuclear submarines he had learned a much more diverting game. Now he hunted people.

Two hours later an alarm bell went off on the ELF radio in the sub's communications room. Like all nuclear submarines, the *Dallas* was trailing a lengthy wire antenna attuned to the extremely low-frequency transmitter in the central United States. The channel had a frustratingly narrow data band width. Unlike a TV channel, which transmitted thousands of bits of data per frame, thirty frames per second, the ELF radio passed on data slowly, about one character every thirty seconds. The duty radioman waited patiently while the information was recorded on tape. When the message was finished, he ran the tape at high speed and transcribed the message, handing it to the communications officer who was waiting with his code book.

The signal was actually not a code but a "one-time-pad" cipher. A book, published every six months and distributed to every nuclear submarine, was filled with randomly generated transpositions for each letter of the signal. Each scrambled three-letter group in this book corresponded to a preselected word or phrase in another book. Deciphering the message by hand took under three minutes, and when that was completed it was carried to the captain in the attack center.

```
        NHG                  JPR                YTR
  FROM COMSUBLANT     TO LANTSUBS AT SEA     STANDBY
     OPY     TBD             QEQ              GER
  POSSIBLE  MAJOR  REDEPLOYMENT ORDER   LARGE-SCALE
     MAL                     ASF                NME
  UNEXPECTED       REDFLEET OPERATION    IN PROGRESS
     TYQ                     ORV
  NATURE UNKNOWN        NEXT ELF MESSAGE
     HWZ
  COMMUNICATE SSIX
```

COMSUBLANT—commander of the Submarine Force in the Atlantic—was Mancuso's big boss, Vice Admiral Vincent Gallery. The old man was evidently contemplating a reshuffling of his entire force, no minor affair. The next wake-up signal, AAA—encrypted, of course—would alert them to go to periscope-antenna depth to get more detailed instructions from SSIX, the submarine satellite information exchange, a geosynchronous communications satellite used exclusively by submarines.

The tactical situation was becoming clearer, though its strategic implications were beyond his ability to judge. The ten-mile move eastward had given them adequate range information for their initial three contacts and another *Alfa* which had turned up a few minutes later. The first of the contacts, *Vic 6*, was now within torpedo range. A Mark 48 was locked in on her, and there was no way that her skipper could know the *Dallas* was here. *Vic 6* was a deer in his sights—but it wasn't hunting season.

Though not much faster than the *Victor*s and *Charlie*s, and ten knots slower than the smaller *Alfa*s, the *Dallas* and her sisters could move almost silently at nearly twenty knots. This was a triumph of engineering and design, the product of decades of work. But moving without being detected was useful only if the hunter could at the same time detect his quarry. Sonars lost effectiveness as their carrier platform increased speed. The *Dallas'* BQQ-5 retained twenty percent effectiveness at twenty knots, nothing to cheer about. Submarines running at high speed from one point to another were blind and unable to harm anyone. As a result, the operating pattern of an attack submarine was much like that of a combat infantryman. With a rifleman it was called dash-and-cover; with a sub, sprint-and-drift. After detecting a target, a sub would race to a more advantageous position, stop to reacquire her prey, then dash again until a firing position had been achieved. The sub's quarry would be moving too, and if the submarine could gain position in front of it, she had then only to lie in wait like a great hunting cat to strike.

The submariner's trade required more than skill. It required instinct, and an artist's touch; monomaniacal confidence, and the aggressiveness of a professional boxer. Mancuso had all of these things. He had spent fifteen years learning his craft, watching a generation of commanders as a junior officer, listening carefully at the frequent round-table discussions which made submarining a very human profession, its lessons passed on by verbal tradition. Time on shore had been spent training in a variety of computerized simulators, attending seminars, comparing notes and ideas with his peers. Aboard surface ships and ASW aircraft he learned how the "enemy"—the surface sailors—played his own hunting game.

Submariners lived by a simple motto: There are two kinds of ships, submarines... and targets. What would *Dallas* be hunting? Mancuso wondered. Russian subs? Well, if that was the game and the Russians kept racing around like this, it ought to be easy enough. He and the *Swiftsure* had just bested a team of NATO ASW experts, men whose countries depended on their ability to keep the sea-lanes open. His boat and his crew were performing as well as any man could ask. In Jones he had one of the ten best sonar operators in the fleet. Mancuso was ready, whatever the game might be. As on the opening day of hunting season, outside considerations were dwindling away. He was becoming a weapon.

CIA Headquarters

It was 4:45 in the morning, and Ryan was dozing fitfully in the back of a CIA Chevy taking him from the Marriott to Langley. He'd been over for what? twenty hours? About that, enough time to see his boss, see Skip, get the presents for Sally, and check the house. The house looked to be in good shape. He had rented it to an instructor at the Naval Academy. He could have gotten five times the rent from someone else, but he didn't want any wild parties in his home. The officer was a Bible-thumper from Kansas, and made an acceptable custodian.

Five and a half hours of sleep in the past—thirty? Something like that; he was too tired to look at his watch. It wasn't fair. Sleeplessness murders judgment. But it made little sense telling himself that, and telling the admiral would make less.

He was in Greer's office five minutes later.

"Sorry to have to wake you up, Jack."

"Oh, that's all right, sir," Ryan returned the lie. "What's up?"

"Come on over and grab some coffee. It's going to be a long day."

Ryan dropped his topcoat on the sofa and walked over to pour a mug of navy brew. He decided against Coffee Mate or sugar. Better to endure it naked and get the caffeine full force.

"Any place I can shave around here, sir?"

"Head's behind the door, over in the corner." Greer handed him a yellow sheet torn from a telex machine. "Look at this."

TOP SECRET
102200Z*****38976

NSA SIGINT BULLETIN

REDNAV OPS

MESSAGE FOLLOWS

AT 083145Z NSA MONITOR STATIONS [DELETED] [DELETED] AND [DELETED] RECORDED AN ELF BROADCAST FROM REDFLEET ELF FACILITY SEMIPOLIPINSK XX MESSAGE DURATION 10 MINUTES XX 6 ELEMENTS XX

ELF SIGNAL IS EVALUATED AS "PREP" BROAD-CAST TO REDFLEET SUBMARINES AT SEA XX

AT 090000Z AN "ALL SHIPS" BROADCAST WAS MADE BY REDFLEET HEADQUARTERS CENTRAL COMMO STATION TULA AND SATELLITES THREE AND FIVE XX BANDS USED: HF VHF UHF XX MESSAGE DURATION 39 SECONDS WITH 2 RE-PEATS IDENTICAL CONTENT MADE AT 091000Z AND 092000Z XX 475 5-ELEMENT CIPHER GROUPS XX

SIGNAL COVERAGE AS FOLLOWS: NORTHERN FLEET AREA BALTIC FLEET AREA AND MED SQUADRON AREA XX NOTE FAR EAST FLEET NOT REPEAT NOT AFFECTED BY THIS BROADCAST XX

NUMEROUS ACKNOWLEDGMENT SIGNALS EM-ANATED FROM ADDRESSES IN AREAS CITED ABOVE XX ORIGIN AND TRAFFIC ANALYSIS TO

FOLLOW XX NOT COMPLETED AT THIS TIME XX
BEGINNING AT 100000Z NSA MONITOR STATIONS
[DELETED] [DELETED] AND [DELETED] RE-
CORDED INCREASED HF AND VHF TRAFFIC AT
REDFLEET BASES POLYARNYY SEVEROMORSK
PECHENGA TALLINN KRONSTADT AND EAST-
ERN MED AREA XX ADDITIONAL HF AND VHF
TRAFFIC FROM REDFLEET ASSETS AT SEA XX
AMPLIFICATION TO FOLLOW XX

EVALUATION: A MAJOR UNPLANNED REDFLEET
OPERATION HAS BEEN ORDERED WITH FLEET
ASSETS REPORTING AVAILABILITY AND STATUS
XX

END BULLETIN

NSA SENDS

102215Z

BREAKBREAK

Ryan looked at his watch. "Fast work by the boys at NSA, and fast work by our duty watch officers, getting everybody up." He drained his mug and went over for a refill. "What's the word on signal traffic analysis?"

"Here." Greer handed him a second telex sheet.

Ryan scanned it. "That's a lot of ships. Must be nearly everything they have at sea. Not much on the ones in port, though."

"Landline," Greer observed. "The ones in port can phone fleet ops, Moscow. By the way, that *is* every ship they have at sea in the Western Hemisphere. Every damned one. Any ideas?"

"Let's see, we have that increased activity in the Barents Sea. Looks like a medium-sized ASW exercise. Maybe they're expanding it. Doesn't explain the increased activity in the Baltic and Med, though. Do they have a war game laid on?"

"Nope. They just finished CRIMSON STORM a month ago."

Ryan nodded. "Yeah, they usually take a couple of months to evaluate that much data—and who'd want to play games up there at this time of the year? The weather's supposed to be a bitch. Have they ever run a major game in December?"

"Not a big one, but most of these acknowledgments are from submarines, son, and subs don't care a whole lot about the weather."

"Well, given some other preconditions, you might call this ominous. No idea what the signal said, eh?"

"No. They're using computer-based ciphers, same as us. If the spooks at the NSA can read them, they're not telling me about it." In theory the National Security Agency came under the titular control of the director of Central Intelligence. In fact it was a law unto itself. "That's what traffic analysis is all about, Jack. You try to guess intentions by who's talking to whom."

"Yes, sir, but when everybody's talking to everybody—"

"Yeah."

"Anything else on alert? Their army? Voyska PVO?" Ryan referred to the Soviet air defense network.

"Nope, just the fleet. Subs, ships, and naval aviation."

Ryan stretched. "That makes it sound like an exercise, sir. We'll want a little more data on what they're doing, though. Have you talked to Admiral Davenport?"

"That's the next step. Haven't had time. I've only been in long enough to shave myself and turn the coffee on." Greer sat down and set his phone receiver in the desk speaker before punching in the numbers.

"Vice Admiral Davenport." The voice was curt.

"Morning, Charlie, James here. Did you get that NSA -976?"

"Sure did, but that's not what got me up. Our SOSUS net went berserk a few hours ago."

"Oh?" Greer looked at the phone, then at Ryan.

"Yeah, nearly every sub they have at sea just put the pedal to the metal, and all at about the same time."

"Doing what exactly, Charlie?" Greer prompted.

"We're still figuring that out. It looks like a lot of boats are heading into the North Atlantic. Their units in the Norwegian Sea are racing southwest. Three from the western Med are heading that way, too, but we haven't got a clear picture yet. We need a few more hours."

"What do they have operating off our coast, sir?" Ryan asked.

"They woke you up, Ryan? Good. Two old *November*s.

One's a raven conversion doing an ELINT job off the cape. The other one's sitting off King's Bay making a damned nuisance of itself."

Ryan smiled to himself. An American or allied ship was a *she;* the Russians used the male pronoun for a ship; and the intelligence community usually referred to a Soviet ship as *it*.

"There's a *Yankee* boat," Davenport went on, "a thousand miles south of Iceland, and the initial report is that it's heading north. Probably wrong. Reciprocal bearing, transcription error, something like that. We're checking. Must be a goof, because it was heading south earlier."

Ryan looked up. "What about their other missile boats?"

"Their *Delta*s and *Typhoon*s are in the Barents Sea and the Sea of Okhotsk, as usual. No news on them. Oh, we have attack boats up there, of course, but Gallery doesn't want them to break radio silence, and he's right. So all we have at the moment is the report on the stray *Yankee*."

"What are we doing, Charlie?" Greer asked.

"Gallery has a general alert out to his boats. They're standing by in case we need to redeploy. NORAD has gone to a slightly increased alert status, they tell me." Davenport referred to the North American Aerospace Defense Command. "CINCLANT and CINCPAC fleet staffs are up and running around in circles, like you'd expect. Some extra P-3s are working out of Iceland. Nothing much else at the moment. First we have to figure out what they're up to."

"Okay, keep me posted."

"Roger, if we hear anything, I'll let you know, and I trust—"

"We will." Greer killed the phone. He shook a finger at Ryan. "Don't you go to sleep on me, Jack."

"On top of this stuff?" Ryan waved his mug.

"You're not concerned, I see."

"Sir, there's nothing to be concerned about yet. It's what, one in the afternoon over there now? Probably some admiral, maybe old Sergey himself, decided to toss a drill at his boys. He wasn't supposed to be all that pleased with how CRIMSON STORM worked out, and maybe he decided to rattle a few cages—ours included, of course. Hell, their army and air force aren't involved, and it's for damned sure that if they were planning anything nasty the other services would know about it. We'll have to keep an eye on this, but so far I don't see anything to—" Ryan almost said lose sleep over "—sweat about."

"How old were you at Pearl Harbor?"

"My father was nineteen, sir. He didn't marry until after the war, and I wasn't the first little Ryan." Jack smiled. Greer knew all this. "As I recall you weren't all that old yourself."

"I was a seaman second on the old *Texas*." Greer had never made it into that war. Soon after it started he'd been accepted by the Naval Academy. By the time he had graduated from there and finished training at submarine school, the war was almost over. He reached the Japanese coast on his first cruise the day after the war ended. "But you know what I mean."

"Indeed I do, sir, and that's why we have the CIA, DIA, NSA, and NRO, among others. If the Russkies can fool all of us, maybe we ought to read up on our Marx."

"All those subs heading into the Atlantic ..."

"I feel better with word that the *Yankee* is heading north. They've had enough time to make that a hard piece of data. Davenport probably doesn't want to believe it without confirmation. If Ivan was looking to play hardball, that *Yankee*'d be heading south. The missiles on those old boats can't reach very far. Sooo—we stay up and watch. Fortunately, sir, you make a decent cup of coffee."

"How does breakfast grab you?"

"Might as well. If we can finish up on the Afghanistan stuff, maybe I can fly back tomorr—tonight."

"You still might. Maybe this way you'll learn to sleep on the plane."

Breakfast was sent up twenty minutes later. Both men were accustomed to big ones, and the food was surprisingly good. Ordinarily CIA cafeteria food was government-undistinguished, and Ryan wondered if the night crew, with fewer people to serve, might take the time to do their job right. Or maybe they had sent out for it. The two men sat around until Davenport phoned at quarter to seven.

"It's definite. All the boomers are heading towards port. We have good tracks on two *Yankee*s, three *Delta*s, and a *Typhoon*. *Memphis* reported when her *Delta* took off for home at twenty knots after being on station for five days, and then Gallery queried *Queenfish*. Same story—looks like they're all headed for the barn. Also we just got some photos from a Big Bird pass over the fjord—for once it wasn't covered with clouds—

and we have a bunch of surface ships with bright infrared signatures, like they're getting steam up."

"How about *Red October?*" Ryan asked.

"Nothing. Maybe our information was bad, and she didn't sail. Wouldn't be the first time."

"You don't suppose they've lost her?" Ryan wondered aloud.

Davenport had already thought of that. "That would explain the activity up north, but what about the Baltic and Med business?"

"Two years ago we had that scare with *Tullibee*," Ryan pointed out. "And the CNO was so pissed he threw an all-hands rescue drill on both oceans."

"Maybe," Davenport conceded. The blood in Norfolk was supposed to have been ankle deep after that fiasco. The USS *Tullibee*, a small one-of-a-kind attack sub, had long carried a reputation for bad luck. In this case it had spilled over onto a lot of others.

"Anyway, it looks a whole lot less scary than it did two hours back. They wouldn't be recalling their boomers if they were planning anything against us, would they?" Ryan said.

"I see that Ryan still has your crystal ball, James."

"That's what I pay him for, Charlie."

"Still, it is odd," Ryan commented. "Why recall all of the missile boats? Have they ever done this before? What about the ones in the Pacific?"

"Haven't heard about those yet," Davenport replied. "I've asked CINCPAC for data, but they haven't gotten back to me yet. On the other question, no, they've never recalled all their boomers at once, but they do occasionally reshuffle all their positions at once. That's probably what this is. I said they're heading towards port, not into it. We won't know that for a couple of days."

"What if they're afraid they've lost one?" Ryan ventured.

"No such luck," Davenport scoffed. "They haven't lost a boomer since that *Golf* we lifted off Hawaii, back when you were in high school, Ryan. Ramius is too good a skipper to let that happen."

So was Captain Smith of the *Titanic*, Ryan thought.

"Thanks for the info, Charlie." Greer hung up. "Looks like you were right, Jack. Nothing to worry about yet. Let's get that data on Afghanistan in here—and just for the hell of it, we'll look at Charlie's pictures of their Northern Fleet when we're finished."

Ten minutes later a messenger arrived with a cart from central files. Greer was the sort who liked to see the raw data himself. This suited Ryan. He'd known of a few analysts who had based their reports on selective data and been cut off at the knees for it by this man. The information on the cart was from a variety of sources, but to Ryan the most significant were tactical radio intercepts from listening posts on the Pakistani border, and, he gathered, from inside Afghanistan itself. The nature and tempo of Soviet operations did not indicate a backing off, as seemed to be suggested by a pair of recent articles in *Red Star* and some intelligence sources inside the Soviet Union. They spent three hours reviewing the data.

"I think Sir Basil is placing too much stock in political intelligence and too little in what our listening posts are getting in the field. It would not be unprecedented for the Soviets not to let their field commanders know what's going on in Moscow, of course, but on the whole I do not see a clear picture," Ryan concluded.

The admiral looked at him. "I pay you for answers, Jack."

"Sir, the truth is that Moscow moved in there by mistake. We know that from both military and political intelligence reports. The tenor of the data is pretty clear. From where I sit, I don't see that *they* know what they want to do. In a case like this the bureaucratic mind finds it most easy to do nothing. So, their field commanders are told to continue the mission, while the senior party bosses fumble around looking for a solution and covering their asses for getting into the mess in the first place."

"Okay, so we know that we don't know."

"Yes, sir. I don't like it either, but saying anything else would be a lie."

The admiral snorted. There was a lot of that at Langley, intelligence types giving answers when they didn't even know the questions. Ryan was still new enough to the game that when he didn't know, he said so. Greer wondered if that would change in time. He hoped not.

After lunch a package arrived by messenger from the National Reconnaissance Office. It contained the photographs taken earlier in the day on two successive passes by a KH-11 satellite.

They'd be the last such photos for a while because of the restrictions imposed by orbital mechanics and the generally miserable weather on the Kola Peninsula. The first set of visible light shots taken an hour after the FLASH signal had gone out from Moscow showed the fleet at anchor or tied to the docks. On infrared a number of them were glowing brightly from internal heat, indicating that their boilers or gas-turbine engine plants were operating. The second set of photos had been taken on the next orbital pass at a very low angle.

Ryan scrutinized the blowups. "Wow! *Kirov, Moskva, Kiev,* three *Kara*s, five *Kresta*s, four *Krivak*s, eight *Udaloy*s, and five *Sovremenny*s."

"Search and rescue exercise, eh?" Greer gave Ryan a hard look. "Look at the bottom here. Every fast oiler they have is following them out. That's most of the striking force of the Northern Fleet right there, and if they need oilers, they figure to be out for a while."

"Davenport could have been more specific. But we still have their boomers heading back in. No amphibious ships in this photo, just combatants. Only the new ones, too, the ones with range and speed."

"And the best weapons."

"Yeah," Ryan nodded. "And all scrambled in a few hours. Sir, if they had this planned in advance, we'd have known about it. This must have been laid on today. Interesting."

"You've picked up the English habit of understatement, Jack." Greer stood up to stretch. "I want you to stay over an extra day."

"Okay, sir." He looked at his watch. "Mind if I phone the wife? I don't want her to drive out to the airport for a plane I'm not on."

"Sure, and after you're finished that, I want you to go down and see someone at DIA who used to work for me. See how much operational data they're getting on this sortie. If this is a drill, we'll know soon enough, and you can still take your Surfing Barbie home tomorrow."

It was a Skiing Barbie, but Ryan didn't say so.

THE SIXTH DAY

WEDNESDAY, 8 DECEMBER

CIA Headquarters

Ryan had been to the office of the director of central intelligence several times before to deliver briefings and occasional personal messages from Sir Basil Charleston to his highness, the DCI. It was larger than Greer's, with a better view of the Potomac Valley, and appeared to have been decorated by a professional in a style compatible with the DCI's origins. Arthur Moore was a former judge of the Texas State Supreme Court, and the room reflected his southwestern heritage. He and Admiral Greer were sitting on a sofa near the picture window. Greer waved Ryan over and passed him a folder.

The folder was made of red plastic and had a snap closure. Its edges were bordered with white tape and the cover had a simple white paper label bearing the legends EYES ONLY Δ and WILLOW. Neither notation was unusual. A computer in the basement of the Langley headquarters selected random names at the touch of a key; this prevented a foreign agent from inferring anything from the name of the operation. Ryan opened the folder and looked first at the index sheet. Evidently there were only three copies of the WILLOW document, each initialed by its owner. This one was initialed by the DCI himself. A CIA document with only three copies was unusual enough that Ryan, whose highest clearance was NEBULA, had never encountered one. From the grave looks of Moore and Greer, he guessed that these were two of the Δ-cleared officers; the other, he assumed, was the deputy director of operations (DDO), another Texan named Robert Ritter.

Ryan turned the index sheet. The report was a xeroxed copy of something that had been typed on a manual machine, and it had too many strikeovers to have been done by a real secretary. If Nancy Cummings and the other elite executive secretaries had not been allowed to see this . . . Ryan looked up.

"It's all right, Jack," Greer said. "You've just been cleared for WILLOW."

Ryan sat back, and despite his excitement began to read the document slowly and carefully.

The agent's code name was actually CARDINAL. The highest ranking agent-in-place the CIA had ever had, he was the stuff that legends are made of. CARDINAL had been recruited more than twenty years earlier by Oleg Penkovskiy. Another legend—a dead one—Penkovskiy had at the time been a colonel in the GRU, the Soviet military intelligence agency, a larger and more active counterpart to America's Defense Intelligence Agency (DIA). His position had given him access to daily information on all facets of the Soviet military, from the Red Army's command structure to the operational status of intercontinental missiles. The information he smuggled out through his British contact, Greville Wynne, was supremely valuable, and Western countries had come to depend on it—too much. Penkovskiy was discovered during the Cuban Missile Crisis in 1962. It was his data, ordered and delivered under great pressure and haste, that told President Kennedy that Soviet strategic systems were not ready for war. This information enabled the president to back Khrushchev into a corner from which there was no easy exit. The famous blink ascribed to Kennedy's steady nerves was, as in many such events throughout history, facilitated by his ability to see the other man's cards. This advantage was given him by a courageous agent whom he would never meet. Penkovskiy's response to the FLASH request from Washington was too rash. Already under suspicion, this finished him. He paid for his treason with his life. It was CARDINAL who first learned that he was being watched more closely than was the norm for a society where everyone is watched. He warned Penkovskiy—too late. When it became clear that the colonel could not be extracted from the Soviet Union, he himself urged CARDINAL to betray him. It was the final ironic joke of a brave man that his own death would advance the career of an agent whom he had recruited.

CARDINAL's job was necessarily as secret as his name. A senior adviser and confidant of a Politburo member, CARDINAL often acted as his representative within the Soviet military establishment. He thus had access to political and military intelligence of the highest order. This made his information extraordinarily valuable—and, paradoxically, highly suspect. Those few experienced CIA case officers who knew of him found it impossible to believe that he had not been "turned" somewhere along the line by one of the thousands of KGB counterintelligence officers whose sole duty it is to watch everyone and everything. For this reason CARDINAL-coded material was generally cross-checked against the reports of other spies and sources. But he had outlived many small-fry agents.

The name CARDINAL was known in Washington only to the top three CIA executives. On the first day of each month a new code name was chosen for his data, a name made known only to the highest echelon of CIA officers and analysts. This month it was WILLOW. Before being passed on, grudgingly, to outsiders, CARDINAL data was laundered as carefully as Mafia income to disguise its source. There were also a number of security measures that protected the agent and were unique to him. For fear of cryptographic exposure of his identity, CARDINAL material was hand delivered, never transmitted by radio or landline. CARDINAL himself was a very careful man—Penkovskiy's fate had taught him that. His information was conveyed through a series of intermediaries to the chief of the CIA's Moscow station. He had outlived twelve station chiefs; one of these, a retired field officer, had a brother who was a Jesuit. Every morning the priest, an instructor in philosophy and theology at Fordham University in New York, said mass for the safety and the soul of a man whose name he would never know. It was as good an explanation as any for CARDINAL's continued survival.

Four separate times he had been offered extraction from the Soviet Union. Each time he had refused. To some this was proof that he'd been turned, but to others it was proof that like most successful agents CARDINAL was a man driven by something he alone knew—and therefore, like most successful agents, he was probably a little crazy.

The document Ryan was reading had been in transit for twenty hours. It had taken five for the film to reach the American embassy in Moscow, where it was delivered at once to the station chief. An experienced field officer and former reporter for the *New York Times,* he worked under the cover of press attaché. He developed the film himself in his private darkroom. Thirty minutes after its arrival, he inspected the five exposed frames through a magnifying glass and sent a FLASH-priority dispatch to Washington saying that a CARDINAL signal was en route. Next he transcribed the message from the film to flash paper on his own portable typewriter, translating from the Russian as he went. This security measure erased both the agent's handwriting and, by the paraphrasing automatic to translation, any personal peculiarities of his language. The film was then burned to ashes, the report folded into a metal container much like a cigarette case. This held a small pyrotechnic charge that would go off if the case were improperly opened or suddenly shaken; two CARDINAL signals had been lost when their cases were accidentally dropped. Next the station chief took the case to the embassy's courier-in-residence, who had already been booked on a three-hour Aeroflot flight to London. At Heathrow Airport the courier sprinted to make connections with a Pan Am 747 to New York's Kennedy International, where he connected with the Eastern shuttle to Washington's National Airport. By eight that morning the diplomatic bag was in the State Department. There a CIA officer removed the case, drove it immediately to Langley, and handed it to the DCI. It was opened by an instructor from the CIA's technical services branch. The DCI made three copies on his personal Xerox machine and burned the flash paper in his ashtray. These security measures had struck a few of the men who had succeeded to the office of the DCI as laughable. The laughs had never outlasted the first CARDINAL report.

When Ryan finished the report he referred back to the second page and read it through again, shaking his head slowly. The

WILLOW document was the strongest reinforcement yet of his desire not to know how intelligence information reached him. He closed the folder and handed it back to Admiral Greer.

"Christ, sir."

"Jack, I know I don't have to say this—but what you have just read, nobody, not the president, not Sir Basil, not God if He asks, *nobody* learns of it without the authorization of the director. Is that understood?" Greer had not lost his command voice.

"Yes, sir." Ryan bobbed his head like a schoolboy.

Judge Moore pulled a cigar from his jacket pocket and lit it, looking past the flame into Ryan's eyes. The judge, everyone said, had been a hell of a field officer in his day. He'd worked with Hans Tofte during the Korean War and had been instrumental in bringing off one of the CIA's legendary missions, the disappearance of a Norwegian ship that had been carrying a cargo of medical personnel and supplies for the Chinese. The loss had delayed a Chinese offensive for several months, saving thousands of American and allied lives. But it had been a bloody operation. All of the Chinese personnel and all of the Norwegian crewmen had vanished. It was a bargain in the simple mathematics of war, but the morality of the mission was another matter. For this reason, or perhaps another, Moore had soon thereafter left government service to become a trial lawyer in his native Texas. His career had been spectacularly successful, and he'd advanced from wealthy courtroom lawyer to distinguished appellate judge. He had been recalled to the CIA three years earlier because of his unique combination of absolute personal integrity and experience in black operations. Judge Moore hid a Harvard law degree and a highly ordered mind behind the facade of a West Texas cowboy, something he had never been but simulated with ease.

"So, Dr. Ryan, what do you think of this?" Moore said as the deputy director of operations came in. "Hi, Bob, come on over here. We just showed Ryan here the WILLOW file."

"Oh?" Ritter slid a chair over, neatly trapping Ryan in the corner. "And what does the admiral's fair-haired boy think of that?"

"Gentlemen, I assume that you all regard this information as genuine," Ryan said cautiously, getting nods. "Sir, if this information was hand delivered by the Archangel Michael, I'd have trouble believing it—but since you gentlemen say it's reliable . . ." They wanted his opinion. The problem was, his conclusion was too incredible. Well, he decided, *I've gotten this far by giving my honest opinions . . .*

Ryan took a deep breath and gave them his evaluation.

"Very well, Dr. Ryan," Judge Moore nodded sagaciously. "First I want to hear what else it might be, then I want to defend your analysis."

"Sir, the most obvious alternative doesn't bear much thinking about. Besides, they've been able to do it since Friday and they haven't done it," Ryan said, keeping his voice low and reasonable. Ryan had trained himself to be objective. He ran through the four alternatives he had considered, careful to examine each in detail. This was no time to allow personal views to intrude on his thinking. He spoke for ten minutes.

"I suppose there's one more possibility, Judge," he concluded. "This could be disinformation aimed at blowing this source. I cannot evaluate that possibility."

"The thought has occurred to us. All right, now that you've gone this far, you might as well give your operational recommendation."

"Sir, the admiral can tell you what the navy'll say."

"I sorta figured that one out, boy," Moore laughed. "What do you think?"

"Judge, setting up the decision tree on this will not be easy—there are too many variables, too many possible contingencies. But I'd say yes. If it's possible, if we can work out the details, we ought to try. The biggest question is the availability of our own assets. Do we have the pieces in place?"

Greer answered. "Our assets are slim. One carrier, *Kennedy*. I checked. *Saratoga*'s in Norfolk with an engineering casualty. On the other hand, HMS *Invincible* was just over here for the NATO exercise, sailed from Norfolk Monday night. Admiral White, I believe, commanding a small battle group."

"Lord White, sir?" Ryan asked. "The earl of Weston?"

"You know him?" Moore asked.

"Yes, sir. Our wives are friendly. I hunted with him last September, a grouse shoot inn Scotland. He makes noises like a good operator, and I hear he has a good reputation."

"You're thinking we might want to borrow their ships, James?" Moore asked. "If so, we'll have to tell them about this. But we have to tell our side first. There's a meeting of the National Security Council at one this afternoon. Ryan, you will prepare the briefing papers and deliver the briefing yourself."

Ryan blinked. "That's not much time, sir."

"James here says you work well under pressure. Prove it." He looked at Greer. "Get a copy of his briefing papers and be ready to fly to London. That's the president's decision. If we want their boats, we'll have to tell them why. That means briefing the prime minister, and that's your job. Bob, I want you to confirm this report. Do what you have to do, but do not get WILLOW involved."

"Right," Ritter replied.

Moore looked at his watch. "We'll meet back here at 3:30, depending on how the meeting goes. Ryan, you have ninety minutes. Get cracking."

What am I being measured for? Ryan wondered. There was talk in the CIA that Judge Moore would be leaving soon for a comfortable ambassadorship, perhaps to the Court of St. James's, a fitting reward for a man who had worked long and hard to reestablish a close relationship with the British. If the judge left, Admiral Greer would probably move into his office. He had the virtues of age—he wouldn't be around that long—and of friends on Capitol Hill. Ritter had neither. He had complained too long and too openly about congressmen who leaked information on his operations and his field agents, getting men killed in the process of demonstrating their importance on the local cocktail circuit. He also had an ongoing feud with the chairman of the Select Intelligence Committee.

With that sort of reshuffling at the top and this sudden access to new and fantastic information . . . What does it mean for me? Ryan asked himself. They couldn't want him to be the next DDI. He knew he didn't have anything like the experience required for that job—though maybe in another five or six years . . .

Reykjanes Ridge

Ramius inspected his status board. The *Red October* was heading southwest on track eight, the westernmost surveyed route on what Northern Fleet submariners called Gorshkov's Railroad. His speed was thirteen knots. It never occurred to him that this was an unlucky number, an Anglo-Saxon superstition. They would hold this course and speed for another twenty hours. Immediately behind him, Kamarov was seated at the submarine's gravitometer board, a large rolled chart behind him. The young lieutenant was chain-smoking, and looked tense as he ticked off their position on the chart. Ramius did not disturb him. Kamarov knew this job, and Borodin would relieve him in another two hours.

Installed in the *Red October*'s keel was a highly sensitive device called a gradiometer, essentially two large lead weights separated by a space of one hundred yards. A laser-computer system measured the space between the weights down to a fraction of an angstrom. Distortions of that distance or lateral movement of the weights indicated variations in the local gravitational field. The navigator compared these highly precise local values to the values on his chart. With careful use of gravitometers in the ship's inertial navigation system, he could plot the vessel's location to within a hundred meters, half the length of the ship.

The mass-sensing system was being added to all the submarines that could accommodate it. Younger attack boat commanders, Ramius knew, had used it to run the Railroad at high speed. Good for the commander's ego, Ramius judged, but a little hard on the navigator. He felt no need for recklessness. Perhaps the letter had been a mistake . . . No, it prevented second thoughts. And the sensor suites on attack submarines simply were not good enough to detect the *Red October* so long as he maintained his silent routine. Ramius was certain of this; he had used them all. He would get where he wanted to go, do what he wanted to do, and nobody, not his own countrymen, not even the Americans, would be able to do a thing about it. That's why earlier he had listened to the passage of an *Alfa* thirty miles to his east and smiled.

The White House

Judge Moore's CIA car was a Cadillac limousine that came with a driver and a security man who kept an Uzi submachinegun under the dashboard. The driver turned right off Pennsylvania Avenue onto Executive Drive. More a parking lot than a street, this served the needs of senior officials and reporters who worked at the White House and the Executive

Office Building. "Old State," that shining example of Insti-
tutional Grotesque that towered over the executive mansion.
The driver pulled smoothly into a vacant VIP slot and jumped
out to open the doors after the security man had swept the area
with his eyes. The judge got out first and went ahead, and as
Ryan caught up he found himself walking on the man's left,
half a step behind. It took a moment to remember that this
instinctive action was exactly what the marine corps had taught
him at Quantico was the proper way for a junior officer to
accompany his betters. It forced Ryan to consider just how
junior he was.

"Ever been in here before, Jack?"

"No, sir, I haven't."

Moore was amused. "That's right, you come from around
here. Now, if you came from farther away, you'd have made
the trip a few times." A marine guard held the door open for
them. Inside a Secret Service agent signed them in. Moore
nodded and walked on.

"Is this to be in the Cabinet Room, sir?"

"Uh-uh. Situation Room, downstairs. It's more comfortable
and better equipped for this sort of thing. The slides you need
are already down there, all set up. Nervous?"

"Yes, sir, I sure am."

Moore chuckled. "Settle down, boy. The president has wanted
to meet you for some time now. He liked that report on terrorism
you did a few years back, and I've shown him some more of
your work, the one on Russian missile submarine operations,
and the one you just did on management practices in their arms
industries. All in all, I think you'll find he's a pretty regular
guy. Just be ready when he asks questions. He'll hear every word
you say, and he has a way of hitting you with good ones
when he wants." Moore turned to descend a staircase. Ryan followed him down three flights, then they came to a door which
led to a corridor. The judge turned left and walked to yet another door, this one guarded by another Secret Service agent.

"Afternoon, Judge. The president will be down shortly."

"Thank you. This is Dr. Ryan. I'll vouch for him."

"Right." The agent waved them in.

It was not nearly as spectacular as Ryan had expected. The
Situation Room was probably no larger than the Oval Office
upstairs. There was expensive-looking wood paneling over what
were probably concrete walls. This part of the White House

dated back to the complete rebuilding job done under Truman.
Ryan's lectern was to his left as he went in. It stood in front
and slightly to the right of a roughly diamond-shaped table,
and behind it was the projection screen. A note on the lectern
said the slide projector in the middle of the table was already
loaded and focused, and gave the order of the slides, which
had been delivered from the National Reconnaissance Office.

Most of the people were already here, all of the Joint Chiefs
of Staff and the secretary of defense. The secretary of state,
he remembered, was still shuttling back and forth between
Athens and Ankara trying to settle the latest Cyprus situation.
This perennial thorn in NATO's southern flank had flared up
a few weeks earlier when a Greek student had run over a Turkish
child with his car and been killed by a gang minutes later. By
the end of the day fifty people had been injured, and the putatively allied countries were once more at each other's throats.
Now two American aircraft carriers were cruising the Aegean
as the secretary of state labored to calm both sides. It was bad
enough that two young people had died, Ryan thought, but not
something to get a country's army mobilized for.

Also at the table were General Thomas Hilton, chairman of
the Joint Chiefs of Staff, and Jeffrey Pelt, the president's national security adviser, a pompous man Ryan had met years
before at Georgetown University's Center for Strategic and
International Studies. Pelt was going through some papers and
dispatches. The chiefs were chatting amicably among themselves when the commandant of the marine corps looked up
and spotted Ryan. He got up and walked over.

"You Jack Ryan?" General David Maxwell asked.

"Yes, sir." Maxwell was a short, tough fireplug of a man
whose stubbly haircut seemed to spark with aggressive energy.
He looked Ryan over before shaking hands.

"Pleased to meet you, son. I liked what you did over in
London. Good for the corps." He referred to the terrorist incident in which Ryan had very nearly been killed. "That was
good, quick action you took, Lieutenant."

"Thank you, sir. I was lucky."

"Good officer's supposed to be lucky. I hear you got some
interesting news for us."

"Yes sir. I think you will find it worth your time."

"Nervous?" The general saw the answer and smiled thinly.
"Relax, son. Everybody in this damned cellar puts his pants

on the same way as you." He backhanded Ryan to the stomach and went back to his seat. The general whispered something to Admiral Daniel Foster, chief of naval operations. The CNO looked Ryan over for a moment before going back to what he was doing.

The president arrived a minute later. Everyone in the room stood as he walked to his chair, on Ryan's right. He said a few quick things to Dr. Pelt, then looked pointedly at the DCI.

"Gentlemen, if we can bring this meeting to order, I think Judge Moore has some news for us."

"Thank you, Mr. President. Gentlemen, we've had an interesting development today with respect to the Soviet naval operation that started yesterday. I have asked Dr. Ryan here to deliver the briefing."

The president turned to Ryan. The younger man could feel himself being appraised. "You may proceed."

Ryan took a sip of ice water from a glass hidden in the lectern. He had a wireless control for the slide projector and a choice of pointers. A separate high-intensity light illuminated his notes. The pages were full of errors and scribbled corrections. There had not been time to edit the copy.

"Thank you, Mr. President. Gentlemen, my name is Jack Ryan, and the subject of this briefing is recent Soviet naval activity in the North Atlantic. Before I get to that it will be necessary for me to lay a little groundwork. I trust you will bear with me for a few minutes, and please feel free to interrupt with questions at any time." Ryan clicked on the slide projector. The overhead lights near the screen dimmed automatically.

"These photographs come to us courtesy of the British," Ryan said. He now had everyone's attention. "The ship you see here is the Soviet fleet ballistic missile submarine *Red October*, photographed by a British agent in her dock at their submarine base at Polyarnyy, near Murmansk in northern Russia. As you can see, she is a very large vessel, about 650 feet long, a beam of roughly 85 feet, and an estimated submerged displacement of 32,000 tons. These figures are roughly comparable to those of a World War I battleship."

Ryan lifted a pointer. "In addition to being considerably larger than our own *Ohio*-class Trident submarines, *Red October* has a number of technical differences. She carries twenty-six missiles instead of our twenty-four. The earlier *Typhoon*-class vessels, from which she was developed, only have twenty.

October carries the new SS-N-20 sea-launched ballistic missile, the Seahawk. It's a solid-fuel missile with a range of about six thousand nautical miles, and it carries eight multiple independently targetable reentry vehicles, MIRVs, each with an estimated yield of five hundred kilotons. It's the same RV carried by their SS-18s, but there are less of them per launcher.

"As you can see, the missile tubes are located forward of the sail instead of aft, as in our subs. The forward diving planes fold into slots in the hull here; ours go on the sail. She has twin screws; ours have one propeller. And finally, her hull is oblate. Instead of being cylindrical like ours, it is flattened out markedly top and bottom."

Ryan clicked to the next slide. It showed two views superimposed, bow over stern. "These frames were delivered to us undeveloped. They were processed by the National Reconnaissance Office. Please note the doors here at the bow and here at the stern. The British were a little puzzled by these, and that's why I was permitted to bring the shots over earlier this week. We weren't able to figure out this function at the CIA either, and it was decided to seek the opinion of an outside consultant."

"Who decided?" the secretary of defense demanded angrily. "Hell, I haven't even seen them yet!"

"We only got them Monday, Bert," Judge Moore replied soothingly. "These two on the screen are only four hours old. Ryan suggested an outside expert, and James Greer approved it. I concurred."

"His name is Oliver W. Tyler. Dr. Tyler is a former naval officer who is now associate professor of engineering at the Naval Academy and a paid consultant to Sea Systems Command. He's an expert in the analysis of Soviet naval technology. Skip— Dr. Tyler—concluded that these doors are the intake and exhaust vents for a new silent propulsion system. He is currently developing a computer model of the system, and we hope to have this information by the end of the week. The system itself is rather interesting." Ryan explained Tyler's analysis briefly.

"Okay, Dr. Ryan." The president leaned forward. "You've just told us that the Soviets have built a missile submarine that's supposed to be hard for our men to locate. I don't suppose that's news. Go on."

"*Red October*'s captain is a man named Marko Ramius. That is a Lithuanian name, although we believe his internal passport designates his nationality as Great Russian. He is the son of a high Party official, and as good a submarine commander as they have. He's taken out the lead ship of every Soviet submarine class for the past ten years.

"*Red October* sailed last Friday. We do not know exactly what her orders were, but ordinarily their missile subs—that is, those with the newer long-range missiles—confine their activities to the Barents Sea and adjacent areas in which they can be protected from our attack boats by land-based ASW aircraft, their own surface ships, and attack submarines. About noon local time on Sunday, we noted increased search activity in the Barents Sea. At the time we took this to be a local ASW exercise, and by late Monday it looked to be a test of *October*'s new drive system.

"As you all know, early yesterday saw a vast increase in Soviet naval activity. Nearly all of the blue-water ships assigned to their Northern Fleet are now at sea, accompanied by all of their fast fleet-replenishment vessels. Additional fleet auxiliaries sailed from the Baltic Fleet bases and the western Mediterranean. Even more disquieting is the fact that nearly every nuclear submarine assigned to the Northern Fleet—their largest—appears to be heading into the North Atlantic. This includes three from the Med, since submarines there come from the Northern Fleet, not the Black Sea Fleet. Now we think we know why all this happened." Ryan clicked to the next slide. This one showed the North Atlantic, from Florida to the Pole, with Soviet ships marked in red.

"The day *Red October* sailed, Captain Ramius evidently posted a letter to Admiral Yuri Ilych Padorin. Padorin is chief of the Main Political Administration of their navy. We do not know what that letter said, but here we can see its results. This began to happen not four hours after that letter was opened. Fifty-eight nuclear-powered submarines and twenty-eight major surface combatants all headed our way. This is a remarkable reaction in four hours. This morning we learned what their orders are.

"Gentlemen, these ships have been ordered to locate *Red October,* and if necessary, to sink her." Ryan paused for effect. "As you can see, the Soviet surface force is here, about halfway between the European mainland and Iceland. Their submarines, these in particular, are all heading southwest towards the U.S. coast. Please note, there is no unusual activity on the Pacific side of either country—except we have information that Soviet fleet ballistic missile submarines in *both* oceans are being recalled to port.

"Therefore, while we do not know exactly what Captain Ramius said, we can draw some conclusions from these patterns of activity. It would appear that they think he's heading in our direction. Given his estimated speed as something between ten and thirty knots, he could be anywhere from here, below Iceland, to here, just off our coast. You will note that in either case he has successfully avoided detection by all four of these SOSUS barriers—"

"Wait a minute. You say they have issued orders to their ships to sink one of their submarines?"

"Yes, Mr. President."

The president looked at the DCI. "This is reliable information, Judge?"

"Yes, Mr. President, we believe it to be solid."

"Okay, Dr. Ryan, we're all waiting. What's this Ramius fellow up to?"

"Mr. President, our evaluation of this intelligence data is that *Red October* is attempting to defect to the United States."

The room went very quiet for a moment. Ryan could hear the whirring of the fan in the slide projector as the National Security Council pondered that. He held his hands on the lectern to keep them from shaking under the stare of the ten men in front of him.

"That's a very interesting conclusion, Doctor." The president smiled. "Defend it."

"Mr. President, no other conclusion fits the data. The really crucial thing, of course, is the recall of their other missile boats. They've never done that before. Add to that the fact that they have issued orders to sink their newest and most powerful missile sub, and that they are chasing in this direction, and one is left with the conclusion that they think she has left the reservation and is heading this way."

"Very well. What else could it be?"

"Sir, he could have told them that he's going to fire his missiles. At us, at them, the Chinese, or just about anyone else."

"And you don't think so?"

"No, Mr. President. The SS-N-20 has a range of six thousand miles. That means he could have hit any target in the

Northern Hemisphere from the moment he left the dock. He's had six days to do that, but he has not fired. Moreover, if he had threatened to launch his birds, he would have to consider the possibility that the Soviets would enlist our assistance to locate and sink him. After all, if our surveillance systems detect the launch of nuclear-armed missiles in any direction, things could get very tense, very quickly."

"You know he could fire his birds in both directions and start World War III," the secretary of defense observed.

"Yes, Mr. Secretary. In that case we'd be dealing with a total madman—more than one, in fact. On our missile boats there are five officers, who must all agree and act in unison to fire their missiles. The Soviets have the same number. For political reasons their nuclear warhead security procedures are even more elaborate than ours. Five or more people, all of whom wish to end the world?" Ryan shook his head. "That seems most unlikely, sir, and again, the Soviets would be well advised to inform us and enlist our aid."

"Do you really think they would inform us?" Dr. Pelt asked. His tone indicated what he thought.

"Sir, that's more a psychological question than a technical one, and I deal principally with technical intelligence. Some of the men in this room have met their Soviet counterparts and are better equipped to answer that than I am. My answer to your question, however, is yes. That would be the only rational thing for them to do, and while I do not regard the Soviets as entirely rational by our standards, they are rational by their own. They are not given to this sort of high-stakes gambling."

"Who is?" the president observed. "What else might it be?"

"Several things, sir. It could simply be a major naval exercise aimed at testing their ability to close our sea lines of communication and our ability to respond, both on short notice. We reject this possibility for several reasons. It's too soon after their autumn naval exercise, CRIMSON STORM, and they are only using nuclear submarines; no diesel-powered boats seem to be involved. Clearly speed is at a premium in their operation. And as a practical matter, they do not run major exercises at this time of year."

"And why is that?" the president asked.

Admiral Foster answered for Ryan. "Mr. President, the weather up there at this time of the year is extremely bad. Even we don't schedule exercises under these conditions."

"I seem to recall we just ran a NATO exercise, Admiral," Pelt noted.

"Yes, sir, south of Bermuda, where the weather's a lot nicer. Except for an antisub exercise off the British Isles, all of NIFTY DOLPHIN was held on our side of the lake."

"Okay, let's get back to what else their fleet might be up to," the president ordered.

"Well, sir, it might not be an exercise at all. It could be the real thing. This could be the beginning of a conventional war against NATO, its first step being interdiction of the sea lines of communication. If so, they've achieved complete strategic surprise and are now throwing it away by operating so overtly that we cannot fail to notice or react forcefully. Moreover, there is no corresponding activity whatever in their other armed services. Their army and air force—except for maritime surveillance aircraft—and their Pacific Fleet are engaged in routine training operations.

"Finally, this could be an attempt to provoke or divert us, drawing our attention to this while they are preparing to spring a surprise somewhere else. If so, they're going about it in a strange way. If you try to provoke somebody, you don't do it in his front yard. The Atlantic, Mr. President, is still our ocean. As you can see from this chart, we have bases here in Iceland, the Azores, all up and down our coast. We have allies on both sides of the ocean, and we can establish air superiority over the entire Atlantic if we so choose. Their navy is numerically large, larger than ours in some critical areas, but they cannot project force as well as we can—not yet, anyway—and certainly not right off our coast." Ryan took a sip of water.

"So, gentlemen, we have a Soviet missile submarine at sea when all the others, in both oceans, are being recalled. We have their fleet at sea with orders to sink that sub, and evidently they are chasing it in our direction. As I said, this is the only conclusion that fits the data."

"How many men on the sub, Doctor?" the president asked.

"We believe 110 or so, sir."

"So, 110 men all decide to defect to the United States at one time. Not an altogether bad idea," the president observed wryly, "but hardly a likely one."

Ryan was ready for that. "There is precedent for this, sir. On November 8, 1975, the *Storozhevoy,* a Soviet *Krivak*-class missile frigate, attempted to run from Riga, Latvia, to the Swedish island of Gotland. The political officer aboard, Valery Sablin, led a mutiny of the enlisted personnel. They locked their officers in their cabins and raced away from the dock. They came close to making it. Air and fleet units attacked them and forced them to halt within fifty miles of Swedish territorial waters. Two more hours and they would have made it. Sablin and twenty-six others were court-martialed and shot. More recently we have had reports of mutinous episodes on several Soviet vessels—especially submarines. In 1980 an *Echo*-class Soviet attack submarine surfaced off Japan. The captain claimed to have had a fire aboard, but photographs taken by naval reconnaissance aircraft—ours and Japanese—did not show smoke or fire-damaged debris being jettisoned from the submarine. However, the crewmen on deck did show sufficient evidence of trauma to support the conclusion that a riot had taken place aboard. We have had similar, sketchier reports for some years now. While I admit this is an extreme example, our conclusion is decidedly not without precedent."

Admiral Foster reached inside his jacket and came out with a plastic-tipped cigar. His eyes sparkled behind the match. "You know, I could almost believe this."

"Then I wish you'd tell us all why, Admiral," the president said, "because I still don't."

"Mr. President, most mutinies are led by officers, not enlisted men. The reason for this is simply that the enlisted men do not know how to navigate the ship. Moreover, officers have the advantages and educational background to know that successful rebellion is a possibility. Both of these factors would be even more true in the Soviet Navy. What if just the officers are doing this?"

"And the rest of the crew is going along with them?" Pelt asked. "Knowing what would happen to them and their families?"

Foster puffed a few times on his cigar. "Ever been to sea, Dr. Pelt? No? Let's imagine for the moment that you're taking a world cruise, on the *Queen Elizabeth 2*, say. One fine day you're in the middle of the Pacific Ocean—but how do you know exactly where you are? You don't know. You know what the officers tell you. Oh, sure, if you know a little astronomy, you might be able to estimate your latitude to within a few hundred miles. With a good watch and some knowledge of spherical trigonometry you might even guess your longitude to within a few hundred. Okay? That's on a ship that you can see from.

"These guys are on a submarine. You can't see a whole lot. Now, what if the officers—not even all the officers—are doing this? How will the crew know what's going on?" Foster shook his head. "They won't. They can't. Even our guys might not, and our men are trained a lot better than theirs. Their seamen are nearly all conscripts, remember. On a nuclear submarine you are absolutely cut off from the outside world. No radios except for ELF and VLF—and that's all encrypted; messages have to come through the communications officer. So, he has to be in on it. Same thing with the boat's navigator. They use inertial navigation systems, same as us. We have one of theirs, from that *Golf* we lifted off Hawaii. In their machine the data is also encrypted. The quartermaster reads the numbers off the machine, and the navigator gets their position from a book. In the Red Army, on *land,* maps are classified documents. Same thing in their navy. The enlisted men don't get to see charts and are not encouraged to know where they are. This would be especially true on missile submarines, right?

"On top of all that, these guys are working sailors, nucs. When you're at sea, you have a job to do, and you do it. On their ships, that means from fourteen to eighteen hours a day. These kids are all draftees with very simple training. They're taught to perform one or two tasks—and to follow their orders exactly. The Soviets train people to do their jobs by rote, with as little thinking as possible. That's why on major repair jobs you see officers holding tools. Their men will have neither the time nor the inclination to question their officers about what's going on. You do your job, and depend on everybody else to do his. That's what discipline at sea is all about." Foster tapped his cigar ash into an ashtray. "Yes, sir, you get the officers together, maybe not even all of them, and this would work. Getting ten or twelve dissidents together is a whole lot easier than assembling a hundred."

"Eas*ier*, but hardly easy, Dan," General Hilton objected. "For Christ's sake, they have at least one political officer aboard, plus moles from their intelligence outfits. You really think a Party hack would go along with this?"

"Why not? You heard Ryan—that frigate's mutiny was led by the political officer."

"Yeah, and since then they have shaken up that whole directorate," Hilton responded.

"We have defecting KGB types all the time, all good Party members," Foster said. Clearly he liked the idea of a defecting Russian sub.

The president took all this in, then turned to Ryan. "Dr. Ryan, you have managed to persuade me that your scenario is a theoretical possibility. Now, what does the CIA think we ought to do about it?"

"Mr. President, I'm an intelligence analyst, not—"

"I know very well what you are, Dr. Ryan. I've read enough of your work. I can see you have an opinion. I want to hear it."

Ryan didn't even look at Judge Moore. "We grab her, sir."

"Just like that?"

"No, Mr. President, probably not. However, Ramius could surface off the Virginia Capes in a day or two and request political asylum. We ought to be prepared for that contingency, sir, and my opinion is that we should welcome him with open arms." Ryan saw nods from all the chiefs. Finally somebody was on his side.

"You've stuck your neck out on this one," the president observed kindly.

"Sir, you asked me for an opinion. It will probably not be that easy. These *Alfa*s and *Victor*s appear to be racing for our coast, almost certainly with the intention of establishing an interdiction force—effectively a blockade of our Atlantic coast."

"Blockade," the president said, "an ugly word."

"Judge," General Hilton said, "I suppose it's occurred to you that this is a piece of disinformation aimed at blowing whatever highly placed source generated this report?"

Judge Moore affected a sleepy smile. "It has, Gener'l. If this is a sham, it's a damned elaborate one. Dr. Ryan was directed to prepare this briefing on the assumption that this data is genuine. If it is not, the responsibility is mine." God bless you, Judge, Ryan said to himself, wondering just how gold-plated the WILLOW source was. The judge went on, "In any case, gentlemen, we will have to respond to this Soviet activity whether our analysis is accurate or not."

"Are you getting confirmation on this, Judge?" the president asked.

"Yes, sir, we are working on that."

"Good." The president was sitting straight, and Ryan noted his voice become crisper. "The judge is correct. We have to react to this, whatever they're really up to. Gentlemen, the Soviet Navy is heading for our coast. What are we doing about it?"

Admiral Foster answered first. "Mr. President, our fleet is pulling to sea at this moment. Everything that'll steam is out already, or will be by tomorrow night. We've recalled our carriers from the South Atlantic, and we are redeploying our nuclear submarines to deal with this threat. We began this morning to saturate the air over their surface force with P-3C Orion patrol aircraft, assisted by British Nimrods operating out of Scotland. General?" Foster turned to Hilton.

"At this moment we have E-3A Sentry AWACS-type aircraft circling them along with Dan's Orions, both accompanied by F-15 Eagle fighters out of Iceland. By this time Friday we'll have a squadron of B-52s operating from Loring Air Base in Maine. These will be armed with Harpoon air-to-surface missiles, and they'll be orbiting the Soviets in relays. Nothing aggressive, you understand," Hilton smiled. "Just to let them know we're interested. If they continue to come this way, we will redeploy some tactical air assets to the East Coast, and, subject to your approval, we can activate some national guard and reserve squadrons quietly."

"Just how will you do that quietly?" Pelt asked.

"Dr. Pelt, we have a number of guard outfits scheduled to run through our Red Flag facility at Nellis in Nevada starting this Sunday, a routine training rotation. They go to Maine instead of Nevada. The bases are pretty big, and they belong to SAC." Hilton referred to the Strategic Air Command. "They have good security."

"How many carriers do we have handy?" the president asked.

"Only one at the moment, sir, *Kennedy*. *Saratoga* stripped a main turbine last week, and it'll take a month to replace. *Nimitz* and *America* are both in the South Atlantic right now, *America* coming back from the Indian Ocean, *Nimitz* heading out to the Pacific. Bad luck. Can we recall a carrier from the eastern Med?"

"No." The president shook his head. "This Cyprus thing is

still too sensitive. Do we really need to? If anything . . . untoward happens, can we handle their surface force with what
we have at hand?"

"Yes, sir!" General Hilton said at once. "Dr. Ryan said it:
the Atlantic is our ocean. The air force alone will have over
five hundred aircraft designated for this operation, and another
three or four hundred from the navy. If any sort of shooting
match develops, that Soviet fleet will have an exciting and
short life."

"We will try to avoid that, of course," the president said
quietly. "The first press reports surfaced this morning. We had
a call from Bud Wilkins of the *Times* right before lunch. If the
American people find out too soon what the scope of this is
. . . Jeff?"

"Mr. President, let's assume for the moment that Dr. Ryan's
analysis is correct. I don't see what we can do about it," Pelt
said.

"What?" Ryan blurted. "I, ah, beg your pardon, sir."

"We can't exactly steal a Russian missile sub."

"Why not!" Foster demanded. "Hell, we have enough of
their tanks and aircraft." The other chiefs agreed.

"An aircraft with a crew of one or two is one thing, Admiral.
A nuclear-powered submarine with twenty-six rockets and a
crew of over a hundred is something else. Naturally, we can
give asylum to the defecting officers."

"So, you're saying that if the thing does come sailing into
Norfolk," Hilton joined in, "we give it back! Christ, man, it
carries two hundred warheads! They just might use those goddamned things against us someday, you know. Are you *sure*
you want to give them back?"

"That's a billion-dollar asset, General," Pelt said diffidently.

Ryan saw the president smile. He was said to like lively
discussions. "Judge, what are the legal ramifications?"

"That's admiralty law, Mr. President." Moore looked uneasy
for once. "I've never had an admiralty practice, takes me all
the way back to law school. Admiralty is *jus gentium*—the
same legal codes theoretically apply to all countries. American
and British admiralty courts routinely cite each other's rulings.
But as for the rights that attach to a mutinous crew—I have
no idea."

"Judge, we are not dealing with mutiny or piracy," Foster
noted. "The correct term is *barratry*, I believe. Mutiny is when

the crew rebels against lawful authority. Gross misconduct of the officers is called barratry. Anyway, I hardly think we need to attack legal folderol to a situation involving nuclear weapons."

"We might, Admiral," the president mused. "As Jeff said, this is a highly valuable asset, legally their property, and they will know we have her. I think we are agreed that not all the crew is likely to be in on this. If so, those not party to the mutiny—barratry, whatever—will want to return home after it's all over. And we'll have to let them go, won't we?"

"Have to?" General Maxwell was doodling on a pad. "Have to?"

"General," the president said firmly, "we will not, repeat *not*, be party to the imprisonment or murder of men whose only desire is to return to home and family. Is that understood?" He looked around the table. "If they know we have her, they'll want her back. And they will know we have her from the crewmen who want to return home. In any case, big as this thing is, how could we hide her?"

"We might be able to," Foster said neutrally, "but as you say, the crew is a complication. I presume we'll have the chance to look her over?"

"You mean conduct a quarantine inspection, check her for seaworthiness, maybe make sure they're not smuggling drugs into the country?" The president grinned. "I think we might arrange that. But we are getting ahead of ourselves. There's a lot of ground to cover before we get to that point. What about or allies?"

"The English just had one of their carriers over here. Could you use her, Dan?" General Hilton asked.

"If they let us borrow her, yes. We just finished that ASW exercise south of Bermuda, and the Brits acquitted themselves well. We could use *Invincible*, the four escorts, and the three attack boats. The force is being recalled at high speed because of this."

"Do they know of this development, Judge?" the president asked.

"Not unless they've developed it themselves. This information is only a few hours old." Moore did not reveal that Sir Basil had his own ear in the Kremlin. Ryan didn't know much about it himself, had only heard some disconnected rumblings.

"With your permission, I have asked Admiral Greer to be ready to fly to England to brief the prime minister."

"Why not just send—"

Judge Moore was shaking his head. "Mr. President, this information—let's say it's only delivered by hand." Eyebrows went up all around the table.

"When is he leaving?"

"This evening, if you wish. There are a couple of VIP flights leaving Andrews tonight. Congressional flights." It was the usual end-of-session junket season. Christmas in Europe, on fact-finding missions.

"General, do we have anything quicker?" the president asked Hilton.

"We can scratch up a VC-141. Lockheed JetStar, almost as fast as a -135, and we can have it up in half an hour."

"Do it."

"Yes, sir, I'll call them in right now." Hilton rose and walked to a phone in the corner.

"Judge, tell Greer to pack his bags. I'll have a cover letter waiting for him on the plane to give to the prime minister. Admiral, you want the *Invincible?*"

"Yes, sir."

"I'll get her for you. Next, what do we tell our people at sea?"

"If *October* just sails in, it won't be necessary, but if we have to communicate with her—"

"Excuse me, Judge," Ryan said, "that is rather likely—that we'll have to. They'll probably have these attack boats on the coast before she gets here. If so, we'll have to warn her off if only to save the defecting officers. They are out to locate and sink her."

"We haven't detected her. What makes you think they can?" Foster asked, miffed at the suggestion.

"They did build her, Admiral. So they might know things about her that will enable them to locate her more easily than us."

"Makes sense," the president said. "That means somebody goes out to brief the fleet commanders. We can't broadcast this, can we, Judge?"

"Mr. President, this source is too valuable to compromise in any way. That's all I can say here, sir."

"Very well, somebody flies out. Next thing is, we'll have to talk to the Soviets about this. For the moment they can say that they're operating in home waters. When will they pass Iceland?"

"Tomorrow night, unless they change course," Foster answered.

"Okay, we give it a day, for them to call this off and for us to confirm this report. Judge, I want something to back up this fairy tale in twenty-four hours. If they haven't turned back by midnight tomorrow, I'll call Ambassador Arbatov into my office Friday morning." He turned to the chiefs. "Gentlemen, I want to see contingency plans for dealing with this situation by tomorrow afternoon. We will meet here tomorrow at two. One more thing: *no leaks!* This information does not go beyond this room without my personal approval. If this story breaks to the press, I'll have heads on my desk. Yes, General?"

"Mr. President, in order to develop those plans," Hilton said after sitting back down, "we have to work through our field commanders and some of our own operations people. Certainly we'll need Admiral Blackburn." Blackburn was CINCLANT, commander in chief of the Atlantic.

"Let me think that one over. I'll be back to you in an hour. How many people at the CIA know about this?"

"Four, sir. Ritter, Greer, Ryan, and myself, sir. That's all."

"Keep it that way." The president had been bedeviled by security leaks for months.

"Yes, Mr. President."

"Meeting is adjourned."

The president stood. Moore walked around the table to keep him from leaving at once. Dr. Pelt stayed also as the rest filed out of the room. Ryan stood outside the door.

"That was all right." General Maxwell grabbed his hand. He waited until everyone else was a few yards down the hall before going on. "I think you're crazy, son, but you sure put a burr under Dan Foster's saddle. No, even better: I think he got a hard-on." The little general chuckled. "And if we get the sub, maybe we can change the president's mind and arrange for the crew to disappear. The judge did that once, you know." It was a thought that chilled Ryan as he watched Maxwell swagger down the hall.

"Jack, you want to come back in here a minute?" Moore's voice called.

"You're an historian, right?" the president asked, reviewing his notes. Ryan hadn't even noticed him holding a pen.

"Yes, Mr. President. That's what my graduate degree's in." Ryan shook his hand.

"You have a fine sense of the dramatic, Jack. You would have made a decent trial lawyer." The president had made his reputation as a hard-driving state's attorney. He had survived an unsuccessful Mafia assassination attempt early in his career which hadn't hurt his political ambitions one bit. "Damned nice briefing."

"Thank you, Mr. President." Ryan beamed.

"The judge tells me you know the commander of that British task force."

It was like a sandbag hitting his head. "Yes, sir. Admiral White. I've hunted with him, and our wives are good friends. They're close to the Royal Family."

"Good. Somebody has to fly out to brief our fleet commander, then go on to talk to the Brits, if we get their carrier, as I expect we will. The judge says we ought to let Admiral Davenport go out with you. So, you fly out to *Kennedy* tonight, then on to *Invincible*."

"Mr. President, I—"

"Come now, Dr. Ryan," Pelt smiled thinly. "You are uniquely suited to this. You already have access to the intelligence, you know the British commander, and you're a naval intelligence specialist. You fit. Tell me, how eager do you think the navy is about getting this *Red October?*"

"Of course they're interested in it, sir. To get a chance to look at it, better yet to run it, take it apart, and run it some more. It would be the intelligence coup of all time."

"That's true. But maybe they're a little too eager."

"I don't understand what you mean, sir," Ryan said, though he understood it just fine. Pelt was the president's favorite. He was not the Pentagon's favorite.

"They might take a chance that we might not want them to take."

"Dr. Pelt, if you're saying that a uniformed officer would—"

"He's not saying that. At least not exactly. What he's saying is that it might be useful for me to have somebody out there who can give me an independent, civilian point of view."

"Sir, you don't know me."

"I've read a lot of your reports." The chief executive was smiling. It was said he could turn dazzling charm on and off like a spotlight. Ryan was being blinded, knew it, and couldn't do a thing about it. "I like your work. You have a good feel for things, for facts. Good judgment. Now, one reason I got to where I am is good judgment, too, and I think you can handle what I have in mind. The question is, will you do it, or won't you?"

"Do what, exactly, sir?"

"After you get out there, you stay put for a few days, and report directly to me. Not through channels, directly to me. You'll get the cooperation you need. I'll see to that."

Ryan didn't say anything. He'd just become a spy, a field officer, by presidential fiat. Worse, he'd be spying on his own side.

"You don't like the idea of reporting on your own people, right? You won't be, not really. Like I said, I want an independent, civilian opinion. We'd prefer to send an experienced case officer out, but we want to minimize the number of people involved in this. Sending Ritter or Greer out would be far too obvious, whereas you, on the other hand, are a relative—"

"Nobody?" Jack asked.

"As far as they're concerned, yes," Judge Moore replied. "The Soviets have a file on you. I've seen parts of it. They think you're an upper-class drone, Jack."

I am a drone, Ryan thought, unmoved by the implicit challenge. In this company I sure as hell am.

"Agreed, Mr. President. Please forgive me for hesitating. I've never been a field officer before."

"I understand." The president was magnanimous in victory. "One more thing. If I understand how submarines operate, Ramius could just have taken off, not saying anything. Why tip them off? Why the letter? The way I read this, it's counterproductive."

It was Ryan's turn to smile. "Ever meet a sub driver, sir? No? How about an astronaut?"

"Sure, I've met a bunch of the Shuttle pilots."

"They're the same breed of cat, Mr. President. As to why he left the letter, there's two parts to that. First, he's probably mad about something, exactly what we'll find out when we see him. Second, he figures he can pull this off regardless of what they try to stop him with—and he wants them to know that. Mr. President, the men who drive subs for a living are aggressive, confident, and very, very smart. They like nothing better than making somebody else, a surface ship operator for example, look like an idiot."

"You just scored another point, Jack. The astronauts I've met, on most things they're downright humble, but they think they're gods when it comes to flying. I'll keep that in mind. Jeff, let's get back to work. Jack, keep me posted."

Ryan shook his hand again. After the president and his senior adviser left, he turned to Judge Moore. "Judge, what the hell did you tell him about me?"

"Only the truth, Jack." Actually, the judge had wanted this operation to be run by one of the CIA's senior case officers. Ryan had not been part of this scheme, but presidents have been known to spoil many carefully laid plans. The judge took this philosophically. "This is a big move up in the world for you, if you do your job right. Hell, you might even like it."

Ryan was sure he wouldn't, and he was right.

CIA Headquarters

He didn't speak the whole way back to Langley. The director's car pulled into the basement parking garage, where they got out and entered a private elevator that took them directly to Moore's office. The elevator door was disguised as a wall panel, which was convenient but melodramatic, Ryan thought. The DCI went right to his desk and lifted a phone.

"Bob, I need you in here right now." He glanced at Ryan, standing in the middle of the room. "Looking forward to this, Jack?"

"Sure, Judge," Ryan said without enthusiasm.

"I can see how you feel about this spying business, but the whole thing could develop into an extremely sensitive situation. You ought to be damned flattered you're being trusted with it."

Ryan caught the between-the-line message just as Ritter breezed in.

"What's up, Judge?"

"We're laying an operation on. Ryan is flying out to the

Kennedy with Charlie Davenport to brief the fleet commanders on this *October* business. The president bought it."

"Guess so. Greer left for Andrews just before you pulled in. Ryan gets to fly out, eh?"

"Yes. Jack, the rules is this: you can brief the fleet commander and Davenport, that's all. Same for the Brits, just the boss-sailor. If Bob can confirm WILLOW, the data can be spread out, but only as much as is absolutely necessary. Clear?"

"Yes, sir. I suppose somebody has told the president that it's hard to accomplish anything if nobody knows what the hell is going on. Especially the guys who're doing the work."

"I know what you're saying, Jack. We have to change the president's mind on that. We will, but until we do, remember—he is the boss. Bob, we'll need to rustle something up so he'll fit in."

"Naval officer's uniform? Let's make him a commander, three stripes, usual ribbons." Ritter looked Ryan over. "Say a forty-two long. We can have him outfitted in an hour, I expect. This operation have a name?"

"That's next." Moore lifted his phone again and tapped in five numbers. "I need two words . . . Uh-huh, thank you." He wrote a few things down. "Okay, gentlemen, you're calling this Operation MANDOLIN. You, Ryan, are Magi. Ought to be easy to remember, given the time of year. We'll work up a series of code words based on those while you're being fitted. Bob, take him down there yourself. I'll call Davenport and have him arrange the flight."

Ryan followed Ritter to the elevator. It was going too fast, everyone was being too clever, he thought. This Operation MANDOLIN was racing forward before they knew what the hell they were going to do, much less how. And the choice of his code name struck Ryan as singularly inappropriate. He wasn't anyone's wise man. The name should have been something more like "Halloween."

THE SEVENTH DAY

THURSDAY, 9 DECEMBER

The North Atlantic

When Samuel Johnson compared sailing in a ship to "being in jail, with the chance of being drowned," at least he had the consolation of travelling to his ship in a safe carriage, Ryan thought. Now he was going to sea, and before he got to his ship Ryan stood the chance of being smashed to red pulp in a plane crash. Jack sat hunched in a bucket seat on the port side of a Grumman Greyhound, known to the fleet without affection as a COD (for carrier onboard delivery), a flying delivery truck. The seats, facing aft, were too close together, and his knees jutted up against his chin. The cabin was far more amenable to cargo than to people. There were three tons of engine and electronics parts stowed in crates aft—there, no doubt, so that the impact of a plane crash on the valuable equipment would be softened by the four bodies in the passenger section. The cabin was not heated. There were no windows. A thin aluminum skin separated him from a two-hundred-knot wind that shrieked in time with the twin turbine engines. Worst of all, they were flying through a storm at five thousand feet, and the

COD was jerking up and down in hundred-foot gulps like a berserk roller coaster. The only good thing was the lack of lighting, Ryan thought—at least nobody can see how green my face is. Right behind him were two pilots, talking away loudly so they could be heard over the engine noise. The bastards were enjoying themselves!

The noise lessened somewhat, or so it seemed. It was hard to tell. He'd been issued foam-rubber ear protectors along with a yellow, inflatable life preserver and a lecture on what to do in the event of a crash. The lecture had been perfunctory enough that it took no great intellect to estimate their chances of survival if they did crash on a night like this. Ryan hated flying. He had once been a marine second lieutenant, and his active career had ended after only three months when his platoon's helicopter had crashed on Crete during a NATO exercise. He had injured his back, nearly been crippled for life, and ever since regarded flying as something to be avoided. The COD, he thought, was bouncing more down than up. It probably meant they were close to the *Kennedy*. The alternative did not bear thinking about. They were only ninety minutes out of Oceana Naval Air Station at Virginia Beach. It felt like a month, and Ryan swore to himself that he'd never be afraid on a civilian airliner again.

The nose dropped about twenty degrees, and the aircraft seemed to be flying right at something. They were landing, the most dangerous part of carrier flight operations. He remembered a study conducted during the Vietnam War in which carrier pilots had been fitted with portable electrocardiographs to monitor stress, and it had surprised a lot of people that the most stressful time for carrier pilots wasn't while they were being shot at—it was while they were landing, particularly at night.

Christ, you're full of happy thoughts! Ryan told himself. He closed his eyes. One way or another, it would be over in a few seconds.

The deck was slick with rain and heaving up and down, a black hole surrounded by perimeter lights. The carrier landing was a controlled crash. Massive landing gear struts and shock absorbers were needed to lessen the bone-crushing impact. The aircraft surged forward only to be jerked to a halt by the arresting wire. They were down. They were safe. Probably. After a moment's pause, the COD began moving forward again. Ryan heard some odd noises as the plane taxied and realized that they came from the wings folding up. The one danger he had not considered was flying on an aircraft whose wings were supposed to collapse. It was, he decided, just as well. The plane finally stopped moving, and the rear hatch opened.

Ryan flipped off his seatbelts and stood rapidly, banging his head on the low ceiling. He didn't wait for Davenport. With his canvas bag clutched to his chest he darted out of the rear of the aircraft. He looked around, and was pointed to the *Kennedy*'s island structure by a yellow-shirted deck crewman. The rain was falling heavily, and he felt rather than saw that the carrier was indeed moving on the fifteen-foot seas. He ran towards an open, lighted hatch fifty feet away. He had to wait for Davenport to catch up. The admiral didn't run. He walked with a precise thirty-inch step, dignified as a flag officer should be, and Ryan decided that he was probably annoyed that his semisecret arrival prohibited the usual ceremony of bosun's pipes and side boys. There was a marine standing inside the hatch, a corporal, resplendent in striped blue trousers, khaki shirt and tie, and snow-white pistol belt. He saluted, welcoming both aboard.

"Corporal, I want to see Admiral Painter."

"The admiral's in flag quarters, sir. Do you require escort?"

"No, son. I used to command this ship. Come along, Jack." Ryan got to carry both bags.

"Gawd, sir, you actually used to do this for a living?" Ryan asked.

"Night carrier landings? Sure, I've done a couple of hundred. What's the big deal?" Davenport seemed surprised at Ryan's awe. Jack was sure it was an act.

The inside of the *Kennedy* was much like the interior of the USS *Guam,* the helicopter assault ship Ryan had been assigned to during his brief military career. It was the usual navy maze of steel bulkheads and pipes, everything painted the same shade of cave-gray. The pipes had some colored bands and stenciled acronyms which probably meant something to the men who ran the ship. To Ryan they might as well have been neolithic cave paintings. Davenport led him through a corridor, around a corner, down a "ladder" made entirely of steel and so steep he almost lost his balance, down another passageway, and around another corner. By this time Ryan was thoroughly lost. They came to a door with a marine stationed in front. The sergeant saluted perfectly, and opened the door for them.

Ryan followed Davenport in—and was amazed. Flag quarters on the USS *Kennedy* might have been transported as a block from a Beacon Hill mansion. To his right was a wall-sized mural large enough to dominate a big living room. A half-dozen oils, one of them a portrait of the ship's namesake, President John Fitzgerald Kennedy, dotted the other walls, themselves covered with expensive-looking paneling. The deck was covered in thick crimson wool, and the furniture was pure civilian, French provincial, oak and brocade. One could almost imagine they were not aboard a ship at all, except that the ceiling—"overhead"—had the usual collection of pipes, all painted gray. It was a decidedly odd contrast to the rest of the room.

"Hi ya, Charlie!" Rear Admiral Joshua Painter emerged from the next room, drying his hands with a towel. "How was it coming in?"

"Little rocky," Davenport allowed, shaking hands. "This is Jack Ryan."

Ryan had never met Painter but knew him by reputation. A Phantom pilot during the Vietnam War, he had written a book, *Paddystrikes,* on the conduct of the air campaigns. It had been a truthful book, not the sort of thing that wins friends. He was a small, feisty man who could not have weighed more than a hundred thirty pounds. He was also a gifted tactician and a man of puritanical integrity.

"One of yours, Charlie?"

"No, Admiral, I work for James Greer. I am not a naval officer. Please accept my apologies. I don't like pretending to be what I'm not. The uniform was the CIA's idea." This drew a frown.

"Oh? Well, I suppose that means you're going to tell me what Ivan's up to. Good, I hope to hell somebody knows. First time on a carrier? How did you like the flight in?"

"It might be a good way to interrogate prisoners of war," Ryan said as offhandedly as he could. The two flag officers had a good laugh at his expense, and Painter called for some food to be sent in.

The double doors to the passageway opened serveral minutes

later and a pair of stewards—"mess management specialists"—
came in, one bearing a tray of food, the other two pots of
coffee. The three men were served in a style appropriate to
their rank. The food, served on silver-trimmed plates, was
simple but appetizing to Ryan, who hadn't eaten in twelve
hours. He dished cole slaw and potato salad onto his plate and
selected a pair of corned-beef-on-ryes.

"Thank you. That's all for now," Painter said. The stewards
came to attention before leaving. "Okay, let's get down to
business."

Ryan gulped down half a sandwich. "Admiral, this information is only twenty hours old." He took the briefing folders
from his bag and handed them around. His delivery took twenty
minutes, during which he managed to consume the two sandwiches and a goodly portion of his cole slaw and spill coffee
on his hand-written notes. The two flag officers were a perfect
audience, not interrupting once, only darting a few disbelieving
looks at him.

"God Almighty," Painter said when Ryan finished. Davenport just stared poker-faced as he contemplated the possibility
of examining a Soviet missile sub from the inside. Jack decided
he'd be a formidable opponent over cards. Painter went on,
"Do you really believe this?"

"Yes, sir, I do." Ryan poured himself another cup of coffee.
He would have preferred a beer to go with his corned beef. It
hadn't been bad at all, and good kosher corned beef was something he'd been unable to find in London.

Painter leaned back and looked at Davenport. "Charlie, you
tell Greer to teach this lad a few lessons—like how a bureaucrat
ain't supposed to stick his neck this far out on the block. Don't
you think this is a little far-fetched?"

"Josh, Ryan here's the guy who did the report last June on
Soviet missile-sub patrol patterns."

"Oh? That was a nice piece of work. It confirmed something
I've been saying for two or three years." Painter rose and
walked to the corner to look out at the stormy sea. "So, what
are we supposed to do about all this?"

"The exact details of the operation have not been determined. What I expect is that you will be directed to locate *Red
October* and attempt to establish communications with her skipper. After that? We'll have to figure a way to get her to a safe

place. You see, the president doesn't think we'll be able to hold onto her once we get her—if we get her."

"What?" Painter spun around and spoke a tenth of a second before Davenport did. Ryan explained for several minutes.

"Dear God above! You give me one impossible task, then you tell me that if we succeed in it, we gotta give the goddamned thing back to them!"

"Admiral, my recommendation—the president asked me for one—was that we keep the submarine. For what it's worth, the Joint Chiefs are on your side, too, along with the CIA. As it is, though, if the crewmen want to go back home, we have to send them back, and then the Soviets will know we have the boat for sure. As a practical matter, I can see the other side's point. The vessel is worth a pile of money, and it is their property. And how would we hide a 30,000-ton submarine?"

"You hide a submarine by sinking it," Painter said angrily. "They're designed to do that, you know. 'Their property!' We're not talking about a damned passenger liner. That's something designed to kill people—our people!"

"Admiral, I am on your side," Ryan said quietly. "Sir, you said we've given you an impossible task, Why?"

"Ryan, finding a boomer that does not want to be found is not the easiest thing in the world. We practice against our own. We damned near always fail, and you say this one's already passed all the northeast SOSUS lines. The Atlantic's a rather large ocean, and a missile sub's noise footprint is very small."

"Yes, sir." Ryan noted to himself that he might have been overly optimistic about their chances for success.

"What sort of shape are you in, Josh?" Davenport asked.

"Pretty good, really. The exercise we just ran, NIFTY DOLPHIN, worked out all right. Our part of it," Painter corrected himself. *"Dallas* raised some hell on the other side. My ASW crews are functioning very well. What sort of help are we getting?"

"When I left the Pentagon, the CNO was checking the availability of P-3s out on the Pacific, so you'll probably be seeing more of those. Everything that'll move is putting to sea. You're the only carrier, so you've got overall tactical command, right? Come on, Josh, you're our best ASW operator."

Painter poured some coffee for himself. "Okay, we have one carrier deck. *America* and *Nimitz* are still a good week

vay. Ryan, you said you're flying out to *Invincible*. We get
r, too, right?"

"The president was working on that. Want her?"

"Sure. Admiral White has a good nose for ASW, and his
oys really lucked out during DOLPHIN. They killed two of
ir attack boats, and Vince Gallery was some kind of pissed
out that. Luck's a big part of this game. That would give us
vo decks instead of one. I wonder if we can get some more
-3s?" Painter referred to the Lockheed Vikings, carrier-borne
ntisubmarine aircraft.

"Why?" Davenport asked.

"I can transfer my F-18s to shore, and that'll give us room
r twenty more Vikings. I don't like losing the striking power,
it what we're going to need is more ASW muscle. That means
ore S-3s. Jack, you know that if you're wrong, that Russkie
rface force is going to be a handful to deal with. You know
ow many surface-to-surface missiles they're packing?"

"No, sir." Ryan was certain it was too many.

"We're one carrier, and that makes us their primary target.
they start shooting at us, it'll get awful lonesome—then it'll
t awful exciting." The phone rang. "Painter here . . . Yes.
aank you. Well, *Invincible* just turned around. Good, they're
ving her to us along with two tin cans. The rest of the escorts
d the three attack subs are still heading home." He frowned.
can't really fault them for that. That means we have to give
em some escorts, but it's a good trade. I want that flight
ck."

"Can we chopper Jack out to her?" Ryan wondered if
avenport knew what the president had ordered him to do.
ne admiral seemed interested in getting him off the *Kennedy*.
Painter shook his head. "Too far for a chopper. Maybe they
n send a Harrier back for him."

"The Harrier's a fighter, sir," Ryan commented.

"They have an experimental two-seat version set up for
SW patrolling. It's supposed to work reasonably well outside
eir helo perimeter. That's how they bagged one of our attack
ats, caught her napping." Painter finished off the last of his
ffee.

"Okay, gentlemen, let's get ourselves down to ASW control
d try and figure a way to run this circus act. CINCLANT
ll want to hear what I have in mind. I suppose I'd better

decide for myself. We'll also call *Invincible* and have then
send a bird back to ferry you out, Ryan."

Ryan followed the two admirals out of the room. He spen
two hours watching Painter move ships around the ocean lik
a chess master with his pieces.

The USS Dallas

Bart Mancuso had been on duty in the attack center for mor
than twenty hours. Only a few hours of sleep separated hi
stretch from the previous one. He had been eating sandwiche
and drinking coffee, and two cups of soup had been thrown i
by his cooks for variety's sake. He examined his latest cup c
freeze-dried without affection.

"Cap'n?" He turned. It was Roger Thompson, his sona
officer.

"Yes, what is it?" Mancuso pulled himself away from th
tactical display that had occupied his attention for several days
Thompson was standing at the rear of the compartment. Jone
was standing beside him holding a clipboard and what looke
like a tape machine.

"Sir, Jonesy has something I think you ought to look at.'

Mancuso didn't want to be bothered—extended time o
duty always taxed his patience. But Jones looked eager an
excited. "Okay, come on over to the chart table."

The *Dallas*' chart table was a new gadget wired into th
BC-10 and projected onto a TV-type glass screen four fee
square. The display moved as the *Dallas* moved. This mad
paper charts obsolete, though they were kept anyway. Char
can't break.

"Thanks, Skipper," Jones said, more humbly than usual. '
know you're kinda busy, but I think I got something here. Tha
anomalous contact we had the other day's been bothering me
I had to leave it after the ruckus the other Russkie subs kicke
up, but I was able to come back to it three times to make sur
it was still there. The fourth time it was gone, faded out.
want to show you what I worked up. Can you punch up o
course track for back then on this baby, sir?"

The chart table was interfaced through the BC-10 into th
ship's inertial navigation system, SINS. Mancuso punched th
command in himself. It was getting so that they couldn't flus

e head without a computer command . . . The *Dallas'* course ack showed up as a convoluted red line, with tick marks isplayed at fifteen-minute intervals.

"Great!" Jones commented. "I've never seen it do that be-re. That's all right. Okay." Jones pulled a handful of pencils om his back pocket. "Now, I got the contact first at 0915 or , and the bearing was about two-six-nine." He set a pencil own, eraser at *Dallas'* position, point directed west towards e target. "Then at 0930 it was bearing a two-six-zero. At 948, it was two-five-zero. There's some error built into these, ap'n. It was a tough signal to lock in on, but the errors should verage out. Right about then we got all this other activity, and had to go after them, but I came back to it about 1000, and e bearing was two-four-two." Jones set down another pencil n the due-east line traced when the *Dallas* had moved away om the Icelandic coast. "At 1015 it was two-three-four, and 1030 it was two-two-seven. These last two are shaky, sir. he signal was real faint, and I didn't have a very good lock n it." Jones looked up. He appeared nervous.

"So far, so good. Relax, Jonesy. Light up if you want."

"Thanks, Cap'n." Jones fished out a cigarette and lit it with a utane lighter. He had never approached the captain quite this ay. He knew Mancuso to be a tolerant, easygoing com-ander—if you had something to say. He was not a man who ked his time wasted, and it was sure as hell he wouldn't want it asted now. "Okay, sir, we gotta figure he couldn't be too far way from us, right? I mean, he had to be between us and Ice-nd. So let's say he was about halfway between. That gives him course about like this." Jones set down some more pencils.

"Hold it, Jonesy. Where does the course come from?"

"Oh, yeah." Jones flipped open his clipboard. "Yesterday orning, night, whatever it was, after I got off watch, it started othering me, so I used the move we made offshore as a aseline to do a little course track for him. I know how, Skipper. read the manual. It's easy, just like we used to do at Cal Tech chart star motion. I took an astronomy course in my freshman ear."

Mancuso stifled a groan. It was the first time he had ever eard this called easy, but on looking at Jones' figures and iagrams, it appeared that he had done it right. "Go on."

Jones pulled a Hewlitt Packard scientific calculator from his pocket and what looked like a National Geographic map liberally coated with pencil marks and scribblings. "You want to check my figures, sir?"

"We will, but I'll trust you for now. What's the map?"

"Skipper, I know it's against the rules an' all, but I keep this as a personal record of the tracks the bad guys use. It doesn't leave the boat, sir, honest. I may be a little off, but all this translates to a course of about two-two-zero and a speed of ten knots. And *that* aims him right at the entrance of Route One. Okay?"

"Go on." Mancuso had already figured that one. Jonesy was on to something.

"Well, I couldn't sleep after that, so I skipped back to sonar and pulled the tape on the contact. I had to run it through the computer a few times to filter out all the crap—sea sounds, the other subs, you know—then I rerecorded it at ten times normal speed." He set his cassette recorder on the chart table. "Listen to this, Skipper."

The tape was scratchy, but every few seconds there was a *thrum*. Two minutes of listening seemed to indicate a regular interval of about five seconds. By this time Lieutenant Mannion was looking over Thompson's shoulder, listening, and nodding speculatively.

"Skipper, that's gotta be a man-made sound. It's just too regular for anything else. At normal speed it didn't make much sense, but once I speeded it up, I had the sucker."

"Okay, Jonesy, finish it," Mancuso said.

"Captain, what you just heard was the acoustical signature of a Russian submarine. He was heading for Route One, taking the inshore track off the Icelandic coast. You can bet money on that, Skipper."

"Roger?"

"He sold me, Captain," Thompson replied.

Mancuso took another look at the course track, trying to figure an alternative. There wasn't any. "Me, too. Roger, Jonesy makes sonarman first class today. I want to see the paper work done by the turn of the next watch, along with a nice letter of commendation for my signature. Ron," he poked the sonarman in the shoulder, "that's all right. Damned well done!"

"Thanks, Skipper." Jones' smile stretched from ear to ear.

"Pat, please call Lieutenant Butler to the attack center."

Mannion went to the phones to call the boat's chief engineer. "Any idea what it is, Jonesy?" Mancuso turned back.

The sonarman shook his head. "It isn't screw sounds. I've never heard anything like it." He ran the tape back and played it again.

Two minutes later, Lieutenant Earl Butler came into the attack center. "You rang, Skipper?"

"Listen to this, Earl." Mancuso rewound the tape and played it a third time.

Butler was a graduate of the University of Texas and every school the navy had for submarines and their engine systems. "What's that supposed to be?"

"Jonesy says it's a Russian sub. I think he's right."

"Tell me about the tape," Butler said to Jones.

"Sir, it's speeded up ten times, and I washed it through the BC-10 five times. At normal speed it doesn't sound like much of anything." With uncharacteristic modesty, Jones did not point out that it had sounded like something to him.

"Some sort of harmonic? I mean, if it was a propeller, it'd have to be a hundred feet across, and we'd be hearing one blade at a time. The regular interval suggests some sort of harmonic." Butler's face screwed up. "But a harmonic what?"

"Whatever it was, it was headed right here." Mancuso tapped Thor's Twins with his pencil.

"That makes him a Russian, all right," Butler agreed. "Then they're using something new. Again."

"Mr. Butler's right," Jones said. "It does sound like a harmonic rumble. The other funny thing is, well, there was this background noise, kinda like water going through a pipe. I don't know, it didn't pick up on this. I guess the computer filtered it off. It was real faint to start with—anyway, that's outside my field."

"That's all right. You've done enough for one day. How do you feel?" Mancuso asked.

"A little tired, Skipper. I've been working on this for a while."

"If we get close to this guy again, you think you can track him down?" Mancuso knew the answer.

"You bet, Cap'n! Now that we know what to listen for, you bet I'll bag the sucker!"

Mancuso looked at the chart table. "Okay, if he was heading

for the Twins, and then ran the route at, say twenty-eight or thirty knots, and then settled down to his base course and speed of about ten or so . . . that puts him about here now. Long ways off. Now, if we run at top speed . . . forty-eight hours will put us here, and that'll put us in front of him. Pat?"

"That's about right, sir," Lieutenant Mannion concurred. "You're figuring he ran the route at full speed, then settled down—makes sense. He wouldn't need the quiet drive in that damned maze. It gives him a free shot for four or five hundred miles, so why not uncrank his engines? That's what I'd do."

"That's what we'll try and do, then. We'll radio in for permission to leave Toll Booth station and track this character down. Jonesy, running at max speed means you sonarmen will be out of work for a while. Set up the contact tape on the simulator and make sure the operators all know what this guy sounds like, but get some rest. All of you. I want you at a hundred percent when we try to reacquire this guy. Have yourself a shower. Make that a Hollywood shower—you've earned it—and rack out. When we do go after this character, it'll be a long, tough hunt."

"No sweat, Captain. We'll get him for you. Bet on it. You want to keep my tape, sir?"

"Yeah." Mancuso ejected the tape and looked up in surprise. "You sacrificed a Bach for this?"

"Not a good one, sir. I have a Christopher Hogwood of this piece that's much better."

Mancuso pocketed the tape. "Dismissed, Jonesy. Nice work."

"A pleasure, Cap'n." Jones left the attack center counting the extra money for jumping a rate.

"Roger, make sure your people are well rested over the next two days. When we do go after this guy, it's going to be a bastard."

"Aye, Captain."

"Pat, get us up to periscope depth. We're going to call this one into Norfolk right now. Earl, I want you thinking about what's making that noise."

"Right, Captain."

While Mancuso drafted his message, Lieutenant Mannion brought the *Dallas* to periscope-antenna depth with an upward angle on the diving planes. It took five minutes to get from five hundred feet to just below the stormy surface. The submarine was subject to wave action, and while it was very gentle by surface ship standards, the crew noted her rocking. Mannion raised the periscope and ESM (electronic support measures) antenna, the latter used for the broad-band receiver designed to detect possible radar emissions. There was nothing in view— he could see about five miles—and the ESM instruments showed nothing except for aircraft sets, which were too far away to matter. Next Mannion raised two more masts. One was a reed-like UHF (ultrahigh frequency) receiving antenna. The other was new, a laser transmitter. This rotated and locked onto the carrier wave signal of the Atlantic SSIX, the communications satellite used exclusively by submarines. With the laser, they could send high-density transmissions without giving away the sub's position.

"All ready, sir," the duty radioman reported.

"Transmit."

The radioman pressed a button. The signal, sent in a fraction of a second, was received by photovoltaic cells, read over to a UHF transmitter, and shot back down by a parabolic dish antenna towards Atlantic Fleet Communications headquarters. At Norfolk another radioman noted the reception and pressed a button that transmitted the same signal up to the satellite and back to the *Dallas*. It was a simple way to identify garbles.

The *Dallas* operator compared the received signal with the one he'd just sent. "Good copy, sir."

Mancuso ordered Mannion to lower everything but the ESM and UHF antennae.

Atlantic Fleet Communications

In Norfolk the first line of the dispatch revealed the page and line of the one-time-pad cipher sequence, which was recorded on computer tape in the maximum security section of the communications complex. An officer typed the proper numbers into his computer terminal, and an instant later the machine generated a clear text. The officer checked it again for garbles. Satisfied there were none, he took the printout to the other side of the room where a yeoman was seated at a telex. The officer handed him the dispatch.

The yeoman keyed up the proper addressee and transmitted the message by dedicated landline to COMSUBLANT Operations, half a mile away. The landline was fiber optic, located in a steel conduit under a paved street. It was checked three times a week for security purposes. Not even the secrets of nuclear weapons performance were as closely guarded as day-to-day tactical communications.

COMSUBLANT *Operations*

A bell went off in the operations room as the message came up on the "hot" printer. It bore a Z prefix, which indicated FLASH-priority status.

Z090414ZDEC

T O P   S E C R E T   T H E O

FM: USS DALLAS

TO: COMSUBLANT

INFO: CINCLANTFLT

//NOOOOO//

REDFLEET SUBOPS
1. REPORT ANOMALOUS SONAR CONTACT ABOUT 0900Z 7DEC AND LOST AFTER INCREASE IN REDFLEET SUB ACTIVITY. CONTACT SUBSE-QUENTLY EVALUATED AS REDFLEET SSN/SSBN TRANSITING ICELAND INSHORE TRACK TO-WARDS ROUTE ONE. COURSE SOUTHWEST SPEED TEN DEPTH UNKNOWN.
2. CONTACT EVIDENCED UNUSUAL REPEAT UN-USUAL ACOUSTICAL CHARACTERISTICS. SIG-NATURE UNLIKE ANY KNOWN REDFLEET SUBMARINE.
3. REQUEST PERMISSION TO LEAVE TOLL BOOTH TO PURSUE AND INVESTIGATE. BELIEVE A NEW DRIVE SYSTEM WITH UNUSUAL SOUND CHAR-ACTERISTICS BEING USED THIS SUB. BELIEVE GOOD PROBABILITY CAN LOCATE AND IDEN-TIFY.

A lieutenant junior grade took the dispatch to the office of Vice Admiral Vincent Gallery. COMSUBLANT had been on duty since the Soviet subs had started moving. He was in an evil mood.

"A FLASH priority from *Dallas,* sir."

"Uh-huh." Gallery took the yellow form and read it twice. "What do you suppose this means?"

"No telling, sir. Looks like he heard something, took his time figuring it out, and wants another crack at it. He seems to think he's onto something unusual."

"Okay, what do I tell him? Come on, mister. You might be an admiral yourself someday and have to make decisions." An unlikely prospect, Gallery thought.

"Sir, *Dallas* is in an ideal position to shadow their surface force when it gets to Iceland. We need her where she is."

"Good textbook answer." Gallery smiled up at the youngster, preparing to cut him off at the knees. "On the other hand, *Dallas* is commanded by a fairly competent man who wouldn't be bothering us unless he really thought he had something. He doesn't go into specifics, probably because it's too complicated for a tactical FLASH dispatch, and also because he thinks that we know his judgment is good enough to take his word on something. 'New drive system with unusual sound characteristics.' That may be a crock, but he's the man on the scene, and he wants an answer. We tell him yes."

"Aye aye, sir," the lieutenant said, wondering if the skinny old bastard made decisions by flipping a coin when his back was turned.

The Dallas

Z090432ZDEC

T O P   S E C R E T

FM: COMSUBLANT

TO: USS DALLAS

A. USS DALLAS Z090414ZDEC

B. COMSUBLANT INST 2000.5

OPAREA ASSIGNMENT //N04220//

1. REQUEST REF A GRANTED.
2. AREAS BRAVO ECHO GOLF REF B ASSIGNED
FOR UNRESTRICTED OPS 090500Z TO 140001Z.
REPORT AS NECESSARY. VADM GALLERY SENDS.

"Hot damn!" Mancuso chuckled. That was one nice thing
about Gallery. When you asked him a question, by God, you
got an answer, yes or no, before you could rig your antenna
in. Of course, he reflected, if it turned out that Jonesy was
wrong and this was a wild-goose chase, he'd have some explaining to do. Gallery had handed more than one sub skipper
his head in a bag and set him on the beach.

Which was where he was headed regardless, Mancuso knew.
Since his first year at Annapolis all he had ever wanted was
command of his own attack boat. He had that now, and he
knew that the rest of his career would be downhill. In the rest
of the navy your first command was just that, a first command.
You could move up the ladder and command a fleet at sea
eventually, if you were lucky and had the right stuff. Not
submariners, though. Whether he did well with the *Dallas* or
poorly, he'd lose her soon enough. He had this one and only
chance. And afterwards, what? The best he could hope for was
command of a missile boat. He'd served on those before and
was sure that commanding one, even a new *Ohio*, was about
as exciting as watching paint dry. The boomer's job was to stay
hidden. Mancuso wanted to be the hunter, that was the exciting
end of the business. And after commanding a missile boat? He
could get a "major surface command," perhaps a nice oiler—
it would be like switching mounts from Secretariat to Elsie the
Cow. Or he could get a squadron command and sit in an office
onboard a tender, pushing paper. At best in that position he'd
go to sea once a month, his main purpose being to bother sub
skippers who didn't want him there. Or he could get a desk
job in the Pentagon—what fun! Mancuso understood why some
of the astronauts had cracked up after coming back from the
moon. He, too, had worked many years for this command, and
in another year his boat would be gone. He'd have to give the
Dallas to someone else. But he did have her now.

"Pat, let's lower all masts and take her down to twelve
hundred feet."

"Aye aye, sir. Lower the masts," Mannion ordered. A petty officer pulled on the hydraulic control levers.

"ESM and UHF masts lowered, sir," the duty electrician reported.

"Very well. Diving officer, make your depth twelve hundred feet."

"Twelve hundred feet, aye," the diving officer responded. "Fifteen degrees down-angle on the planes."

"Fifteen degrees down, aye."

"Let's move her, Pat."

"Aye, Skipper. All ahead full."

"All ahead full, aye." The helmsman reached up to turn the annunciator.

Mancuso watched his crew at work. They did their jobs with mechanistic precision. But they were not machines. They were men. His.

In the reactor spaces aft, Lieutenant Butler had his enginemen acknowledge the command and gave the necessary orders. The reactor coolant pumps went to fast speed. An increased amount of hot, pressurized water entered the exchanger, where its heat was transferred to the steam on the outside loop. When the coolant returned to the reactor it was cooler than it had been and therefore denser. Being denser, it trapped more neutrons in the reactor pile, increasing the ferocity of the fission reactic and giving off yet more power. Farther aft, saturated steam in the "outside" or nonradioactive loop of the heat exchange system emerged through clusters of control valves to strike the blades of the high-pressure turbine. The *Dallas'* huge bronze screw began to turn more quickly, driving her forward and down.

The engineers went about their duties calmly. The noise in the engine spaces rose noticeably as the systems began to put out more power, and the technicians kept track of this by continuously monitoring the banks of instruments under their hands. The routine was quiet and exact. There was no extraneous conversation, no distraction. Compared to a submarine's reactor spaces, a hospital operating room was a den of libertines.

Forward, Mannion watched the depth gauge go below six hundred feet. The diving officer would wait until they got to nine hundred feet before starting to level off, the object being to zero the dive out exactly at the ordered depth. Commander Mancuso wanted the *Dallas* below the thermocline. This was the border between different temperatures. Water settled in isothermal layers of uniform stratification. The relatively flat boundary where warmer surface water met colder depth water was a semipermeable barrier which tended to reflect sound waves. Those waves that did manage to penetrate the thermocline were mostly trapped below it. Thus, though the *Dallas* was now running below the thermocline at over thirty knots and making as much noise as she was capable of, she would still be difficult to detect with surface sonar. She would also be largely blind, but then, there was not much down there to run into.

Mancuso lifted the microphone for the PA system. "This is the captain speaking. We have just started a speed run that will last forty-eight hours. We are heading towards a point where we hope to locate a Russian sub that went past us two days ago. This Russkie is evidently using a new and rather quiet propulsion system that nobody's run across before. We're going to try and get ahead of him and track on him as he passes us again. This time we know what to listen for, and we'll get a nice clear picture of him. Okay, I want everyone on this boat to be well rested. When we get there, it'll be a long, tough hunt. I want everybody at a hundred percent. This one will probably be interesting." He switched off the microphone. "What's the movie tonight?"

The diving officer watched the depth gauge stop moving before answering. As chief of the boat, he was also manager of the *Dallas*' cable TV system, three video-cassette recorders in the mess room which led to televisions in the wardroom, and various other crew accommodations. "Skipper, you got a choice. *Return of the Jedi* or two football tapes: Oklahoma-Nebraska and Miami-Dallas. Both those games were played while we were on the exercise, sir. It'll be like watching them live." He laughed. "Commercials and all. The cooks are already making the popcorn."

"Good. I want everybody nice and loose." Why couldn't they ever get Navy tapes, Mancuso wondered. Of course, Army had creamed them this year . . .

"Morning, Skipper." Wally Chambers, the executive officer, came into the attack center. "What gives?"

"Come on back to the wardroom, Wally. I want you to listen

to something." Mancuso took the cassette from his shirt pocket and led Chambers aft.

The V. K. Konovalov

Two hundred miles northeast of the *Dallas,* in the Norwegian Sea, the *Konovalov* was racing southwest at forty-one knots. Captain Tupolev sat alone in the wardroom rereading the dispatch he'd received two days before. His emotions alternated between rage and grief. The Schoolmaster had done *that!* He was dumbfounded.

But what was there to do? Tupolev's orders were explicit, the more so since, as his *zampolit* had pointed out, he was a former pupil of the traitor Ramius. He, too, could find himself in a very bad position. If the slug succeeded.

So, Marko had pulled a trick on everyone, not just the *Konovalov.* Tupolev had been slinking about the Barents Sea like a fool while Marko had been heading the other way. Laughing at everyone, Tupolev was sure. Such treachery, such a hellish threat against the *Rodina.* It was inconceivable—and all too conceivable. All the advantages Marko had. A four-room apartment, a dacha, his own Zhiguli. Tupolev did not yet have his own automobile. He had earned his way to a command, and now it was all threatened by—this! He'd be lucky to keep what he had.

I have to kill a friend, he thought. Friend? Yes, he admitted to himself, Marko had been a good friend and a fine teacher. Where had he gone wrong?

Natalia Bogdanova.

Yes, that had to be it. A big stink, the way that had happened. How many times had he had dinner with them, how many times had Natalia laughed about her fine, strong, big sons? He shook his head. A fine woman killed by a damned incompetent fool of a surgeon. Nothing could be done about it, he was the son of a Central Committee member. It was an outrage the way things like that still happened, even after three generations of building socialism. But nothing was sufficient to justify this madness.

Tupolev bent over the chart he'd brought back. He'd be on his station in five days, in less time if the engine plant held together and Marko wasn't in too much of a hurry—and he

wouldn't be. Marko was a fox, not a bull. The other *Alfa*s
would get there ahead of his, Tupolev knew, but it didn't matter.
He had to do this himself. He'd get ahead of Marko and wait.
Marko would try to slink past, and the *Konovalov* would be
there. And the *Red October* would die.

The North Atlantic

The British Sea Harrier FRS.4 appeared a minute early. It
hovered briefly off the *Kennedy*'s port beam as the pilot sized
up his landing target, the wind, and sea conditions. Maintaining
a steady thirty-knot forward speed to compensate for the carrier's forward speed, he side-slipped his fighter neatly to the
right, then dropped it gently amidships, slightly forward of the
Kennedy's island structure, exactly in the center of the flight
deck. Instantly a gang of deck crewmen raced for the aircraft,
three carrying heavy metal chocks, another a metal ladder which
he set up by the cockpit, whose canopy was already coming
open. A team of four snaked a fueling hose towards the aircraft,
eager to demonstrate the speed with which the U.S. Navy
services aircraft. The pilot was dressed in an orange coverall
and yellow life jacket. He set his helmet on the back of the
front seat and came down the ladder. He watched briefly to be
sure his fighter was in capable hands before sprinting to the
island. He met Ryan at the hatch.

"You Ryan? I'm Tony Parker. Where's the loo?" Jack gave
him the proper directions and the pilot darted off, leaving Ryan
standing there in a flight suit, holding his bag and feeling stupid.
A white plastic flight helmet dangled from his other hand as
they watched the crewmen fueling the Harrier. He wondered
if they knew what they were doing.

Parker was back in three minutes. "Commander," he said,
"there's one thing they've never put in a fighter, and that's a
bloody toilet. They fill you up with coffee and tea and send
you off, and you've no place to go."

"I know the feeling. Anything else you have to do?"

"No, sir. Your admiral chatted with me on the radio when
I was flying in. Looks like your chaps have finished fueling
my bird. Shall we be off?"

"What do I do with this?" Ryan held up his bag, expecting
to have to hold it in his lap. His briefing papers were inside

the flight suit, tucked against his chest.

"We put it in the boot, of course. Come along, sir."

Parker walked out to the fighter jauntily. The dawn was a feeble one. There was a solid overcast at one or two thousand feet. It wasn't raining, but looked as though it might. The sea, still rolling at about eight feet, was a gray, crinkled surface dotted with whitecaps. Ryan could feel the *Kennedy* moving, surprised that something so huge could be made to move at all. When they got to the Harrier, Parker took the duffle in one hand and reached for a recessed handle on the underside of the fighter. Twisting and pulling the lever, he revealed a cramped space about the size of a small refrigerator. Parker stuffed the bag into it, slamming the door shut behind it, making sure the locking lever was fully engaged. A deck crewman in a yellow shirt conferred with the pilot. Aft a helicopter was revving its engines, and a Tomcat fighter was taxiing towards a midships catapult. On top of this a thirty-knot wind was blowing. The carrier was a noisy place.

Parker waved Ryan up the ladder. Jack, who liked ladders about as much as he liked flying, nearly fell into his seat. He struggled to get situated properly, while a deck crewman strapped him into the four-point restraint system. The man put the helmet on Ryan's head and pointed to the jack for its intercom system. Maybe American crews really did know something about Harriers. Next to the plug was a switch. Ryan flipped it.

"Can you hear me, Parker?"

"Yes, Commander. All settled in?"

"I suppose."

"Right." Parker's head swiveled to check the engine intakes. "Starting the engine."

The canopies stayed up. Three crewmen stood close by with large carbon dioxide extinguishers, presumably in case the engine exploded. A dozen others were standing by the island, watching the strange aircraft as the Pegasus engine screamed to life. Then the canopy came down.

"Ready, Commander?"

"If you are."

The Harrier was not a large fighter, but it was certainly the loudest. Ryan could feel the engine noise ripple through his body as Parker adjusted his thrust-vector controls. The aircraft wobbled, dipped at the nose, then rose shakily into the air.

Ryan saw a man by the island point and gesture to them. The Harrier slid to port, moving away from the island as it gained in height.

"That wasn't too bad," Parker said. He adjusted the thrust controls, and the Harrier began true forward flight. There was little feeling of acceleration, but Ryan saw that the *Kennedy* was rapidly falling behind. A few seconds later they were beyond the inner ring of escorts.

"Let's get on top of this muck," Parker said. He pulled back on the stick and headed for the clouds. In seconds they were in them, and Ryan's field of view was reduced from five miles to five feet in an instant.

Jack looked around his cockpit, which had flight controls and instruments. Their airspeed showed one hundred fifty knots and rising, altitude four hundred feet. This Harrier had evidently been a trainer, but the instrument panel had been altered to include the read-out instruments for a sensor pod that could be attached to the belly. A poor man's way of doing things, but from what Admiral Painter said it had evidently worked well enough. He figured the TV-type screen was the FLIR readout, which monitored a forward-looking infrared heat sensor. The airspeed gauge now said three hundred knots, and the climb indicator showed a twenty-degree angle of attack. It felt like more than that.

"Should be hitting the top of this soon," Parker said. "Now!"

The altimeter showed twenty-six thousand feet when Ryan was blasted by pure sunlight. One thing about flying that he never got used to was that no matter how awful the weather was on the ground, if you flew high enough you could always find the sun. The light was intense, but the sky's color was noticeably deeper than the soft blue seen from the ground. The ride became airliner smooth as they escaped the lower turbulence. Ryan fumbled with his visor to shield his eyes.

"That better, sir?"

"Fine, Lieutenant. It's better than I expected."

"What do you mean, sir?" Parker inquired.

"I guess it beats flying on a commercial bird. You can see more. That helps."

"Sorry we don't have any extra fuel, or I'd show you some aerobatics. The Harrier will do almost anything you ask of her."

"That's all right."

"And your admiral," Parker went on conversationally, "said hat you don't fancy flying."

Ryan's hands grabbed the armrests as the Harrier went through hree complete revolutions before snapping back to level flight. Ie surprised himself by laughing. "Ah, the British sense of umor."

"Orders from your admiral, sir," Parker semi-apologized. "We wouldn't want you to think the Harrier's another bloody ous."

"Which admiral, Ryan wondered, Painter or Davenport? Probably both. The top of the clouds was like a rolling field of cotton. He'd never appreciated that before, looking through a foot-square window on an airliner. In the back seat he almost elt as if he were sitting outside.

"May I ask a question, sir?"

"Sure."

"What's the flap?"

"What do you mean?"

"I mean, sir, that they turned my ship around. Then I get orders to ferry a VIP from *Kennedy* to *Invincible*."

"Oh, okay. Can't say, Parker. I'm delivering some messages o your boss. I'm just the mailman," Ryan lied. Roll that one hree times.

"Excuse me, Commander, but you see, my wife is expecting a child, our first, soon after Christmas. I hope to be there, sir."

"Where do you live?"

"Chatham, that's—"

"I know. I live in England myself at the moment. Our place s in Marlow, upriver from London. My second kid got started over there."

"Born there?"

"Started there. My wife says it's those strange hotel beds, lo it to her every time. If I were a betting man, I'd give you good odds, Parker. First babies are always late anyway."

"You say you live in Marlow?"

"That's right, we built a house there earlier this year."

"Jack Ryan—John Ryan? The same chap who—"

"Correct. You don't have to tell anybody that, Lieutenant."

"Understood, sir. I didn't know you were a naval officer."

"That's why you don't have to tell anyone."

"Yes, sir. Sorry for the stunt earlier."

"That's all right. Admirals must have their little laughs. I understand you guys just ran an exercise with our guys."

"Indeed we did, Commander. I sank one of your submarines, the *Tullibee*. My systems operator and I, that is. We caught her near the surface at night with our FLIR and dropped noise-makers all round her. You see, we didn't let anyone know about our new equipment. All's fair, as you know. I understand her commander was bloody furious. I'd hoped to meet him in Norfolk, but he didn't arrive until the day we sailed."

"You guys have a good time in Norfolk?"

"Yes, Commander. We were able to get in a day's shooting on your Chesapeake Bay, the Eastern Shore, I believe you call it."

"Oh yeah? I used to hunt there. How was it?"

"Not bad. I got my three geese in half an hour. Bag limit was three—stupid."

"You called in and blasted three geese in a half hour this late in the season?"

"That is how I earn my modest living, Commander, shooting," Parker commented.

"I was up for a grouse shoot with your admiral last September. They made me use a double. If you show up with my kind of gun—I use a Remington automatic—they look at you like you're some kind of terrorist. I got stuck with a pair of Purdeys that didn't fit. Got fifteen birds. Seemed an awful lazy way to hunt, though, with one guy loading my gun for me, and another platoon of ghillies driving the game. We just about annihilated the bird population, too."

"We have more game per acre than you do."

"That's what the admiral said. How far to *Invincible*?"

"Forty minutes."

Ryan looked at the fuel gauges. They were half empty already. In a car he'd be thinking about a fill-up. All that fuel gone in half an hour. Well, Parker didn't seem excited.

The landing on HMS *Invincible* was different from the COD's arrival on the *Kennedy*. The ride became rocky as Parker descended through the clouds, and it occurred to Ryan that they were on the leading edge of the same storm he'd endured the night before. The canopy was coated with rain, and he heard the impact of thousands of raindrops on the airframe—or was

t hail? Watching the instruments, he saw that Parker leveled
out at a thousand feet, while they were still in clouds, then
descended more slowly, breaking into the clear at a hundred
feet. The *Invincible* was scarcely a half the *Kennedy*'s size. He
watched her bobbing actively on the fifteen-foot seas. Parker
used the same technique as before. He hovered briefly on the
carrier's port side, then slid to the right, dropping the fighter
twenty feet onto a painted circle. The landing was hard, but
Ryan was able to see it coming. The canopy came up at once.

"You can get out here," Parker said. "I have to taxi to the
elevator."

A ladder was already in place. He unbuckled and got out.
A crewman had already retrieved his bag. Ryan followed him
to the island and was met by an ensign—a sublieutenant, the
British call the rank.

"Welcome aboard, sir." The youngster couldn't be more
than twenty, Ryan thought. "Let me help you out of the flight
suit."

The sublieutenant stood by as Ryan unzipped and took off
his helmet, Mae West, and coverall. He retrieved his cap from
the bag. In the process he bounced off the bulkhead a few
times. The *Invincible* seemed to be corkscrewing in a following
sea. A bow wind and a following sea? In the North Atlantic
in winter, nothing was too crazy. The officer took his bag, and
Ryan held onto the briefing material.

"Lead on, *lef*tenant," Ryan gestured. The youngster shot
up a series of three ladders, leaving Jack painting behind,
thinking about the jogging he wasn't getting in. The combination of the ship's motion and an inner ear badly scrambled
from the day's flying made him dizzy, and he found himself
bumping into things. How did professional pilots do it?

"Here's the flag bridge, sir." The sublieutenant held the door
open.

"Hello, Jack!" boomed the voice of Vice Admiral John
White, eighth earl of Weston. He was a tall, well-built man of
fifty with a florid complexion set off by a white scarf at his
neck. Jack had first met him earlier in the year, and since then
his wife Cathy and the countess, Antonia, had become close
friends, members of the same circle of amateur musicians.
Cathy Ryan played classical piano. Toni White, an attractive
woman of forty-four, owned a Guarnieri del Jesu violin. Her

husband was a man whose peerage was treated as the convenient afterthought. His career in the Royal Navy had been built entirely on merit. Jack walked over to take his hand.

"Good day, Admiral."

"How was your flight?"

"Different. I've never been in a fighter before, much less one with ambitions to mate with a hummingbird," Ryan smiled. The bridge was overheated, and it felt good.

"Jolly good. Let's go aft to my sea cabin." White dismissed the sublieutenant, who handed Jack his bag before withdrawing. The admiral led him aft through a short passageway and left into a small compartment.

It was surprisingly austere, considering that the English liked their comforts and that White was a peer. There were two curtained portholes, a desk, and a couple of chairs. The only human touch was a color photograph of his wife. The entire port wall was covered with a chart of the North Atlantic.

"You look tired, Jack." White waved him to the upholstered chair.

"I am tired. I've been on the go since—hell, since 6:00 A.M. yesterday. I don't know about time changes, I think my watch is still on European time."

"I have a message for you." White pulled a slip of paper from his pocket and handed it over.

"Greer to Ryan. WILLOW confirmed," Ryan read. "Basil sends regards. Ends." Somebody had confirmed WILLOW. Who? Maybe Sir Basil, maybe Ritter. Ryan would not quote odds on that one.

Jack tucked it in his pocket. "This is good news, sir."

"Why the uniform?"

"Not my idea, Admiral. You know who I work for, right? They figured I'd be less conspicuous this way."

"At least it fits." The admiral lifted a phone and ordered refreshments sent to them. "How's the family, Jack?"

"Fine, thank you, sjr. The day before I came over Cathy and Toni were playing over at Nigel Ford's place. I missed it. You know, if they get much better, we ought to have a record cut. There aren't too many violin players better than your wife."

A steward arrived with a plateful of sandwiches. Jack had never figured out the British taste for cucumbers on bread.

"So, what's the flap?"

"Admiral, the significance of the message you just gave me is that I can tell this to you and three other officers. This is very hot stuff, sir. You'll want to make your choices accordingly."

"Hot enough to turn my little fleet around." White thought it over before lifting the phone and ordering three of his officers to the cabin. He hung up. "Captain Carstairs, Captain Hunter, and Commander Barclay—they are, respectively, *Invincible*'s commanding officer, my fleet operations officer, and my fleet intelligence officer."

"No chief of staff?"

"Flew home, death in the family. Something for your coffee?" White extracted what looked like a brandy bottle from a desk drawer.

"Thank you, Admiral." He was grateful for the brandy. The coffee needed the help. He watched the admiral pour a generous amount, perhaps with the ulterior motive of making him speak more freely. White had been a British sailor longer than he'd been Ryan's friend.

The three officers arrived together, two carrying folding metal chairs.

"Admiral," Ryan began, "you might want to leave that bottle out. After you hear this story, we might all need a drink." He passed out his two remaining briefing folders and talked from memory. His delivery took fifteen minutes.

"Gentlemen," he concluded, "I must insist that this information be kept strictly confidential. For the moment no one outside this room may learn it."

"That is too bad," Carstairs said. "This makes for a bloody good sea story."

"And our mission?" White was holding the photographs. He poured Ryan another shot of brandy, gave the bottle a brief look, then stowed it back in the desk.

"Thank you, Admiral. For the moment our mission is to locate *Red October*. After that we're not sure. I imagine just locating her will be hard enough."

"An astute observation, Commander Ryan," Hunter said.

"The good news is that Admiral Painter has requested that CINCLANT assign you control of several U.S. Navy vessels,

probably three 1052-class frigates, and a pair of FFG *Perry*s.
They all carry a chopper or two."

"Well, Geoffrey?" White asked.

"It's a start," Hunter agreed.

"They'll be arriving in a day or two. Admiral Painter asked
me to express his confidence in your group and its personnel."

"A whole fucking Russian missile submarine..." Barclay
said almost to himself. Ryan laughed.

"Like the idea, Commander?" At least he had one convert.

"What if the sub is heading for the U.K.? Does it then
become a British operation?" Barclay asked pointedly.

"I suppose it would, but from the way I read the map, if
Ramius was heading for England, he'd already be there. I saw
a copy of the president's letter to the prime minister. In return
for your assistance, the Royal Navy gets the same access to
the data we develop as our guys get. We're on the same side,
gentlemen. The question is, can we do it?"

"Hunter?" the admiral asked.

"If this intelligence is correct... I'd say we have a good
chance, perhaps as good as fifty percent. On one hand, we
have a missile submarine attempting to evade detection. On
the other, we have a great deal of ASW arrayed to locate her,
and she will be heading towards one of only a few discrete
locations. Norfolk, of course, Newport, Groton, King's Bay,
Port Everglades, Charleston. A civilian port such as New York
is less likely, I think. The problem is, what with Ivan sending
all his *Alfa*s racing to your coast, they will get there ahead of
October. They may have a specific port target in mind. We'll
know that in another day. So, I'd say they have an equal chance.
They'll be able to operate far enough off your coast that your
government will have no viable legal reason to object to whatever they do. If anything, I'd say the Soviets have the advantage. They have both a clearer idea of the submarine's capabilities
and a simpler overall mission. That more than balances their
less capable sensors."

"Why isn't Ramius coming on faster?" Ryan asked. "That's
the one thing I can't figure. Once he clears the SOSUS lines
off Iceland, he's clear into the deep basin—so why not crack
his throttles wide open and race for our coast?"

"At least two reasons," Barclay answered. "How much operational intelligence data do you see?"

"I handle individual assignments. That means I hop around a lot from one thing to another. I know a good deal about their boomers, for example, but not as much about their attack boats." Ryan didn't have to explain he was CIA.

"Well, you know how compartmentalized the Sovs are. Ramius probably doesn't know where their attack submarines are, not all of them. So, if he were to race about, he'd run the off chance of blundering into a stray *Victor* and being sunk without ever knowing what was happening. Second, what if the Soviets did enlist American assistance, saying perhaps that a missile sub had been taken over by a mutinous crew of Maoist counterrevolutionaries—and then your navy detects a missile submarine racing down the North Atlantic towards the American coast. What would your president do?"

"Yeah," Ryan nodded. "We'd blow it the hell out of the water."

"There you have it. Ramius is in the trade of stealth, and he'll likely stick to what he knows," Barclay concluded. "Fortunately or unfortunately, he's jolly good at it."

"How soon will we have performance data on this quiet drive system?" Carstairs wanted to know.

"Next couple of days, we hope."

"Where does Admiral Painter want us?" White asked.

"The plan he submitted to Norfolk puts you on the right flank. He wants *Kennedy* inshore to handle the threat from their surface force. He wants your force farther out. You see, Painter thinks there's the chance that Ramius will come straight south from the G-I-U.K. gap into the Atlantic basin and just sit for a while. The odds favor his not being detected there, and if the Soviets send the fleet after him, he's got the time and supplies to sit out there longer than they can maintain a force off our coast—both for technical and political reasons. Additionally, he wants your striking power out here to threaten their flank. It has to be approved by the commander in chief of the Atlantic Fleet, and a lot of details remain to be worked out. For example, Painter requested some E-3 Sentries to support you out here."

"A month in the middle of the North Atlantic in winter?" Carstairs winced. He had been the *Invincible*'s executive officer during the war around the Falklands and had ridden in the violent South Atlantic for endless weeks.

"Be happy for the E-3s." The admiral smiled. "Hunter, I want to see plans for using all these ships the Yanks are giving us, and how we can cover a maximum area. Barclay, I want to see your evaluation of what our friend Ramius will do. Assume he's still the clever bastard we've come to know and love."

"Aye aye, sir." Barclay stood with the others.

"Jack, how long will you be with us?"

"I don't know, Admiral. Until they recall me to the *Kennedy,* I guess. From where I sit, this operation was laid on too fast. Nobody really knows what the hell we're supposed to do."

"Well, why don't you let us see to this for a while? You look exhausted. Get some sleep."

"True enough, Admiral." Ryan was beginning to feel the brandy.

"There's a cot in the locker over there. I'll have someone set it up for you, and you can sleep in here for the time being. If anything comes in for you, we'll get you up."

"That's kind of you, sir." Admiral White was a good guy, Jack thought, and his wife was something very special. In ten minutes, Ryan was on the cot and asleep.

The Red October

Every two days the *starpom* collected the radiation badges. This was part of a semiformal inspection. After seeing to it that every crewman's shoes were spit-shined, every bunk was properly made, and every footlocker was arranged according to the book, the executive officer would take the two-day-old badges and hand the sailors new ones, usually along with some terse advice to square themselves away as New Soviet Men ought. Borodin had this procedure down to a science. Today, as always, the trip from one compartment to another took two hours. When he was finished, the bag on his left hip was full of old badges, and the one on his right depleted of new ones. He took the badges to the ship's medical officer.

"Comrade Petrov, I have a gift for you." Borodin set the leather bag on the physician's desk.

"Good." The doctor smiled up at the executive officer. "With all the healthy young men I have little to do but read my journals."

Borodin left Petrov to his task. First the doctor set the badges out in order. Each bore a three-digit number. The first digit identified the badge series, so that if any radiation were detected there would be a time reference. The second digit showed where the sailor worked, the third where he slept. This system was easier to work with than the old one, which had used individual numbers for each man.

The developing process was cookbook-simple. Petrov could do it without a thought. First he switched off the white overhead light and replaced it with a red one. Then he locked his office door. Next he took the development rack from its holder on the bulkhead, broke open the plastic holders, and transferred the film strips to spring clips on the rack.

Petrov took the rack into the adjacent laboratory and hung it on the handle of the single filing cabinet. He filled three large square basins with chemicals. Though a qualified physician, he had forgotten most of his inorganic chemistry and didn't remember exactly what the developing chemicals were. Basin number one was filled from bottle number one. Basin two was filled from bottle two, and basin three, he remembered, was filled with water. Petrov was in no hurry. The midday meal was not for two more hours, and his duties were truly boring. The last two days he had been reading his medical texts on tropical diseases. The doctor was looking forward to visiting Cuba as much as anyone aboard. With luck a crewman would come down with some obscure malady, and he'd have something interesting to work on for once.

Petrov set the lab timer for seventy-five seconds and submerged the film strips in the first basin as he pressed the start button. He watched the timer under the red light, wondering if the Cubans still made rum. He had been there, too, years before, and acquired a taste for the exotic liquor. Like any good Soviet citizen, he loved his vodka but had the occasional hankering for something different.

The timer went off and he lifted the rack, shaking it carefully over the tank. No sense getting the chemical—silver nitrate? something like that—on his uniform. The rack went into the second tank, and he set the timer again. Pity the orders had been so damned secret—he could have brought his tropical uniform. He'd sweat like a pig in the Cuban heat. Of course, none of those savages ever bothered to wash. Maybe they had learned something in the past fifteen years? He'd see.

The timer *ding*ed again, and Petrov lifted the rack a second time, shaking it and setting it in the water-filled basin. Another boring job completed. Why couldn't a sailor fall down a ladder and break something? He wanted to use his East German X-ray machine on a live patient. He didn't trust the Germans, Marxists or not, but they did make good medical equipment, including his X-ray, autoclave, and most of his pharmaceuticals. Time. Petrov lifted the rack and held it up against the X-ray reading plate, which he switched on.

"Nichevo!" Petrov breathed. He had to think. His badge was fogged. Its number was 3-4-8: third badge series, frame fifty-four (the medical office, galley section), aft (officers') accommodations.

Though only two centimeters across, the badges were made with variable sensitivity. Ten vertically segmented columns were used to quantify the exposure level. Petrov saw that his was fogged all the way to segment four. The engine room crewmen's were fogged to segment five, and the torpedomen, who spent all their time forward, showed contamination only in segment one.

"Son of a bitch." He knew the sensitivity levels by heart. He took the manual down to check them anyway. Fortunately, the segments were logarithmic. His exposure was twelve rads. Fifteen to twenty-five for the engineers. Twelve to twenty-five rads in two days, not enough to be dangerous. Not really life threatening, but . . . Petrov went back into his office, careful to leave the films in the labs. He picked up the phone.

"Captain Ramius? Petrov here. Could you come aft to my office, please?"

"On the way, Comrade Doctor."

Ramius took his time. He knew what the call was about. The day before they sailed, while Petrov had been ashore procuring drugs for his cupboard, Borodin had contaminated the badges with the X-ray machine.

"Yes, Petrov?" Ramius closed the door behind him.

"Comrade Captain, we have a radiation leak."

"Nonsense. Our instruments would have detected it at once."

Petrov got the films from the lab and handed them to the captain. "Look here."

Ramius held them up to the light, scanning the film strips

top to bottom. He frowned. "Who knows of this?"

"You and I, Comrade Captain."

"You will tell no one—no one." Ramius paused. "Any chance that the films were—that they have something wrong, that you made an error in the developing process?"

Petrov shook his head emphatically. "No, Comrade Captain. Only you, Comrade Borodin, and I have access to these. As you know, I tested random samples from each batch three days before we sailed." Petrov wouldn't admit that, like everyone, he had taken the samples from the top of the box they were stored in. They weren't really random.

"The maximum exposure I see here is ... ten to twenty?" Ramius understated it. "Whose numbers?"

"Bulganin and Surzpoi. The torpedomen forward are all under three rads."

"Very well. What we have here, Comrade Doctor, is a possible minor—minor, Petrov—leak in the reactor spaces. At worst a gas leak of some sort. This has happened before, and no one has ever died from it. The leak will be found and fixed. We will keep this little secret. There is no reason to get the men excited over nothing."

Petrov nodded agreement, knowing that men had died in 1970 in an accident on the submarine *Voroshilov,* more in the icebreaker *Lenin.* Both accidents were a long time ago, though, and he was sure Ramius could handle things. Wasn't he?

The Pentagon

The E ring was the outermost and largest of the Pentagon's rings, and since its outside windows offered something other than a view of sunless courtyards, this was where the most senior defense officials had their offices. One of these was the office of the director of operations for the Joint Chiefs of Staff, the J-3. He wasn't there. He was down in a subbasement room known colloquially as the Tank because its metal walls were dotted with electronic noisemakers to foil other electronic devices.

He had been there for twenty-four hours, though one would not have known this from his appearance. His green trousers were still creased, his khaki shirt still showed the folds made by the laundry, its collar starched plywood-stiff, and his tie was held neatly in place by a gold marine corps tiepin. Lieutenant General Edwin Harris was neither a diplomat nor a service academy graduate, but he was playing peacemaker. An odd position for a marine.

"God damn it!" It was the voice of Admiral Blackburn, CINCLANT. Also present was his own operations officer, Rear Admiral Pete Stanford. "Is this any way to run an operation?"

The Joint Chiefs were all there, and none of them thought so.

"Look, Blackie, I told you where the orders come from." General Hilton, chairman of the Joint Chiefs of Staff, sounded tired.

"I understand that, General, but this is largely a submarine operation, right? I gotta get Vince Gallery in on this, and you should have Sam Dodge working up at this end. Dan and I are both fighter jocks, Pete's an ASW expert. We need a sub driver in on this."

"Gentlemen," Harris said calmly, "for the moment the plan we have to take to the president need only deal with the Soviet threat. Let's hold this story about the defecting boomer in abeyance for the moment, shall we?"

"I agree," Stanford nodded. "We have enough to worry about right here."

The attention of the eight flag officers turned to the map table. Fifty-eight Soviet submarines and twenty-eight surface warships, plus a gaggle of oilers and replenishment ships, were unmistakably heading for the American coast. To face this, the U.S. Navy had one available carrier. The *Invincible* did not rate as such. The threat was considerable. Among them the Soviet vessels carried over three hundred surface-to-surface cruise missiles. Though principally designed as antiship weapons, the third of them believed to carry nuclear warheads were sufficient to devastate the cities of the East Coast. From a position off New Jersey, these missiles could range from Norfolk to Boston.

"Josh Painter proposes that we keep *Kennedy* inshore," Admiral Blackburn said. "He wants to run the ASW operation from his carrier, transferring his light attack squadrons to shore and replacing them with S-3s. He wants *Invincible* out on their seaward flank."

"I don't like it," General Harris said. Neither did Pete Stanford, and they had agreed earlier that the J-3 would launch the counterplan. "Gentlemen, if we're only going to have one deck to use, we damned well ought to have a carrier and not an oversized ASW platform."

"We're listening, Eddie," Hilton said.

"Let's move *Kennedy* out here." He moved the counter to a position west of the Azores. "Josh keeps his attack squadrons. We move *Invincible* inshore to handle the ASW work. It's what the Brits designed her for, right? They're supposed to be good at it. *Kennedy* is an offensive weapon, her mission is to threaten them. Okay, if we deploy like this, she is the threat. From over here she can range against their surface force from outside their surface-to-surface missile perimeter—"

"Better yet," Stanford interjected, pointing to some vessels on the map, "threaten this service force here. If they lose these oilers, they ain't going home. To meet that threat they'll have to redeploy themselves. For starters, they'll have to move *Kiev* offshore to give themselves some kind of air defense against *Kennedy*. We can use the spare S-3s from shore bases. They can still patrol the same areas." He traced a line about five hundred miles off the coast.

"Leaves *Invincible* kind of naked, though," the CNO, Admiral Foster, noted.

"Josh was asking about some E-3 coverage for the Brits." Blackburn looked at the air force chief of staff, General Claire Barnes.

"You want help, you get help," Barnes said. "We'll have a Sentry operating over *Invincible* at dawn tomorrow, and if you move her inshore we can maintain that round the clock. I'll throw in a wing of F-16s if you want."

"What do you want in return, Max?" Foster asked. Nobody called him Claire.

"The way I see this, you have *Saratoga*'s air wing sitting around doing nothing. Okay, by Saturday I'll have five hundred tactical fighters deployed from Dover to Loring. My boys don't know much about antiship stuff. They'll have to learn in a hurry. I want you to send your kids to work with mine, and I also want your Tomcats. I like the fighter-missile combination. Let one squadron work out of Iceland, the other out of New England to track the Bears Ivan's starting to send our way. I'll sweeten that. If you want, we'll send some tankers to Lajes to help keep *Kennedy*'s birds flying."

"Blackie?" Foster asked.

"Deal," Blackburn nodded. "The only thing that bothers me is that *Invincible* doesn't have all that much ASW capacity."

"So we get more," Stanford said. "Admiral, what say we take *Tarawa* out of Little Creek, team her with *New Jersey*'s group, with a dozen ASW choppers aboard and seven or eight Harriers?"

"I like it," Harris said quickly. "Then we have two baby carriers with a noteworthy striking force right in front of their groups, *Kennedy* playing stalking tiger to their east, and a few hundred tactical fighters to the west. They have to come into a three-way box. This actually gives us more ASW patrolling capacity than we'd have otherwise."

"Can *Kennedy* handle her mission alone out there?" Hilton asked.

"Depend on it," Blackburn replied. "We can kill any one, maybe any two of these four groups in an hour. The ones nearest shore will be your job, Max."

"How long did you two characters rehearse this?" General Maxwell, commandant of the marine corps, asked the operations officer. Everyone chuckled.

The Red October

Chief Engineer Melekhin cleared the reactor compartment before beginning the check for the leak. Ramius and Petrov were there also, plus the engineering duty officers and one of the young lieutenants, Svyadov. Three of the officers carried Geiger counters.

The reactor room was quite large. It had to be to accommodate the massive, barrel-shaped steel vessel. The object was warm to the touch despite being inactive. Automatic radiation detectors were in every corner of the room, each surrounded by a red circle. More were hanging on the fore and aft bulkheads. Of all the compartments on the submarine, this was the cleanest. The deck and bulkheads were spotless white-painted steel. The reason was obvious: the smallest leak of reactor coolant had to be instantly visible even if all the detectors failed.

Svyadov climbed an aluminum ladder affixed to the side of the reactor vessel to run the detachable probe from his counter over every welded pipe joint. The speaker-annunciator on the hand-held box was turned to maximum so that everyone in the compartment could hear it, and Svyadov had an earpiece plugged in for even greater sensitivity. A youngster of twenty-one, he was nervous. Only a fool would feel entirely safe looking for a radiation leak. There is a joke in the Soviet Navy: How do you tell a sailor from the Northern Fleet? He glows in the dark. It had been a good laugh on the beach, but not now. He knew that he was conducting the search because he was the youngest, least experienced, and most expendable officer. It was an effort to keep his knees from wobbling as he strained to reach all over and around the reactor piping.

The counter was not entirely silent, and Svyadov's stomach cringed at each click generated by the passage of a random particle through the tube of ionized gas. Every few seconds his eyes flickered to the dial that measured intensity. It was well inside the safe range, hardly registering at all. The reactor vessel was a quadruple-layer design, each layer several centimeters of tough stainless steel. The three inner spaces were filled with a barium-water mixture, then a barrier of lead, then polyethylene, all designed to prevent the escape of neutrons and gamma particles. The combination of steel, barium, lead, and plastic successfully contained the dangerous elements of the reaction, allowing only a few degrees of heat to escape, and the dial showed, much to his relief, that the radiation level was less than that on the beach at Sochi. The highest reading was made next to a light bulb. This made the lieutenant smile.

"All readings in normal range, comrades," Svyadov reported.

"Start over," Melekhin ordered, "from the beginning."

Twenty minutes later Svyadov, now sweating from the warm air that gathered at the top of the compartment, made an identical report. He came down awkwardly, his arms and legs tired.

"Have a cigarette," Ramius suggested. "You did well, Svyadov."

"Thank you, Comrade Captain. It's warm up there from the lights and the coolant pipes." The lieutenant handed the counter to Melekhin. The lower dial showed a cumulative count, well within the safe range.

"Probably some contaminated badges," the chief engineer commented sourly. "It would not be the first time. Some joker in the factory or at the yard supply office—something for our friends in the GRU to check into. 'Wreckers!' A joke like this ought to earn somebody a bullet."

"Perhaps," Ramius chuckled. "Remember the incident on *Lenin?*" He referred to the nuclear-powered icebreaker that had spent two years tied to the dock, unusable because of a reactor mishap. "A ship's cook had some badly crusted pans, and a madman of an engineer suggested that he use live steam to get them cleaned. So the idiot·walked down to the steam generator and opened an inspection valve, with his pots under it!"

Melekhin rolled his eyes. "I remember it! I was a staff engineering officer then. The captain had asked for a Kazakh cook—"

"He liked horsemeat with his kasha," Ramius said.

"—and the fool didn't know the first thing about a ship. Killed himself and three other men, contaminated the whole fucking compartment for twenty months. The captain only got out of the gulag last year."

"I bet the cook got his pans cleaned, though," Ramius observed.

"Indeed, Marko Aleksandrovich—they may even be safe to use in another fifty years." Melekhin laughed raucously.

That was a hell of a thing to say in front of a young officer, Petrov thought. There was nothing, nothing at all funny about a reactor leak. But Melekhin was known for his heavy sense of humor, and the doctor imagined that twenty years of working on reactors allowed him and the captain to view the potential dangers phlegmatically. Then, there was the implicit lesson in the story: never let someone who does not belong into the reactor spaces.

"Very well," Melekhin said, "now we check the pipes in the generator room. Come, Svyadov, we still need your young legs."

The next compartment aft contained the heat exchanger/ steam generator, turboalternators, and auxiliary equipment. The main turbines were in the next compartment, now inactive while the electrically driven caterpillar was operating. In any case, the steam that turned them was supposed to be clean. The only radioactivity was in the inside loop. The reactor coolant, which carried short-lived but dangerous radioactivity, never flashed to steam. This was in the outside loop and boiled from uncontaminated water. The two water supplies met but never mixed inside the heat exchanger, the most likely site for a coolant leak because of its more numerous fittings and valves.

The more complex piping required a full fifty minutes to check. These pipes were not as well insulated as those forward. Svyadov nearly burned himself twice, and his face was bathed in perspiration by the time he finished his first sweep.

"Readings all safe again, comrades."

"Good," Melekhin said. "Come down and rest a moment before you check it again."

Svyadov almost thanked his chief for that, but this would not have done at all. As a young, dedicated officer and member of the Komsomol, no exertion was too great. He came down carefully, and Melekhin handed him another cigarette. The chief engineer was a gray-haired perfectionist who took decent care of his men.

"Why, thank you, Comrade," Svyadov said.

Petrov got a folding chair. "Sit, Comrade Lieutenant, rest your legs."

The lieutenant sat down at once, stretching his legs to work out the knots. The officers at VVMUPP had told him how lucky he was to draw this assignment. Ramius and Melekhin were the two best teachers in the fleet, men whose crews appreciated their kindness along with their competence.

"They really should insulate those pipes," Ramius said. Melekhin shook his head.

"Then they'd be too hard to inspect." He handed the counter to his captain.

"Entirely safe," the captain read off the cumulative dial. "You get more exposure tending a garden."

"Indeed," Melekhin said. "Coal miners get more exposure than we do, from the release of radon gas in the mines. Bad badges, that's what it has to be. Why not take out a whole batch and check it?"

"I could, Comrade," Petrov answered. "But then, due to the extended nature of our cruise, we'd have to run for several days without any. Contrary to regulations. I'm afraid."

"You are correct. In any case the badges are only a backup to our instruments." Ramius gestured to the red-circled detectors all over the compartment.

"Do you really want to recheck the piping?" Melekhin asked.

"I think we should," Ramius said.

Svyadov swore to himself, looking down at the deck.

"There is no extravagance in the pursuit of safety," Petrov quoted doctrine. "Sorry, Lieutenant." The doctor was not a bit sorry. He had been genuinely worried, and was now feeling a lot better.

An hour later the second check had been completed. Petrov took Svyadov forward for salt tablets and tea to rehydrate himself. The senior officers left, and Melekhin ordered the reactor plant restarted.

The enlisted men filed back to their duty stations, looking at one another. Their officers had just checked the "hot" compartments with radiation instruments. The medical corpsman had looked pale a while earlier and refused to say anything. More than one engine attendant fingered his radiation badge and checked his wristwatch to see how long it would be before he went off duty.

THE EIGHTH DAY

FRIDAY, 10 DECEMBER

HMS Invincible

Ryan awoke in the dark. The curtains were drawn on the cabin's two small portholes. He shook his head a few times to clear it and began to assess what was going on around him. The *Invincible* was moving on the seas, but not as much as before. He got up to look out of a porthole and saw the last red glow of sunset aft under scudding clouds. He checked his watch and did some clumsy mental arithmetic, concluding that it was six in the evening, local time. That translated to about six hours of sleep. He felt pretty good, considering. A minor headache from the brandy—so much for the theory that good stuff doesn't give you a hangover—and his muscles were stiff. He did a few sit-ups to work out the knots.

There was a small bathroom—head, he corrected himself—adjoining the cabin. Ryan splashed some water on his face and washed his mouth out, not wanting to look in the mirror. He decided he had to. Counterfeit or not, he was wearing his country's uniform and he had to look presentable. It took a minute to get his hair in place and the uniform arranged properly. The CIA had done a nice job of tailoring, given such short notice. Finished, he went out the door towards the flag bridge.

"Feeling better, Jack?" Admiral White pointed him to a tray full of cups. It was only tea, but it was a start.

"Thank you, Admiral. Those few hours really helped. I guess I'm in time for dinner."

"Breakfast," White corrected him with a laugh.

"What—uh, pardon me, Admiral?" Ryan shook his head again. He was still a little groggy.

"That's a sun*rise*, Commander. Change in orders, we're heading west again. *Kennedy*'s moving east at high speed, and we're to take station inshore."

"Who said, sir?"

"CINCLANT. I gather Joshua was not at all pleased. You are to remain with us for the moment, and under the circumstances it seemed the reasonable thing to let you sleep. You did appear to need it."

Must have been eighteen hours, Ryan thought. No wonder he felt stiff.

"You do look much better," Admiral White noted from his leather swivel chair. He got up, took Ryan's arm, and guided him aft. "Now for breakfast. I've been waiting for you. Captain Hunter will brief you on your revised orders. Weather's clearing up for a few days, they tell me. Escort assignments are being reshuffled. We're to operate in conjunction with your *New Jersey* group. Our antisubmarine operations begin in earnest in another twelve hours. It's a good thing you got that extra sleep, lad. You'll bloody need it."

Ryan ran his hand over his face. "Can I shave, sir?"

"We still permit beards. Let it wait until after breakfast."

Flag quarters on HMS *Invincible* were not quite to the standard of those on the *Kennedy*—but close. White had a private dining area. A steward in a white livery served them expertly, setting a third place for Hunter, who appeared within a few minutes. When they started talking, the steward was excused.

"We rendezvous with a pair of young *Knox*-class frigates in two hours. We already have them on radar. Two more 1052s, plus an oiler and two *Perry*s will join us in another thirty-six hours. They were on their way home from the Med. With our own escorts, a total of nine warships. A noteworthy collection, I think. We'll be working five hundred miles offshore, with the *New Jersey–Tarawa* force two hundred miles to our west."

"*Tarawa?* What do we need a regiment of marines for?" Ryan asked.

Hunter explained briefly. "Not a bad idea, that. The funny thing is, with *Kennedy* racing for the Azores, that rather leaves us guarding the American coast." Hunter grinned. "This may be the first time the Royal Navy has ever done that—certainly since it belonged to us."

"What are we up against?"

"The first of the *Alfa*s will be on your coast tonight, four of them ahead of all the others. The Soviet surface force passed Iceland last night. It's divided into three groups. One is built around their carrier *Kiev,* two cruisers and four destroyers; the second, probably the force flag, is built around *Kirov,* with three additional cruisers and six destroyers; and the third is centered on *Moskva,* three more cruisers and seven destroyers. I gather that the Soviets will want to use the *Kiev* and *Moskva* groups inshore, with *Kirov* guarding them out to sea—but *Kennedy*'s relocation will make them rethink that. Regardless, the total force carries a considerable number of surface-to-surface missiles, and potentially, we are very exposed. To help out with that, your air force has an E-3 Sentry detailed to arrive here in an hour to exercise with our Harriers, and when we get farther west, we'll have additional land-based air support. On the whole our position is hardly an enviable one, but Ivan's is rather less so. So far as the question of finding *Red October* is concerned?" Hunter shrugged. "How we conduct our search will depend on how Ivan deploys. At the moment we're conducting some tracking drills. The lead *Alfa* is eighty miles northwest of us, steaming at forty-plus knots, and we have a helicopter in pursuit—which is roughly what it amounts to," the fleet operations officer concluded. "Will you join us below?"

"Admiral?" Ryan wanted to see *Invincible*'s combat information center.

"Certainly."

Thirty minutes later Ryan was in a darkened, quiet room whose walls were a solid bank of electronic instruments and glass plotting panels. The Atlantic Ocean was full of Russian submarines.

The White House

The Soviet ambassador entered the Oval Office a minute early, at 10:59 A.M. He was a short, overweight man with a broad Slavic face and eyes that would have done a professional gambler proud. They revealed nothing. He was a career diplomat, having served in a number of posts throughout the Western world, and a thirty-year member of the Communist party's Foreign Department.

"Good morning, Mr. President, Dr. Pelt," Alexei Arbatov nodded politely to both men. The president, he noted at once, was seated behind his desk. Every other time he'd been here the president had come around the desk to shake hands, then sat down beside him.

"Help yourself to some coffee, Mr. Ambassador," Pelt offered. The special assistant to the president for national security affairs was well known to Arbatov. Jeffrey Pelt was an academic from the Georgetown University's Center for Strategic and International Studies—an enemy, but a well-mannered, *kulturny* enemy. Arbatov had a fondness for the niceties of formal behavior. Today, Pelt was standing at his boss's side, unwilling to come too close to the Russian bear. Arbatov did not get himself any coffee.

"Mr. Ambassador," Pelt began, "we have noted a troubling increase in Soviet naval activity in the North Atlantic."

"Oh?" Arbatov's eyebrows shot up in a display of surprise that fooled no one, and he knew it. "I have no knowledge of this. As you know, I have never been a sailor."

"Shall we dispense with the bullshit, Mr. Ambassador?" the president said. Arbatov did not permit himself to be surprised by the vulgarity. It made the American president seem very Russian, and like Soviet officials he seemed to need a professional like Pelt around to smooth the edges. "You certainly have nearly a hundred naval vessels operating in the North Atlantic or heading in that direction. Chairman Narmonov and my predecessor agreed years ago that no such operation would take place without prior notification. The purpose of this agreement, as you know, was to prevent acts that might appear to be unduly provocative to one side or the other. This agreement has been kept—until now.

"Now, my military advisers tell me that what is going on looks very much like a war exercise, indeed, could be the precursor to a war. How are we to tell the difference? Your ships are now passing east of Iceland, and will soon be in a position from which they can threaten our trade routes to Europe. This situation is at the least unsettling, and at the most a grave and wholly unwarranted provocation. The scope of this action has not yet been made public. That will change, and when it does, Alex, the American people will demand action on my part." The president paused, expecting a response but getting only a nod.

Pelt went on for him. "Mr. Ambassador, your country has seen fit to cast aside an agreement which for years has been a model of East-West cooperation. How can you expect us to regard this as anything other than a provocation?"

"Mr. President, Dr. Pelt, truly I have no knowledge of this." Arbatov lied with the utmost sincerity. "I will contact Moscow at once to ascertain the facts. Is there any message you wish me to pass along?"

"Yes. As you and your superiors in Moscow will understand," the president said, "we will deploy our ships and aircraft to observe yours. Prudence requires this. We have no wish to interfere with whatever legitimate operations your forces may be engaged in. It is not our intention to make a provocation of our own, but under the terms of our agreement we have the right to know what is going on, Mr. Ambassador. Until we do, we are unable to issue the proper orders to our men. It would be well for your government to consider that having so many of your ships and our ships, your aircraft and our aircraft in close proximity is an inherently dangerous situation. Accidents can happen. An action by one side or the other which at another time would seem harmless might seem to be something else entirely. Wars have begun in this way, Mr. Ambassador." The president leaned back to let that thought hang in the air for a moment. When he went on, he spoke more gently. "Of course, I regard this possibility as remote, but is it not irresponsible to take such chances?"

"Mr. President, you make your point well, as always, but as you know, the sea is free for the passage of all, and—"

"Mr. Ambassador," Pelt interrupted, "consider a simple analogy. Your next-door neighbor begins to patrol his front yard with a loaded shotgun while your children are at play in your own front yard. In this country such action would be technically legal. Even so, would it not be a matter of concern?"

"So it would, Dr. Pelt, but the situation you describe is very different—"

Now the president interrupted. "Indeed it is. The situation at hand is far more dangerous. It is the breach of an agreement, and I find that especially disquieting. I had hoped that we were entering a new era of Soviet-American relations. We have settled our trade differences. We have just concluded a new grain agreement. You had a major part in that. We have been moving forward, Mr. Ambassador—is this at an end?" The president shook his head emphatically. "I hope not, but the choice is yours. The relationship between our countries can only be based on trust.

"Mr. Ambassador, I trust that I have not alarmed you. As you know, it is my habit to speak plainly. I personally dislike the greasy dissimulation of diplomacy. At times like this, we must communicate quickly and clearly. We have a dangerous situation before us, and we must work together, rapidly, to resolve it. My military commanders are greatly concerned, and I need to know—today—what your naval forces are up to. I expect a reply by seven this evening. Failing that I will be on the direct line to Moscow to demand one."

Arbatov stood. "Mr. President, I will transmit your message within the hour. Please keep in mind, however, the time differential between Washington and Moscow—"

"I know that a weekend has just begun, and that the Soviet Union is a worker's paradise, but I expect that some of your country's managers may still be at work. In any case, I will detain you no further. Good day."

Pelt led Arbatov out, then came back and sat down.

"Maybe I was just a little tough on him," the president said.

"Yes, sir." Pelt thought that he had been too damned tough. He had little affection for the Russian but he too liked the niceties of diplomatic exchange. "I think we can say that you succeeded in getting your message across."

"He knows."

"He knows. But he doesn't know we know."

"We think," the president grimaced. "What a crazy goddamned game this is! And to think I had a nice, safe career going for me putting mafiosi in jail . . . Do you think he'll snap at the bait I offered?"

"'Legitimate operations?' Did you see his hands twitch at that? He'll go after it like a marlin after a squid." Pelt walked over to pour himself half a cup of coffee. It pleased him that the china service was gold trimmed. "I wonder what they'll call it? Legitimate operations . . . probably a rescue mission. If they call it a fleet exercise they admit to violating the notification protocol. A rescue operation justifies the level of activity, the speed with which it was laid on, and the lack of publicity. Their press never reports this sort of thing. As a guess, I'd say they'll call it a rescue, say a submarine is missing, maybe even to the point of calling it a missile sub."

"No, they won't go that far. We also have that agreement about keeping our missile subs five hundred miles offshore. Arbatov probably has his instructions on what to tell us already, but he'll play for all the time he can. It's also vaguely possible that he's in the dark. We know how they compartmentalize information. You suppose we're reading too much into this talent for obfuscation?"

"I think not, sir. It is a principle of diplomacy," Pelt observed, "that one must know something of the truth in order to lie convincingly."

The president smiled. "Well, they've had enough time to play this game. I hope my belated reaction will not disappoint them."

"No, sir. Alex must have half expected you to kick him out the door."

"The thought's occurred to me more than once. His diplomatic charm has always been lost on me. That's the one thing about the Russians—they remind me so much of the mafia chieftains I used to prosecute. The same smattering of culture and good manners, and the same absence of morality." The president shook his head. He was talking like a hawk again. "Stay close, Jeff. I have George Farmer coming in here in a few minutes, but I want you around when our friend comes back."

Pelt walked back to his office pondering the president's remark. It was, he admitted to himself, crudely accurate. The most wounding insult to an educated Russian was to be called *nekulturny,* uncultured—the term didn't translate adequately—

yet the same men who sat in the gilt boxes at the Moscow State Opera weeping at the end of a performance of *Boris Gudunov* could immediately turn around and order the execution or imprisonment of a hundred men without blinking. A strange people, made more strange by their political philosophy. But the president had too many sharp edges, and Pelt wished he'd learn to soften them. A speech in front of the American Legion was one thing, a discussion with the ambassador of a foreign power was something else.

CIA Headquarters

"CARDINAL's in trouble, Judge." Ritter sat down.

"No surprise there." Moore removed his glasses and rubbed his eyes. Something Ryan had not seen was the cover note from the station chief in Moscow saying that to get his latest signal out, CARDINAL had bypassed half the courier chain that ran from the Kremlin to the U.S. embassy. The agent was getting bold in his old age. "What does the station chief say exactly?"

"CARDINAL's supposed to be in the hospital with pneumonia. Maybe it's true, but..."

"He's getting old, and it is winter over there, but who believes in coincidences?" Moore looked down at his desk. "What do you suppose they'd do if they've turned him?"

"He'd die quietly. Depends on who turned him. If it was the KGB, they might want to make something out of it, especially since our friend Andropov took a lot of their prestige with him when he left. But I don't think so. Given who his sponsor is, it would raise too much of a ruckus. Same thing if the GRU turns him. No, they'd grill him for a few weeks, then quietly do away with him. A public trial would be too counterproductive."

Judge Moore frowned. They sounded like doctors discussing a terminally ill patient. He didn't even know what CARDINAL looked like. There was a photograph somewhere in the file, but he had never seen it. It was easier that way. As an appellate court judge he had never had to look a defendant in the eye; he'd just reviewed the law in a detached way. He tried to keep his stewardship of the CIA the same way. Moore knew that this might be perceived as cowardly, and was very different from what people expect of a DCI—but even spies got old, and old men developed consciences and doubts that rarely troubled the young. It was time to leave the "Company." Nearly three years, it was enough. He'd accomplished what he was supposed to do.

"Tell the station chief to lay off. No inquiries of any kind directed at CARDINAL. If he's really sick, we'll be hearing from him again. If not, we'll know that soon enough, too."

"Right."

Ritter had succeeded in confirming CARDINAL's reports. One agent had reported that the fleet was sailing with additional political officers, another that the surface force was commanded by an academic sailor and crony of Gorshkov, who had flown the Severomorsk and boarded the *Kirov* minutes before the fleet had sailed. The naval architect who was believed to have designed the *Red October* was supposed to have gone with him. A British agent had reported that detonators for the various weapons carried by the surface ships had been hastily taken aboard from their usual storage depots ashore. Finally, there was an unconfirmed report that Admiral Korov, commander of the Northern Fleet, was not at his command post; his whereabouts were unknown. Together the information was enough to confirm the WILLOW report, and more was still coming in.

The U.S. Naval Academy

"Skip?"

"Oh, howdy, Admiral. Will you join me?" Tyler waved to a vacant chair across the table.

"I got a message from the Pentagon for you." The superintendent of the Naval Academy, a former submarine officer, sat down. "You have an appointment tonight at 1930 hours. That's all they said."

"Great!" Tyler was just finishing his lunch. He'd been working on the simulation program nearly around the clock since Monday. The appointment meant that he would have access to the air force's Cray-2 tonight. His program was just about ready.

"What's this all about anyway?"

"Sorry, sir, I can't say. You know how it is."

The White House

The Soviet ambassador was back at four in the afternoon. To avoid press notice he had been taken into the Treasury building across the street from the White House and brought through a connecting tunnel which few knew existed. The president hoped that he had found this unsettling. Pelt hustled in to be there when Arbatov arrived.

"Mr. President," Arbatov reported, standing at attention. The president had not known that he had any military experience. "I am instructed to convey to you the regrets of my government that there has not been time to inform you of this. One of our nuclear submarines is missing and presumed lost. We are conducting an emergency rescue operation."

The president nodded soberly, motioning the ambassador to a chair. Pelt sat next to him.

"This is somewhat embarrassing, Mr. President. You see, in our navy as in yours, duty on a nuclear submarine is a posting of the greatest importance, and consequently those selected for it are among our best educated and trusted men. In this particular case several members of the crew—the officers, that is—are sons of high Party officials. One is even the son of a Central Committee member—I cannot say which, of course. The Soviet Navy's great effort to find her sons is understandable, though I admit a bit undisciplined." Arbatov feigned embarrassment beautifully, speaking as though he were confiding a great family secret. "Therefore, this has developed into what your people call an 'all hands' operation. As you undoubtedly know, it was undertaken virtually overnight."

"I see," the president said sympathetically. "That makes me feel a little better, Alex. Jeff, I think it's late enough in the day. How about you fix us all a drink. Bourbon, Alex?"

"Yes, thank you, sir."

Pelt walked over to a rosewood cabinet against the wall. The ornate antique contained a small bar, complete with an ice bucket which was stocked every afternoon. The president often liked to have a drink or two before dinner, something else that reminded Arbatov of his countrymen. Dr. Pelt had had ample experience playing presidential bartender. In a few minutes he came back with three glasses in his hands.

"To tell you the truth, we rather suspected this was a rescue operation," Pelt said.

"I don't know how we get our young men to do this sort of work." The president sipped at his drink. Arbatov worked hard on his. He had said frequently at local cocktail parties that he preferred American bourbon to his native vodka. Maybe it was true. "We've lost a pair of nuclear boats, I believe. How many does this make for you, three, four?"

"I don't know, Mr. President. I expect your information on this is better than my own." The president noted that he had just told the truth for the first time today. "Certainly I can agree with you that such duty is both dangerous and demanding."

"How many men aboard, Alex?" the president asked.

"I have no idea. A hundred more or less, I suppose. I've never been aboard a naval vessel."

"Mostly kids, probably, just like our crews. It is indeed a sad commentary on both our countries that our mutual suspicions must condemn so many of our best young men to such hazards, when we know that some won't be coming back. But—how can it be otherwise?" The president paused, turning to look out the windows. The snow was melting on the South Lawn. It was time for his next line.

"Perhaps we can help," the president offered speculatively. "Yes, perhaps we can use this tragedy as an opportunity to reduce those suspicions by some small amount. Perhaps we can make something good come from this to demonstrate that our relations really have improved."

Pelt turned away, fumbling for his pipe. In their many years of friendship he could never understand how the president got away with so much. Pelt had met him at Washington University, when he was majoring in political science, the president in prelaw. Back then the chief executive had been president of the dramatics society. Certainly amateur theatrics had helped his legal career. It was said that at least one Mafia don had been sent up the river by sheer rhetoric. The president referred to it as his sincere act.

"Mr. Ambassador, I offer you the assistance and the resources of the United States in the search for your missing countrymen."

"That is most kind of you, Mr. President, but—"

The president held his hand up. "No buts, Alex. If we cannot cooperate in something like this, how can we hope to cooperate in more serious matters? If memory serves, last year when one of our navy patrol aircraft crashed off the Aleutians, one of your fishing vessels"—it had been an intelligence trawler—"picked up the crew, saved their lives. Alex, we owe you a debt for that, a debt of honor, and the United States will not be said to be ungrateful." He paused for effect. "They're probably all dead, you know. I don't suppose there's more chance of surviving a sub accident than of surviving a plane crash. But at least the crew's families will know. Jeff, don't we have some specialized submarine rescue equipment?"

"With all the money we give the navy? We damned well ought to. I'll call Foster about it."

"Good," the president said. "Alex, it is too much to expect that your mutual suspicions will be allayed by something so small as this. Your history and ours conspire against us. But let's make a small beginning with this. If we can shake hands in space or over a conference table in Vienna, maybe we can do it here also. I will give the necessary instructions to my commanders as soon as we're finished here."

"Thank you, Mr. President." Arbatov concealed his uneasiness.

"And please convey my respects to Chairman Narmonov and my sympathy for the families of your missing men. I appreciate his effort, and yours, in getting this information to us."

"Yes. Mr. President." Arbatov rose. He left after shaking hands. What were the Americans really up to? He'd warned Moscow: call it a rescue mission and they'd demand to help. It was their stupid Christmas season, and Americans were addicted to happy endings. It was madness not to call it something else—to hell with the protocol.

At the same time he was forced to admire the American president. A strange man, very open, yet full of guile. A friendly man most of the time, yet always ready to seize the advantage. He remembered stories his grandmother had told, about how the gypsies switched babies. The American president was very Russian.

"Well," the president said after the doors closed, "now we can keep a nice close eye on them, and they can't complain. They're lying and we know it—but they don't know we know.

And we're lying, and they certainly suspect it, but not why we're lying. Gawd! and I told him this morning that not knowing was dangerous! Jeff, I've been thinking about this. I do not like the fact that so much of their navy is operating off our coast. Ryan was right, the Atlantic is our ocean. I want the air force and the navy to cover them like a goddamned blanket! That's our ocean, and I damned well want them to know it." The president finished off his drink. "On the question of the sub, I want our people to have a good look at it, and whoever of the crew wants to defect, we take care of. Quietly, of course."

"Of course. As a practical matter, having the officers is as great a coup as having the submarine."

"But the navy still want to keep it."

"I just don't see how we can do that, not without eliminating the crewmen, and we can't do that."

"Agreed." The president buzzed his secretary. "Get me General Hilton."

The Pentagon

The air force's computer center was in a subbasement of the Pentagon. The room temperature was well below seventy degrees. It was enough to make Tyler's leg ache where it met the metal-plastic prosthesis. He was used to that.

Tyler was sitting at a control console. He had just finished a trial run of his program, named MORAY after the vicious eel that inhabited oceanic reefs. Skip Tyler was proud of his programming ability. He'd taken the old dinosaur program from the files of the Taylor Lab, adapted it to the common Defense Department computer language, ADA—named for Lady Ada Lovelace, daughter of Lord Byron—and then tightened it up. For most people this would have been a month's work. He'd done it in four days, working almost around the clock not only because the money was an attractive incentive but also because the project was a professional challenge. He ended the job quietly satisfied that he could still meet an impossible deadline with time to spare. It was eight in the evening. MORAY had just run through a one-variable-value test and not crashed. He was ready.

He'd never seen the Cray-2 before, except in photographs, and he was pleased to have a chance to use it. The -2 was five units of raw electrical power, each one roughly pentagonal in shape, about six feet high and four across. The largest unit was the main-frame processor bank; the other four were memory banks, arrayed around it in a cruciform configuration. Tyler typed in the command to load his variable sets. For each of the *Red October*'s main dimensions—length, beam, height—he input ten discrete numerical values. Then came six subtly different values for her hull form block and prismatic coefficients. There were five sets of tunnel dimensions. This aggregated to over thirty thousand possible permutations. Next he keyed in eighteen power variables to cover the range of possible engine systems. The Cray-2 absorbed this information and placed each number in its proper slot. It was ready to run.

"Okay," he announced to the system operator, an air force master sergeant.

"Roge." The sergeant typed "XQT" into his terminal. The Cray-2 went to work.

Tyler walked over to the sergeant's console.

"That's a right lengthy program you've input, sir." The sergeant laid a ten-dollar bill on the top of the console. "Betcha my baby can run it in ten minutes."

"Not a chance." Tyler laid his own bill next to the sergeant's. "Fifteen minutes, easy."

"Split the difference?"

"Alright. Where's the head around here?"

"Out the door, sir, turn right, go down the hall and it's on the left."

Tyler moved towards the door. It annoyed him that he could not walk gracefully, but after four years the inconvenience was a minor one. He was alive—that's what counted. The accident had occurred on a cold, clear night in Groton, Connecticut, only a block from the shipyard's main gate. On Friday at three in the morning he was driving home after a twenty-hour day getting his new command ready for sea. The civilian yard worker had had a long day also, stopping off at a favorite watering hole for a few too many, as the police established afterwards. He got into his car, started it, and ran a red light, ramming Tyler's Pontiac broadside at fifty miles per hour. For him the accident was fatal. Skip was luckier. It was at an intersection, and he had the green light; when he saw the front end of the Ford not a foot from his left-side door, it was far too late. He did not remember going through a pawnshop window, and the next week, when he hovered near death at the Yale–New Haven hospital, was a complete blank. His most vivid memory was of waking up, eight days later he was to learn, to see his wife, Jean, holding his hand. His marriage up to that point had been a troubled one, not an uncommon problem for nuclear submarine officers. His first sight of her was not a complimentary one—her eyes were bloodshot, her hair was tousled—but she had never looked quite so good. He had never appreciated just how important she was. A lot more important than half a leg.

"Skip? Skip Tyler!"

The former submariner turned awkwardly to see a naval officer running towards him.

"Johnnie Coleman! How the hell are you!"

It was Captain Coleman now, Tyler noted. They had served together twice, a year on the *Tecumseh,* another on the *Shark.* Coleman, a weapons expert, had commanded a pair of nuclear subs.

"How's the family, Skip?"

"Jean's fine. Five kids now, and another on the way."

"Damn!" they shook hands with enthusiasm. "You always were a randy bugger. I hear you're teaching at Annapolis."

"Yeah, and a little engineering stuff on the side."

"What are you doing here?"

"I'm running a program on the air force computer. Checking a new ship configuration for Sea Systems Command." It was an accurate enough cover story. "What do they have you doing?"

"OP-02's office. I'm chief of staff for Admiral Dodge."

"Indeed?" Tyler was impressed. Vice Admiral Sam Dodge was the current OP-02. The office of the deputy chief of naval operations for submarine warfare had administrative control of all aspects of submarine operations. "Keeping you busy?"

"You know it! The crap's really hit the fan."

"What do you mean?" Tyler hadn't seen the news or read a paper since Monday.

"You kidding?"

"I've been working on this computer program twenty hours a day since Monday, and I don't get ops dispatches anymore." Tyler frowned. He had heard something the other day at the Academy but not paid any attention to it. He was the sort who could focus his whole mind on a single problem.

Coleman looked up and down the corridor. It was late on a Friday evening, and they had it entirely to themselves. "Guess I can tell you. Our Russian friends have some sort of major exercise laid on. Their whole Northern Fleet's at sea, or damned near. They have subs all over the place."

"Doing what?"

"We're not sure. Looks like they might have a major search and rescue operation. The question is, after what? They have four *Alfa*s doing a max speed run for our coast right now, with a gaggle of *Victor*s and *Charlie*s charging in behind them. At first we were worried that they wanted to block the trade routes, but they blitzed right past those. They're definitely heading for our coast, and whatever they're up to, we're getting tons of information."

"What do they have moving?" Tyler asked.

"Fifty-eight nuclear subs, and thirty or so surface ships."

"Gawd! CINCLANT must be going ape!"

"You know it, Skip. The fleet's at sea, all of it. Every nuke we have is scrambling for a redeployment. Every P-3 Lockheed ever made is either over the Atlantic or heading that way." Coleman paused. "You're still cleared, right?"

"Sure, for the work I do for the Crystal City gang. I had a piece of the evaluation of the new *Kirov*."

"I thought that sounded like your work. You always were a pretty good engineer. You know, the old man still talks about that job you did for him on the old *Tecumseh*. Maybe I can get you in to see what's happening. Yeah, I'll ask him."

Tyler's first cruise after graduating from nuc school in Idaho had been with Dodge. He'd done a tricky repair job on some ancillary reactor equipment two weeks earlier than estimated with a little creative effort and some back-channel procurement of spare parts. This had earned him and Dodge a flowery letter of commendation.

"I bet the old man would love to see you. When will you be finished down here?"

"Maybe half an hour."

"You know where to find me?"

"Have they moved OP-02?"

"Same place. Call me when you're finished. My extension is 78730. Okay? I gotta get back."

"Right." Tyler watched his old friend disappear down the

corridor, then proceeded on his way to the men's room, wondering what the Russians were up to. Whatever it was, it was enough to keep a three-star admiral and his four-striped captain working on a Friday night in Christmas season.

"Eleven minutes, 53.18 seconds, sir," the sergeant reported, pocketing both bills.

The computer printout was over two hundred pages of data. The cover sheet plotted a rough-looking bell curve of speed solutions, and below it was the noise prediction curve. The case-by-case solutions were printed individually on the remaining sheets. The curves were predictably messy. The speed curve showed the majority of solutions in the ten- to twelve-knot range, the total range going from seven to eighteen knots. The noise curve was surprisingly low.

"Sergeant, that's one hell of a machine you have here."

"Believe it, sir. And reliable. We haven't had an electronic fault all month."

"Can I use a phone?"

"Sure, take your pick, sir."

"Okay, Sarge." Tyler picked up the nearest phone. "Oh, and dump the program."

"Okay." He typed in some instructions. "MORAY is . . . gone. Hope you kept a copy, sir."

Tyler nodded and dialed the phone.

"OP-02A, Captain Coleman."

"Johnnie, this is Skip."

"Great! Hey, the old man wants to see you. Come right up."

Tyler placed the printout in his briefcase and locked it. He thanked the sergeant one more time before hobbling out the door, giving the Cray-2 one last look. He'd have to get in here again.

He could not find an operating elevator and had to struggle up a gently sloped ramp. Five minutes later he found a marine guarding the corridor.

"You Commander Tyler, sir?" the guard asked. "Can I see some ID, please?"

Tyler showed the corporal his Pentagon pass, wondering how many one-legged former submarine officers there might be.

"Thank you, Commander. Please go down the corridor. You know the room, sir?"

"Sure. Thanks, Corporal."

Vice Admiral Dodge was sitting on the corner of a desk reading over some message flimsies. Dodge was a small, combative man who'd made his mark commanding three separate boats, then pushing the *Los Angeles*–class attack submarines through their lengthy development program. Now he was "Grand Dolphin," the senior admiral who fought all the battles with Congress.

"Skip Tyler! You're looking good, laddy." Dodge gave Tyler's leg a furtive glance as he came over to take his hand. "I hear you're doing a great job at the Academy."

"It's all right, sir. They even let me scout the occasional ballgame."

"Hmph, shame they didn't let you scout Army."

Tyler hung his head theatrically. "I did scout Army, sir. They were just too tough this year. You heard about their middle linebacker, didn't you?"

"No, what about him?" Dodge asked.

"He picked armor as his duty assignment, and they gave him an early trip to Fort Knox—not to learn about tanks. To *be* a tank."

"Ha!" Dodge laughed. "Johnnie says you have a bunch of new kids."

"Number six is due the end of February," Tyler said proudly.

"Six? You're not a Catholic or a Mormon, are you? What's with all this bird hatching?"

Tyler gave his former boss a wry look. He'd never understood that prejudice in the nuclear navy. It came from Rickover, who had invented the disparaging term *bird hatching* for fathering more than one child. What the hell was wrong with having kids?

"Admiral, since I'm not a nuc anymore, I have to do *something* on nights and weekends." Tyler arched his eyebrows lecherously. "I hear the Russkies are playing games."

Dodge was instantly serious. "They sure are. Fifty-eight attack boats—every nuclear boat in the Northern Fleet—heading this way with a big surface group, and most of their service forces tagging along."

"Doing what?"

"Maybe you can tell me. Come on back to my inner sanctum." Dodge led Tyler into a room where he saw another new gadget, a projection screen that displayed the North Atlantic from the Tropic of Cancer to the polar ice pack. Hundreds of ships were represented. The merchantmen were white, with flags to identify their nationality; the Soviet ships were red, and their shapes depicted their ship type; the American and allied ships were blue. The ocean was getting crowded.

"Christ."

"You got that one right, lad," Tyler nodded grimly. "How are you cleared?"

"Top secret and some special things, sir. I see everything we have on their hardware, and I do a lot of work with Sea Systems on the side."

"Johnnie said you did the evaluation of the new *Kirov* they just sent out to the Pacific—not bad, by the way."

"These two *Alfa*s heading for Norfolk?"

"Looks like it. And they're burning a lot of neutrons doing it." Dodge pointed. "That one's heading to Long Island Sound as though to block the entrance to New London and that one's heading to Boston, I think. These *Victor*s are not far behind. They already have most of the British ports staked out. By Monday they'll have two or more subs off every major port we have."

"I don't like the looks of this, sir."

"Neither do I. As you see, we're nearly a hundred percent at sea ourselves. The interesting thing, though—what they're doing just doesn't figure. I—" Captain Coleman came in.

"I see you let the prodigal son in, sir," Coleman said.

"Be nice to him, Johnnie. I seem to remember when he was a right fair sub driver. Anyway, at first it looked like they were going to block the SLOCs, but they went right past. What with these *Alfa*s, they might be trying to blockade our coast."

"What about out west?"

"Nothing. Nothing at all, just routine activity."

"That doesn't make any sense," Tyler objected. "You don't ignore half the fleet. Of course, if you're going to war you don't announce it by kicking every boat to max power either."

"The Russians are a funny bunch, Skip," Coleman pointed out.

"Admiral, if we start shooting at them—"

"We hurt 'em," Dodge said. "With all the noise they're

making we have good locations on near all of 'em. They have to know that, too. That's the one thing that makes me believe they're not up to anything really bad. They're smart enough not to be that obvious—unless that's what they want us to think."

"Have they said anything?" Tyler asked.

"Their ambassador says they've lost a boat, and since it has a bunch of big shots' kids aboard, they laid on an all-hands rescue mission. For what that's worth."

Tyler set his briefcase down and walked closer to the screen. "I can see the pattern for a search and rescue, but why blockade our ports?" He paused, thinking rapidly as his eyes scanned the top of the display. "Sir, I don't see any boomers up here."

"They're in port—all of 'em, on both oceans. The last *Delta* tied up a few hours ago. That's funny, too," Dodge said, looking at the screen again.

"All of them, sir?" Tyler asked as offhandedly as he could. Something had just occurred to him. The display screen showed the *Bremerton* in the Barents Sea but not her supposed quarry. He waited a few seconds for an answer. Getting none, he turned to see the two officers observing him closely.

"Why do you ask, son?" Dodge said quietly. In Sam Dodge, gentleness could be a real warning flag.

Tyler thought this one over for a few seconds. He'd given Ryan his word. Could he phrase his answer without compromising it and still find out what he wanted? Yes, he decided. There was an investigative side to Skip Tyler's character, and once he was onto something, his psyche compelled him to run it down.

"Admiral, do they have a missile sub at sea, a brand new one?"

Dodge stood very straight. Even so he still had to look up at the younger man. When he spoke, his voice was glacial. "Exactly where did you get that information, Commander?"

Tyler shook his head. "Admiral, I'm sorry, but I can't say. It's compartmented, sir. I think this is something you ought to know, and I'll try to get it to you."

Dodge backed off to try a different tack. "You used to work for me, Skip." The admiral was unhappy. He'd bent a rule to show something to his former subordinate because he knew him well and was sorry that he had not received the command he had worked so hard for. Tyler was technically a civilian, even though his suits were still navy blue. What made it really bad was that he knew something himself. Dodge had given him some information, and Tyler wasn't giving any back.

"Sir, I gave my word," Skip apologized. "I will try to get this to you. That's a promise, sir. May I use a phone?"

"Outer office," Dodge said flatly. There were four telephones within sight.

Tyler went out and sat at a secretary's desk. He took his notebook from a coat pocket and dialed the number on the card Ryan had left him.

"Acres," a female voice answered.

"Could I speak to Dr. Ryan, please?"

"Dr. Ryan is not here at the moment."

"Then . . . give me Admiral Greer, please."

"One moment, please."

"James Greer?" Dodge was behind him. "Is that who you're working for?"

"This is Greer. Your name Skip Tyler?"

"Yes, sir."

"You have that information for me?"

"Yes, sir, I do."

"Where are you?"

"In the Pentagon, sir."

"Okay, I want you to drive right up here. You know how to find the place? The guards at the main gate will be waiting for you. Get moving, son." Greer hung up.

"You're working for the CIA?" Dodge asked.

"Sir—I can't say. If you will excuse me, sir, I have some information to deliver."

"Mine?" the admiral demanded.

"No, sir. I already had it when I came in here. That's the truth, Admiral. And I will try to get this back to you."

"Call me," Dodge ordered. "We'll be here all night."

CIA Headquarters

The drive up the George Washington Parkway was easier than he expected. The decrepit old highway was crowded with shoppers but moved along at a steady crawl. He got off at the right exit and presently found himself at the guard post for the main highway entrance to the CIA. The barrier was down.

"Your name Tyler, Oliver W.?" the guard asked. "ID please." Tyler handed him his Pentagon pass.

"Okay, Commander. Pull your car right to the main entrance. Somebody will be there to meet you."

It was another two minutes to the main entrance through mostly empty parking lots glazed with ice from yesterday's melted snow. The armed guard who was waiting for him tried to help him out of the car. Tyler didn't like to be helped. He shrugged him off. Another man was waiting for him under the canopied main entrance. They were waved right through to the elevator.

He found Admiral Greer sitting in front of his office fireplace, seemingly half asleep. Skip didn't know that the DDI had only returned from England a few hours earlier. The admiral came to and ordered his plain-clothes security officer to withdraw. "You must be Skip Tyler. Come on over and sit down."

"That's quite a fire you have going there, sir."

"I shouldn't bother. Looking at a fire makes me go to sleep. Of course, I could use a little sleep right now. So, what do you have for me?"

"May I ask where Jack is?"

"You may ask. He's away."

"Oh." Tyler unlocked his briefcase and removed the printout. "Sir, I ran the performance model for this Russian sub. May I ask her name?"

Greer chuckled. "Okay, you've earned that much. Her name is *Red October*. You'll have to excuse me, son. I've had a busy couple of days, and being tired makes me forget my manners. Jack says you're pretty sharp. So does your personnel file. Now, you tell me. What'll she do?"

"Well, Admiral, we have a wide choice of data here, and—"

"The short version, Commander. I don't play with computers. I have people who do that for me."

"From seven to eighteen knots, the best bet is ten to twelve. With that speed range, you can figure a radiated noise level about the same as that of a *Yankee* doing six knots, but you'd have to factor reactor plant noise into that also. Moreover, the character of the noise will be different from what we're used to. These multiple impeller models don't put out normal propulsion noises. They seem to generate an irregular harmonic rumble. Did Jack tell you about this? It results from a backpressure wave in the tunnels. This fights the water flow, and that makes the rumble. Evidently there's no way around it. Our guys spent two years trying to find one. What they got was a new principle of hydrodynamics. The water almost acts like air in a jet engine at idle or low speed, except that water doesn't compress like air does. So, our guys will be able to detect something, but it will be different. They're going to have to get used to a wholly new acoustical signature. Add to that the lower signal intensity, and you have a boat that will be harder to detect than anything they have at this time."

"So that's what all this says." Greer riffled through the pages.

"Yes, sir. You'll want to have your own people look through it. The model—the program, that is—could stand a little improvement. I didn't have much time. Jack said you wanted this in a hurry. May I ask a question, sir?"

"You can try." Greer leaned back, rubbing his eyes.

"Is, ah, *Red October* at sea? That's it, isn't it? They're trying to locate her right now?" Tyler asked innocently.

"Uh huh, something like that. We couldn't figure what these doors meant. Ryan said you might be able to, and I suppose he was right. You've earned your money, Commander. This data might just enable us to find her."

"Admiral, I think *Red October* is up to something, maybe even trying to defect to the United States."

Greer's head came around. "Whatever makes you think that?"

"The Russkies have a major fleet operation in progress. They have subs all over the Atlantic, and it looks like they're trying to blockade our coast. The story is a rescue job for a lost boat. Okay, but Jack shows up Monday with pictures of a new missile boat—and today I hear that all of their other missile boats have been recalled to port." Tyler smiled. "That's kind of an odd set of coincidences, sir."

Greer turned and stared at the fire. He had just joined the DIA when the army and air force had pulled off the daring raid on the Song Tay prison camp twenty miles west of Hanoi. The raid had been a failure because the North Vietnamese had

removed all of the captured pilots a few weeks before, something that aerial photographs could not determine. But everything else had gone perfectly. After penetrating hundreds of
miles into hostile territory, the raiding force appeared entirely
by surprise and caught many of the camp guards literally with
their pants down. The Green Berets did a letter-perfect job of
getting in and out. In the process they killed several hundred
enemy troops, themselves sustaining a single casualty, a broken
ankle. The most impressive part of the mission, however, was
its secrecy. Operation KINGPIN had been rehearsed for months,
and despite this its nature and objective had not been guessed
by friend or enemy—until the day of the raid itself. On that
day a young air force captain of intelligence went into his
general's office to ask if a deep-penetration raid into North
Vietnam had been laid on for the Song Tay prisoner-of-war
camp. His astonished commander proceeded to grill the captain
at length, only to learn that the bright young officer had seen
enough disjointed bits and pieces to construct a clear picture
of what was about to happen. Events like this gave security
officers peptic ulcers.

"*Red October*'s going to defect, isn't she?" Tyler persisted.

If the admiral had had more sleep he might have bluffed it
out. As it was, his response was a mistake. "Did Ryan tell you
this?"

"Sir, I haven't spoken with Jack since Monday. That's the
truth, sir."

"Then where did you get this other information?" Greer
snapped.

"Admiral, I used to wear the blue suit. Most of my friends
still do. I hear things," Tyler evaded. "The whole picture dropped
into place an hour ago. The Russkies have never recalled all
of their boomers at once. I know, I used to hunt them."

Greer sighed. "Jack thinks the same as you. He's out with
the fleet right now. Commander, if you tell that to anyone, I'll
have your other leg mounted overtop that fireplace. Do you
understand me?"

"Aye aye, sir. What are we going to do with her?" Tyler
smiled to himself, thinking that as a senior consultant to Sea
Systems Command, he'd sure as hell get a chance to look at
a for-real Russian submarine.

"Give her back. After we've had a chance to look her over,

of course. But there's a lot of things that could happen to prevent our ever seeing her."

It took Skip a moment to grasp what he'd just been told. "Give her back! Why, for Christ's sake?"

"Commander, just how likely do you think this scenario is? Do you think the whole crew of a submarine has decided to come over to us all at once?" Greer shook his head. "Smart money is that it's only the officers, maybe not all of them, and that they're trying to get over here without the crew's knowing what they're up to."

"Oh." Tyler considered that. "I suppose that does make sense—but why give her back? This isn't Japan. If somebody landed a MiG-25 here we wouldn't give it back."

"This is not like holding onto a stray fighter plane. The boat is worth a billion dollars, more if you throw in the missiles and warheads. And legally, the president says, it's their property. So if they find out we have her, they'll ask for her back, and we'll have to give her back. Okay, how will they know we have her? Those crew members who don't want to defect will ask to go home. Whoever asks, we send."

"You know, sir, that whoever does want to go back will be in a whole shitload of trouble—excuse me, sir."

"A shitload and a half." Tyler hadn't known that Greer was a mustang and could swear like a real sailor. "Some will want to stay, but most won't. They have families. Next you'll ask me if we might arrange for the crew to disappear."

"The thought has occurred to me," Tyler said.

"It's occurred to us, too. But we won't. Murder a hundred men? Even if we wanted to, there's no way we could conceal it in this day and age. Hell, I doubt even the Soviets could. Besides that, this simply is not the sort of thing you do in peacetime. That's one difference between us and them. You can take those reasons in any order you want."

"So, except for the crew, we'd keep her . . ."

"Yes, if we could hide her. And if a pig had wings, it could fly."

"Lots of places to hide her, Admiral. I can think of a few right here on the Chesapeake, and if we could get her round to Horn, there's a million little atolls we could use, and they all belong to us."

"But the crew will know, and when we send them home,

they'll tell their bosses," Greer explained patiently. "And Moscow will ask for her back. Oh, sure, we'll have a week or so to conduct, uh, safety and quarantine inspections, to make sure they weren't trying to smuggle cocaine into the country." The admiral laughed. "A British admiral suggested we invoke the old slave-trading treaty. Somebody did that back in World War II, to put the grab on a German blockade runner right before we got into it. So, we'll get a ton of intelligence regardless."

"Better to keep her, and run her, and take her apart..." Tyler said quietly, staring into the orange-white flames on the oak logs. How do we keep her? he wondered. An idea began to rattle around in his head. "Admiral, what if we could get the crew off without them knowing that we have the submarine?"

"Your full name is Oliver Wendell Tyler? Well, son, if you were named after Harry Houdini instead of a justice of the Supreme Court, I—" Greer looked into the engineer's face. "What do you have in mind?"

While Tyler explained Greer listened intently.

"To do this, sir, we'll have to get the navy in on it right quick. Specifically, we'll need the cooperation of Admiral Dodge, and if my speed figures for this boat are anything like accurate, we'll have to move smartly."

Greer rose and walked around the couch a few times to get his circulation going. "Interesting. The timing would be almost impossible, though."

"I didn't say it would be easy, sir, just that we *could* do it."

"Call home, Tyler. Tell your wife you won't be making it home. If I don't get any sleep tonight, neither do you. There's coffee behind my desk. First I have to call the judge, then we'll talk to Sam Dodge."

The USS Pogy

"Pogy, this is Black Gull 4. We're getting low on fuel. Have to return to the barn," the Orion's tactical coordinator reported, stretching after ten hours at his control console. "Anything you want us to get you? Over."

"Yeah, have a couple cases of beer sent out," Commander Wood replied. It was the current joke between P-3C and submarine crews. "Thanks for the data. We'll take it from here. Out."

Overhead, the Lockheed Orion increased power and turned southwest. The crewmen aboard would each hoist an extra beer or two at dinner, saying it was for their friends on the submarine.

"Mr. Dyson, take her two hundred feet. One-third speed."

The officer of the deck gave the proper orders as Commander Wood moved over to the plot.

The USS *Pogy* was three hundred miles northeast of Norfolk, awaiting the arrival of two Soviet *Alfa*-class submarines which several relays of antisubmarine patrol aircraft had tracked all the way from Iceland. The *Pogy* was named for a distinguished World War II fleet submarine, named in turn for an undistinguished game fish. She had been at sea for eighteen hours, and was fresh from an extended overhaul at the Newport News shipyard. Nearly everything aboard was either straight from manufacturers' crates or had been completely worked over by the skilled shipfitters on the James River. This was not to say that everything worked properly. Many items had failed in one way or another on the post-overhaul shakedown the previous week, a fact less unusual than lamentable, Commander Wood thought. The *Pogy*'s crew was new, too. Wood was on his first deployment as a commanding officer after a year of desk duty in Washington, and too many of the enlisted men were green, just out of sub school at New London, still getting accustomed to their first cruise on a submarine. It takes time for men used to blue skies and fresh air to learn the regime inside a thirty-two-foot-diameter steel pipe. Even the experienced men were making adjustments to their new boat and officers.

The *Pogy* had met her top speed of thirty-three knots on post-overhaul trials. This was fast for a ship but slower than the speed of the *Alfa*s she was listening to. Like all American submarines, her long suit was stealth. The *Alfa*s had no way of knowing she was there and that they would be easy targets for her weapons, the more so since the patrolling Orion had fed the *Pogy* exact range information, something that ordinarily takes time to deduce from a passive sonar plot.

Lieutenant Commander Tom Reynolds, the executive officer

and fire control coordinator, stood casually over the tactical plot. "Thirty-six miles to the near one, and forty on the far one." On the display they were labeled Pogy-Bait 1 and 2. Everyone found the use of this service epithet amusing.

"Speed forty-two?" Wood asked.

"Yes, Captain." Reynolds had handled the radio exchange until Black Gull 4 had announced its intention to return to base. "They're driving those boats for all they're worth. Right for us. We have hard solutions on both . . . zap! What do you suppose they're up to?"

"The word from CINCLANT is that their ambassador says they're on a SAR mission for a lost boat." His voice indicated what he thought of that.

"Search and rescue, eh?" Reynolds shrugged. "Well, maybe they think they lost a boat off Point Comfort, 'cause if they don't slow down real fast, that's where they'll end up. I've never heard of *Alfa*s operating this close to our coast. Have you, sir?"

"Nope." Wood frowned. The thing about the *Alfa*s was that they were fast and noisy. Soviet tactical doctrine seemed to call for them mainly in defensive roles: as "interceptor submarines" they could protect their own missile subs, and with their high speed they could engage American attack submarines, then evade counterattack. Wood didn't think the doctrine was sound, but that was all right with him.

"Maybe they want to blockade Norfolk," Reynolds suggested.

"You might have a point there," Wood said. "Well, in any case, we'll just sit tight and let them burn right past us. They'll have to slow as they cross the continental shelf line, and we'll tag along behind them, nice and quiet."

"Aye," Reynolds said.

If they had to shoot, both men reflected, they'd find out just how tough the *Alfa* really was. There had been much talk about the strength of the titanium used for her hull, whether it really would withstand the force of several hundred pounds of high explosive in direct contact. A new shaped-charge warhead for the Mark 48 torpedo had been developed for just this purpose and for handling the equally tough *Typhoon* hull. Both officers set this thought aside. Their assigned mission was to track and shadow.

The E. S. Politovskiy

Pogy-Bait 2 was known to the Soviet Navy as the *E. S. Politovskiy*. This *Alfa*-class attack sub was named for the chief engineering officer of the Russian fleet who had sailed all the way around the world to meet his appointment with destiny in the Tsushima Straits. Evgeni Sigismondavich Politovskiy had served the czar's navy with skill and a devotion to duty equal to that of any officer in history, but in his diary, which was discovered years later in Leningrad, the brilliant officer had decried in the most violent terms the corruption and excesses of the czarist regime, giving a grim counterpoint to the selfless patriotism he had shown as he sailed knowingly to his death. This made him a genuine hero for Soviet seamen to emulate, and the State had named its greatest engineering achievement in his memory. Unfortunately the *Politovskiy* had enjoyed no better luck than he had enjoyed in the face of Togo's guns.

The *Politovskiy*'s acoustical signature was labeled *Alfa 3* by the Americans. This was incorrect; she had been the first of the *Alfas*. The small, spindle-shaped attack submarine had reached forty-three knots three hours into her initial builder's trials. Those trials had been cut short only a minute later by an incredible mishap: a fifty-ton right whale had somehow blundered in her path, and the *Politovskiy* had rammed the unfortunate creature broadside. The impact had smashed ten square meters of bow plating, annihilated the sonar dome, knocked a torpedo tube askew, and nearly flooded the torpedo room. This did not count shock damage to nearly every interior system from electronic equipment to the galley stove, and it was said that if anyone but the famous Vilnius headmaster had been in command, the submarine would surely have been lost. A two-meter segment of the whale's rib was now a permanent fixture at the officer's club in Severomorsk, dramatic testament to the strength of Soviet submarines; in fact the damage had taken over a year to repair, and by the time the *Politovskiy* sailed again there were already two other *Alfas* in service. Two days after sailing on her next shakedown, she suffered another major casualty, the total failure of her high-pressure turbine. This had taken six months to replace. There had been three more minor incidents since, and the submarine was forever marked as a bad luck ship.

Chief Engineer Vladimir Petchukocov was a loyal Party member and a committed atheist, but he was also a sailor and therefore profoundly superstitious. In the old days, his ship would have been blessed on launching and thereafter every time she sailed. It would have been an impressive ceremony, with a bearded priest, clouds of incense, and evocative hymns. He had sailed without any of that and found himself wishing otherwise. He needed some luck. Petchukocov was having trouble with his reactor.

The *Alfa* reactor plant was small. It had to fit into a relatively small hull. It was also powerful for its size, and this one had been running at one hundred percent rated power for just over four days. They were racing for the American coast at 42.3 knots, as fast as the eight-year-old plant would permit. The *Politovskiy* was due for a comprehensive overhaul: new sonar, new computers, and a redesigned reactor control suite were all planned for the coming months. Petchukocov thought it irresponsible—reckless—to push his submarine so hard, even if everything were functioning properly. No *Alfa* plant on a submarine had ever been pushed this hard, not even a new one. And on this one, things were beginning to come apart.

The primary high-pressure reactor coolant pump was beginning to vibrate ominously. This was particularly worrying to the engineer. There was a backup, but the secondary pump had a lower rated power, and using it meant losing eight knots of speed. The *Alfa* plant achieved its high power not with a sodium-cooled system—as the Americans thought—but by running at a far higher pressure than any reactor system afloat and using a revolutionary heat exchange system that boosted the plant's overall thermal efficiency to forty-one percent, well in excess of that for any other submarine. But the price of this was a reactor that at full power was red-lined on every monitor gauge—and in this case the red lines were not mere symbolism. They signified genuine danger.

This fact, added to the vibrating pump, had Petchukocov seriously concerned; an hour earlier he had pleaded with the captain to reduce power for a few hours so that his skilled crew of engineers could make repairs. It was probably only a bad bearing, after all, and they had spares. The pump had been designed so that it would be easy to fix. The captain had wavered, wanting to grant the request, but the political officer had intervened, pointing out that their orders were both urgent and explicit: they had to be on station as quickly as possible; to do otherwise would be "politically unsound." And that was that.

Petchukocov bitterly remembered the look in his captain's eyes. What was the purpose of a commanding officer if his every order had to be approved by a political flunky? Petchukocov had been a faithful Communist since joining the Octobrists as a boy—but damn it! what was the point of having specialists and engineers? Did the Party really think that physical laws could be overturned by the whim of some apparatchik with a heavy desk and a dacha in the Moscow suburbs? The engineer swore to himself.

He stood alone at the master control board. This was located in the engine room, aft of the compartment that held the reactor and the heat exchanger/steam generator, the latter placed right at the submarine's center of gravity. The reactor was pressurized to twenty kilograms per square centimeter, about twenty-eight hundred pounds per square inch. Only a fraction of this pressure came from the pump. The higher pressure caused a higher boiling point for the coolant. In this case, the water was heated to over 900° Celsius, a temperature sufficient to generate steam, which gathered at the top of the reactor vessel; the steam bubble applied pressure to the water beneath, preventing the generation of more steam. The steam and water regulated one another in a delicate balance. The water was dangerously radioactive as a result of the fission reaction taking place within the uranium fuel rods. The function of the control rods was to regulate the reaction. Again, the control was delicate. At most the rods could absorb just less than one percent of the neutron flux, but this was enough either to permit the reaction or to prevent it.

Petchukocov could recite all this data in his sleep. He could draw a wholly accurate schematic diagram of the entire engine plant from memory and could instantly grasp the significance of the slightest change in his instrument readings. He stood perfectly straight over the control board, his eyes tracing the myriad dials and gauges in a regular pattern, one hand poised over the SCRAM switch, the other over the emergency cooling controls.

He could hear the vibration. It had to be a bad bearing getting worse as it wore more and more unevenly. If the crankshaft bearings went bad, the pump would seize, and they'd have to stop. This would be an emergency, though not really a dangerous one. It would mean that repairing the pump—if they could repair it at all—would take days instead of hours, eating up valuable time and spare parts. That was bad enough. What was worse, and what Petchukocov did not know, was that the vibration was generating pressure waves in the coolant.

To make use of the newly developed heat exchanger, the *Alfa* plant had to move water rapidly through its many loops and baffles. This required a high-pressure pump which accounted for one hundred fifty pounds of the total system pressure—almost ten times what was considered safe in Western reactors. With the pump so powerful, the whole engine room complex, normally very noisy at high speed, was like a boiler factory, and the pump's vibration was disturbing the performance of the monitor instruments. It was making the needles on his gauges waver, Petchukocov noted. He was right, and wrong. The pressure gauges were really wavering because of the thirty-pound overpressure waves pulsing through the system. The chief engineer did not recognize this for what it was. He had been on duty too many hours.

Within the reactor vessel, these pressure waves were approaching the frequency at which a piece of equipment resonated. Roughly halfway down the interior surface of the vessel was a titanium fitting, part of the backup cooling system. In the event of a coolant loss, and *after* a successful SCRAM, valves inside and outside the vessel would open, cooling the reactor either with a mixture of water and barium or, as a last measure, with seawater which could be vented in and out of the vessel—at the cost of ruining the entire reactor. This had been done once, and though it had been costly, the action of a junior engineer had prevented the loss of a *Victor*-class attack sub by catastrophic meltdown.

Today the inside valve was closed, along with the corresponding through-hull fitting. The valves were made of titanium because they had to function reliably after prolonged exposure to high temperature, and also because titanium was very corrosion-resistant—high-temperature water was murderously corrosive. What had not been fully considered was that the metal was also exposed to intense nuclear radiation, and this particular titanium alloy was not completely stable under extended neutron bombardment. The metal had become brittle over the years. The minute waves of hydraulic pressure were beating against the clapper in the valve. As the pump's frequency of vibration changed it began to approach the frequency at which the clapper vibrated. This caused the clapper to snap harder and harder against its retaining ring. The metal at its edges began to crack.

A *michman* at the forward end of the compartment heard it first, a low buzz coming through the bulkhead. At first he thought it was feedback noise from the PA speaker, and he waited too long to check it. The clapper broke free and dropped out of the valve nozzle. It was not very large, only ten centimeters in diameter and five millimeters thick. This type of fitting is called a butterfly valve, and the clapper looked just like a butterfly, suspended and twirling in the water flow. If it had been made of stainless steel it would have been heavy enough to fall to the bottom of the vessel. But it was made of titanium, which was both stronger than steel and very much lighter. The coolant flow moved it up, towards the exhaust pipe.

The outward-moving water carried the clapper into the pipe, which had a fifteen-centimeter inside diameter. The pipe was made of stainless steel, two-meter sections welded together for easy replacement in the cramped quarters. The clapper was borne along rapidly towards the heat exchanger. Here the pipe took a forty-five-degree downward turn and the clapper jammed momentarily. This blocked half of the pipe's channel, and before the surge of pressure could dislodge the clapper too many things happened. The moving water had its own momentum. On being blocked, it generated a back-pressure wave within the pipe. Total pressure jumped momentarily to thirty-four hundred pounds. This caused the pipe to flex a few millimeters. The increased pressure, lateral displacement of a weld joint, and cumulative effect of years of high-temperature erosion of the steel damaged the joint. A hole the size of a pencil point

opened. The escaping water flashed instantly into steam, setting
off alarms in the reactor compartment and neighboring spaces.
It ate at the remainder of the weld, rapidly expanding the failure
until reactor coolant was erupting as though from a horizontal
fountain. One jet of steam demolished the adjacent reactor-
control wiring conduits.

What had just begun was a catastrophic loss-of-coolant accident.

The reactor was fully depressurized within three seconds.
Its many gallons of coolant exploded into steam, seeking release
into the surrounding compartment. A dozen alarms sounded at
once on the master control board, and in the blink of an eye
Vladimir Petchukocov faced his ultimate nightmare. The engineer's automatic trained reaction was to jam his finger on the
SCRAM switch, but the steam in the reactor vessel had disabled
the rod control system, and there wasn't time to solve the
problem. In an instant, Petchukocov knew that his ship was
doomed. Next he opened the emergency coolant controls, ad-
mitting seawater into the reactor vessel. This automatically set
off alarms throughout the hull.

In the control room forward, the captain grasped the nature
of the emergency at once. The *Politovskiy* was running at one
hundred fifty meters. He had to get her to the surface immediately, and he shouted orders to blow all ballast and make full
rise on the diving planes.

The reactor emergency was regulated by physical laws. With
no reactor coolant to absorb the heat of the uranium rods, the
nuclear reaction actually stopped—there was no water to at-
tenuate the neutron flux. This was no solution, however, since
the residual decay heat was sufficient to melt everything in the
compartment. The cold water admitted into the vessel drew off
the heat but also slowed down too many neutrons, keeping
them in the reactor core. This caused a runaway reaction that
generated even more heat, more than any amount of coolant
could control. What had started as a loss-of-coolant accident
became something worse: a cold-water accident. It was now
only a matter of minutes before the entire core melted, and the
Politovskiy had that long to get to the surface.

Petchukocov stayed at his post in the engine room, doing
what he could. His own life, he knew, was almost certainly
lost. He had to give his captain time to surface the boat. There

was a drill for this sort of emergency, and he barked orders to implement it. It only made things worse.

His duty electrician moved along the electrical control panels switching from main power to emergency, since residual steam power in the turboalternators would die in a few more seconds. In a moment the submarine's power completely depended on standby batteries.

In the control room power was lost to the electrically controlled trim tabs on the trailing edge of the diving planes, which automatically switched back to electrohydraulic control. This powered not just the small trim tabs but the diving planes as well. The control assemblies moved instantly to a fifteen-degree up-angle—and she was still moving at thirty-nine knots. With all her ballast tanks now blasted free of water by compressed air, the submarine was very light, and she rose like a climbing aircraft. In seconds the astonished control room crew felt their boat rise to an up-angle that was forty-five degrees and getting worse. A moment later they were too busy trying to stand to come to grips with the problem. Now the *Alfa* was climbing almost vertically at thirty miles per hour. Every man and unsecured item aboard fell sternward.

In the motor control room aft, a crewman crashed against the main electrical switchboard, short-circuiting it with his body, and all power aboard was lost. A cook who had been inventorying survival gear in the torpedo room forward struggled into the escape trunk as he fought his way into an exposure suit. Even with only a year's experience, he was quick to understand the meaning of the hooting alarms and unprecedented actions of his boat. He yanked the hatch shut and began to work the escape controls as he had been taught in submarine school.

The *Politovskiy* soared through the surface of the Atlantic like a broaching whale, coming three quarters of her length out of the water before crashing back.

The USS Pogy

"Conn, sonar."

"Conn, aye, Captain speaking."

"Skipper, you better hear this. Something just went crazy on Bait 2," *Pogy*'s chief reported. Wood was in the sonar room in seconds, putting on earphones plugged into a tape recorder which had a two-minute offset. Commander Wood heard a whooshing sound. The engine noises stopped. A few seconds later there was an explosion of compressed air, and a staccato of hull popping noises as a submarine changed depth rapidly.

"What's going on?" Wood asked quickly.

The E. S. Politovskiy

In the *Politovskiy*'s reactor, the runaway fission reaction had virtually annihilated both the incoming seawater and the uranium fuel rods. Their debris settled on the after wall of the reactor vessel. In a minute there was a meter-wide puddle of radioactive slag, enough to form its own critical mass. The reaction continued unabated, this time directly attacking the tough stainless steel of the vessel. Nothing man made could long withstand five thousand degrees of direct heat. In ten seconds the vessel wall failed. The uranium mass dropped free, against the aft bulkhead.

Petchukocov knew he was dead. He saw the paint on the forward bulkhead turn black, and his last impression was of a dark mass surrounded with the blue glow. The engineer's body vaporized an instant later, and the mass of slag dropped to the next bulkhead aft.

Forward, the submarine's nearly vertical angle in the water eased. The high-pressure air in the ballast tanks spilled out of the bottom floods and the tanks filled with water, dropping the angle of the boat and submerging her. In the forward part of the submarine men were screaming. The captain struggled to his feet, ignoring his broken leg, trying to get control, to get his men organized and out of the submarine before it was too late, but the luck of Evgeni Sigismondavich Politovskiy would plague his namesake one last time. Only one man escaped. The cook opened the escape trunk hatch and got out. Following what he had learned during the drill, he began to seal the hatch so that men behind him could use it, but a wave slapped him off the hull as the sub slid backwards.

In the engine room, the changing angle dropped the melted core to the deck. The hot mass attacked the steel deck first, burning through that, then the titanium of the hull. Five seconds later the engine room was vented to the sea. The *Politovskiy*'s largest compartment filled rapidly with water. This destroyed what little reserve buoyancy the ship had, and the acute down-angle returned. The *Alfa* began her last dive.

The stern dropped just as the captain began to get his control room crew to react to orders again. His head struck an instrument console. What slim hopes his crew had died with him. The *Politovskiy* was falling backwards, her propeller wind-milling the wrong way as she slid to the bottom of the sea.

The *Pogy*

"Skipper, I was on the *Chopper* back in sixty-nine," the *Pogy*'s chief said, referring to a horrifying accident on a diesel-powered submarine.

"That's what it sounds like," his captain said. He was now listening to direct sonar input. There was no mistaking it. The submarine was flooding. They had heard the ballast tanks refill; this could only mean interior compartments were filling with water. If they had been closer, they might have heard the screams of men in that doomed hull. Wood was just as happy he couldn't. The continuing rush of water was dreadful enough. Men were dying. Russians, his enemy, but men not unlike himself, and there was not a thing that could be done about it.

Bait 1, he saw, was proceeding, unmindful of what had happened to her trailing sister.

The E. S. *Politovskiy*

It took nine minutes for the *Politovskiy* to fall the two thousand feet to the ocean floor. She impacted savagely on the hard sand bottom at the edge of the continental shelf. It was a tribute to her builders that her interior bulkheads held. All the compartments from the reactor room aft were flooded and half the crew killed in them, but the forward compartments were dry. Even this was more curse than blessing. With the aft air storage banks unusable and only emergency battery power to run the complex environmental control systems, the forty men had only a limited supply of air. They were spared a rapid death from the crushing North Atlantic only to face a slower one from asphyxiation.

THE NINTH DAY

SATURDAY, 11 DECEMBER

The Pentagon

A female yeoman first class held the door open for Tyler. He walked in to find General Harris standing alone over the large chart table pondering the placement of tiny ship models.

"You must be Skip Tyler." Harris looked up.

"Yes, sir." Tyler was standing as rigidly at attention as his prosthetic leg allowed. Harris came over quickly to shake hands.

"Greer says you used to play ball."

"Yes, General, I played right tackle at Annapolis. Those were good years." Tyler smiled, flexing his fingers. Harris looked like an iron-pumper.

"Okay, if you used to play ball, you can call me Ed." Harris poked him in the chest. "Your number was seventy-eight, and you made All American, right?"

"Second string, sir. Nice to know somebody remembers."

"I was on temporary duty at the Academy for a few months back then, and I caught a couple games. I never forget a good offensive lineman. I made All Conference at Montana—long time ago. What happened to the leg?"

"Drunk driver clipped me. I was the lucky one. The drunk didn't make it."

"Serves the bastard right."

Tyler nodded agreement, but remembered that the drunken shipfitter had had his own wife and family, according to the police. "Where is everybody?"

"The chiefs are at their normal—well, normal for a weekday, not a Saturday—intelligence briefing. They ought to be down in a few minutes. So, you're teaching engineering at Annapolis now, eh?"

"Yes, sir. I got a doctorate in that along the way."

"Name's Ed, Skip. And this morning you're going to tell us how we can hold onto that maverick Russian sub?"

"Yes, sir—Ed."

"Tell me about it, but let's get some coffee first." The two men went to a table in the corner with coffee and donuts. Harris listened to the younger man for five minutes, sipping his coffee and devouring a couple of jelly donuts. It took a lot of food to support his frame.

"Son of a gun," the J-3 observed when Tyler finished. He walked over to the chart. "That's interesting. Your idea depends a lot on sleight of hand. We'd have to keep them away from where we're pulling this off. About here, you say?" He tapped the chart.

"Yes, General. The thing is, the way they seem to be operating we can do this to seaward of them—"

"And do a double shuffle. I like it. Yeah, I like it, but Dan Foster won't like losing one of our own boats."

"I'd say it's worth the trade."

"So would I," Harris agreed. "But they're not my boats. After we do this, where do we hide her—if we get her?"

"General, there are some nice places right here on the Chesapeake Bay. There's a deep spot on the York River and another on the Patuxent, both owned by the navy, both marked Keep Out on the charts. Nice thing about subs, they're supposed to be invisible. You just find a deep enough spot and flood your tanks. That's temporary, of course. For a more permanent spot, maybe Truk or Kwajalein in the Pacific. Nice and far from any place."

"And the Soviets would never notice the presence of a sub tender and three hundred submarine technicians there all of a sudden? Besides, those islands don't really belong to us anymore, remember?"

Tyler hadn't expected this man to be a dummy. "So, what if they do find out in a few months? What will they do, announce it to the whole world? I don't think so. By that time we'll have all the information we want, and we can always produce the defecting officers in a nice news conference. How would that look for them? Anyway, it figures that after we've had her for a while, we'll break her up. The reactor'll go to Idaho for tests. The missiles and warheads will get taken off. The electronics gear will be taken to California for testing, and the CIA, NSA, and navy will have gunfights over the crypto gear. The stripped hulk will be taken to a nice deep spot and scuttled. No evidence. We don't have to keep this a secret forever, just for a few months."

Harris set his cup down. "You'll have to forgive me for playing devil's advocate. I see you've thought this out. Fine, I think it's worth a hard look. It means coordinating a lot of hardware, but it doesn't really interfere with what we're already doing. Okay, you have my vote."

The Joint Chiefs arrived three minutes later. Tyler had never seen so many stars in one room.

"You wanted to see all of us, Eddie?" Hilton asked.

"Yes, General. This is Dr. Skip Tyler."

Admiral Foster came over first to take his hand. "You got us that performance data on *Red October* that we were just briefed on. Good work, Commander."

"Dr. Tyler thinks we should hold onto her if we get her," Harris said deadpan. "And he thinks he has a way we can do it."

"We already thought of killing the crew," Commandant Maxwell said. "The president won't let us."

"Gentlemen, what if I told you that there was a way to send the crewmen home without them knowing that we have her? That's the issue, right? We have to send the crewmen back to Mother Russia. I say there's a way to do that, and the remaining question is where to hide her."

"We're listening," Hilton said suspiciously.

"Well, sir, we'll have to move quickly to get everything in

place. We'll need *Avalon* from the West Coast. *Mystic* is already aboard the *Pigeon* in Charleston. We need both of them, and we need an old boomer of our own that we can afford to do without. That's the hardware. The real trick, however, is the timing—and we have to find her. That may be the hardest part."

"Maybe not," Foster said. "Admiral Gallery reported this morning that *Dallas* may be onto her. Her report dovetails nicely with your engineering model. We'll know more in a few days. Go on."

Tyler explained. It took ten minutes since he had to answer questions and use the chart to diagram time and space constraints. When he was finished, General Barnes was at the phone calling the commander of the Military Airlift Command. Foster left the room to call Norfolk, and Hilton was on his way to the White House.

The Red October

Except for those on watch, every officer was in the wardroom. Several pots of tea were on the table, all untouched, and again the door was locked.

"Comrades," Petrov reported, "the second set of badges was contaminated, worse than the first."

Ramius noted that Petrov was rattled. It wasn't the first set of badges, or the second. It was the third and fourth since sailing. He had chosen his ship's doctor well.

"Bad badges," Melekhin growled. "Some bastard of a trickster in Severomorsk—or perhaps an imperialist spy playing a typical enemy trick on us. When they catch the son of a bitch I will shoot him myself—whoever he is! This sort of thing is treasonous!"

"Regulations require that I report this," Petrov noted. "Even though the instruments show safe levels."

"Your adherence to the rules is noted, Comrade Doctor. You have acted correctly," Ramius said. "And now regulations stipulate that we make yet another check. Melekhin, I want you and Borodin to do it personally. First check the radiation instruments themselves. If they are working properly, we will be certain that the badges are defective—or have been tampered with. If so, my report on this incident will demand someone's head." It was not unknown for drunken shipyard workers to be sent to the gulag. "Comrades, in my opinion there is nothing at all to concern us. If there were a leak, Comrade Melekhin would have discovered it days ago. So. We all have work to do."

They were all back in the wardroom half an hour later. Passing crewmen noticed this, and already the whispering started.

"Comrades," Melekhin announced, "we have a major problem."

The officers, especially the younger ones, looked a little pale. On the table was a Geiger counter stripped into a score of small parts. Next to it was a radiation detector taken off the reactor room bulkhead, its inspection cover removed.

"Sabotage," Melekhin hissed. It was a word fearsome enough to make any Soviet citizen shudder. The room went deathly still, and Ramius noted that Svyadov was holding his face under rigid control.

"Comrades, mechanically speaking these instruments are quite simple. As you know, this counter has ten different settings. We can choose from ten sensitivity ranges, using the same instrument to detect a minor leak or to quantify a major one. We do that by dialing this selector, which engages one of ten electrical resistors of increasing value. A child could design this, or maintain and repair it." The chief enginer tapped the underside of the selector dial. "In this case the proper resistors have been clipped off, and new ones soldered on. Settings one to eight have the same impedance value. All of our counters were inspected by the same dockyard technician three days before we sailed. Here is his inspection sheet." Melekhin tossed it on the table contemptuously.

"Either he or another spy sabotaged this and all the other counters I've looked at. It would have taken a skilled man no more than an hour. In the case of this instrument." The engineer turned the fixed detector over. "You see that the electrical parts have been disconnected, except for the test circuit, which was rewired. Borodin and I removed this from the forward bulkhead. This is skilled work; whoever did this is no amateur. I believe that an imperialist agent has sabotaged our ship. First he disabled our radiation monitor instruments, then he probably arranged a low-level leak in our hot piping. It would appear, comrades, that Comrade Petrov was correct. We may have a leak. My apologies, Doctor."

Petrov nodded jerkily. Compliments like this he could easily forego.

"Total exposure, Comrade Petrov?" Ramius asked.

"The greatest is for the enginemen, of course. The maximum is fifty rads for Comrades Melekhin and Svyadov. The other engine crewmen run from twenty to forty-five rads, and the cumulative exposure drops rapidly as one moves forward. The torpedomen have only five rads or so, mostly less. The officers exclusive of engineers run from ten to twenty-five." Petrov paused, telling himself to be more positive. "Comrades, these are not lethal doses. In fact, one can tolerate a dose of up to a hundred rads without any near-term physiological effects, and one can survive several hundred. We do face a serious problem here, but it is not yet a life-threatening emergency."

"Melekhin?" the captain asked.

"It is my engine plant, and my responsibility. We do not yet *know* that we have a leak. The badges could still be defective or sabotaged. This could all be a vicious psychological trick played on us by the main enemy to damage our morale. Borodin will assist me. We will personally repair these and conduct a thorough inspection of all reactor systems. I am too old to have children. For the moment, I suggest that we deactivate the reactor and proceed on battery. The inspection will take us four hours at most. I also recommend that we reduce reactor watches to two hours. Agreed, Captain?"

"Certainly, Comrade. I know that there is nothing you cannot repair."

"Excuse me, Comrade Captain," Ivanov spoke up. "Should we report this to fleet headquarters?"

"Our orders are not to break radio silence," Ramius said.

"If the imperialists were able to sabotage our instruments . . . What if they knew our orders beforehand and are attempting to make us use the radio so they can locate us?" Borodin asked.

"A possibility," Ramius replied. "First we will determine if we have a problem, then its severity. Comrades, we have a fine crew and the best officers in the fleet. We will see to our own problems, conquer them, and continue our mission. We all have a date in Cuba that I intend to meet—to hell with imperialist plots!"

"Well said," Melekhin concurred.

"Comrades, we will keep this secret. There is no reason to excite the crew over what may be nothing, and at most is something we can handle on our own." Ramius ended the meeting.

Petrov was less sure, and Svyadov was trying very hard not to shake. He had a sweetheart at home and wanted one day to have children. The young lieutenant had been painstakingly trained to understand everything that went on in the reactor systems and to know what to do if things went awry. And it was some consolation to know that most of the solutions to reactor problems to be found in the book had been written by some of the men in this room. Even so, something that could neither be seen nor felt was invading his body, and no rational person would be happy with that.

The meeting adjourned. Melekhin and Borodin went aft to the engineering stores. A *michman* electrician came with them to get the proper parts. He noted that they were reading from the maintenance manual for a radiation detector. When he went off duty an hour later, the whole crew knew that the reactor had been shut down yet again. The electrician conferred with his bunkmate, a missile maintenance technician. Together they discussed the reason for working on a half dozen Geiger counters and other instruments, and their conclusion was an obvious one.

The submarine's bosun overheard the discussion and pondered the conclusion himself. He had been on nuclear submarines for ten years. Despite this he was not an educated man and regarded any activity in the reactor spaces as something to the left of witchcraft. It worked the ship, how he did not know, though he was certain that there was something unholy about it. Now he began to wonder if the devils he never saw inside that steel drum—were coming loose? Within two hours the entire crew knew that something was wrong and that their officers had not yet figured out a way to deal with it.

The cooks bringing food forward from the galley to the crew spaces were seen to linger in the bow as long as they could. Men standing watch in the control room shifted on their feet more than usual, Ramius noted, hurrying forward at the change of watch.

The USS New Jersey

It took some getting used to, Commodore Zachary Eaton reflected. When his flagship was built, he was sailing boats in a bathtub. Back then the Russians were allies, but allies of convenience, who shared a common enemy instead of a common goal. Like the Chinese today, he judged. The enemy then had been the Germans and the Japanese. In his twenty-six-year career, he had been to both countries many times, and his first command, a destroyer, had been home-ported at Yokoshuka. It was a strange world.

There were several nice things about his flagship. Big as she was, her movement on the ten-foot seas was just enough to remind him that he was at sea, not at a desk. Visibility was about ten miles, and somewhere out there, about eight hundred miles away, was the Russian fleet. His battleship was going to meet them just like in the old old days, as if the aircraft carrier had never come along. The destroyers *Caron* and *Stump* were in sight, five miles off either bow. Further forward, the cruisers *Biddle* and *Wainwright* were doing radar picket duty. The surface action group was marking time instead of proceeding forward as he would have preferred. Off the New Jersey coast, the helicopter assault ship *Tarawa* and two frigates were racing to join up, bringing ten AV-8B Harrier attack fighters and fourteen ASW helicopters to supplement his air strength. This was useful, but not of critical concern to Eaton. The *Saratoga*'s air wing was now operating out of Maine, along with a goodly collection of air force birds working hard to learn the maritime strike business. HMS *Invincible* was two hundred miles to his east, conducting aggressive ASW patrols, and eight hundred miles east of that force was the *Kennedy,* hiding under a weather front off the Azores. It slightly irked the commodore that the Brits were helping out. Since when did the U.S. Navy need help defending the American coast? Not that they didn't owe us the favor, though.

The Russians had split into three groups, with the carrier *Kiev* easternmost to face the *Kennedy*'s battle group. His expected responsibility was the *Moskva* group, with the *Invincible* handling the *Kirov*'s. Data on all three was being fed to him continuously and digested by his operations staff down in flag plot. What were the Soviets up to? he wondered.

He knew the story that they were searching for a lost sub, but Eaton believed that as much as if they'd explained that they had a bridge they wanted to sell. Probably, he thought, they want to demonstrate that they can trail their coats down our coast whenever they want, to show that they have a seagoing fleet and to establish a precedent for doing this again.

Eaton did not like that.

He did not much care for his assigned mission either. He had two tasks that were not fully compatible. Keeping an eye on their submarine activity would be difficult enough. The *Saratoga*'s Vikings were not working his area, despite his request, and most of the Orions were working farther out, closer to the *Invincible*. His own ASW assets were barely adequate for local defense, much less active sub hunting. The *Tarawa* would change that, but also change his screening requirements. His other mission was to establish and maintain sensor contact with the *Moskva* group and to report at once any unusual activity to CINCLANTFLT, the commander in chief of the Atlantic Fleet. This made sense, sort of. If their surface ships did anything untoward, Eaton had the means to deal with them. It was being decided now how closely he should shadow them.

The problem was whether he should be nearby or far away. Near meant twenty miles—gun range. The *Moskva* had ten escorts, none of which could possibly survive more than two of his sixteen-inch projectiles. At twenty miles he had the choice of using full-sized or subcaliber rounds, the latter guided to their targets by a laser designator installed atop the main director tower. Tests the previous year had determined that he could maintain a steady firing rate of one round every twenty seconds, with the laser shifting fire from one target to another until there were no more. But this would expose the *New Jersey* and her escorts to torpedo and missile fire from the Russian ships.

Backing farther off, he could still fire sabot rounds from fifty miles, and they could be directed to the target by a laser designator aboard the battlewagon's helicopter. This would expose the chopper to surface-to-air missile fire and to Soviet helicopters suspected of having air-to-air missile capability. To help out with this, the *Tarawa* was bringing a pair of Apache attack helicopters, which carried lasers, air-to-air missiles, and their own air-to-surface missiles; they were antitank weapons expected to work well against small warships.

His ships would be exposed to missile fire, but he didn't fear for his flagship. Unless the Russians were carrying nuclear warheads, their antiship missiles would not be able to damage his ship gravely—the *New Jersey* had upwards of a foot of class B armor plate. They would, however, play hell with his radar and communications gear, and worse, they would be lethal to his thin-hulled escorts. His ships carried their own antiship missiles, Harpoons and Tomahawks, though not as many as he would have liked.

And what about a Russian sub hunting them? Eaton had been told of none, but you never knew where one might be hiding. Oh well—he couldn't worry about everything. A submarine could sink the *New Jersey,* but she would have to work at it. If the Russians were really up to something nasty, they'd get the first shot, but Eaton would have enough warning to launch his own missiles and get off a few rounds of gunfire while calling for air support—none of which would happen, he was sure.

He decided that the Russians were on some sort of fishing expedition. His job was to show them that the fish in these waters were dangerous.

Naval Air Station, North Island, California

The oversized tractor-trailer crept at two miles per hour into the cargo bay of the C-5A Galaxy transport under the watchful eyes of the aircraft's loadmaster, two flight officers, and six naval officers. Oddly, only the latter, none of whom wore aviator's wings, were fully versed in the procedure. The vehicle's center of gravity was precisely marked, and they watched the mark approach a particular number engraved on the cargo bay floor. The work had to be done exactly. Any mistake could fatally impair the aircraft's trim and imperil the lives of the flight crew and passengers.

"Okay, freeze it right there," the senior officer called. The driver was only too glad to stop. He left the keys in the ignition, set all the brakes, and put the truck in gear before getting out. Someone else would drive it out of the aircraft on the other side of the country. The loadmaster and six airmen immediately went to work, snaking steel cables to eyebolts on the truck and trailer to secure the heavy load. Shifting cargo was something else an aircraft rarely survived, and the C-5A did not have ejection seats.

The loadmaster saw to it that his ground crewmen were properly at work before walking over to the pilot. He was a twenty-five-year sergeant who loved the C-5s despite their blemished history.

"Cap'n, what the hell is this thing?"

"It's called a DSRV, Sarge, deep submergence rescue vehicle."

"Says *Avalon* on the back, sir," the sergeant pointed out.

"Yeah, so it has a name. It's a sort of a lifeboat for submarines. Goes down to get the crew out if something screws up."

"Oh." The sergeant considered that. He'd flown tanks, helicopters, general cargo, once a whole battalion of troops on his—he thought of the aircraft as his—Galaxy before. This was the first time he had ever flown a ship. If it had a name, he reasoned, it was a ship. Damn, the Galaxy could do anything! "Where we takin' it, sir?"

"Norfolk Naval Air Station, and I've never been there either." The pilot watched the securing process closely. Already a dozen cables were attached. When a dozen more were in place, they'd put tension on the cables to prevent the minutest shift. "We figure a trip of five hours, forty minutes, all on internal fuel. We got the jet stream on our side today. Weather's supposed to be okay until we hit the coast. We lay over for a day, then come back Monday morning."

"Your boys work pretty fast," said the senior naval officer, Lieutenant Ames, coming over.

"Yes, Lieutenant, another twenty minutes." The pilot checked his watch. "We ought to be taking off on the hour."

"No hurry, Captain. If this thing shifts in flight, I guess it would ruin our whole day. Where do I send my people?"

"Upper deck forward. There's room for fifteen or so just aft of the flight deck." Lieutenant Ames knew this but didn't say so. He'd flown with his DSRV across the Atlantic several times and across the Pacific once, every time on a different C-5.

"May I ask what the big deal is?" the pilot inquired.

"I don't know," Ames said. "They want me and my baby in Norfolk."

"You really take that little bitty thing underwater, sir?" the loadmaster asked.

"That's what they pay me for. I've had her down to forty-eight hundred feet, almost a mile." Ames regarded his vessel with affection.

"A mile *under* water, sir? Jesus—uh, pardon me, sir, but I mean, isn't that a little hairy—the water pressure, I mean?"

"Not really. I've been down to twenty thousand aboard *Trieste*. It's really pretty interesting down there. You see all kinds of strange fish." Though a fully qualified submariner, Ames' first love was research. He had a degree in oceanography and had commanded or served in all of the navy's deep-submergence vehicles except the nuclear-powered *NR-1*. "Of course, the water pressure would do bad things to you if anything went wrong, but it would be so fast you'd never know it. If you fellows want a check ride, I could probably arrange it. It's a different world down there."

"That's okay, sir." The sergeant went back to swearing at his men.

"You weren't serious," the pilot observed.

"Why not? It's no big deal. We take civilians down all the time, and believe me, it's a lot less hairy than riding this damned white whale during a midair refueling."

"Uh-huh," the pilot noted dubiously. He'd done hundreds of those. It was entirely routine, and he was surprised that anyone would find it dangerous. You had to be careful, of course, but, hell, you had to be careful driving every morning. He was sure that an accident on this pocket submarine wouldn't leave enough of a man to make a decent meal for a shrimp. It takes all kinds, he decided. "You don't go to sea by yourself in that, do you?"

"No, ordinarily we work off a submarine rescue ship, *Pigeon* or *Ortolan*. We can also operate off a regular submarine. That gadget you see there on the trailer is our mating collar. We can nest on the back of a sub at the after escape trunk, and the sub takes us where we need to go."

"Does this have to do with the flap on the East Coast?"

"That's a good bet, but nobody's said anything official to us. The papers say the Russians have lost a sub. If so, we might go down to look at her, maybe rescue any survivors. We can take off twenty or twenty-five men at a time, and our mating collar is designed to fit Russian subs as well as our own."

"Same size?"

"Close enough." Ames cocked an eyebrow. "We plan for all kinds of contingencies."

"Interesting."

The North Atlantic

The YAK-36 Forger had left the *Kiev* half an hour before, guided first by gyro compass and now by the ESM pod on the fighter's stubby rudder fin. Senior Lieutenant Viktor Shavrov's mission was not an easy one. He was to approach the American E-3A Sentry radar surveillance aircraft, one of which had been shadowing his fleet for three days now. The AWACS (airborne warning and control system) aircraft had been careful to circle well beyond SAM range, but had stayed close enough to maintain constant coverage of the Soviet fleet, reporting every maneuver and radio transmission to their command base. It was like having a burglar watching one's apartment and being unable to do anything about it.

Shavrov's mission was to do something about it. He couldn't shoot, of course. His orders from Admiral Stralbo on the *Kirov* had been explicit about that. But he was carrying a pair of Atoll heat-seeking missiles which he would be sure to show the imperialists. He and his admiral expected that this would teach them a lesson: the Soviet Navy did not like having imperialist snoopers about, and accidents had been known to happen. It was a mission worthy of the effort it took.

This effort was considerable. To avoid detection by the airborne radar Shavrov had to fly as low and slow as his fighter could operate, a bare twenty meters above the rough Atlantic; this way he would get lost in the sea return. His speed was two hundred knots. This made for excellent fuel economy, though his mission was at the ragged edge of his fuel load. It also made for very rough flying as his fighter bounced through the roiled air at the wave tops. There was a low-hanging mist that cut visibility to a few kilometers. So much the better, he thought. The nature of the mission had chosen him, rather than the other way around. He was one of the few Soviet pilots experienced in low-level flying. Shavrov had not become a sailor-pilot by himself. He'd started flying attack helicopters for frontal aviation in Afghanistan, graduating to fixed-wing aircraft after a year's bloody apprenticeship. Shavrov was an expert in nap-of-the-earth flying, having learned it by necessity, hunting the bandits and counterrevolutionaries that hid in the towering mountains like hydrophobic rats. This skill had made him attractive to the fleet, which had transferred him to sea duty without his having had much say in the matter. After a few months he had no complaints, his perqs and extra pay being more attractive than his former frontal aviation base on the Chinese border. Being one of the few hundred carrier-qualified Soviet airmen had softened the blow of missing his chance to fly the new MiG-27, though with luck, if the new full-sized carrier were ever finished, he'd have the chance to fly the naval version of that wonderful bird. Shavrov could wait for that, and with a few successful missions like this one he might have his squadron command.

He stopped daydreaming—the mission was too demanding for that. This was real flying. He'd never flown against Americans, only against the weapons they gave to the Afghan bandits. He had lost friends to those weapons, some of whom had survived their crashes only to be done to death by the Afghan savages in ways that would have made even a German puke. It would be good to teach the imperialists a lesson personally.

The radar signal was growing stronger. Beneath his ejection seat a tape recorder was making a continuous record of the signal characteristics of the American aircraft so that the scientific people would be able to devise a means of jamming and foiling the vaunted American flying eye. The aircraft was only a converted 707, a glorified passenger plane, hardly a worthy opponent for a crack fighter pilot! Shavrov checked his chart. He'd have to find it soon. Next he checked his fuel. He'd dropped his last external tank a few minutes earlier, and all he had now was his internal fuel. The turbofan was guzzling fuel, something he had to keep an eye on. He planned to have only five or ten minutes of fuel left when he returned to his ship.

This did not trouble him. He already had over a hundred carrier landings.

There! His hawk's eyes caught the glint of sun off metal at one o'clock high. Shavrov eased back on his stick and increased power gently, bringing his Forger into a climb. A minute later he was at two thousand meters. He could see the Sentry now, its blue paint blending neatly into the darkening sky. He was coming up beneath its tail, and with luck the empennage would shield him from the rotating radar antenna. Perfect! He'd blaze by her a few times, letting the flight crew see his Atolls, and—

It took Shavrov a moment to realize that he had a wingman. Two wingmen.

Fifty meters to his left and right, a pair of American F-15 Eagle fighters. The visored face of one pilot was staring at him.

"YAK-106, YAK-106, please acknowledge." The voice on the SSB (single side band) radio circuit spoke flawless Russian. Shavrov did not acknowledge. They had read the number off his engine intake housing before he had known they were there.

"106, 106, this is the Sentry aircraft you are now approaching. Please identify yourself and your intentions. We get a little anxious when a stray fighter comes our way, so we've had three following you for the past hundred kilometers."

Three? Shavrov turned his head around. A third Eagle with four sparrow missiles was hanging fifty meters from his tail, his "six."

"Our men compliment you on your ability to fly low and slow, 106."

Lieutenant Shavrov was shaking with rage as he passed four thousand meters, still eight thousand from the American AWACS. He had checked his six every thirty seconds on the way in. The Americans must have been riding back there, hidden in the mist, and vectored in on him by instructions from the Sentry. He swore to himself and held course. He'd teach that AWACS a lesson!

"Break off, 106." It was a cool voice, without emotion except perhaps a trace of irony. "106, if you do not break off, we will consider your mission to be hostile. Think about it, 106. You are beyond radar coverage of your own ships, and you are not yet within missile range of us."

Shavrov looked to his right. The Eagle was breaking off—so was the one to the left. Was it a gesture, taking the heat off of him and expecting some courtesy in return? Or were they clearing the way for the one behind him—he checked, still there—to shoot? There was no telling what these imperialist criminals would do; he was at least a minute from the fringe of their missile range. Shavrov was anything but a coward. Neither was he a fool. He moved his stick, curving his fighter a few degrees to the right.

"Thank you, 106," the voice acknowledged. "You see, we have some trainee operators aboard. Two of them are women, and we don't want them to get rattled their first time out." Suddenly it was too much. Shavrov thumbed the radio switch on his stick.

"Shall I tell you what you can do with your women, Yankee?"

"You are *nekulturny*, 106," the voice replied softly. "Perhaps the long overwater flight has made you nervous. You must be about at the limit of your internal fuel. Bastard of a day to fly, what with all these crazy, shifting winds. Do you need a position check, over?"

"Negative, Yankee!"

"Course back to *Kiev* is one-eight-five, true. Have to be careful using a magnetic compass this far north, you know. Distance to *Kiev* is 318.6 kilometers. Warning—there is a rapidly moving cold front moving in from the southwest. That's going to make flying a little rough in a few hours. Do you require an escort back to *Kiev*?"

"Pig!" Shavrov swore to himself. He switched his radio off, cursing himself for his lack of discipline. He had allowed the Americans to wound his pride. Like most fighter pilots, he had a surfeit of that.

"106, we did not copy your last transmission. Two of my Eagles are heading that way. They will form up on you and see that you get home safely. Have a happy day, Comrade. Sentry-November, out."

The American lieutenant turned to his colonel. He couldn't keep a straight face any longer. "God, I thought I'd strangle talking like that!" He sipped some Coke from a plastic cup. "He really thought he'd sneak up on us."

"In case you didn't notice, he did get within a mile of Atoll range, and we don't have authorization to shoot at him until he flips one at us—which might wreck our day," the colonel grumped. "Nice job of twisting his tail, Lieutenant."

"A pleasure, Colonel." The operator looked at his screen. "Well, he's heading back to momma, with Cobras 3 and 4 on his six. He's going to be one unhappy Russkie when he gets home. If he gets home. Even with those drop tanks, he must be near his range limit." He thought for a moment. "Colonel, if they do this again, how 'bout we offer to take the guy home with us?"

"Get a Forger—what for? I suppose the navy'd like to have one to play with, they don't get much of Ivan's hardware, but the Forger's a piece of junk."

Shavrov was tempted to firewall his engine but restrained himself. He'd already shown enough personal weakness for one day. Besides, his YAK could only break Mach 1 in a dive. Those Eagles could do it straight up, and they had plenty of fuel. He saw that they both carried FAST-pack comformal fuel cells. They could cross whole oceans with those. Damn the Americans and their arrogance! Damn his own intelligence officer for telling him he could sneak up on the Sentry! Let the air-to-air armed Backfires go after them. They could handle that famed overbred passenger bus, could get to it faster than its fighter guardians could react.

The Americans, he saw, were not lying about the weather front. A line of cold weather squawls racing northeast was just on the horizon as he approached the *Kiev*. The Eagles backed off as he approached the formation. One American pilot pulled alongside briefly to wave goodbye. His head bobbed at Shavrov's return gesture. The Eagles paired up and turned back north.

Five minutes later he was aboard the *Kiev*, still pale with rage. As soon as the wheels were choked he jumped to the carrier deck, stomping off to see his squadron commander.

The Kremlin

The city of Moscow was justly famous for its subway system. For a pittance, people could ride nearly anywhere they wanted

on a modern, safe, garishly decorated electric railway system.
In case of war, the underground tunnels could serve as a bomb
shelter for the citizens of Moscow. This secondary use was the
result of the efforts of Nikita Khrushchev, who when construction was begun in the mid-thirties had suggested to Stalin that the
system be driven deep. Stalin had approved. The shelter con-
sideration had been decades ahead of its time; nuclear fission
had then only been a theory, fusion hardly thought of at all.

On a spur of the line running from Sverdlov Square to the
old airport, which ran near the Kremlin, workers bored a tunnel
that was later closed off with a ten-meter-thick steel and concrete plug. The hundred-meter-long space was connected to
the Kremlin by a pair of elevator shafts, and over time it had
been converted to an emergency command center from which
the Politburo could control the entire Soviet empire. The tunnel
was also a convenient means of going unseen from the city to
a small airport from which Politburo members could be flown
to their ultimate redoubt, beneath the granite monolith at Zhiguli. Neither command post was a secret to the West—both
had existed far too long for that—but the KGB confidently
reported that nothing in the Western arsenals could smash through
the hundreds of feet of rock which in both places separated the
Politburo from the surface.

This fact was of little comfort to Admiral Yuri Ilych Padorin.
He found himself seated at the far end of a ten-meter-long
conference table looking at the grim faces of the ten Politburo
members, the inner circle that alone made the strategic decisions affecting the fate of his country. None of them were
officers. Those in uniform reported to these men. Up the table
to his left was Admiral Sergey Gorshkov, who had disassociated
himself from this affair with consummate skill, even producing
a letter in which he had opposed Ramius' appointment to command the *Red October*. Padorin, as chief of the Main Political
Administration, had successfully blocked Ramius' transfer,
pointing out that Gorshkov's candidate for command was occasionally late in paying his Party dues and did not speak up
at the regular meetings often enough for an officer of his rank.
The truth was that Gorshkov's candidate was not so proficient
an officer as Ramius, whom Gorshkov had wanted for his own
operations staff, a post that Ramius had successfully evaded
for years.

Party General Secretary and President of the Union of Soviet Socialist Republics Andre Narmonov shifted his gaze to Padorin. His face gave nothing away. It never did, unless he wished it to—which was rare enough. Narmonov had succeeded Andropov when the latter had suffered a heart attack. There were rumors about that, but in the Soviet Union there are always rumors. Not since the days of Laventri Beria had the security chieftain come so close to power, and senior Party officials had allowed themselves to forget that. It would not be forgotten again. Bringing the KGB to heel had taken a year, a necessary measure to secure the privileges of the Party elite from the supposed reforms of the Andropov clique.

Narmonov was the apparatchik par excellence. He had first gained prominence as a factory manager, an engineer with a reputation for fulfilling his quota early, a man who produced results. He had risen steadily by using his own talents and those of others, rewarding those he had to, ignoring those he could. His position as general secretary of the Communist Party was not entirely secure. It was still early in his stewardship of the Party, and he depended on a loose coalition of colleagues— not friends, these men did not make friends. His succession to this chair had resulted more from ties within the Party structure than from personal ability, and his position would depend on consensus rule for years, until such time as his will could dictate policy.

Narmonov's dark eyes, Padorin could see, were red from tobacco smoke. The ventilation system down here had never worked properly. The general secretary squinted at Padorin from the other end of the table as he decided what to say, what would please the members of this cabal, these ten old, passionless men.

"Comrade Admiral," he began coldly, "we have heard from Comrade Gorshkov what the chances are of finding and destroying this rebellious submarine before it can complete its unimaginable crime. We are not pleased. Nor are we pleased with the fantastic error in judgment that gave command of our most valuable ship to this slug. What I want to know from you, Comrade, is what happened to the *zampolit* aboard, and what security measures were taken by your office to prevent this infamy from taking place!"

There was no fear in Narmonov's voice, but Padorin knew

it had to be there. This "fantastic error" could ultimately be laid at the chairman's feet by members who wanted another in that chair—unless he were able somehow to separate himself from it. If this meant Padorin's skin, that was the admiral's problem. Narmonov had had men flayed before.

Padorin had prepared himself for this over several days. He was a man who had lived through months of intensive combat operations and had several boats sunk from under him. If his body was softer now, his mind was not. Whatever his fate might be, Padorin was determined to meet it with dignity. If they remember me as a fool, he thought, it will be as a courageous fool. He had little left to live for in any case. "Comrade General Secretary," he began, "the political officer aboard *Red October* was Captain Ivan Yurievich Putin, a stalwart and faithful Party member. I cannot imagine—"

"Comrade Padorin," Defense Minister Ustinov interrupted, "we presume that you also could not imagine the unbelievable treachery of this Ramius. You now expect us to trust your judgment on this man also?"

"The most disturbing thing of all," added Mikhail Alexandrov, the Party theoretician who had replaced the dead Mikhail Suslov and was even more determined than the departed ideologue to be simon-pure on Party doctrine, "is how tolerant the Main Political Administration has been toward this renegade. It is amazing, particularly in view of his obvious efforts to construct his own personality cult throughout the submarine service, even in the political arm, it would seem. Your criminal willingness to overlook this—this *obvious* aberration from Party policy—does not make your judgment appear very sound."

"Comrades, you are correct in judging that I erred badly in approving Ramius for command, and also that we allowed him to select most of *Red October*'s senior officers. At the same time, we chose some years ago to do things in this way, to keep officers associated with a single ship for many years, and to give the captain great sway over their careers. This is an operational question, not a political one."

"We have already considered that," Narmonov replied. "It is true that in this case there is enough blame for more than one man." Gorshkov didn't move, but the message was explicit: his effort to separate himself from this scandal had failed.

Narmonov didn't care how many heads it took to prop up his chair.

"Comrade Chairman," Gorshkov objected, "the efficiency of the fleet—"

"Efficiency?" Alexandrov said. "Efficiency. This Lithuanian half-breed is *efficiently* making fools of our fleet with his chosen officers while our remaining ships blunder about like newly castrated cattle." Alexandrov alluded to his first job on a state farm. A fitting beginning, it was generally thought, for the man who held the position of chief ideologue was as popular in Moscow as the plague, but the Politburo had to have him or one like him. The ideological chieftain was always the kingmaker. Whose side was he on now—in addition to his own?"

"The most likely explanation is that Putin was murdered," Padorin continued. "He alone of the officers left behind a wife and family."

"That's another question, Comrade Admiral." Narmonov seized this issue. "Why is it that none of these men are married? Didn't that tell you something? Must we of the Politburo supervise everything? Can't you think for yourselves?"

As if you want us to, Padorin thought. "Comrade General Secretary, most of our submarine commanders prefer young, unmarried officers in their wardrooms. Duty at sea is demanding, and single men have fewer distractions. Moreover, each of the senior officers aboard is a Party member in good standing with a praiseworthy record. Ramius had been treacherous, there is no denying that, and I would gladly kill the son of a bitch with my own hands—but he has deceived more good men than there are in this room."

"Indeed," Alexandrov observed. "And now that we are in this mess, how do we get out of it?"

Padorin took a deep breath. He'd been waiting for this. "Comrades, we have another man aboard *Red October,* unknown to either Putin or Captain Ramius, an agent of the Main Political Administration."

"What?" Gorshkov said. "And why did I not know of this?"

Alexandrov smiled. "That's the first intelligent thing we've heard today. Go on."

"This individual is covered as an enlisted man. He reports

directly to our office, bypassing all operational and political channels. His name is Igor Loginov. He is twenty-four, a—"

"*Twenty-four!*" Narmonov shouted. "You trust a child with this responsibility?"

"Comrade, Loginov's mission is to blend in with the conscripted crewmen, to listen in on conversations, to identify likely traitors, spies, and saboteurs. In truth he looks younger still. He serves alongside young men, and he must be young himself. He is, in fact, a graduate of the higher naval school for political officers at Kiev and the GRU intelligence academy. He is the son of Arkady Ivanovich Loginov, chief of the Lenin Steel Plant at Kazan. Many of you here know his father." Narmonov was among those who nodded, a flickering of interest in his eyes. "Only an elite few are chosen for this duty. I have met and interviewed this boy myself. His record is clear, he is a Soviet patriot without question."

"I know his father," Narmonov confirmed. "Arkady Ivanovich is an honorable man who has raised several good sons. What are this boy's orders?"

"As I said, Comrade General Secretary, his ordinary duties are to observe the crewmen and report on what he sees. He's been doing this for two years, and he is good at it. He does not report to the *zampolit* aboard, but only to Moscow or to one of my representatives. In a genuine emergency, his orders are to report to the *zampolit*. If Putin is alive—and I do not believe this, comrades—he would be part of the conspiracy, and Loginov would know not to do this. In a true emergency, therefore, his orders are to destroy the ship and make his escape."

"This is possible?" Narmonov asked. "Gorshkov?"

"Comrades, all of our ships carry powerful scuttling charges, submarines especially."

"Unfortunately," Padorin said, "these are generally not armed, and only the captain can activate them. Ever since the incident on *Storozhevoy*, we in the Main Political Administration have had to consider that an incident such as this one was indeed a possibility, and that its most damaging manifestation would involve a missile-carrying submarine."

"Ah," Narmonov observed, "he is a missile mechanic."

"No, Comrade, he is a ship's cook," Padorin replied.

"Wonderful! He spends all his day boiling potatoes!" Narmonov's hands flew up in the air, his hopeful demeanor gone in an instant, replaced with palpable wrath. "You wish your bullet now, Padorin?"

"Comrade Chairman, this is a better cover assignment than you may imagine." Padorin did not flinch, wanting to show these men what he was made of. "On *Red October* the officers' accommodations and galley are aft. The crew's quarters are forward—the crew eat there since they do not have a separate messroom—with the missile room in between. As a cook he must travel back and forth many times each day, and his presence in any particular area will not be thought unusual. The food freezer is located adjacent to the lower missile deck forward. It is not our plan that he should activate the scuttling charges. We have allowed for the possibility that the captain could disarm them. Comrades, these measures have been carefully thought out."

"Go on," Narmonov grunted.

"As Comrade Gorshkov explained earlier, *Red October* carries twenty-six Seahawk missiles. These are solid-fuel rockets, and one has a range-safety package installed."

"Range safety?" Narmonov was puzzled.

Up to this point the other military officers at the meeting, none of them Politburo members, had kept their peace. Padorin was surprised when General V.M. Vishenkov, commander of the Strategic Rocket Forces, spoke up. "Comrades, these details were worked out through my office some years ago. As you know, when we test our missiles, we have safety packages aboard to explode them if they go off course. Otherwise they might land on one of our own cities. Our operational missiles do not ordinarily carry them—for the obvious reason, the imperialists might learn a way to explode them in flight."

"So, our young GRU comrade will blow up the missile. What of the warheads?" Narmonov asked. An engineer by training, he could always be distracted by technical discourse, always impressed by a clever one.

"Comrade," Vishenkov went on, "the missile warheads are armed by accelerometers. Thus they cannot be armed until the missile reaches its full programmed speed. The Americans use the same system, and for the same reason, to prevent sabotage. These safety systems are absolutely reliable. You could drop one of the reentry vehicles from the top of the Moscow television transmitter onto a steel plate and it would not fire." The general referred to the massive TV tower whose construction Narmonov had personally supervised while head of the Central Communications Directorate. Vishenkov was a skilled political operator.

"In the case of a solid-fuel rocket," Padorin continued, recognizing his debt to Vishenkov, wondering what he'd ask for in return, and hoping he'd live long enough to deliver, "a safety package ignites all of the missile's three stages simultaneously."

"So the missile just takes off?" Alexandrov asked.

"No, Comrade Academician. The upper stage might, if it could break through the missile tube hatch, and this would flood the missile room, sinking the submarine. But even if it did not, there is sufficient thermal energy in either of the first two stages to reduce the entire submarine to a puddle of molten iron, twenty times what is necessary to sink it. Loginov has been trained to bypass the alarm system on the missile tube hatch, to activate the safety package, set a timer, and escape."

"Not just to destroy the ship?" Narmonov asked.

"Comrade General Secretary," Padorin said, "it is too much to ask a young man to do his duty, knowing that it means certain death. We would be unrealistic to expect this. He must have at least the possibility of escape, otherwise human weakness might lead to failure."

"This is reasonable," Alexandrov said. "Young men are motivated by hope, not fear. In this case, young Loginov would hope for a considerable reward."

"And get it," Narmonov said. "We will make every effort to save this young man, Gorshkov."

"If he is truly reliable," Alexandrov noted.

"I know that my life depends on this, Comrade Academician," Padorin said, his back still straight. He did not get a verbal answer, only nods from half the heads at the table. He had faced death before and was at the age where it remains the last thing a man need face.

The White House

Arbatov came into the Oval Office at 4:50 P.M. He found the president and Dr. Pelt sitting in easy chairs across from the chief executive's desk.

"Come on over, Alex. Coffee?" The president pointed to a tray on the corner of his desk. He was not drinking today, Arbatov noted.

"No, thank you, Mr. President. May I ask—"

"We think we found your sub, Alex," Pelt answered. "They just brought these dispatches over, and we're checking them now." The adviser held up a ring binder of message forms.

"Where is it, may I ask?" The ambassador's face was dead-pan.

"Roughly three hundred miles northeast of Norfolk. We have not located it exactly. One of our ships noted an underwater explosion in the area—no, that's not right. It was recorded on a ship, and when the tapes were checked a few hours later, they thought they heard a submarine explode and sink. Sorry, Alex," Pelt said. "I should have known better than to read through all this stuff without an interpreter. Does your navy talk in its own language, too?"

"Officers do not like for civilians to understand them," Arbatov smiled. "This has doubtless been true since the first man picked up a stone."

"Anyway, we have ships and aircraft searching the area now."

The president looked up. "Alex, I talked to the chief of naval operations, Dan Foster, a few minutes ago. He said not to expect any survivors. The water there's over a thousand feet deep, and you know what the weather is like. They said it's right on the edge of the continental shelf."

"The Norfolk Canyon, sir," Pelt added.

"We are conducting a thorough search," the president continued. "The navy is bringing in some specialized rescue equipment, search gear, all that sort of thing. If the submarine is located, we'll get somebody down to them on the chance there might be survivors. From what the CNO tells me it is just possible that there might be if the interior partitions—bulkheads, I think he called them—are intact. The other question is their air supply, he said. Time is very much against us, I'm afraid. All this fantastically expensive equipment we buy them, and they can't locate one damned object right off our coast."

Arbatov made a mental record of these words. It would make a worthwhile intelligence report. The president occasionally let—

"By the way, Mr. Ambassador, what exactly was your sub marine doing there?"

"I have no idea, Dr. Pelt."

"I trust it was not a missile sub," Pelt said. "We have a agreement to keep those five hundred miles offshore. The wreck will of course be inspected by our rescue craft. Were we t learn that it is indeed a missile sub . . ."

"Your point is noted. Still, those are international waters.'

The president turned and spoke softly. "So is the Gulf o Finland, Alex, and, I believe, the Black Sea." He let thi observation hang in the air for a moment. "I sincerely hop that we are not heading back to that kind of situation. Are w talking about a missile submarine, Alex?"

"Truly, Mr. President, I have no idea. Certainly I shoul hope not."

The president could see how carefully the lie was phrased He wondered if the Russians would admit that there was captain out there who had disregarded his orders. No, the would probably claim a navigation error.

"Very well. In any case, we will be conducting our ow search and rescue operation. We'll know soon enough wha sort of vessel we're talking about." The president looked sud denly uneasy. "One more thing Foster talked about. If we fin bodies—pardon the crudity on a Saturday afternoon—I expec that you will want them returned to your country."

"I have had no instructions on this," the ambassador an swered truthfully, caught off guard.

"It was explained to me in too much detail what a death like this does to a man. In simple terms, they're crushed b the water pressure, not a very pretty thing to see, they tell me But they were men, and they deserve some dignity even i death."

Arbatov conceded the point. "If this is possible, then, believe that the Soviet people would appreciate this humani tarian gesture."

"We'll do our best."

And the American best, Arbatov remembered, included a ship named the *Glomar Explorer*. This notorious exploration ship had been built by the CIA for the specific purpose o recovering a Soviet *Golf*-class missile submarine from the floor of the Pacific Ocean. She had been placed in storage, no doub to await the next such opportunity. There would be nothing the Soviet Union could do to prevent the operation, a few hundred miles off the American coast, three hundred miles from the United States' largest naval base.

"I trust that the precepts of international law will be observed, gentlemen. That is, with respect to the vessel's remains and the crew's bodies."

"Of course, Alex." The president smiled, gesturing to a memorandum on his desk. Arbatov struggled for control. He'd been led down this path like a schoolboy, forgetting that the American president had been a skilled courtroom tactician—not something that life in the Soviet Union prepares a man for—and knew all about legal tricks. Why was this bastard so easy to underestimate?

The president was also struggling to control himself. It was not often that he saw Alex flustered. This was a clever opponent, not easily caught off balance. Laughing would spoil it.

The memorandum from the attorney general had arrived only that morning. It read:

Mr. President,

Pursuant to your request, I have asked the chief of our admiralty law department to review the question of international law regarding the ownership of sunken or derelict vessels, and the law of salvage pertaining to such vessels. There is a good deal of case law on the subject. One simple example is *Dalmas v Stathos* (84FSuff. 828, 1949 A.M.C. 770 [S.D.N.Y. 1949]):

No problem of foreign law is here involved, for it is well settled that "salvage is a question arising out of the *jus gentium* and does not ordinarily depend on the municipal law of particular countries."

The international basis for this is the Salvage Convention of 1910 (Brussels), which codified the transnational nature and admiralty and salvage law. This was ratified by the United States in the Salvage Act of

1912, 37 Stat. 242, (1912), 46 U.S.C.A. §§ 727-731;
and also in 37 Stat. 1658 (1913).

"International law will be observed, Alex," the president
promised. "In all particulars." And whatever we get, he thought,
will be taken to the nearest port, Norfolk, where it will be
turned over to the receiver of wrecks, an overworked federal
official. If the Soviets want anything back, they can bring action
in admiralty court, which means the federal district court sitting
in Norfolk, where, if the suit were successful—*after* the value
of the salvaged property was determined, and *after* the U.S.
Navy was paid a proper fee for its salvage effort, also determined by the court—the wreck would be returned to its rightful
owners. Of course, the federal district court in question had,
at last check, an eleven-month backlog of cases.

Arbatov would cable Moscow on this. For what good it
would do. He was certain the president would take perverse
pleasure in manipulating the grotesque American legal system
to his own advantage, all the time pointing out that, as president, he was constitutionally unable to interfere with the working of the courts.

Pelt looked at his watch. It was about time for the next
surprise. He had to admire the president. For a man with only
limited knowledge of international affairs only a few years
earlier, he'd learned fast. This outwardly simple, quiet-talking
man was at his best in face to face situations, and after a
lifetime's experience as a prosecutor, he still loved to play the
game of negotiation and tactical exchange. He seemed able to
manipulate people with frighteningly casual skill. The phone
rang and Pelt got it, right on cue.

"This is Dr. Pelt speaking. Yes, Admiral—where? When?
Just one? I see . . . Norfolk? Thank you, Admiral, that is very
good news. I will inform the president immediately. Please
keep us advised." Pelt turned around. "We got one, alive, by
God!"

"A survivor off the lost sub?" The president stood.

"Well, he's a Russian sailor. A helicopter picked him up an
hour ago, and they're flying him to the Norfolk base hospital.
They picked him up 290 miles northeast of Norfolk, so I guess
that makes it fit. The men on the ship say he's in pretty bad
shape, but the hospital is ready for him."

The president walked to his desk and lifted the phone. "Grace, ring me Dan Foster right now . . . Admiral, this is the president. The man they picked up, how soon to Norfolk? Another two hours?" He grimaced. "Admiral, you get on the phone to the naval hospital, and you tell them that *I* say they are to do everything they can for that man. I want him treated like he was my own son, is that clear? Good. I want hourly reports on his condition. I want the best people we have in on this, the very best. Thank you, Admiral." He hung up. "All right!"

"Maybe we were too pessimistic, Alex," Pelt chirped up.

"Certainly," the president answered. "You have a doctor at the embassy, don't you?"

"Yes, we do, Mr. President."

"Take him down, too. He'll be extended every courtesy. I'll see to that. Jeff, are they searching for other survivors?"

"Yes, Mr. President. There's a dozen aircraft in the area right now, and two more ships on the way."

"Good!" The president clapped his hands together, enthusiastic as a kid in a toystore. "Now, if we can find some more survivors, maybe we can give your country a meaningful Christmas present, Alex. We will do everything we can, you have my word on that."

"That is very kind of you, Mr. President. I will communicate this happy news to my country at once."

"Not so fast, Alex." The chief executive held his hand up. "I'd say this calls for a drink."

THE TENTH DAY

SUNDAY, 12 DECEMBER

SOSUS Control

At SOSUS Control in Norfolk, the picture was becoming increasingly difficult. The United States simply did not have the technology to keep track of submarines in the deep ocean basins. The SOSUS receptors were principally laid at shallow-water choke points, on the bottom of undersea ridges and highlands. The strategy of the NATO countries was a direct consequence of this technological limitation. In a major war with the Soviets, NATO would use the Greenland–Iceland–United Kingdom SOSUS barrier as a huge tripwire, a burglar alarm system. Allied submarines and ASW patrol aircraft would try to seek out, attack, and destroy Soviet submarines as they approached it, before they could cross the lines.

The barrier had never been expected to halt more than half of the attacking submarines, however, and those that succeeded in slipping through would have to be handled differently. The deep ocean basins were simply too wide and too deep—the average depth was over two miles—to be littered with sensors as the shallow choke points were. This was a fact that cut both ways. The NATO mission would be to maintain the Atlantic Bridge and continue transoceanic trade, and the obvious Soviet mission would be to interdict this trade. Submarines would have to spread out over the vast ocean to cover the many possible convoy routes. NATO strategy behind the SOSUS barriers, then, was to assemble large convoys, each ringed with destroyers, helicopters, and fixed-wing aircraft. The escorts would try to establish a protective bubble about a hundred miles across. Enemy submarines would not be able to exist within that bubble; if in it they would be hunted down and killed— or merely driven off long enough for the convoy to speed past. Thus while SOSUS was designed to neutralize a huge, fixed expanse of sea, deep-basin strategy was founded on mobility, a moving zone of protection for the vital North Atlantic shipping.

This was an altogether sensible strategy, but one that could not be tested under realistic conditions, and, unfortunately, one that was largely useless at the moment. With all of the Soviet *Alfa*s and *Victor*s already on the coast, and the last of the *Charlie*s, *Echoe*s, and *November*s just arriving on their stations, the master screen Commander Quentin was staring at was no longer filled with discrete little red dots but rather with large circles. Each dot or circle designated the position of a Soviet submarine. A circle respresented an estimated position, calculated from the speed with which a sub could move without giving off enough noise to be localized by the many sensors being employed. Some circles were ten miles across, some as much as fifty; an area anywhere from seventy-eight to two thousand square miles had to be searched if the submarine were again to be pinned down. And there were just too damned many of the boats.

Hunting the submarines was principally the job of the P-3C Orion. Each Orion carried sonobuoys, air-deployable active and passive sonar sets that were dropped from the belly of the aircraft. On detecting something, a sonobuoy reported to its mother aircraft and then automatically sank lest it fall into unfriendly hands. The sonobuoys had limited electrical power and thus limited range. Worse, their supply was finite. The sonobuoy inventory was already being depleted alarmingly, and soon they would have to cut back on expenditures. Additionally, each P-3C carried FLIRs, forward-looking infrared scanners, to identify the heat signature of a nuclear sub, and MADs, magnetic anomaly detectors that located the disturbance in the earth's magnetic field caused by a large chunk of ferrous metal like a submarine. MAD gear could only detect a magnetic disturbance six hundred yards to the left and right of an aircraft's course track, and to do this the aircraft had to fly low, consuming fuel and limiting the crew's visual search range. FLIR had roughly the same limitation.

Thus the technology used to localize a target first detected by SOSUS, or to "delouse" a discrete piece of ocean preparatory to the passage of a convoy, simply was not up to a random search of the deep ocean.

Quentin leaned forward. A circle had just changed to a dot. A P-3C had just dropped an explosive sounding charge and localized an *Echo*-class attack sub five hundred miles south of the Grand Banks. For an hour they had a near-certain shooting solution on that *Echo;* her name was written on the Orion's Mark 46 ASW torpedoes.

Quentin sipped at his coffee. His stomach rebelled at the additional caffeine, remembering the abuse of four months of hellish chemotherapy. If there were to be a war, this was one way it might start. All at once, their submarines would stop, perhaps just like this. Not sneaking to kill convoys in midocean but attacking them closer to shore, the way the Germans had done . . . and all the American sensors would be in the wrong place. Once stopped the dots would grow to circles, ever wider, making the task of finding the subs all the more difficult. Their engines quiet, the boats would be invisible traps for the passing merchant vessels and warships racing to bring life-saving supplies to the men in Europe. Submarines were like cancer. Just like the disease that he had only barely defeated. The invisible, malignant vessels would find a place, stop to infect it, and on his screen the malignancies would grow until they were attacked by the aircraft he controlled from this room. But he could not attack them now. Only watch.

"PK EST 1 HOUR—RUN," he typed into his computer console.

"23," the computer answered at once.

Quentin grunted. Twenty-four hours earlier the PK, probability of a kill, had been forty—forty probable kills in the first hour after getting a shooting authorization. Now it was barely half that, and this number had to be taken with a large grain of salt, since it assumed that everything would work, a happy state of affairs found only in fiction. Soon, he judged, the number would be under ten. This did not include kills from friendly submarines that were trailing the Russians under strict orders not to reveal their positions. His sometime allies in the *Sturgeon*s, *Permit*s, and *Los Angeles*es were playing their own ASW game by their own set of rules. A different breed. He tried to think of them as friends, but it never quite worked. In his twenty years of naval service submarines had always been the enemy. In war they would be useful enemies, but in a war it was widely recognized that there was no such thing as a friendly submarine.

A B-52

The bomber crew knew exactly where the Russians were. Navy Orions and air force Sentries had been shadowing them for days now, and the day before, he'd been told, the Soviets had sent an armed fighter from the *Kiev* to the nearest Sentry. Possibly an attack mission, probably not, it had in any case been a provocation.

Four hours earlier the squadron of fourteen had flown out of Plattsburg, New York, at 0330, leaving behind black trails of exhaust smoke hidden in the predawn gloom. Each aircraft carried a full load of fuel and twelve missiles whose total weight was far less than the -52's design bombload. This made for good, long range.

Which was exactly what they needed. Knowing where the Russians were was only half the battle. Hitting them was the other. The mission profile was simple in concept, rather more difficult in execution. As had been learned in missions over Hanoi—in which the B-52 had participated and sustained SAM (surface-to-air missile) damage—the best method of attacking a heavily defended target was to converge from all points of the compass at once, "like the enveloping arms of an angry bear," the squadron commander had put it at the briefing, indulging his poetic nature. This gave half the squadron relatively direct courses to their target; the other half had to curve around,

careful to keep well beyond effective radar coverage; all had
to turn exactly on cue.

The B-52s had turned ten minutes earlier, on command from
the Sentry quarterbacking the mission. The pilot had added a
twist. His course to the Soviet formation took his bomber right
down a commercial air route. On making his turn, he had
switched his IFF transponder from its normal setting to international. He was fifty miles behind a commercial 747, thirty
miles ahead of another, and on Soviet radar all three Boeing
products would look exactly alike—harmless.

It was still dark down on the surface. There was no indication that the Russians were alerted yet. Their fighters were
only supposed to be VFR (visual flight rules) capable, and the
pilot imagined that taking off and landing on a carrier in the
dark was pretty risky business, doubly so in bad weather.

"Skipper," the electronic warfare officer called on the intercom, "we're getting L- and S-band emissions. They're right
where they're supposed to be."

"Roger. Enough for a return off us?"

"That's affirm, but they probably think we're flying Pan
Am. No fire control stuff yet, just routine air search."

"Range to target?"

"One-three-zero miles."

It was almost time. The mission profile was such that all
would hit the 125-mile circle at the same moment.

"Everything ready?"

"That's a roge."

The pilot relaxed for another minute, waiting for the signal
from the entry.

"FLASHLIGHT, FLASHLIGHT, FLASHLIGHT." The signal came over the digital radio channel.

"That's it! Let 'em know we're here," the aircraft commander ordered.

"Right." The electronic warfare officer flipped the clear
plastic cover off his set of toggle switches and dials controlling
the aircraft's jamming systems. First he powered up his systems. This took a few seconds. The -52's electronics were all
old seventies-vintage equipment, else the squadron would not
be part of the junior varsity. Good learning tools, though, and
the lieutenant was hoping to move up to the new B-1Bs now

beginning to come off the Rockwell assembly line in California. For the past ten minutes the ESM pods on the bomber's nose and wingtips had been recording the Soviet radar signals, classifying their exact frequencies, pulse repetition rates, power, and the individual signature characteristics of the transmitters. The lieutenant was brand new to this game. He was a recent graduate of electronic warfare school, first in his class. He considered what he should do first, then selected a jamming mode, not his best, from a range of memorized options.

The Nikolayev

One hundred twenty-five miles away on the *Kara*-class cruiser *Nikolayev*, a radar *michman* was examining some blips that seemed to be in a circle around his formation. In an instant his screen was covered with twenty ghostly splotches tracing crazily in various directions. He shouted the alarm, echoed a second later by a brother operator. The officer of the watch hurried over to check the screen.

By the time he got there the jamming mode had changed and six lines like the spokes of a wheel were rotating slowly around a central axis.

"Plot the strobes," the officer ordered.

Now there were blotches, lines, and sparkles.

"More than one aircraft, Comrade." The *michman* tried flipping through his frequency settings.

"Attack warning!" another *michman* shouted. His ESM receiver had just reported the signals of aircraft search-radar sets of the type used to acquire targets for air-to-surface missiles.

The B-52

"We got hard targets," the weapons officer on the -52 reported. "I got a lock on the first three birds."

"Roger that," the pilot acknowledged. "Hold for ten more seconds."

"Ten seconds," the officer replied. "Cutting switches . . . *now.*"

"Okay, kill the jamming."

"ECM systems off."

The Nikolayev

"Missile acquisition radars have ceased," the combat information center officer reported to the cruiser's captain, just now arrived from the bridge. Around them the *Nikolayev*'s crew was racing to battle stations. "Jamming has also ceased."

"What is out there?" the captain asked. Out of a clear sky his beautiful clipper-bowed cruiser had been threatened—and now all was well?

"At least eight enemy aircraft in a circle around us."

The captain examined the now normal S-band air search screen. There were numerous blips, mainly civilian aircraft. The half circle of others had to be hostile, though.

"Could they have fired missiles?"

"No, Comrade Captain, we would have detected it. They jammed our search radars for thirty seconds and illuminated us with their own search systems for twenty. Then everything stopped."

"So, they provoke us and now pretend nothing has happened?" the captain growled. "When will they be within SAM range?"

"This one and these two will be within range in four minutes if they do not change course."

"Illuminate them with our missile control systems. Teach the bastards a lesson."

The officer gave the necessary instructions, wondering who was being taught what. Two thousand feet above one of the B-52s was an EC-135 whose computerized electronic sensors were recording all signals form the Soviet cruiser and taking them apart, the better to know how to jam them. It was the first good look at the new SA-N-8 missile system.

Two F-14 Tomcats

The double-zero code number on its fuselage marked the Tomcat as the squadron commander's personal bird; the black ace of spades on the twin-rudder tail indicated his squadron, Fighting 41, "The Black Aces." The pilot was Commander Robby Jackson, and his radio call sign was Spade 1.

Jackson was leading a two-plane section under the direction

of one of the *Kennedy*'s E-2C Hawkeyes, the navy's more diminutive version of the air force's AWACS and close brother to the COD, a twin-prop aircraft whose radome makes it look like an airplane being terrorized by a UFO. The weather was bad—depressingly normal for the North Atlantic in December—but was supposed to improve as they headed west. Jackson and his wingman, Lieutenant (j.g.) Bud Sanchez, were flying through nearly solid clouds, and they had eased their formation out somewhat. In the limited visibility both remembered that each Tomcat had a crew of two and a price of over thirty million dollars.

They were doing what the Tomcat does best. An all-weather interceptor, the F-14 has transoceanic range, Mach 2 speed, and a radar computer fire control system that can lock onto and attack six separate targets with long-range Phoenix air-to-air missiles. Each fighter was now carrying two of those along with a pair each of AIM-9M Sidewinder heat-seekers. Their prey was a flight of YAK-36 Forgers, the bastard V/STOL fighters that operated from the carrier *Kiev*. After harassing the Sentry the previous day, Ivan had decided to close with the *Kennedy* force, no doubt guided in with data from a reconnaissance satellite. The Soviet aircraft had come up short, their range being fifty miles less than they needed to sight the *Kennedy*. Washington decided that Ivan was getting a little too obnoxious on this side of the ocean. Admiral Painter had been given permission to return the favor, in a friendly sort of way.

Jackson figured that he and Sanchez could handle this, even outnumbered. No Soviet aircraft, least of all the Forger, was equal to the Tomcat—certainly not while I'm flying it, Jackson thought.

"Spade 1, your target is at your twelve o'clock and level, distance now twenty miles," reported the voice of Hummer 1, the Hawkeye a hundred miles aft. Jackson did not acknowledge.

"Got anything, Chris?" he asked his radar intercept officer, Lieutenant Commander Christiansen.

"An occasional flash, but nothing I can use." They were tracking the Forgers with passive systems only, in this case an infrared sensor.

Jackson considered illuminating their targets with his powerful fire control radar. The Forgers' ESM pods would sense this at once, reporting to their pilots that their death warrant had been written but not yet signed. "How about *Kiev?*"

"Nothing. The *Kiev* group is under total EMCON."

"Cute," Jackson commented. He guessed that the SAC raid on the *Kirov-Nikolayev* group had taught them to be more careful. It was not generally known that warships often made no use whatever of their radar systems, a protective measure called EMCON, for emission control. The reason was that a radar beam could be detected at several times the distance at which it generated a return signal to its transmitter and could thus tell an enemy more than it told its operators. "You suppose these guys can find their way home without help?"

"If they don't, you know who's gonna get blamed." Christiansen chuckled.

"That's a roge," Jackson agreed.

"Okay, I got infrared acquisition. Clouds must be thinning out some." Christiansen was concentrating on his instruments, oblivious of the view out of the canopy.

"Spade 1, this is Hummer 1, your target is twelve o'clock, at your level, range now ten miles." The report came over the secure radio circuit.

Not bad, picking up the Forgers' heat signature through this slop, Jackson thought, especially since they had small, inefficient engines.

"Radar coming on, Skipper," Christiansen advised. *"Kiev* has an S-band air search just come on. They have us for sure."

"Right." Jackson thumbed his mike switch. "Spade 2, illuminate targets—now."

"Roger, lead," Sanchez acknowledged. No point hiding now.

Both fighters activated their powerful AN/AWG-9 radars. It was now two minutes to intercept.

The radar signals, received by the ESM threat-receivers on the Forgers' tail fins, set off a musical tone in the pilot headsets which had to be turned off manually, and lit up a red warning light on each control panel.

The Kingfisher Flight

"Kingfisher flight, this is *Kiev,"* called the carrier's air operations officer. "We show two American fighters closing you at high speed from the rear."

"Acknowledged." The Russian flight leader checked his mirror. He'd hoped to avoid this, though he hadn't expected to. His orders were to take no action unless fired upon. They had just broken into the clear. Too bad, he'd have felt safer in the clouds.

The pilot of Kingfisher 3, Lieutenant Shavrov, reached down to arm his four Atolls. Not this time, Yankee, he thought.

The Tomcats

"One minute, Spade 1, you ought to have visual any time," Hummer 1 called in.

"Roger . . . Tallyho!" Jackson and Sanchez broke into the clear. The Forgers were a few miles ahead, and the Tomcats' 250-knot speed advantage was eating that distance up rapidly. *The Russian pilots are keeping a nice, tight formation,* Jackson thought, *but anybody can drive a bus.*

"Spade 2, let's go to burners on my mark. Three, two, one—mark!"

Both pilots advanced their engine controls and engaged their afterburners, which dumped raw fuel into the tail pipes of their new F-110 engines. The fighters lept forward with a sudden double thrust and went quickly through Mach 1.

The Kingfisher Flight

"Kingfisher, warning, warning, the *Amerikantsi* have increased speed," *Kiev* cautioned.

Kingfisher 4 turned in his seat. He saw the Tomcats a mile aft, twin dart-like shapes racing before trails of black smoke. Sunlight glinted off one canopy, and it almost looked like the flashes of a—

"They're attacking!"

"What?" The flight leader checked his mirror again. "Negative, negative—hold formation!"

The Tomcats screeched fifty feet overhead, the sonic booms they trailed sounding just like explosions. Shavrov acted entirely on his combat-trained instincts. He jerked back on his stick and triggered his four missiles at the departing American fighters.

"Three, what did you do?" the Russian flight leader demanded.

"They were attacking us, didn't you hear?" Shavrov protested.

The Tomcats

"Oh shit! Spade Flight, you have four Atolls after you," the voice of the Hawkeye's controller said.

"Two, break right," Jackson ordered. "Chris, activate countermeasures." Jackson threw his fighter into a violent evasive turn to the left. Sanchez broke the other way.

In the seat behind Jackson's, the radar intercept officer flipped switches to activate the aircraft's defense systems. As the Tomcat twisted in midair, a series of flares and balloons was ejected from the tail section, each an infrared or radar lure for the pursuing missiles. All four were targeted on Jackson's fighter.

"Spade 2 is clear, Spade 2 is clear. Spade 1, you still have four birds in pursuit," the voice from the Hawkeye said.

"Roger." Jackson was surprised at how calmly he took it. The Tomcat was doing over eight hundred miles per hour and accelerating. He wondered how much range the Atoll had. His rearward-looking-radar warning light flicked on.

"Two, get after them!" Jackson ordered.

"Roger, lead." Sanchez swept into a climbing turn, fell off into a hammerhead, and dove at the retreating Soviet fighters.

When Jackson turned, two of the missiles lost lock and kept going straight into open air. A third, decoyed into hitting a flare, exploded harmlessly. The fourth kept its infrared seeker head on Spade 1's glowing tail pipes and bored right in. The missile struck the Spade 1 at the base of its starboard rudder fin.

The impact tossed the fighter completely out of control. Most of the explosive force was spent as the missile blasted through the boron surface into open air. The fin was blown completely off, along with the right-side stabilizer. The left fin was badly holed by fragments, which smashed through the back of the fighter's canopy, hitting Christiansen's helmet. The right engine's fire warning lights came on at once.

Jackson heard the *oomph* over his intercom. He killed every engine switch on the right side and activated the in-frame fire extinguisher. Next he chopped power to his port engine, still on afterburner. By this time the Tomcat was in an inverted spin. The variable-geometry wings angled out to low-speed configuration. This gave Jackson aeleron control, and he worked quickly to get back to normal attitude. His altitude was four thousand feet. There wasn't much time.

"Okay, baby," he coaxed. A quick burst of power gave him back aerodynamic control, and the former test pilot snapped his fighter over—too hard. It went through two complete rolls before he could catch it in level flight. "Gotcha! You with me, Chris?"

Nothing. There was no way he could look around, and there were still four hostile fighters behind him.

"Spade 2, this is lead."

"Roger, lead." Sanchez had the four Fighters bore-sighted. They had just fired at his commander.

Hummer 1

On Hummer 1, the controller was thinking fast. The Forgers were holding formation, and there was a lot of Russian chatter on the radio circuit.

"Spade 2, this is Hummer 1, break off, I say again, break off, do not, repeat do not fire. Acknowledge. Spade 2, Spade 1 is at your nine o'clock, two thousand feet below you." The officer swore and looked at one of the enlisted men he worked with.

"That was too fast, sir, just too fuckin' fast. We got tapes of the Russkies. I can't understand it, but it sounds like *Kiev* is right pissed."

"They're not the only ones," the controller said, wondering if he had done the right thing calling Spade 2 off. It sure as hell didn't feel that way.

The Tomcats

Sanchez' head jerked in surprise. "Roger, breaking off." His thumb came off the switch. "Goddammit!" He pulled his stick back, throwing the Tomcat into a savage loop. "Where are you, lead?"

Sanchez brought his fighter under Jackson's and did a slow circle to survey the visible damage.

"Fire's out, Skipper. Right side rudder and stabilizer are gone. Left side fin—shit, I can see through it, but it looks like it oughta hold together. Wait a minute. Chris is slumped over, Skipper. Can you talk to him?"

"Negative, I've tried. Let's go back home."

Nothing would have pleased Sanchez more than to blast the Forgers right out of the sky, and with his four missiles he could have done this easily. But like most pilots, he was highly disciplined.

"Roger, lead."

"Spade 1, this is Hummer 1, advise your condition, over."

"Hummer 1, we'll make it unless something else falls off. Tell them to have docs standing by. Chris is hurt. I don't know how bad."

It took an hour to get to the *Kennedy*. Jackson's fighter flew badly, would not hold course in any specific attitude. He had to adjust trim constantly. Sanchez reported some movement in the aft cockpit. Maybe it was just the intercom shot out, Jackson thought hopefully.

Sanchez was ordered to land first so that the deck would be cleared for Commander Jackson. On the final approach the Tomcat started to handle badly. The pilot struggled with his fighter, planting it hard on the deck and catching the number one wire. The right-side landing gear collapsed at once, and the thirty-million-dollar fighter slid sideways into the barrier that had been erected. A hundred men with fire-fighting gear raced toward it from all directions.

The canopy went up on emergency hydraulic power. After unbuckling himself Jackson fought his way around and tried to grab for his backseater. They had been friends for many years.

Chris was alive. It looked like a quart of blood had poured down the front of his flight suit, and when the first corpsman took the helmet off, he saw that it was still pumping out. The second corpsman pushed Jackson out of the way and attached a cervical collar to the wounded airman. Christiansen was lifted gently and lowered onto a stretcher whose bearers ran towards the island. Jackson hesitated a moment before following it.

Norfolk Naval Medical Center

Captain Randall Tait of the Navy Medical Corps walked down the corridor to meet with the Russians. He looked younger than his forty-five years because his full head of black hair showed not the first sign of gray. Tait was a Mormon, educated at Brigham Young University and Stanford Medical School, who had joined the navy because he had wanted to see more of the world than one could from an office at the foot of the Wasatch Mountains. He had accomplished that much, and until today had also avoided anything resembling diplomatic duty. As the new chief of the Department of Medicine at Bethesda Naval Medical Center he knew that couldn't last. He had flown down to Norfolk only a few hours earlier to handle the case. The Russians had driven down, and taken their time doing it.

"Good morning, gentlemen. I'm Dr. Tait." They shook hands all around, and the lieutenant who had brought them up walked back to the elevator.

"Dr. Ivanov," the shortest one said. "I am physician to the embassy."

"Captain Smirnov." Tait knew him to be assistant naval attaché, a career intelligence officer. The doctor had been briefed on the helicopter trip down by a Pentagon intelligence officer who was now drinking coffee in the hospital commissary.

"Vasily Petchkin, Doctor. I am second secretary to the embassy." This one was a senior KGB officer, a "legal" spy with a diplomatic cover. "May we see our man?"

"Certainly. Will you follow me please?" Tait led them back down the corridor. He'd been on the go for twenty hours. This was part of the territory as chief of service at Bethesda. He got all the hard calls. One of the first things a doctor learns is how not to sleep.

The whole floor was set up for intensive care, Norfolk Naval Medical Center having been built with war casualties in mind. Intensive Care Unit Number Three was a room twenty-five feet square. The only windows were on the corridor wall, and the curtains had been drawn back. There were four beds, only one occupied. The young man in it was almost totally concealed. The only thing not hidden by the oxygen mask covering his face was an unruly clump of wheat-colored hair. The rest of his body was fully draped. An IV stand was next to the bed, its two bottles of fluid merging in a single line that led under the covers. A nurse dressed like Tait in surgical greens was standing at the foot of the bed, her green eyes locked on the electrocardiograph readout over the patient's head, dropping momentarily to make a notation on his chart. On the far side of the bed was a machine whose function was not immediately obvious. The patient was unconscious.

"His condition?" Ivanov asked.

"Critical," Tait replied. "It's a miracle he got here alive at all. He was in the water for at least twelve hours, probably more like twenty. Even accounting for the fact that he was wearing a rubber exposure suit, given the ambient air and water temperatures there's just no way he ought to have been alive. On admission his core temperature was 23.8°C." Tait shook his head. "I've read about worse hypothermia cases in the literature, but this is by far the worst I've ever seen."

"Prognosis?" Ivanov looked into the room.

Tait shrugged. "Hard to say. Maybe as good as fifty-fifty, maybe not. He's still extremely shocky. He's a fundamentally healthy person. You can't see it from here, but he's in superb physical shape, like a track and field man. He has a particularly strong heart; that's probably what kept him alive long enough to get here. We have the hypothermia pretty much under control now. The problem is, with hypothermia so many things go wrong at once. We have to fight a number of separate but connected battles against different systemic enemies to keep them from overwhelming his natural defenses. If anything's going to kill him, it'll be the shock. We're treating that with electrolytes, the normal routine, but he's going to be on the edge for several days at least I—"

Tait looked up. Another man was pacing down the hall. Younger than Tait, and taller, he had a white lab coat over his greens. He carried a metal chart.

"Gentlemen, this is Doctor—Lieutenant—Jameson. He's the physician of record on the case. He admitted your man. What do you have, Jamie?"

"The sputum sample showed pneumonia. Bad news. Worse, his blood chemistry isn't getting any better, and his white count is *dropping.*"

"Great." Tait leaned against the window frame and swore to himself.

"Here's the printout from the blood analyzer." Jameson handed the chart over.

"May I see this, please?" Ivanov came around.

"Sure." Tait flipped the metal cloud chart open and held it so that everyone could see it. Ivanov had never worked with a computerized blood analyzer, and it took several seconds for him to orient himself.

"This is not good."

"Not at all," Tait agreed.

"We're going to have to jump on that pneumonia, hard," Jameson said. "This kid's got too many things going wrong. If the pneumonia really takes hold . . ." He shook his head.

"Keflin?" Tait asked.

"Yeah." Jameson pulled a vial from his pocket. "As much as he'll handle. I'm guessing that he had a mild case before he got dumped in the water, and I hear that some penicillin-resistant strains have been cropping up in Russia. You use mostly penicillin over there, right?" Jameson looked down at Ivanov.

"Correct. What is this keflin?"

"It's a big gun, a synthetic antibiotic, and it works well on resistant strains."

"Right now, Jamie," Tait ordered.

Jameson walked around the corner to enter the room. He injected the antibiotic into a 100cc piggyback IV bottle and hung it on a stand.

"He's so young," Ivanov noted. "He treated our man initially?"

"His name's Albert Jameson. We call him Jamie. He's twenty-nine, graduated Harvard third in his class, and he's been with us ever since. He's board-certified in internal medicine and virology. He's as good as they come." Tait suddenly realized how uncomfortable he was dealing with the Russians. His education and years of naval service taught him that these men were the enemy. That didn't matter. Years before he had sworn an oath to treat patients without regard to outside considerations. Would they believe or did they think he'd let their man die because he was a Russian? "Gentlemen, I want you to understand this: we're giving your man the very best care we can. We're not holding anything back. If there's a way to give him back to you alive, we'll find it. But I can't make any promises."

The Soviets could see that. While waiting for instructions from Moscow, Petchkin had checked up on Tait and found him to be, though a religious fanatic, an efficient and honorable physician, one of the best in government service.

"Has he said anything?" Petchkin asked, casually.

"Not since I've been here. Jamie said that right after they started warming him up he was semiconscious and babbled for a few minutes. We taped it, of course, and had a Russian-speaking officer listen to it. Something about a girl with brown eyes, didn't make any sense. Probably his sweetheart—he's a good-looking kid, he probably has a girl at home. It was totally incoherent, though. A patient in his condition has no idea what's going on."

"Can we listen to the tape?" Petchkin said.

"Certainly. I'll have it sent up."

Jameson came around the corner. "Done. A gram of keflin every six hours. Hope it works."

"How about his hands and feet?" Smirnov asked. The captain knew something about frostbite.

"We're not even bothering about that," Jameson answered. "We have cotton around the digits to prevent maceration. If he survives the next few days, we'll get blebs and maybe have some tissue loss, but that's the least of our problems. You guys know what his name is?" Petchkin's head snapped around. "He wasn't wearing any dogtags when he arrived. His clothes didn't have the ship's name. No wallet, no identification, not even any coins in the pockets. It doesn't matter very much for his initial treatment, but I'd feel better if you could pull his medical records. It would be good to know if he has any allergies or underlying medical conditions. We don't want him to go into shock from an allergic reaction to drug treatment."

"What was he wearing?" Smirnov asked.

"A rubber exposure suit," Jameson answered. "The guys

who found him left it on him, thank God. I cut it off him when
he arrived. Under that, shirt, pants, handerchief. Don't you
guys wear dogtags?"

"Yes," Smirnov responded. "How did you find him?"

"From what I hear, it was pure luck. A helicopter off a
frigate was patrolling and spotted him in the water. They didn't
have any rescue gear aboard, so they marked the spot with a
dye marker and went back to their ship. A bosun volunteered
to go in after him. They loaded him and a raft cannister into
the chopper and flew him back, with the frigate hustling down
south. The bosun kicked out the raft, jumped in after it—and
landed on it. Bad luck. He broke both his legs, but he did get
your sailor into the raft. The tin can picked them up an hour
later and they were both flown directly here."

"How is your man?"

"He'll be all right. The left leg wasn't too bad, but the right
tibia was badly splintered," Jameson went on. "He'll recover
in a few months. Won't be doing much dancing for a while,
though."

The Russians thought the Americans had deliberately removed their man's identification. Jameson and Tait suspected
that the man had disposed of his tags, possibly hoping to defect.
There was a red mark on the neck that indicated forcible re-
moval.

"If it is permitted," Smirnov said, "I would like to see your
man, to thank him."

"Permission granted, Captain," Tait nodded. "That would
be kind of you."

"He must be a brave man."

"A sailor doing his job. Your people would do the same
thing." Tait wondered if this were true. "We have our differences, gentlemen, but the sea doesn't care about that. The sea—
well, she tries to kill us all regardless what flag we fly."

Petchkin was back looking through the window, trying to
make out the patient's face.

"Could we see his clothing and personal effects?" he asked.

"Sure, but it won't tell you much. He's a cook. That's all
we know," Jameson said.

"A cook?" Petchkin turned around.

"The officer who listened in on the tape—obviously he was

an intelligence officer, right? He looked at the number on his shirt and said it made him a cook." The three-digit number indicated that the patient had been a member of the port watch, and that his battle station was damage control. Jameson wondered why the Russians numbered all their enlisted men. To be sure they didn't trespass? Petchkin's head, he noticed, was almost touching the glass pane.

"Dr. Ivanov, do you wish to attend the case?" Tait asked.

"Is this permitted?"

"It is."

"When will he be released?" Petchkin inquired. "When may we speak with him?"

"Released?" Jameson snapped. "Sir, the only way he'll be out of here in less than a month will be in a box. So far as consciousness is concerned, that's anyone's guess. That's one very sick kid you have in there."

"But we must speak to him!" the KGB agent protested.

Tait had to look up at the man. "Mr. Petchkin, I understand your desire to communicate with your man—but he is my patient now. We will do nothing, repeat *nothing,* that might interfere with his treatment and recovery. I got orders to fly down here to handle this. They tell me those orders came from the White House. Fine. Doctors Jameson and Ivanov will assist me, but that patient is now my responsibility, and my job is to see to it that he walks out of this hospital alive and well. Everything else is secondary to that objective. You will be extended every courtesy. But I make the rules here." Tait paused. Diplomacy was not something he was good at. "Tell you what, you want to sit in there yourselves in relays, that's fine with me. But you have to follow the rules. That means you scrub, change into sterile clothing, and follow the instructions of the duty nurse. Fair enough?"

Petchkin nodded. American doctors think they are gods, he said to himself.

Jameson, busy reexamining the blood analyzer printout, had ignored the sermon. "Can you gentlemen tell us what kind of sub he was on?"

"No," Petchkin said at once.

"What are you thinking, Jamie?"

"The dropping white count and some of these other indi-

cators are consistent with radiation exposure. The gross symptoms would have been masked by the overlying hypothermia."
Suddenly Jameson looked at the Soviets. "Gentlemen, we have to know this, was he on a nuclear sub?"

"Yes," Smirnov answered, "he was on a nuclear-powered submarine."

"Jamie, take his clothing to radiology. Have them check the buttons, zipper, anything metal for evidence of contamination."

"Right." Jameson went to collect the patient's effects.

"May we be involved in this?" Smirnov asked.

"Yes, sir," Tait responded, wondering what sort of people these were. The guy had to come off a nuclear submarine, didn't he? Why hadn't they told him at once? Didn't they want him to recover?

Petchkin pondered the significance of this. Didn't they know he had come off a nuclear-powered sub? Of course—he was trying to get Smirnov to blurt out that the man was off a missile submarine. They were trying to cloud the issue with this story about contamination. Nothing that would harm the patient, but something to confuse their class enemies. Clever. He'd always thought the Americans were clever. And he was supposed to report to the embassy in an hour—report what? How was he supposed to know who the sailor was?

Norfolk Naval Shipyard

The USS *Ethan Allen* was about at the end of her string. Commissioned in 1961, she had served her crews and her country for over twenty years, carrying Polaris sea-launched ballistic missiles in endless patrols through sunless seas. Now she was old enough to vote, and this was very old for a submarine. Her missile tubes had been filled with ballast and sealed months before. She had only a token maintenance crew while the Pentagon bureaucrats debated her future. There had been talk of a complicated cruise missile system to make her into a SSGN like the new Russian *Oscar*s. This was judged too expensive. *Ethan Allen*'s was generation-old technology. Her S5W reactor was too dated for much more use. Nuclear radiation had bombarded the metal vessel and its internal fittings with many billions of neutrons. As recent examination of test strips had revealed, over time the character of the metal had changed, becoming dangerously brittle. The system had at most another three years of useful life. A new reactor would be too expensive. The *Ethan Allen* was doomed by her senescence.

The maintenance crew was made up of members of her last operational team, mainly old-timers looking forward to retirement, with a leavening of kids who needed education in repair skills. The *Ethan Allen* could still serve as a school, especially a repair school since so much of her equipment was worn out.

Admiral Gallery had come aboard early that morning. The chiefs had regarded that as particularly ominous. He had been her first skipper many years before, and admirals always seemed to visit their early commands—right before they were scrapped. He'd recognized some of the senior chiefs and asked them if the old girl had any life left in her. To a man, the chiefs said yes. A ship becomes more than a machine to her crew. Each of a hundred ships, built by the same men at the same yard to the same plans, will have her own special characteristics— most of them bad, really, but after her crew becomes accustomed to them they are spoken of affectionately, particularly in retrospect. The admiral had toured the entire length of the *Ethan Allen*'s hull, pausing to run his gnarled, arthritic hands over the periscope he had used to make certain that there really was a world outside the steel hull, to plan the rare "attack" against a ship hunting his sub—or a passing tanker, just for practice. He'd commanded the *Ethan Allen* for three years, alternating his gold crew with another officer's blue crew, working out of Holy Loch, Scotland. Those were good years, he told himself, a damned sight better than sitting at a desk with a lot of vapid aides running around. It was the old navy game, up or out: just when you got something that you were really good at, something you really liked, it was gone. It made good organizational sense. You had to make room for the youngsters coming up—but, God! to be young again, to command one of the new ones that now he only had the opportunity to ride a few hours at a time, a courtesy to the skinny old bastard in Norfolk.

She'd do it, Gallery knew. She'd do fine. It was not the end he would have preferred for *his* fighting ship, but when you came down to it, a decent end for a fighting ship was something rare. Nelson's *Victory*, the *Constitution* in Boston harbor, the odd battleship kept mummified by her namesake state—they'd had honorable treatment. Most warships were sunk as targets or broken up for razor blades. The *Ethan Allen* would die for a purpose. A crazy purpose, perhaps crazy enough to work, he said to himself as he returned to COMSUBLANT headquarters.

Two hours later a truck arrived at the dock where the *Ethan Allen* lay dormant. The chief quartermaster on deck at the time noted that the truck came from Oceana Naval Air Station. Curious, he thought. More curiously, the officer who got out was wearing neither dolphins nor wings. He saluted the quarterdeck first, then the chief who had the deck while *Ethan Allen*'s remaining two officers supervised a repair job on the engine spaces. The officer from the naval air station made arrangements for a work gang to load the sub with four bullet-shaped objects, which went through the deck hatches. They were large, barely able to fit through the torpedo and capsule loading hatches, and it took some handling to get them emplaced. Next came plastic pallets to set them on and metal straps to secure them. They look like bombs, the chief electrician thought as the younger men did the donkey work. But they couldn't be that; they were too light, obviously made of ordinary sheet metal. An hour later a truck with a pressurized tank on its loadbed arrived. The submarine was cleared of her personnel and carefully ventilated. Then three men snaked a hose to each of the four objects. Finished, they ventilated the hull again, leaving gas detectors near each object. By this time, the crew noted, their dock and the one next to it were being guarded by armed marines so that no one could come over and see what was happening to the *Ethan Allen*.

When the loading, or filling, or whatever, was finished, a chief went below to examine the metal shells more carefully. He wrote down the stenciled acronym PPB76A/J6713 on a pad. A chief yeoman looked the designation up in a catalog and did not like what he found—Pave Pat Blue 76. Pave Pat Blue 76 was a bomb, and the *Ethan Allen* had four of them aboard. Nothing nearly so powerful as the missile warheads she had once carried, but a lot more ominous, the crew agreed. The smoking lamp was out by mutual accord before anyone made an order of it.

Gallery came back soon thereafter and spoke with all of the senior men individually. The youngsters were sent ashore with their personal gear and an admonition that they had not seen, felt, heard, or otherwise noticed anything unusual on the *Ethan Allen*. She was going to be scuttled at sea. That was all. Some political decision in Washington—and if you tell *that* to anyone, start thinking about a twenty-year tour at McMurdo Sound, as one man put it.

It was a tribute to Vincent Gallery that each of the old chiefs stayed aboard. Partly it was a chance for one last cruise on the old girl, a chance to say goodbye to a friend. Mostly it was because Gallery said it was important, and the old-timers remembered that his word had been good once.

The officers showed up at sundown. The lowest-ranking among them was a lieutenant commander. Two four-striped captains would be working the reactor, along with three senior chiefs. Two more four-stripers would handle the navigation, a pair of commanders the electronics. The rest would be spread around to handle the plethora of specialized tasks necessary to the operation of a complex warship. The total complement, not even a quarter the size of a normal crew, might have caused some adverse comment on the part of the senior chiefs, who didn't consider just how much experience these officers had.

One officer would be working the diving planes, the chief quartermaster was scandalized to learn. The chief electrician he discussed this with took it in stride. After all, he noted, the real fun was driving the boats, and officers only got to do that at New London. After that all they got to do was walk around and look important. True, the quartermaster agreed, but could they handle it? If not, the electrician decided, they would take care of things—what else were chiefs for but to protect officers from their mistakes? After that they argued good-naturedly over who would be chief of the boat. Both men had nearly identical experience and time in rate.

The USS *Ethan Allen* sailed for the last time at 2345 hours. No tug helped her away from the dock. The skipper eased her deftly away from the dock with gentle engine commands and strains on his lines that his quartermaster could only admire. He'd served with the skipper before, on the *Skipjack* and the *Will Rogers*. "No tugs, no nothin'," he reported to his bunkmate later. "The old man knows his shit." In an hour they were past the Virginia Capes and ready to dive. Ten minutes later they were gone from sight. Below, on a course of one-one-zero, the small crew of officers and chiefs settled into the demanding routine of running their old boomer shorthanded. The *Ethan Allen* responded like a champ, steaming at twelve knots, her old machinery hardly making any noise at all.

THE ELEVENTH DAY

MONDAY, 13 DECEMBER

An A-10 Thunderbolt

It was a lot more fun than flying DC-9s. Major Andy Richardson had over ten thousand hours in those and only six hundred or so in his A-10 Thunderbolt II strike fighter, but he much preferred the smaller of the twin-engine aircraft. Richardson belonged to the 175th Tactical Fighter Group of the Maryland Air National Guard. Ordinarily his squadron flew out of a small military airfield east of Baltimore. But two days earlier, when his outfit had been activated, the 175th and six other national guard and reserve air groups had crowded the already active SAC base at Loring Air Force Base in Maine. They had taken off at midnight and had refueled in midair only half an hour earlier, a thousand miles out over the North Atlantic. Now Richardson and his flight of four were skimming a hundred feet over the black waters at four hundred knots.

A hundred miles behind the four fighters, ninety aircraft were following at thirty thousand feet in what would look very

much to the Soviets like an alpha strike, a weighted attack
mission of armed tactical fighters. It was exactly that—and
also a feint. The real mission belonged to the low-level team
of four.

Richardson loved the A-10. She was called with backhanded
affection the Warthog or just plain Hog by the men who flew
her. Nearly all tactical aircraft had pleasing lines conferred on
them by the need in combat for speed and maneuverability.
Not the Hog, which was perhaps the ugliest bird ever built for
the U.S. Air Force. Her twin turbofan engines hung like af-
terthoughts at the twin-rudder tail, itself a throwback to the
thirties. Her slablike wings had not a whit of sweepback and
were bent in the middle to accommodate the clumsy landing
gear. The undersides of the wings were studded with many
hard points so ordance could be carried, and the fuselage was
built around the aircraft's primary weapon, the GAU-8 thirty-
millimeter rotary cannon designed specifically to smash Soviet
tanks.

For tonight's mission, Richardson's flight had a full load of
depleted uranium slugs for their Avenger cannons and a pair
of Rockeye cluster bomb cannisters, additional antitank weapons. Directly beneath the fuselage was a LANTIRN (low-
altitude navigation and targeting infrared for night) pod; all the
other ordnance stations save one were occupied by fuel tanks.

The 175th had been the first national guard squadron to
receive LANTIRN. It was a small collection of electronic and
optical systems that enabled the Hog to see at night while flying
at minimum altitude searching for targets. The systems projected a heads-up display (HUD) on the fighter's windshield,
in effect turning night to day and making this mission profile
marginally less hazardous. Beside each LANTIRN pod was a
smaller object which, unlike the cannon shells and Rockeyes,
was intended for use tonight.

Richardson didn't mind—indeed, he relished—the hazards
of the mission. Two of his three comrades were, like him,
airline pilots, the third a crop duster, all experienced men with
plenty of practice in low-level tactics. And their mission was
a good one.

The briefing, conducted by a naval officer, had taken over
an hour. They were paying a visit to the Soviet Navy. Rich-

ardson had read in the papers that the Russians were up to something, and when he had heard at the briefing that they were sending their fleet to trail its coat this close to the American coast, he had been shocked by their boldness. It had angered him to learn that one of their crummy little day fighters had back-shot a navy Tomcat the day before, nearly killing one of its officers. He wondered why the navy was being cut out of the response. Most of the *Saratoga*'s air group was visible on the concrete pads at Loring, sitting alongside the B-52s, A-6E Intruders, and F-18 Hornets with their ordnance carts a few feet away. He guessed that his mission was only the first act, the delicate part. While Soviet eyes were locked on the alpha strike hovering at the edge of their SAM range, his flight of four would dash in under radar cover to the fleet flagship, the nuclear-powered battle cruiser *Kirov*. To deliver a message.

It was surprising that guardsmen had been selected for this mission. Nearly a thousand tactical aircraft were now mobilized on the East Coast, about a third of them reservists of one kind or another, and Richardson guessed that that was part of the message. A very difficult tactical operation was being run by second-line airmen, while the regular squadrons sat ready on the runways of Loring, and McGuire, and Dover, and Pease, and several other bases from Virginia to Maine, fueled, briefed, and ready. Nearly a thousand aircraft! Richardson smiled. There wouldn't be enough targets to go around.

"Linebacker Lead, this is Sentry-Delta. Target bearing zero-four-eight, range fifty miles. Course is one-eight-five, speed twenty."

Richardson did not acknowledge the transmission over the encrypted radio link. The flight was under EMCON. Any electronic noise might alert the Soviets. Even his targeting radar was switched off, and only passive infrared and low-light television sensors were operating. He looked quickly left and right. Second-line flyers, hell! he said to himself. Every man in the flight had at least four thousand miles, more than most regular pilots would ever have, more than most of the astronauts, and their birds were maintained by people who tinkered with airplanes because they liked to. The fact of the matter was that his squadron had better aircraft-availability rates than any regular squadron and had had fewer accidents than the wet-nosed hotdogs who flew the warthogs in England and Korea. They'd show the Russkies that.

He smiled to himself. This sure beat flying his DC-9 from Washington to Providence and Hartford and back every day for U.S. Air! Richardson, who had been an air force fighter pilot, had left the service eight years earlier because he craved the higher pay and flashy lifestyle of a commercial airline pilot. He'd missed Vietnam, and commercial flying did not require anything like this degree of skill; it lacked the *rush* of skimming at treetop level.

So far as he knew, the Hog had never been used for maritime strike missions—another part of the message. It was no surprise that she'd be good at it. Her antitank munitions would be effective against ships. Her cannon slugs and Rockeye clusters were designed to shred armored battle tanks, and he had no doubts what they would do to thin-hulled warships. Too bad this wasn't for real. It was about time somebody taught Ivan a lesson.

A radar sensor light blinked on his threat receiver; S-band radar, it was probably meant for surface search, and was not powerful enough for a return yet. The Soviets did not have any aerial radar platforms, and their ship-carried sets were limited by the earth's curvature. The beam was just over his head; he was getting the fuzzy edge of it. They would have avoided detection better still by flying at fifty feet instead of a hundred, but orders were not to.

"Linebacker flight, this is Sentry-Delta. Scatter and head in," the AWACS commanded.

The A-10s separated from their interval of only a few feet to an extended attack formation that left miles between aircraft. The orders were for them to scatter at thirty miles' distance. About four minutes. Richardson checked his digital clock; the Linebacker flight was right on time. Behind them, the Phantoms and Corsairs in the alpha strike would be turning toward the Soviets, just to get their attention. He ought to be seeing them soon . . .

The HUD showed small bumps on the projected horizon— the outer screen of destroyers, the *Udaloys* and *Sovremennys*. The briefing officer had shown them silhouettes and photos of the warships.

Beep! his threat receiver chirped. An X-band missile guidance radar had just swept over his aircraft and lost it, and was now trying to regain contact. Richardson flipped on his ECM (electronic countermeasures) jamming systems. The destroyers were only five miles away now. Forty seconds. Stay dumb, comrades, he thought.

He began to maneuver his aircraft radically, jinking up, down, left, right, in no particular pattern. It was only a game, but there was no sense in giving Ivan an easy time. If this had been for real, his Hogs would be blazing in behind a swarm of antiradar missiles and would be accompanied by Wild Weasel aircraft trying to scramble and kill Soviet missile control systems. Things were moving very fast now. A screening destroyer loomed in his path, and he nudged his rudder to pass clear of her by a quarter mile. Two miles to the *Kirov*—eighteen seconds.

The HUD system painted an intensified image. The *Kirov*'s pyramidal mast-stack-radar structure was filling his windshield. He could see blinking signal lights all around the battle cruiser. Richardson gave more right rudder. They were supposed to pass within three hundred yards of the ship, no more, no less. His Hog would blaze past the bow, the others past the stern and either beam. He didn't want to cut it too close. The major checked to be certain that his bomb and cannon controls were locked in the safe position. No sense getting carried away. About now in a real attack he'd trigger his cannon and a stream of solid slugs would lance the light armor of the *Kirov*'s forward missile magazines, exploding the SAM and cruise missiles in a huge fireball and slicing through the superstructure as if it were thin as newsprint.

At five hundred yards, the captain reached down to arm the flare pod, attached next to the LANTIRN.

Now! He flipped the switch, which deployed half a dozen high-intensity magnesium parachute flares. All four Linebacker aircraft acted within seconds. Suddenly the *Kirov* was inside a box of blue-white magnesium light. Richardson pulled back on his stick, banking into a climbing turn past the battle cruiser. The brilliant light dazzled him, but he could see the graceful lines of the Soviet warship as she was turning hard on the choppy seas, her men running along the deck like ants.

If we were serious, you'd all be dead now—get the message?

Richardson thumbed his radio switch. "Linebacker Lead to Sentry-Delta," he said in the clear. "Robin Hood, repeat, Robin Hood. Linebacker flight, this is lead, form up on me. Let's go home!"

"Linebacker flight, this is Sentry-Delta. Outstanding!" the controller responded. "Be advised that *Kiev* has a pair of Forgers in the air, thirty miles east, heading your way. They'll have to hustle to catch up. Will advise. Out."

Richardson did some fast arithmetic in his head. They probably could not catch up, and even if they did, twelve Phantoms from the 107th Fighter Interceptor Group were ready for it.

"Hot damn, lead!" Linebacker 4, the crop duster, moved gingerly into his slot. "Did you see those turkeys pointing up at us? God damn, did we rattle their cage!"

"Heads up for Forgers," Richardson cautioned, grinning ear to ear inside his oxygen mask. *Second-line flyers, hell!*

"Let 'em come," Linebacker 4 replied. "Any of those bastards closes me and my thirty, it'll be the last mistake he ever makes!" Four was a little too aggressive for Richardson's liking, but the man did not know how to drive his Hog.

"Linebacker flight, this is Sentry-Delta. The Forgers have turned back. You're in the clear. Out."

"Roger that, out. Okay, flight, let's settle down and head home. I guess we've earned our pay for the month." Richardson looked to make sure he was on an open frequency. "Ladies and gentlemen, this is Captain Barry Friendly," he said, using the in-house U.S. Air public relations joke that had become a tradition in the 175th. "I hope you have enjoyed your flight, and thank you for flying Warthog Air."

The *Kirov*

On the *Kirov,* Admiral Stralbo raced from the combat information center to the flag bridge, too late. They had acquired the low-level raiders only a minute from the outer screen. The box of flares was already behind the battle cruiser, several still burning in the water. The bridge crew, he saw, was rattled.

"Sixty to seventy seconds before they were on us, Comrade

Admiral," the flag captain reported, "we were tracking the orbiting attack force and these four—we think, four—racing in under our radar coverage. We had missile lock on two of them despite their jamming."

Stralbo frowned. That performance was not nearly good enough. If the strike had been real, the *Kirov* would have been badly damaged at least. The Americans would gladly trade a pair of fighters for a nuclear powered cruiser. If all American aircraft attacked like this . . .

"The arrogance of the Americans is fantastic!" The fleet *zampolit* swore.

"It was foolish to provoke them," Stralbo observed sourly. "I knew that something like that would happen, but I expected it from *Kennedy*."

"That was a mistake, a pilot error," the political officer replied.

"Indeed, Vasily. And *this* was no mistake! They just sent us a message, telling us that we are fifteen hundred kilometers from their shore without useful air cover, and that they have over five hundred fighters waiting to pounce on us from the west. In the meantime *Kennedy* is stalking us to the east like a rabid wolf. We are not in an attractive position."

"The Americans would not be so brash."

"Are you sure of that, Comrade Political Officer? Sure? What if one of their aircraft commits a 'pilot error'? And sinks one of our destroyers? And what if the American president gets a direct link to Moscow to apologize before we can ever report it? They swear it was an accident and promise to punish the stupid pilot—then what? You think the imperialists are so predictable this close to their own coastline? I do not. I think they are praying for the smallest excuse to pounce on us. Come to my cabin. We must consider this."

The two men went aft. Stralbo's cabin was a spartan affair. The only decoration on the wall was a print of Lenin speaking to Red Guards.

"What is our mission, Vasily?" Stralbo asked.

"To support our submarines, help them to conduct the search—"

"Exactly. Our mission is to support, not to conduct offensive operations. The Americans do not want us here. Objectively,

I can understand this. With all our missiles we are a threat to them."

"But our orders are not to threaten them," the *zampolit* protested. "Why would we want to strike their homeland?"

"And, of course, the imperialists recognize that we are peaceful socialists! Come now, Vasily, these are our enemies! Of course they do not trust us. Of *course* they wish to attack us, given the smallest excuse. They are already interfering with our search, pretending to help. They do not want us here— and in allowing ourselves to be provoked by their aggressive actions, we fall into their trap." The admiral stared down at his desk. "Well, we shall change that. I will order the fleet to discontinue anything that may appear the least bit aggressive. We will end all air operations beyond normal local patrolling. We will not harass their nearby fleet units. We will use only normal navigational radars."

"And?"

"And we will swallow our pride and be as meek as mice. Whatever provocation they make, we will not react to it."

"Some will call this cowardice, Comrade Admiral," the *zampolit* warned.

Stralbo had expected that. "Vasily, don't you see? In pretending to attack us they have already victimized us. They force us to activate our newest and most secret defense systems so they can gather intelligence on our radars and fire control systems. They examine the performance of our fighters and helicopters, the maneuverability of our ships, and most of all, our command and control. We shall put an end to that. Our primary mission is too important. If they continue to provoke us, we will act as though our mission is indeed peaceful— which it is as far as they are concerned—and protest our innocence. And we make them the aggressors. If they continue to provoke us, we shall watch to see what their tactics are, and give them nothing in return. Or would you prefer that they prevent us from carrying out our mission?"

The *zampolit* mumbled his consent. If they failed in their mission, the charge of cowardice would be a small matter indeed. If they found the renegade submarine, they'd be heroes regardless of what else happened.

The Dallas

How long had he been on duty? Jones wondered. He could have checked easily enough by punching the button on his digital watch, but the sonarman didn't want to. It would be too depressing. Me and my big mouth—*you bet, Skipper,* my ass! he swore to himself. He'd detected the sub at a range of about twenty miles, maybe, had just barely gotten her—and the fuckin' Atlantic Ocean was three thousand miles across, at least sixty footprint diameters. He'd need more than luck now.

Well, he did get a Hollywood shower out of it. Ordinarily a shower on a freshwater-poor ship meant a few seconds of wetting down and a minute or so of lathering, followed by a few more seconds of rinsing the suds off. It got you clean but was not very satisfying. This was an improvement over the old days, the oldtimers liked to say. But back then, Jones often responded, the sailors had to pull oars—or run off diesel and batteries, which amounted to the same thing. A Hollywood shower is something a sailor starts thinking about after a few days at sea. You leave the water running, a long, continuous stream of wonderfully warm water. Commander Mancuso was given to awarding this sensuous pastime in return for above-average performance. It gave people something tangible to work for. You couldn't spend extra money on a sub, and there was no beer or women.

Old movies—they were making an effort on that score. The boat's library wasn't bad, when you had time to sort through the jumble. And the *Dallas* had a pair of Apple computers and a few dozen game programs for amusement. Jones was the boat champion at Choplifter and Zork. The computers were also used for training purposes, of course, for practice exams and programmed learning tests that ate up most of the use time.

The *Dallas* was quartering an area east of the Grand Banks. Any boat transiting Route One tended to come through here. They were moving at five knots, trailing out the BQR-15 towed-array sonar. They'd had all kinds of contacts. First, half the submarines in the Russian Navy had whipped by at high speed, many trailed by American boats. An *Alfa* had burned past them at over forty knots, not three thousand yards away. It would have been so easy, Jones had thought at the time. The *Alfa* had been making so much noise that one could have heard it with a glass against the hull, and he'd had to turn his amplifiers down to minimums to keep the noise from ruining his ears. A pity they couldn't have fired. The setup had been so simple, the firing solution so easy that a kid with an old-fashioned sliderule could have done it. That *Alfa* had been meat on the table. The *Victor*s came running next, and the *Charlie*s and *November*s last of all. Jones had been listening to surface ships a ways to the west, a lot of them doing twenty knots or so, making all kinds of noise as they pounded through the waves. They were way far off, and not his concern.

They had been trying to acquire this particular target for over two days, and Jones had had only an odd hour of sleep here and there. Well, that's what they pay me for, he reflected bleakly. This was not unprecedented, he'd done it before, but he'd be happy when the labor ended.

The large-aperture towed array was at the end of a thousand-foot cable. Jones referred to the use of it as trolling for whales. In addition to being their most sensitive sonar rig, it protected the *Dallas* against intruders shadowing her. Ordinarily a submarine's sonar will work in any direction except aft—an area called the cone of silence, or the baffles. The BQR-15 changed that. Jones had heard all sorts of things on it, subs and surface ships all the time, low-flying aircraft on occasion. Once, during an exercise off Florida, it had been the noise of diving pelicans that he could not figure out until the skipper had raised the periscope for a look. Then off Bermuda they had encountered mating humpbacks, and a very impressive noise that was. Jones had a personal copy of the tape of them for use on the beach; some women had found it interesting, in a kinky sort of way. He smiled to himself.

There was a considerable amount of surface noise. The signal processors filtered most of it out, and every few minutes Jones switched them off his channel, getting the sound unimpeded to make sure that they weren't filtering too much out. Machines were dumb; Jones wondered if SAPS might be letting some of that anomalous signal get lost inside the computer chips. That was a problem with computers, really a problem with programming: you'd tell the machine to do something, and it would go do it to the wrong thing. Jones often amused himself working up programs. He knew a few people from college who drew up game programs for personal computers; one of them was making good money with Sierra On-Line Systems . . .

Daydreaming again, Jonesy, he chided himself. It wasn't easy listening to nothing for hours on end. It would have been a good idea, he thought, to let sonarmen read on duty. He had better sense than to suggest it. Mr. Thompson might go along, but the skipper and all the senior officers were ex-reactor types with the usual rule of iron: You shall watch every instrument with absolute concentration all the time. Jones didn't think this was very smart. It was different with sonarmen. They burned out too easily. To combat this Jones had his music tapes and his games. He could lose himself in any sort of diversion, especially Choplifter. A man had to have something, he reasoned, to lose his mind in, at least once a day. And something on duty in some cases. Even truck drivers, hardly the most intellectual of people, had radios and tape players to keep from becoming mesmerized. But sailors on a nuclear sub costing the best part of a billion . . .

Jones leaned forward, pressing the headphones tight against his head. He tore a page of doodles from his scratch pad and noted the time on a fresh sheet. Next he made some adjustments on his gain controls, already near the top of the scale, and flipped off the processors again. The cacophony of surface noise nearly took his head off. Jones tolerated this for a minute, working the manual muting controls to filter out the worst of the high-frequency noise. Aha! Jones said to himself. Maybe SAPS is messing me up a little—too soon to tell for sure.

When Jones had first been checked out on this gear in sonar school he'd had a burning desire to show it to his brother, who had a masters in electrical engineering and worked as a consultant in the recording industry. He had eleven patents to his name. The stuff on the *Dallas* would have knocked his eyes out. The navy's systems for digitalizing sound were years ahead of any commercial technique. Too bad it was all classified right alongside nuclear stuff . . .

"Mr. Thompson," Jones said quietly, not looking around, "can you ask the skipper if maybe we can swing more easterly and drop down a knot or two?"

"Skipper," Thompson went out into the passageway to relay

the request. New course and engine orders were given in fifteen seconds. Mancuso was in sonar ten seconds after that.

The skipper had been sweating this. It had been obvious two days ago that their erstwhile contact had not acted as expected, had not run the route, or had never slowed down. Commander Mancuso had guessed wrong on something—had he also guessed wrong on their visitor's course? And what did it mean if their friend had not run the route? Jones had figured that one out long before. It made her a boomer. Boomer skippers never go fast.

Jones was sitting as usual, hunched over his table, his left hand up commanding quiet as the towed array came around to a precise east-west azimuth at the end of its cable. His cigarette burned away unnoticed in the ashtray. A reel-to-reel tape recorder was operating continuously in the sonar room, its tapes changed hourly and kept for later analysis on shore. Next to it was another whose recordings were used aboard the *Dallas* for reexamination of contacts. He reached up and switched it on, then turned to see his captain looking down at him. Jones' face broke into a thin, tired smile.

"Yeah," he whispered.

Mancuso pointed to the speaker. Jones shook his head. "Too faint, Cap'n. I just barely got it now. Roughly north, I think, but I need some time on that." Mancuso looked at the intensity needle Jones was tapping. It was down to zero—almost. Every fifty seconds or so it twitched, just a little. Jones was making furious notes. "The goddamned SAPS filters are blanking part of this out!!!!! We need smoother amplifiers and better manual filter controls!!" he wrote.

Mancuso told himself that this was faintly ridiculous. He was watching Jones as he had watched his wife when she'd had Dominic and he was timing the twitches on a needle as he had timed his wife's contractions. But there was no thrill to match this. The comparison he used to explain it to his father was the thrill you got on the first day of hunting season, when you hear the leaves rustle and you know it's not a man making the noise. But it was better than that. He was hunting men, men like himself in a vessel like his own...

"Getting louder, Skipper." Jones leaned back and lit a cigarette. "He's heading our way. I make him three-five-zero, maybe more like three-five-three. Still real faint, but that's our boy. We got him." Jones decided to risk an impertinence. He'd earned a little tolerance. "We wait or we chase, sir?"

"We wait. No sense spooking him. We let him come in nice and close while we do our famous imitation of a hole in the water, then we tag along behind him to wax his tail for a while. I want another tape of this set up, and I want the BC-10 to run a SAPS scan. Use the instruction to bypass the processing algorithms. I want this contact analyzed, not interpreted. Run it every two minutes. I want his signature recorded, digitalized, folded, spindled, and mutilated. I want to know everything there is about him, his propulsion noises, his plant signature, the works. I want to know exactly who he is."

"He's a Russkie, sir," Jones observed.

"But which Russkie?" Mancuso smiled.

"Aye, Cap'n." Jones understood. He'd be on duty another two hours, but the end was in sight. Almost. Mancuso sat down and lifted a spare set of headphones, stealing one of Jones' cigarettes. He'd been trying to break the habit for a month. He'd have a better chance on the beach.

HMS Invincible

Ryan was now wearing a Royal Naval uniform. This was temporary. Another mark of how fast this job had been laid on was that he had only the one uniform and two shirts. All of his wardrobe was now being cleaned and in the interim he had on a pair of English-made trousers and a sweater. Typical, he thought—nobody even knows I'm here. They had forgotten him. No messages from the president—not that he'd ever expected one—and Painter and Davenport were only too glad to forget that he was ever on the *Kennedy*. Greer and the judge were probably going over some damned fool thing or another, maybe chuckling to themselves about Jack Ryan having a pleasure cruise at government expense.

It was not a pleasure cruise. Jack had rediscovered his vulnerability to seasickness. The *Invincible* was off Massachusetts, waiting for the Russian surface force and hunting vigorously after the red subs in the area. They were steaming in circles on an ocean that would not settle down. Everyone was busy—

except him. The pilots were up twice a day or more, exercising with their U.S. Air Force and Navy counterparts working from shore bases. The ships were practicing surface warfare tactics. As Admiral White had said at breakfast, it had developed into a jolly good extension of NIFTY DOLPHIN. Ryan didn't like being a supernumerary. Everyone was polite, of course. Indeed, the hospitality was nearly overpowering. He had access to the command center, and when he watched to see how the Brits hunted subs down, everything was explained to him in sufficient detail that he actually understood about half of it.

At the moment he was reading alone in White's sea cabin, which had become his permanent home aboard. Ritter had thoughtfully tucked a CIA staff study into his duffle bag. Entitled "Lost Children: A Psychological Profile of East Bloc Defectors," the three-hundred-page document had been drafted by a committee of psychologists and psychiatrists who worked with the CIA and other intelligence agencies helping defectors settle into American life—and, he was sure, helping spot security risks in the CIA. Not that there were many of those, but there were two sides to everything the Company did.

Ryan admitted to himself that this was pretty interesting stuff. He had never really thought about what makes a defector, figuring that there were enough things happening on the other side of the Iron Curtain to make any rational person want to take whatever chance he got to run west. But it was not that simple, he read, not that simple at all. Everyone who came over was a fairly unique individual. While one might recognize the inequities of life under Communism and yearn for justice, religious freedom, a chance to develop as an individual, another might simply want to get rich, having read about how greedy capitalists exploit the masses and decided that being an exploiter has its good points. Ryan found this interesting if cynical.

Another defector type was the fake, the imposter, someone planted on the CIA as a living piece of disinformation. But this kind of character could cut both ways. He might ultimately turn out to be a genuine defector. America, Ryan smiled, could be pretty seductive to someone used to the gray life in the Soviet Union. Most of the plants, however, were dangerous enemies. For this reason a defector was never trusted. Never. A man who had changed countries once could do it again. Even the idealists had doubts, great pangs of conscience at having deserted their motherland. In a footnote a doctor commented that the most wounding punishment for Aleksander Solzhenitsyn was exile. As a patriot, being alive far from his home was more of a torment than living in a gulag. Ryan found that curious, but enough so to be true.

The rest of the document addressed the problem of getting them settled. Not a few Soviet defectors had committed suicide after a few years. Some had simply been unable to cope with freedom, the way that long-term prison inmates often fail to function without highly structured control over their lives and commit new crimes hoping to return to their safe environment. Over the years the CIA had developed a protocol for dealing with this problem, and a graph in an appendix showed that the severe maladjustment cases were trending dramatically down. Ryan took his time reading. While getting his doctorate in history at Georgetown University he had used a little free time to audit some psychology classes. He had come away with the gut suspicion that shrinks didn't really know much of anything, that they got together and agreed on random ideas they could all use . . . He shook his head. His wife occasionally said that, too. A clinical instructor in ophthalmic surgery on an exchange program at St. Guy's Hospital in London, Caroline Ryan regarded everything as cut and dried. If someone had eye trouble, she would either fix it or not fix it. A mind was different, Jack decided after reading through the document a second time, and each defector had to be treated as an individual, handled carefully by a sympathetic case officer who had both the time and inclination to look after him properly. He wondered if he'd be good at it.

Admiral White walked in. "Bored, Jack?"

"Not exactly, Admiral. When do we make contact with the Soviets?"

"This evening. Your chaps have given them a very rough time over that Tomcat incident."

"Good. Maybe people will wake up before something really bad happens."

"You think it will?" White sat down.

"Well, Admiral, if they really are hunting a missing sub, yes. If not, then they're here for another purpose entirely, and

I've guessed wrong. Worse than that, I'll have to live with that misjudgment—or die with it."

Norfolk Naval Medical Center

Tait was feeling better. Dr. Jameson had taken over for several hours, allowing him to curl up on a couch in the doctor's lounge for five hours. That was the most sleep he ever seemed to get in one shot, but it was sufficient to make him look indecently chipper to the rest of the floor staff. He made a quick phone call and some milk was sent up. As a Mormon, Tait avoided everything with caffeine—coffee, tea, even cola drinks—and though this type of self-discipline was unusual for a physician, to say nothing of a uniformed officer, he scarcely thought about it except on rare occasions when he pointed out its longevity benefits to his brother practitioners. Tait drank his milk and shaved in the restroom, emerging ready to face another day.

"Any word on the radiation exposure, Jamie?"

The radiology lab had struck out. "They brought a nucleonics officer over from a sub tender, and he scanned the clothes. There was a possible twenty-rad contamination, not enough for frank physiological effects. I think what it might have been was that the nurse took the sample from the back of his hand. The extremities might still have been suffering from the vascular shutdown. That could explain the depleted white count. Maybe."

"How is he otherwise?"

"Better. Not much, but better. I think maybe the keflin's taking hold." The doctor flipped open the chart. "White count is coming back. I put a unit of whole blood into him two hours ago. The blood chemistry is approaching normal limits. Blood pressure is one hundred over sixty-five, heart rate is ninety-four. Temperature ten minutes ago was 100.8—it's been fluctuating for several hours.

"His heart looks pretty good. In fact, I think he's going to make it, unless something unexpected crops up." Jameson reminded himself that in extreme hypothermia cases the unexpected can take a month or more to appear.

Tait examined the chart, remembering what he had been like years ago. A bright young doc, just like Jamie, certain that he could cure the world. It was a good feeling. A pity that experience—in his case, two years at Danang—beat that out of you. Jamie was right, though; there was enough improvement here to make the patient's chances appear measurably better.

"What are the Russians doing?" Tait asked.

"Petchkin has the watch at the moment. When it came his turn, and he changed into scrubs—you know he has that Captain Smirnov holding onto his clothes, like he expected us to steal them or something?"

Tait explained that Petchkin was a KGB agent.

"No kidding? Maybe he has a gun tucked away." Jameson chuckled. "If he does, he'd better watch it. We got three marines up here with us."

"Marines. What for?"

"Forgot to tell you. Some reporter found out we had a Russkie up here and tried to bluff his way onto the floor. A nurse stopped him. Admiral Blackburn found out and went ape. The whole floor's sealed off. What's the big secret, anyway?"

"Beats me, but that's the way it is. What do you think of this Petchkin guy?"

"I don't know. I've never met any Russians before. They don't smile a whole lot. The way they're taking turns watching the patient, you'd think they expect us to make off with him."

"Or maybe that he'll say something they don't want us to hear?" Tait wondered. "Did you get the feeling that they might not want him to make it? I mean, when they didn't want to tell us about what his sub was?"

Jameson thought about that. "No. The Russians are supposed to make a secret of everything, aren't they? Anyway, Smirnov did come through with it."

"Get some sleep, Jamie."

"Aye, Cap'n." Jameson walked off toward the lounge.

We asked them what kind of a sub, the captain thought, meaning whether it was a nuke or not. What if they thought we were asking if it was a missile sub? That makes sense, doesn't it? Yeah. A missile sub right off our coast, and all this activity in the North Atlantic. Christmas season. Dear God! If they were going to do it, they'd do it right now, wouldn't they? He walked down the hall. A nurse came out of the room with a blood sample to be taken down to the lab. This was being done hourly, and it left Petchkin alone with the patient for a few minutes.

Tait walked around the corner and saw Petchkin through the window, sitting in a chair at the corner of the bed and watching his countryman, who was still unconscious. He had on green scrubs. Made to put on in a hurry, these were reversible, with a pocket on both sides so a surgeon didn't have to waste a second to see if they were inside out. As Tait watched, Petchkin reached for something through the low collar.

"Oh, God!" Tait raced around the corner and shot through the swinging door. Petchkin's look of surprise changed to amazement as the doctor batted a cigarette and lighter from his hand, then to outrage as he was lifted from his chair and flung towards the door. Tait was the smaller of the two, but his sudden burst of energy was sufficient to eject the man from the room. "Security!" Tait screamed.

"What is the meaning of this?" Petchkin demanded. Tait was holding him in a bearhug. Immediately he heard feet racing down the hall from the lobby.

"What is it, sir?" A breathless marine lance corporal with a .45 Colt in his right hand skidded to a halt on the tile floor.

"This man just tried to kill my patient!"

"What!" Petchkin's face was crimson.

"Corporal, your post is now at that door. If this man tries to get into that room, you will stop him any way you have to. Understood?"

"Aye aye, sir!" the corporal looked at the Russian. "Sir, would you please step away from the door?"

"What is the meaning of this outrage!"

"Sir, you will step away from the door, right now." The marine holstered his pistol.

"What is going on here?" It was Ivanov, who had sense enough to ask this question in a quiet voice from ten feet away.

"Doctor, do you want your sailor to survive or not?" Tait asked, trying to calm himself.

"What—of course we wish him to survive. How can you ask this?"

"Then why did Comrade Petchkin just try to kill him?"

"I did not do such a thing!" Petchkin shouted.

"What did he do, exactly?" Ivanov asked.

Before Tait could answer, Petchkin spoke rapidly in Russian, then switched to English. "I was reaching for a smoke, that is all. I have no weapon. I wish to kill no one. I only wish to have a cigarette."

"We have No Smoking signs all over the floor, except in the lobby—you didn't see them? You were in a room in intensive care, with a patient on hundred-percent oxygen, the air and bedclothes saturated with oxygen, and you were going to flick your goddamned Bic!" The doctor rarely used profanity. "Oh sure, you'd get burned some, and it would look like an accident—and that kid would be dead! I know what you are, Petchkin, and I don't think you're that stupid. Get off my floor!"

The nurse, who had been watching this, went into the patient's room. She came back out with a pack of cigarettes, two loose ones, a plastic butane lighter, and a curious look on her face.

Petchkin was ashen. "Dr. Tait, I assure you that I had no such intention. What are you saying would happen?"

"Comrade Petchkin," Ivanov said slowly in English, "there would be an explosion and fire. You cannot have a flame near oxygen."

"Nichevo!" Petchkin finally realized what he had done. He had waited for the nurse to leave—medical people never let you smoke when you ask. He didn't know the first thing about hospitals, and as a KGB agent he was accustomed to doing whatever he wanted. He started speaking to Ivanov in Russian. The Soviet doctor looked like a parent listening to a child's explanation for a broken glass. His response was spirited.

For his part, Tait began to wonder if he hadn't overreacted—anyone who smoked was an idiot to begin with.

"Dr. Tait," Petchkin said finally, "I swear to you that I had no idea of this oxygen business. Perhaps I am a fool."

"Nurse," Tait turned, "we will not leave this patient unattended by our personnel at any time—never. Have a corpsman come to pick up the blood samples and anything else. If you have to go to the head, get relief first."

"Yes, Doctor."

"No more screwing around, Mr. Petchkin. Break the rules

again, sir, and you're off the floor again. Do you understand?"

"It will be as you say, Doctor, and allow me, please, to apologize."

"You stay put," Tait said to the marine. He walked away shaking his head angrily, mad at the Russians, embarrassed with himself, wishing he were back at Bethesda where he belonged, and wishing he knew how to swear coherently. He took the service elevator down to the first floor and spent five minutes looking for the intelligence officer who had flown down with him. Ultimately he found him in a game room playing Pac Man. They conferred in the hospital administrator's vacant office.

"You really thought he was trying to kill the guy?" the commander asked incredulously.

"What was I supposed to think?" Tait demanded. "What do you think?"

"I think he just screwed up. They want that kid alive—no, first they want him talking—more than you do."

"How do you know that?"

"Petchkin calls their embassy every hour. We have the phones tapped, of course. How do you think?"

"What if it's a trick?"

"If he's that good an actor he belongs in the movies. You keep that kid alive, Doctor, and leave the rest to us. Good idea to have the marine close, though. That'll rattle 'em a bit. Never pass up a chance to rattle 'em. So, when will he be conscious?"

"No telling. He's still feverish, and very weak. Why do they want him to talk?" Tait asked.

"To find out what sub he was on. Petchkin's KGB contact blurted that out on the phone—sloppy! *Very* sloppy! They must be real excited about this."

"Do we know what sub it was?"

"Sure," the intelligence officer said mischievously.

"Then what's going on, for Lord's sake!"

"Can't say, Doc." The commander smiled as if he knew, though he was as much in the dark as anyone.

Norfolk Naval Shipyard

The USS *Scamp* sat at the dock while a large overhead crane settled the *Avalon* in its support rack. The captain watched impatiently from atop the sail. He and his boat had been called in from hunting a pair of *Victor*s, and he did not like it one bit. The attack boat skipper had only run a DSRV exercise a few weeks before, and right now he had better things to do than play mother whale to this damned useless toy. Besides, having the minisub perched on his after escape trunk would knock ten knots off his top speed. And there'd be four more men to bunk and feed. The *Scamp* was not all that large.

At least they'd get good food out of this. The *Scamp* had been out five weeks when the recall order arrived. Their supply of fresh vegetables was exhausted, and they availed themselves of the opportunity to have fresh food trucked down to the dock. A man tires quickly of three-bean salad. Tonight they'd have real lettuce, tomatoes, fresh corn instead of canned. But that didn't make up for the fact that there were Russians out there to worry about.

"All secure?" the captain called down to the curved after deck.

"Yes, Captain. We're ready when you are," Lieutenant Ames answered.

"Engine room," the captain called down on intercom. "I want you ready to answer bells in ten minutes."

"Ready now, Skipper."

A harbor tug was standing by to help maneuver them from the dock. Ames had their orders, something else that the captain didn't like. Surely they would not be doing any more hunting, not with that damned *Avalon* strapped on.

The Red October

"Look here, Svyadov," Melekhin pointed, "I will show you how a saboteur thinks."

The lieutenant came over and looked. The chief engineer was pointing at an inspection valve on the heat exchanger. Before he got an explanation, Melekhin went to the bulkhead phone.

"Comrade Captain, this is Melekhin. I have found it. I require the reactor to be stopped for an hour. We can operate the caterpillar on batteries, no?"

"Of course, Comrade Chief Engineer," Ramius said, "proceed."

Melekhin turned to the assistant engineering officer. "You will shut the reactor down and connect the batteries to the caterpillar motors."

"At once, Comrade." The officer began to work the controls.

The time taken to find the leak had been a burden on everyone. Once they had discovered that the Geiger counters were sabotaged and Melekhin and Borodin had repaired them, they had begun a complete check of the reactor spaces, a devilishly tricky task. There had never been a question of a major steam leak, else Svyadov would have gone looking for it with a broomstick—even a tiny leak could easily shave off an arm. They reasoned that it had to be a small leak in the low-pressure part of the system. Didn't it? It was the not knowing that had troubled everyone.

The check made by the chief engineer and executive officer had lasted no less than eight hours, during which the reactor had again been shut down. This cut all electricity off throughout the ship except for emergency lights and the caterpillar motors. Even the air systems had been curtailed. That had set the crew muttering to themselves.

The problem was, Melekhin could still not find the leak, and when the badges had been developed a day earlier, there was nothing on them! How was this possible?

"Come, Svyadov, tell me what you see." Melekhin came back over and pointed.

"The water test valve." Opened only in port, when the reactor was cold, it was used to flush the cooling system and to check for unusual water contamination. The thing was grossly unremarkable, a heavy-duty valve with a large wheel. The spout underneath it, below the pressurized part of the pipe, was threaded rather than welded.

"A large wrench, if you please, Lieutenant. Melekhin was drawing the lesson out, Svyadov thought. He was the slowest of teachers when he was trying to communicate something important. Svyadov returned with a meter-long pipe wrench. The chief engineer waited until the plant was closed down, then double-checked a gauge to make sure the pipes were depressurized. He was a careful man. The wrench was set on the fitting, and he turned it. It came off easily.

"You see, Comrade Lieutenant, the threads on the pipe actually go up onto the valve casing. Why is this permitted?"

"The threads are on the outside of the pipe, Comrade. The valve itself bears the pressure. The fitting which is screwed on is merely a directional spigot. The nature of the union does not compromise the pressure loop."

"Correct. A screw fitting is not strong enough for the plant's total pressure." Melekhin worked the fitting all the way off with his hands. It was perfectly machined, the threads still bright from the original engine work. "And there is the sabotage."

"I don't understand."

"Someone thought this one over very carefully, Comrade Lieutenant." Melekhin's voice was half admiration, half rage. "At normal operating pressure, cruising speed, that is, the system is pressurized to eight kilograms per square centimeter, correct?"

"Yes, Comrade, and at full power the pressure is ninety percent higher." Svyadov knew all this by heart.

"But we rarely go to full power. What we have here is a dead-end section of the steam loop. Now, here a small hole has been drilled, not even a millimeter. Look." Melekhin bent over to examine it himself. Svyadov was happy to keep his distance. "Not even a millimeter. The saboteur took the fitting off, drilled the hole, and put it back. The tiny hole permits a minuscule amount of steam to escape, but only very slowly. The steam cannot go up, because the fitting sits against this flange. Look at this machine work! It is perfect, you see, perfect! The steam, therefore, cannot escape upward. It can only force its way down the threads around and around, ultimately escaping inside the spout. Just enough. Just enough to contaminate this compartment by a tiny amount." Melekhin looked up. "Someone was a very clever man. Clever enough to know exactly how this system works. When we reduced power to check for the leak before, there was not enough pressure remaining in the loop to force the steam down the threads, and we could not find the leak. There is only enough pressure at normal power levels—but if you suspect a leak, you power-down the system. And if we had gone to maximum power, who can say what might have happened?" Melekhin shook his head in admiration. "Someone was very, very clever.

I hope I meet him. Oh, I hope I meet this clever man. For when I do, I will take a pair of large steel pliers—," Melekhin's voice lowered to a whisper, "—and I will crush his balls! Get me the small electric welding set, Comrade. I can fix this myself in a few minutes."

Captain First Rank Melekhin was as good as his word. He wouldn't let anyone near the job. It was his plant, and his responsibility. Svyadov was just as happy for that. A tiny bead of stainless steel was worked into the fault, and Melekhin filed it down with jeweler's tools to protect the threads. Then he brushed rubber-based sealant onto the threads and worked the fitting back into place. The whole procedure took twenty-eight minutes by Svyadov's watch. As they had told him in Leningrad, Melekhin was the best engineer in submarines.

"A static pressure test, eight kilograms," he ordered the assistant engineer officer.

The reactor was reactivated. Five minutes later the pressure went all the way to normal power. Melekhin held a counter under the spout for ten minutes—and got nothing, even on the number two setting. He walked to the phone to tell the captain the leak was fixed.

Melekhin had the enlisted men let back into the compartment to return the tools to their places.

"You see how it is done, Lieutenant?"

"Yes, Comrade. Was that one leak sufficient to cause all of our contamination?"

"Obviously."

Svyadov wondered about this. The reactor spaces were nothing but a collection of pipes and fittings, and this bit of sabotage could not have taken long. What if other such time bombs were hidden in the system?

"Perhaps you worry too much, Comrade," Melekhin said. "Yes, I have considered this. When we get to Cuba, I will have a full-power static test made to check the whole system, but for the moment I do not think this is a good idea. We will continue the two-hour watch cycle. There is the possibility that one of our own crewmen is the saboteur. If so, I will not have people in these spaces long enough to commit more mischief. You will watch the crew closely."

THE TWELFTH DAY

TUESDAY, 14 DECEMBER

The Dallas

"Crazy Ivan!" Jones shouted loudly enough to be heard in the attack center. "Turning to starboard!"

"Skipper!" Thompson repeated the warning.

"All stop!" Mancuso ordered quickly. "Rig ship for ultra-quiet!"

A thousand yards ahead of the *Dallas*, her contact had just begun a radical turn to the right. She had been doing so about every two hours since they had regained contact, though not regularly enough for the *Dallas* to settle into a comfortable pattern. *Whoever is driving that boomer knows his business,* Mancuso thought. The Soviet missile submarine was making a complete circle so her bow-mounted sonar could check for anyone hiding in her baffles.

Countering this maneuver was more than just tricky—it was dangerous, especially the way Mancuso did it. When the *Red*

October changed course, her stern, like those of all ships, moved in the direction opposite the turn. She was a steel barrier directly in the *Dallas'* path for as long as it took her to move through the first part of the turn, and the 7,000-ton attack submarine took a lot of space to stop.

The exact number of collisions that had occurred between Soviet and American submarines was a closely guarded secret; that there had been such collisions was not. One characteristically Russian tactic for forcing Americans to keep their distance was a stylized turn called the Crazy Ivan in the U.S. Navy.

The first few hours they had trailed this contact, Mancuso had been careful to keep his distance. He had learned that the submarine was not turning quickly. She was, rather, maneuvering in a leisurely manner, and seemed to ascend fifty to eighty feet as she turned, banking almost like an aircraft. He suspected that the Russian skipper was not using his full maneuverability—an intelligent thing for a captain to do, keeping some of his performance in reserve as a surprise. These facts allowed the *Dallas* to trail very closely indeed and gave Mancuso a chance to chop his speed and drift forward so that he barely avoided the Russian's stern. He was getting good at it— a little too good, his officers were whispering. The last time they had not missed the Russian's screws by more than a hundred fifty yards. The contact's large turning circle was taking her completely around the *Dallas* as the latter sniffed at her prey's trail.

Avoiding collision was the most dangerous part of the maneuver, but not the only part. The *Dallas* also had to remain invisible to her quarry's passive sonar systems. For her to do so the engineers had to cut power in their S6G reactor to a tiny fraction of its total output. Fortunately the reactor was able to run on such low power without the use of a coolant pump, since coolant could be transferred by normal convection circulation. In addition, a strict silent ship routine was enforced. No activity on the *Dallas* that might generate noise was permitted, and the crew took it seriously enough that even ordinary conversations in the mess were muted.

"Speed coming down," Lieutenant Goodman reported. Mancuso decided that the *Dallas* would not be part of a ramming this time and went aft to sonar.

"Target is still turning right," Jones reported quietly. "Ought to be clear now. Distance to the stern, maybe two hundred yards, maybe a shade less . . . Yeah, we're clear now, bearing is changing more rapidly. Speed and engine noises are constant. A slow turn to the right." Jones caught the captain out of the corner of his eye and turned to hazard an observation. "Skipper, this guy is real confident in himself. I mean, *real* confident."

"Explain," Mancuso said, figuring he knew the answer.

"Cap'n, he's not chopping speed the way we do, and we turn a lot sharper than this. It's almost like—like he's doing this out of habit, y'know? Like he's in a hurry to get somewhere, and really doesn't think anybody can track—wait . . . Yeah, okay, he's just about reversed course now, bearing off the starboard bow, say half a mile . . . Still doing the slow turn. He'll go right around us again. Sir, if he knows anybody's back here, he's playing it awful cool. What do you think, Frenchie?"

Chief Sonarman Laval shook his head. "He don't know we're here." The chief didn't want to say anything else. He thought Mancuso's close tailing was reckless. The man had balls, playing with a 688 like this, but one little screw-up and he'd find himself with a pail and shovel, on the beach.

"Passing down the starboard side. No pinging." Jones took out his calculator and punched in some numbers. "Sir, this angular turn rate at this speed makes the range about a thousand yards. You suppose his funny drive system goofs up his rudders any?"

"Maybe." Mancuso took a spare set of phones and plugged them in to listen.

The noise was the same. A swish, and every forty or fifty seconds an odd, low-frequency rumble. This close they could also hear the gurgling and throbbing of the reactor pump. There was a sharp sound, maybe a cook moving a pan on a metal grate. No silent ship drill on this boat. Mancuso smiled to himself. It was like being a cat burglar, hanging this close to an enemy submarine—no, not an enemy, not exactly—hearing everything. In better acoustical conditions they could have heard conversations. Not well enough to understand them, of course, but as if they were at a dinner party listening to the gabble of a dozen couples at once.

"Passing aft and still circling. His turning radius must be a good thousand yards," Mancuso observed.

"Yes, Cap'n, about that," Jones agreed.

"He just can't be using all his rudder, and you're right, Jonesy, he is very damned casual about this. Hmph, the Russians are all supposed to be paranoid—not this boy." So much the better, Mancuso thought.

If he were going to hear the *Dallas* it would be now, with the bow-mounted sonar pointed almost directly at them. Mancuso took off his headphones to listen to his boat. The *Dallas* was a tomb. The words *Crazy Ivan* had been passed, and within seconds his crew had responded. How do you reward a whole crew? Mancuso wondered. He knew he worked them hard, sometimes too hard—but damn! Did they deliver!

"Port beam," Jones said. "Exactly abeam now, speed unchanged, traveling a little straighter, maybe, distance about eleven hundred, I think." The sonarman took a handkerchief from his back pocket and used it to wipe his hands.

There's tension all right, but you'd never know it listening to the kid, the captain thought. Everyone in his crew was acting like a professional.

"He's passed us. On the port bow, and I think the turn has stopped. Betcha he's settled back down on one-nine-zero." Jones looked up with a grin. "We did it again, Skipper."

"Okay. Good work, you men." Mancuso went back to the attack center. Everyone was waiting expectantly. The *Dallas* was dead in the water, drifting slowly downward with her slight negative trim.

"Let's get the engines turned back on. Build her up slowly to thirteen knots." A few seconds later an almost imperceptible noise began as the reactor plant increased power. A moment after that the speed gauge twitched upward. The *Dallas* was moving again.

"Attention, this is the captain speaking," Mancuso said into the sound-powered communications system. The electrically powered speakers were turned off, and his word would be relayed by watchstanders in all compartments. "They circled us again without picking us up. Well done, everybody. We can all breathe again." He placed the handset back in its holder. "Mr. Goodman, let's get back on her tail."

"Aye, Skipper. Left five degrees rudder, helm."

"Left five degrees rudder, aye." The helmsman acknowledged the order, turning his wheel as he did so. Ten minutes later the *Dallas* was back astern of her contact.

A constant fire control solution was set up on the attack director. The Mark 48 torpedoes would barely have sufficient distance to arm themselves before striking the target in twenty-nine seconds.

Ministry of Defense, Moscow

"And how are you feeling, Misha?"

Mikhail Semyonovich Filitov looked up from a large pile of documents. He looked flushed and feverish still. Dmitri Ustinov, the defense minister, worried about his old friend. He should have stayed in the hospital another few days as the doctors had advised. But Misha had never been one to take advice, only orders.

"I feel good, Dmitri. Any time you walk out of a hospital you feel good—even if you are dead," Filitov smiled.

"You still look sick," Ustinov observed.

"Ah! At our age you always look sick. A drink, Comrade Defense Minister?" Filitov hoisted a bottle of Stolychnaya vodka from a desk drawer.

"You drink too much, my friend," Ustinov chided.

"I do not drink enough. A bit more antifreeze and I would not have caught cold last week." He poured two tumblers half full and held one out to his guest. "Here, Dmitri, it is cold outside."

Both men tipped their glasses, took a gulp of the clear liquid, and expelled their breath with an explosive *pah*.

"I feel better already." Filitov's laugh was hoarse. "Tell me, what became of that Lithuanian renegade?"

"We're not sure," Ustinov said.

"Still? Can you tell me now what his letter said?"

Ustinov took another swallow before explaining. When he finished the story Filitov was leaning forward at his desk, shocked.

"Mother of God! And he has still not been found? How many heads?"

"Admiral Korov is dead. He was arrested by the KGB, of

course, and died of a brain hemorrhage soon thereafter."

"A nine-millimeter hemorrhage, I trust," Filitov observed
coldly. "How many times have I said it? What goddamned use
is a navy? Can we use it against the Chinese? Or the NATO
armies that threaten us—no! How many rubles does it cost to
build and fuel those pretty barges for Gorshkov, and what do
we get for it—nothing! Now he loses one submarine and the
whole fucking fleet cannot find it. It is a good thing that Stalin
is not alive."

Ustinov agreed. He was old enough to remember what happened then to anyone who reported results short of total success.
"In any case, Padorin may have saved his skin. There is one
extra element of control on the submarine."

"Padorin!" Filitov took another gulp of his drink. "That
eunuch! I've only met him, what, three times. A cold fish,
even for a commissar. He never laughs, even when he drinks.
Some Russian he is. Why is it, Dmitri, that Gorshkov keeps
so many old farts like that around?"

Ustinov smiled into his drink. "The same reason I do, Misha."
Both men laughed.

"So, how will Comrade Padorin save our secrets and keep
his skin? Invent a time machine?"

Ustinov explained to his old friend. There weren't many
men whom the defense minister could speak to and feel comfortable with. Filitov drew the pension of a full colonel of tanks
and still wore the uniform proudly. He had faced combat for
the first time on the fourth day of the Great Patriotic War, as
the Fascist invaders were driving east. Lieutenant Filitov had
met them southeast of Brest Litovsk with a troop of T-34/76
tanks. A good officer, he had survived his first encounter with
Guderian's panzers, retreated in good order, and fought a constant mobile action for days before being caught in the great
encirclement at Minsk. He had fought his way out of that trap,
and later another at Vyasma, and had commanded a battalion
spearheading Zhukov's counterblow from the suburbs of Moscow. In 1942 Filitov had taken part in the disastrous counter-
offensive toward Kharkov but again escaped, this time on foot,
leading the battered remains of regiment from that dreadful
cauldron on the Dnieper River. With another regiment later
that year he had led the drive that shattered the Italian Army

on the flank of Stalingrad and encircled the Germans. He'd been wounded twice in that campaign. Filitov had acquired the reputation of a commander who was both good and lucky. That luck had run out at Kursk, where he had battled the troopers of SS division *Das Reich*. Leading his men into a furious tank battle, Filitov and his vehicle had run straight into an ambush of eighty-eight-millimeter guns. That he had survived at all was a miracle. His chest still bore the scars from the burning tank, and his right arm was next to useless. This was enough to retire a charging tactical commander who had won the old star of the Hero of the Soviet Union no less than three times, and a dozen other decorations.

After months of being shuttled from one hospital to another, he had become a representative of the Red Army in the armament factories that had been moved to the Urals east of Moscow. The drive that made him a premiere combat soldier would come to serve the State even better behind the lines. A born organizer, Filitov learned to run roughshod over factory bosses to streamline production, and he cajoled design engineers to make the small but often crucial changes in their products that would save crews and win battles.

It was in these factories that Filitov and Ustinov first met, the scarred combat veteran and the gruff apparatchik detailed by Stalin to produce enough tools to drive the hated invaders back. After a few clashes, the young Ustinov came to recognize that Filitov was totally fearless and would not be bullied on a question involving quality control or fighting efficiency. In the midst of one disagreement, Filitov had practically dragged Ustinov into the turret of a tank and taken it through a combat training course to make his point. Ustinov was the sort who only had to be shown something once, and they soon became fast friends. He could not fail to admire the courage of a soldier who could say no to the people's commissar of armaments. By mid-1944 Filitov was a permanent part of his staff, a special inspector—in short, a hatchet man. When there was a problem at a factory, Filitov saw that it was settled, quickly. The three gold stars and the crippling injuries were usually enough to persuade the factory bosses to mend their ways—and if not, Misha had the booming voice and vocabulary to make a sergeant major wince.

Never a high Party official, Filitov gave his boss valuable input from people in the field. He still worked closely with the tank design and production teams, often taking a prototype or randomly chosen production model through a test course with a team of picked veterans to see for himself how well things worked. Crippled arm or not, it was said that Filitov was among the best gunners in the Soviet Union. And he was a humble man. In 1965 Ustinov thought to surprise his friend with general's stars and was somewhat angered by Filitov's reaction—he had not earned them on the field of battle, and that was the only way a man could earn stars. A rather impolitic remark, as Ustinov wore the uniform of a marshal of the Soviet Union, earned for his Party work and industrial management, it nevertheless demonstrated that Filitov was a true New Soviet Man, proud of what he was and mindful of his limitations.

It is unfortunate, Ustinov thought, that Misha has been so unlucky otherwise. He had been married to a lovely woman, Elena Filitov, who had been a minor dancer with the Kirov when the youthful officer had met her. Ustinov remembered her with a trace of envy; she had been the perfect soldier's wife. She had given the State two fine sons. Both were now dead. The elder had died in 1956, still a boy, an officer cadet sent to Hungary because of his political reliability and killed by counterrevolutionaries before his seventeenth birthday. He was a soldier who had taken a soldier's chance. But the younger had been killed in a training accident, blown to pieces by a faulty breech mechanism in a brand-new T-55 tank in 1959. That had been a disgrace. And Elena had died soon thereafter, of grief more than anything else. Too bad.

Filitov had not changed all that much. He drank too much, like many soldiers, but he was a quiet drunk. In 1961 or so, Ustinov remembered, he had taken to cross-country skiing. It made him healthier and tired him out, which was probably what he really wanted, along with the solitude. He was still a fine listener. When Ustinov had a new idea to float before the Politburo, he usually tried it out on Filitov first to get his reaction. Not a sophisticated man, Filitov was an uncommonly shrewd one who had a soldier's instinct for finding weaknesses and exploiting strengths. His value as a liaison officer was unsurpassed. Few men living had three gold stars won on the field of battle. That got him attention, and it still made officers far his senior listen to him.

"So, Dmitri Fedorovich, do you think this would work? Can one man destroy a submarine?" Filitov asked. "You know, rockets, I don't."

"Certainly. It's merely a question of mathematics. There is enough energy in a rocket to melt the submarine."

"And what of our man?" Filitov asked. Always the combat soldier, he would be the type to worry about a brave man alone in enemy territory.

"We will do our best, of course, but there is not much hope."

"He must be rescued, Dmitri! Must! You forget, young men like that have a value beyond their deeds, they are not mere machines who perform their duties. They are symbols for our other young officers, and alive they are worth a hundred new tanks or ships. Combat is like that, Comrade. We have forgotten this—and look what has happened in Afghanistan!"

"You are correct, my friend, but—only a few hundred kilometers from the American coast, if that much?"

"Gorshkov talks so much about what his navy can do, let him do this!" Filitov poured another glass. "One more, I think."

"You are not going skiing again, Misha." Ustinov noted that he often fortified himself before driving his car to the woods east of Moscow. "I will not permit it."

"Not today, Dmitri, I promise—though I think it would do me good. Today I will go to the *banya* to take steam and sweat the rest of the poisons from this old carcass. Will you join me?"

"I have to work late."

"The *banya* is good for you," Filitov persisted. It was a waste of time, and both knew it. Ustinov was a member of the "nobility" and would not mingle in the public steam baths. Misha had no such pretentions.

The Dallas

Exactly twenty-four hours after reacquiring the *Red October*, Mancuso called a conference of his senior officers in the wardroom. Things had settled down somewhat. Mancuso had even managed to squeeze in a couple of four-hour naps and was feeling vaguely human again. They now had time to build an accurate sonar picture of the quarry, and the computer was refining a signature classification that would be out to the other fleet attack boats in a matter of weeks. From trailing they had a very accurate model of the propulsion system's noise characteristics, and from the bihourly circling they had also built a picture of the boat's size and power plant specifications.

The executive officer, Wally Chambers, twirled a pencil in his fingers like a baton. "Jonesy's right. It's the same power plant that the *Oscar*s and *Typhoon*s have. They've quieted it down, but the gross signature characteristics are virtually identical. Question is, what's it turning? It sounds like the propellers are ducted somehow, or shrouded. A directional prop with a collar around it, maybe, or some sort of tunnel drive. Didn't we try that once?"

"Long time ago," Lieutenant Butler, the engineering officer, said. "I heard a story about it while I was at Arco. It didn't work out, but I don't remember why. Whatever it is, it's really knocked down on the propulsion noises. That rumble though . . . It's some sort of harmonic all right—but a harmonic what? You know, except for that we'd never have picked it up in the first place."

"Maybe," Mancuso said. "Jonesy says that the signal processors have tended to filter this noise out, almost as though the Soviets know what SAPS does and have tailored a system to beat it. But that's hard to believe." There was general agreement on this point. Everyone knew the principles on which SAPS operated, but there were probably not fifty men in the country who could really explain the nuts and bolts details.

"We're agreed she's a boomer?" Mancuso asked.

Butler nodded. "No way you could fit that power plant into an attack hull. More important, she acts like a boomer."

"Could be an *Oscar,*" Chambers suggested.

"No. Why send an *Oscar* this far south? *Oscar*'s an antiship platform. Uh-uh, this guy's driving a boomer. He ran the route at the speed he's running now—and that's acting like a missile boat," Lieutenant Mannion noted. "What are they up to with all this other activity? That's the real question. Maybe trying to sneak up on our coast—just to see if they can do it. It's been done before, and all this other activity makes for a hell of a diversion."

They all considered that. The trick had been tried before by both sides. Most recently, in 1978, a Soviet *Yankee*-class missile sub had closed to the edge of the continental shelf off the coast of New England. The evident objective had been to see if the United States could detect it or not. The navy had succeeded, and then the question had been whether or not to react and let the Soviets know.

"Well, I think we can leave the grand strategy to the folks on the beach. Let's phone this one in. Lieutenant Mannion, tell the OOD to get us to periscope depth in twenty minutes. We'll try to slip away and back without his noticing." Mancuso frowned. This was never easy.

A half an hour later the *Dallas* radioed her message.

Z140925ZDEC

TOP SECRET THEO

FR: USS DALLAS

TO: COMSUBLANT

INFO: CINCLANTFLT

A. USS DALLAS Z090414ZDEC

1. ANOMALOUS CONTACT REACQUIRED 0538Z 13DEC. CURRENT POSITION LAT 42° 35' LONG 49° 12'. COURSE 194 SPEED 13 DEPTH 600. HAVE TRACKED 24 HOURS WITHOUT COUNTERDETECTION. CONTACT EVALUATED AS REDFLEET SSBN GROSS SIZE, ENGINE CHARACTERISTICS INDICATIVE TYPHOON CLASS. HOWEVER CONTACT USING NEW DRIVE SYSTEM NOT REPEAT NOT PROPELLERS. HAVE ESTABLISHED DETAILED SIGNATURE PROFILE.
2. RETURNING TO TRACKING OPERATIONS. REQUEST ADDITIONAL OPAREA ASSIGNMENTS. AWAIT REPLY 1030Z.

COMSUBLANT Operations

"Bingo!" Gallery said to himself. He walked back to his office, careful to close the door before lifting the scrambled line to Washington.

"Sam, this is Vince. Listen up: *Dallas* reports she is tracking a Russian boomer with a new kind of quiet drive system, about six hundred miles southwest of the Grand Banks, course one-nine-four, speed thirteen knots."

"All right! That's Mancuso?" Dodge said.

"Bartolomeo Vito Mancuso, my favorite Guinea," Gallery confirmed. Getting him this command had not been easy because of his age. Gallery had gone the distance for him. "I told you the kid was good, Sam."

"Jesus, you see how close they are to the *Kiev* group?" Dodge was looking at his tactical display.

"They are cutting it close," Gallery agreed. *"Invincible's* not too far away, though, and I have *Pogy* out there, too. We moved her off the shelf when we called *Scamp* back in. I figure *Dallas* will need help. The question is how obvious do we want to be."

"Not very. Look, Vince, I have to talk to Dan Foster about this."

"Okay. I have to reply to *Dallas* in, hell, in fifty-five minutes. You know the score. He has to break contact to reach us, then sneak back. Hustle, Sam."

"Right, Vince." Dodge switched buttons on his phone. "This is Admiral Dodge. I need to talk to Admiral Foster right now."

The Pentagon

"Ouch. Between *Kiev* and *Kirov.* Nice." Lieutenant General Harris took a marker from his pocket to represent the *Red October.* It was a sub-shaped piece of wood with a Jolly Roger attached. Harris had an odd sense of humor. "The president says we can try and keep her?" he asked.

"If we can get her to the place we want at the time we want," General Hilton said. "Can *Dallas* signal her?"

"Good trick, General." Foster shook his head. "First things first. Let's get *Pogy* and *Invincible* there for starters, then we figure out how to warn him. From this course track, Christ, he's heading right for Norfolk. You believe the balls on this guy? If worse comes to worse, we can always try to escort him in."

"Then we'd have to give the boat back," Admiral Dodge objected.

"We have to have a fall-back position, Sam. If we can't warn him off, we can try and run a bunch of ships through with him to keep Ivan from shooting."

"The law of the sea is your bailiwick, not mine," General Barnes, the air force chief of staff, commented. "But from where I sit doing that could be called anything from piracy to an overt act of war. Isn't this exercise complicated enough already?"

"Good point, General," Foster said.

"Gentlemen, I think we need time to consider this. Okay, we still have time, but right now let's tell *Dallas* to sit tight and track the bugger," Harris said. "And report any changes in course or speed. I figure we have about fifteen minutes to do that. Next we can get *Pogy* and *Invincible* staked out on their path."

"Right, Eddie." Hilton turned to Admiral Foster. "If you agree, let's do that right now."

"Send the message, Sam," Foster ordered.

"Aye aye." Dodge went to the phone and ordered Admiral Gallery to send the reply.

Z141030ZDEC

TOP SECRET

FR: COMSUBLANT

TO: USS DALLAS

A. USS DALLAS Z140925ZDEC

1. CONTINUE TRACKING. REPORT ANY CHANGES IN COURSE OR SPEED. HELP ON THE WAY.
2. ELF TRANSMISSION "G" DESIGNATES FLASH OPS DIRECTIVE READY FOR YOU.
3. YOUR OPAREA UNRESTRICTED BRAVO ZULU DALLAS KEEP IT UP. VADM GALLERY SENDS.

"Okay, let's look at this," Harris said. "What the Russians are up to never has figured, has it?"

"What do you mean, Eddie?" Hilton asked.

"Their force composition for one thing. Half these surface platforms are antiair and antisurface, not primary ASW assets. And why bring *Kirov* along at all? Granted she makes a nice force flag, but they could do the same thing with *Kiev*."

"We talked about that already," Foster observed. "They ran down the list of what they had that could travel this far at a high speed of advance and took everything that would steam. Same with the subs they sent, half of them are antisurface SSGNs with limited utility against submarines. The reason, Eddie, is that Gorshkov wants every platform here he can get. A half-capable ship is better than nothing. Even one of the old *Echo*es might get lucky, and Sergey is probably hitting the knees every night praying for luck."

"Even so, they've split their surface groups into three forces, each with antiair and antisurface elements, and they're kind of thin on ASW hulls. Nor have they sent their ASW aircraft to stage out of Cuba. Now that is curious," Harris pointed out.

"It would blow their cover story. You don't look for a dead sub with aircraft—well, they might, but if they started using a wing of Bears out of Cuba, the president would go ape," Foster said. "We'd harass them so much they'd never accomplish anything. For us this would be a technical operation, but they factor politics into everything they do."

"Fine, but that still doesn't explain it. What ASW ships and choppers they do have are pinging away like mad. You might look for a dead sub that way, but *October* ain't dead, is she?"

"I don't understand, Eddie," Hilton said.

"How would you look for a stray sub, given these circumstances?" Harris asked Foster.

"Not like this," Foster said after a moment. "Using surface, active sonar would warn the boat off long before they could get a hard contact. Boomers are fat on passive sonar. She'd hear them coming and skedaddle out of the way. You're right, Eddie. It's a sham."

"So what the hell are their surface ships up to?" Barnes asked, puzzled.

"Soviet naval doctrine is to use surface ships to support submarine operations," Harris explained. "Gorshkov is a decent tactical theoretician, and occasionally a very innovative gent.

He said years ago that for submarines to operate effectively they have to have outside help, air or surface assets in direct or proximate support. They can't use air this far from home without staging out of Cuba, and at best finding a boat in open ocean that doesn't want to be found would be a difficult assignment.

"On the other hand, they know where she's heading, a limited number of discrete areas, and those are staked out with fifty-eight submarines. The purpose of the surface forces, therefore, is not to participate in the hunt itself—though if they got lucky, they wouldn't mind. The purpose of the surface forces is to keep us from interfering with their submarines. They can do that by staking out the areas we're likely to be with their surface assets and watching what we're doing." Harris paused for a moment. "That's smart. We have to cover them, right? And since they're on a 'rescue' mission, we have to do more or less what they're doing, so we ping away also, and they can use our own ASW expertise against us for their own purposes. We play right into their hands."

"Why?" Barnes asked again.

"We're committed to helping in the search. If we find their boat, they're close enough to find out, acquire, localize, and shoot—and what can we do about it? Not a thing.

"Like I said, they figure to locate and shoot with their submarines. A surface acquisition would be pure luck, and you don't plan for luck. So, the primary objective of the surface fleet is to ride shotgun for, and draw out forces away from, their subs. Secondarily they can act as beaters, driving the game to the shooters—and again, since we're pinging, we're helping them. We're providing an additional stalking horse." Harris shook his head in grudging admiration. "Not too shabby, is it? If *Red October* hears them coming, she runs a little harder for whatever port the skipper wants, right into a nice, tight trap. Dan, what are the chances they can bag her coming into Norfolk, say?"

Foster looked down at the chart. Russian submarines were staked out on every port from Maine to Florida. "They have more subs than we have ports. Now we know that this guy can be picked up, and there's only so much area to cover off each port, even outside the territorial limit . . . You're right, Eddie.

They have too good a chance of making the kill. Our surface groups are too far away to do anything about it. Our subs don't know what's happening, we have orders not to tell them, and even if we could, how could they interfere? Fire at the Russian subs before they could shoot—and start a war?" Foster let out a long breath. "We gotta warn him off."

"How?" Hilton asked.

"Sonar, a gertrude message maybe," Harris suggested.

Admiral Dodge shook his head. "You can hear that through the hull. If we continue to assume that only the officers are in on this, well, the crew might figure out what's happening, and there's no predicting the consequences. Think we can use *Nimitz* and *America* to force them off the coast? They'll be close enough to enter the operation soon. Damn! I don't want this guy to get this close, then get blown away right off our coast."

"Not a chance," Harris said. "Ever since the raid on *Kirov* they've been acting too docile. That's pretty cute, too. I bet they had that figured out. They know that having so many of their ships operating off our coast is bound to provoke us, so they make the first move, we up the ante, and they just plain fold—so now if we keep leaning on them, we're the bad guys. They're just doing a rescue operation, not threatening anybody. The *Post* reported this morning that we have a Russian survivor in the Norfolk naval hospital. Anyway, the good news is that they've miscalculated *October*'s speed. These two groups will pass her left and right, and with their seven-knot speed advantage they'll just pass her by."

"Disregard the surface groups entirely?" Maxwell asked.

"No," Hilton said, "that tells them we are no longer buying the cover story. They'd wonder why—and we still have to cover their surface groups. They're a threat whether they're acting like honest merchants or not."

"What we can do is pretend to release *Invincible*. With *Nimitz* and *America* ready to enter the game, we can send her home. As they pass *October* we can use that to our advantage. We put *Invincible* to seaward of their surface groups as though she's heading home and interpose her on *October*'s course. We still have to figure out a way to communicate with her, though. I can see how to get the assets in place, but that hurdle remains, gentlemen. For the moment, are we agreed to position *Invincible* and *Pogy* for the intercept?"

The Invincible

"How far is she from us?" Ryan asked.

"Two hundred miles. We can be there in ten hours." Captain Hunter marked the position on the chart. "USS *Pogy* is coming east, and she ought to be able to rendezvous with *Dallas* an hour or so after we do. This will put us about a hundred miles east of this surface group when *October* arrives. Bloody hell, *Kiev* and *Kirov* are a hundred miles east and west of her."

"You suppose her captain knows it?" Ryan looked at the chart, measuring the distances with his eyes.

"Unlikely. He's deep, and their passive sonars are not as good as ours. Sea conditions are against it also. A twenty-knot surface wind can play havoc with sonar, even that deep."

"We have to warn him off." Admiral White looked at the ops dispatch. " 'Without using acoustical devices.' "

"How the hell do you do that? You can't reach down that far with a radio," Ryan noted. "Even I know that. My God, this guy's come four thousand miles, and he's going to get killed within sight of his objective."

"How to communicate with a submarine?"

Commander Barclay straightened up. "Gentlemen, we are not trying to communicate with a submarine, we are trying to communicate with a man."

"What are you thinking?" Hunter asked.

"What do we know about Marko Ramius?" Barclay's eyes narrowed.

"He's a cowboy, typical submarine commander, thinks he can walk on water," Captain Carstairs said.

"Who spent most of his time in attack submarines," Barclay added. "Marko's bet his life that he could sneak into an American port undetected by anyone. We have to shake that confidence to warn him off."

"We have to talk to him first," Ryan said sharply.

"And so we shall," Barclay smiled, the thought now fully formed in his mind. "He's a former *attack* submarine commander. He'll still be thinking about how to attack his enemies, and how does a sub commander do that?"

"Well?" Ryan demanded.

Barclay's answer was the obvious one. They discussed his

idea for another hour, then Ryan transmitted it to Washington for approval. A rapid exchange of technical information followed. The *Invincible* would have to make the rendezvous in daylight, and there was not time for that. The operation was set back twelve hours. The *Pogy* joined formation with the *Invincible,* standing as sonar sentry twenty miles to her east. An hour before midnight, the ELF transmitter in northern Michigan transmitted a message: "G." Twenty minutes later, the *Dallas* approached the surface to get her orders.

THE THIRTEENTH DAY

WEDNESDAY, 15 DECEMBER

The Dallas

"Crazy Ivan," Jones called out again, "turning to port!"

"Okay, all stop," Mancuso ordered, holding a dispatch in his hand which he had been rereading for hours. He was not pleased with it.

"All stop, sir," the helmsman responded.

"All back full."

"All back full, sir." The helmsman dialed in the command and turned, his face a question.

Throughout the *Dallas* the crew heard noise, too much noise as poppet valves opened to vent steam onto the reverse turbine blades, trying to spin the propeller the wrong way. It made for instant vibration and caviation noises aft.

"Right full rudder."

"Right full rudder, aye."

"Conn, sonar, we are cavitating," Jones spoke over the intercom.

"Very well, sonar!" Mancuso answered sharply. He did not understand his new orders, and things he didn't understand made him angry.

"Speed down to four knots," Lieutenant Goodman reported.

"Rudder amidships, all stop."

"Rudder amidships aye, all stop aye," the helmsman responded at once. He didn't want the captain barking at him. "Sir, my rudder is amidships."

"Jesus!" Jones said in the sonar room. "What's the skipper doin'?"

Mancuso was in sonar a second later.

"Still doing the turn to port, Cap'n. He's astern of us 'cause of the turn we made," Jones observed as neutrally as he could. It was close to an accusation, Mancuso noticed.

"Flushing the game, Jonesy," Mancuso said coolly.

You're the boss, Jones thought, smart enough not to say anything else. The captain looked as though he was going to snap somebody's head off, and Jones had just used up a month's worth of tolerance. He switched his phones to the towed array plug.

"Engine noises diminishing, sir. He's slowing down." Jones paused. He had to report the next part. "Sir, it's a fair guess he heard us."

"He was supposed to," Mancuso said.

The Red October

"Captain, an enemy submarine," the *michman* said urgently.

"Enemy?" Ramius asked.

"American. He must have been trailing us, and he had to back down to avoid a collision when we turned. Definitely an American, broad on the port bow, range under a kilometer, I think." He handed Ramius his phones.

"688," Ramius said to Borodin. "Damn! He must have stumbled across us in the past two hours. Bad luck."

The Dallas

"Okay, Jonesy, yankee-search him." Mancuso gave the order for an active sonar search personally. The *Dallas* had slewed farther around before coming to a near halt.

Jones hesitated for a moment, still reading the reactor plant noise on his passive systems. Reaching, he powered up the active transducers in the BQQ-5's main sphere at the bow.

Ping! A wave front of sound energy was directed at the target.

Pong! The wave was reflected back off the hard steel hull and returned to the *Dallas*.

"Range to target 1,050 yards," Jones said. The returning pulse was processed through the BC-10 computer and showed some rough details. "Target configuration is consistent with a *Typhoon*-class boomer. Angle on the bow seventy or so. No doppler. He's stopped." Six more pings confirmed this.

"Secure pinging," Mancuso said. There was some small satisfaction in learning that he had elevated the contact correctly. But not much.

Jones killed power to the system. What the hell did I have to do that for? he wondered. He'd already done everything but read the number off her stern.

The Red October

Every man on the *October* knew now that they had been found. The lash of the sonar waves had resounded through the hull. It was not a sound a submariner liked to hear. Certainly not on top of a troublesome reactor, Ramius thought. Perhaps he could make use of this . . .

The Dallas

"Somebody on the surface," Jones said suddenly. "Where the hell did they come from? Skipper, there was nothing, *nothing*, a minute ago, and now I'm getting engine sounds. Two, maybe more—make that two 'cans . . . and something bigger. Like they were sitting up there waiting for us. A minute ago they were sitting still. Damn! I didn't hear a *thing*."

The Invincible

"We timed that rather nicely," Admiral White said.

"Lucky," Ryan observed.

"Luck is part of the game, Jack."

HMS *Bristol* was the first to pick up the sound of the two

submarines and of the turn the *Red October* had made. Even at five miles the subs were barely readable. The Crazy Ivan maneuver had terminated three miles away, and the surface ships had been able to get good position fixes by reading off the *Dallas'* active sonar emissions.

"Two helicopters en route, sir," Captain Hunter reported. "They'll be on station in another minute."

"Signal *Bristol* and *Fife* to stay to windward of us. I want *Invincible* between them and the contact."

"Aye aye, sir." Hunter relayed the order to the communications room. The destroyermen on the escorts would find that order peculiar, using a carrier to screen destroyers.

A few seconds later a pair of Sea King helicopters stopped and hovered fifty feet over the surface, letting down dipping sonars at the end of a cable as they struggled to hold position. These sonars were far less powerful than ship-carried sonars and had distinctive characteristics. The data they developed was transmitted by digital link to the *Invincible*'s command center.

The Dallas

"Limeys," Jones said at once. "That's a helicopter set, the 195, I think. That means the big ship off to the south is one of their baby carriers, sir, with a two-can escort."

Mancuso nodded. "HMS *Invincible*. She was over our side of the lake for NIFTY DOLPHIN. That means the Brit varsity, their best ASW operators."

"The big one's moving this way, sir. Turns indicate ten knots. The choppers—two of them—have both of us. No other subs around that I hear."

The Invincible

"Positive sonar contact," said the metal speaker. "Two submarines, range two miles from *Invincible*, bearing zero-two-zero."

"Now for the hard part," Admiral White said.

Ryan and the four Royal Navy officers who were privy to the mission were on the flag bridge, with the fleet ASW officer in the command center below, as the *Invincible* steamed slowly north, slightly to the left of the direct course to the contacts.

All five swept the contact area with powerful binoculars.

"Come on, Captain Ramius," Ryan said quietly. "You're supposed to be a hotshot. Prove it."

The Red October

Ramius was back in his control room scowling at his chart. A stray American *Los Angeles* stumbling onto him was one thing, but he had run into a small task force. English ships, at that. Why? Probably an exercise. The Americans and the English often work together, and pure accident had walked *October* right into them. Well. He'd have to evade before he could get on with what he wanted to do. It was that simple. Or was it? A hunter submarine, a carrier, and two destroyers after him. What else? He would have to find out if he were going to lose them all. This would take the best part of a day. But now he'd have to see what he was up against. Besides, it would show them that he was confident, that he could hunt *them* if he wished.

"Borodin, bring the ship to periscope depth. Battle stations."

The Invincible

"Come up, Marko," Barclay urged. "We have a message for you, old boy."

"Helicopter three reports contact is coming up," the speaker said.

"All right!" Ryan pounded his hand on the rail.

White lifted a phone. "Recall one of the helicopters."

The distance to the *Red October* was down to a mile and a half. One of the Sea Kings lifted up and circled around, reeling in its sonar transducer.

"Contact depth is five hundred feet, coming up slowly."

The Red October

Borodin was pumping water slowly from the *October*'s trim tanks. The missile submarine increased speed to four knots, and most of the force required to change her depth came from the diving planes. The *starpom* was careful to bring her up slowly, and Ramius had her heading directly towards the *Invincible*.

The Invincible

"Hunter, are you up on your Morse?" Admiral White inquired.

"I believe so, Admiral," Hunter answered. Everyone was getting excited. What a chance this was!

Ryan swallowed hard. In the past few hours, while the *Invincible* had been lying still on the rolling sea, his stomach had really gone bad. The pills the ship's doctor had given him helped, but now the excitement was making it worse. There was an eighty-foot sheer drop from the flag bridge to the sea. Well, he thought, if I have to puke, there's nothing in the way. Screw it.

The Dallas

"Hull popping noises, sir," Jones said. "Think he's heading up."

"Up?" Mancuso wondered for a second. "Yeah, that fits. He's a cowboy. He wants to see what he's up against before he tries to evade. That fits. I bet he doesn't know where we've been the past few days." The captain went forward to the attack center.

"Looks like he's going up, Skipper," Mannion said, watching the attack director. "Dumb." Mannion had his own opinion of submarine captains depending on their periscopes. Too many of them spent too much time looking out at the world. He wondered how much of this was an implicit reaction to the enforced confinement of submarining, something just to make sure that there really was a world up there, to make sure the instruments were correct. Entirely human, Mannion thought, but it could make you vulnerable . . .

"We go up, too, Skipper?"

"Yeah, slow and easy."

The Invincible

The sky was half-filled with white, fleecy clouds, their undersides gray with the threat of rain. A twenty-knot wind was blowing from the southwest, and a six-foot sea was running, its dark waves streaked with whitecaps. Ryan saw the *Bristol* and *Fife* holding station to windward. Their captains, no doubt, were muttering a few choice words at this disposition. The American escorts, which had been detached the previous day, were now sailing to rendezvous with the USS *New Jersey*.

White was talking into the phone again. "Commander, I want to know the instant we get a radar return from the target area. Train every set aboard onto that patch of ocean. I also want to know of any, repeat any, sonar signals from the area . . . That is correct. Depth of target? Very well. Recall the second helicopter, I want both on station to windward."

They had agreed that the best method of passing the message would be to use a blinker light. Only someone placed in the direct line of sight would be able to read the signal. Hunter moved to the light, holding a sheet of paper Ryan had given him. The yeomen and signalmen normally stationed here were gone.

The Red October

"Thirty meters, Comrade Captain," Borodin reported. The battle watch was set in the control center.

"Periscope," Ramius said calmly. The oiled metal tube hissed upward on hydraulic pressure. The captain handed his cap to the junior officer of the watch as he bent to look into the eyepiece. "So, we have here three imperialist ships. HMS *Invincible*. Such a name for a ship!" He scoffed for his audience. "Two escorts, *Bristol*, and a County-class cruiser."

The Invincible

"Periscope, starboard bow!" the speaker announced.

"I see it!" Barclay's hand shot out to point. "There it is!"

Ryan strained to find it. "I got it." It was like a small broomstick sitting vertically in the water, about a mile away. As the waves rolled past, the bottommost visible part of the periscope flared out.

"Hunter," White said quietly. To Ryan's left the captain began jerking his hand on the lever that controlled the light shutters.

The Red October

Ramius didn't see it at first. He was making a complete circle of the horizon, checking for any other ships or aircraft. When he finished the circuit, the flashing light caught his eye. Quickly he tried to interpret the signal. It took him a moment to realize it was pointed right at him.

> AAA AAA AAA RED OCTOBER RED OCTOBER CAN YOU READ THIS CAN YOU READ THIS PLEASE PING US ONE TIME ON ACTIVE SONAR IF YOU CAN READ THIS PLEASE PING US ONE TIME ON ACTIVE SONAR IF YOU CAN READ THIS AAA AAA AAA RED OCTOBER RED OCTOBER CAN YOU READ THIS CAN YOU READ THIS

The message kept repeating. The signal was jerky and awkward. Ramius didn't notice this. He translated the English signal in his head, at first thinking it was a signal to the American submarine. His knuckles went white on the periscope hand grips as he translated the message in his mind.

"Borodin," he said finally, after reading the message a fourth time, "we set up a practice firing solution on *Invincible*. Damn, the periscope rangefinder is sticking. A single ping, Comrade. Just one, for range."

Ping!

The Invincible

"One ping from the contact area, sir, sounds Soviet," the speaker reported.

White lifted his phone. "Thank you. Keep us informed." He set it back down. "Well, gentlemen . . ."

"He did it!" Ryan sang out. "Send the rest, for Christ's sake!"

"At once." Hunter grinned like a madman.

> RED OCTOBER RED OCTOBER YOUR WHOLE FLEET IS CHASING AFTER YOU YOUR WHOLE FLEET IS CHASING AFTER YOU YOUR PATH IS

BLOCKED BY NUMEROUS VESSELS NUMEROUS
ATTACK SUBMARINES ARE WAITING TO ATTACK
YOU REPEAT NUMEROUS ATTACK SUBMARINES
ARE WAITING TO ATTACK YOU PROCEED TO
RENDEZVOUS 33N 75W WE HAVE SHIPS THERE
WAITING FOR YOU REPEAT PROCEED TO REN-
DEZVOUS 33N 75W WE HAVE SHIPS THERE WAIT-
ING FOR YOU IF YOU UNDERSTAND AND AGREE
PLEASE PING US AGAIN ONE TIME

The Red October

"Distance to target, Borodin?" Ramius asked, wishing he had
more time as the message was repeated again and again.

"Two thousand meters, Comrade Captain. A nice, fat target
for us if we . . ." The *starpom*'s voice trailed off as he saw the
look on his commander's face.

They know our name, Ramius was thinking, *they know our
name! How can this be? They knew where to find us—exactly!
How? What can the Americans have? How long has the* Los
Angeles *been trailing us? Decide—you must decide!*

"Comrade, one more ping on the target, just one."

The Invincible

"One more ping, Admiral."

"Thank you." White looked at Ryan. "Well, Jack, it would
seem that your intelligence estimate was indeed correct. Jolly
good."

"Jolly good my ass, my Lord Earl! I was right. Son of a
bitch!" Ryan's hands flew up in the air, his seasickness forgotten. He calmed down. The occasion called for more de-
corum. "Excuse me, Admiral. We have some things to do."

The Dallas

Whole fleet is chasing after you . . . Proceed to 33N 75W. What
the hell was going on? Mancuso wondered, catching the end
of the second signal.

"Conn, sonar. Getting hull popping noises from the target.
His depth is changing. Engine noise increasing."

"Down scope." Mancuso lifted the phone. "Very well, sonar. Anything else, Jones?"

"No, sir. The helicopters are gone, and there aren't any emissions from the surface ships. What gives, sir?"

"Beats me." Mancuso shook his head as Mannion brought the *Dallas* back in pursuit of the *Red October*. What the hell was happening here? the captain wondered. Why was a Brit carrier signaling to a Russian submarine, and why were they sending her to a rendezvous off the Carolinas? *Whose* subs were blocking her path? It couldn't be. No way. It just couldn't be . . .

The Invincible

Ryan was in the *Invincible*'s communications room. "MAGI TO OLYMPUS," he typed into the special encoding device the CIA had sent out with him, "PLAYED MY MANDOLIN TODAY. SOUNDED PRETTY GOOD. I'M PLANNING A LITTLE CONCERT, AT THE USUAL PLACE. EXPECT GOOD CRITICAL REVIEWS. AWAITING INSTRUCTIONS." Ryan had laughed before at the code words he was supposed to use for this. He was laughing now, for a different reason.

The White House

"So," Pelt observed, "Ryan expects the mission will be successful. Everything's going according to plan, but he didn't use the code group for certain success."

The president leaned back comfortably. "He's honest. Things can always go wrong. You have to admit, though, things do look good."

"This plan the chiefs came up with is crazy, sir."

"Perhaps, but you've been trying to poke a hole in it for several days now, and you haven't succeeded. The pieces will all fall in place shortly."

The president was being clever, Pelt saw. The man liked being clever.

The Invincible

"OLYMPUS TO MAGI. I LIKE OLD-FASHIONED MANDOLIN MUSIC. CONCERT APPROVED," the message said.

Ryan sat back comfortably, sipping at his brandy. "Well, that's good. I wonder what the next part of the plan is."

"I expect that Washington will let us know. For the moment," Admiral White said, "we'll have to move back west to interpose ourselves between *October* and the Soviet fleet."

The Avalon

Lieutenant Ames surveyed the scene through the tiny port on the *Avalon*'s bow. The *Alfa* lay on her port side. She had obviously hit stern first, and hard. One blade was snapped off the propeller, and the lower rudder fin was smashed. The whole stern might have been knocked off true; it was hard to tell in the low visibility.

"Moving forward slowly," he said, adjusting the controls. Behind him an ensign and a senior petty officer were monitoring instruments and preparing to deploy the manipulator arm, attached before they sailed, which carried a television camera and floodlights. These gave them a slightly wider field of view than the navigation ports permitted. The DSRV crept forward at one knot. Visibility was under twenty yards, despite the million candles of illumination from the bow lights.

The sea floor at this point was a treacherous slope of alluvial silt dotted with boulders. It appeared that the only thing that had prevented the *Alfa* from sliding farther down was her sail, driven like a wedge into the bottom.

"Holy gawd!" The petty officer saw it first. There was a crack in the *Alfa*'s hull—or was there?

"Reactor accident," Ames said, his voice detached and clinical. "Something burned through the hull. Lord, and that's *titanium!* Burned right through, from the inside out. There's another one, two burn-throughs. This one's bigger, looks like a good yard across. No mystery what killed her, guys. That's two compartments open to the sea." Ames looked over to the depth gauge: 1,880 feet. "Getting all this on tape?"

"Aye, Skipper," the electrician first class answered. "Crummy way to die. Poor bastards."

"Yeah, depending on what they were up to." Ames maneuvered the *Avalon* around the *Alfa*'s bow, working the directional propeller carefully and adjusting trim to cruise down the other side, actually the top of the dead sub. "See any evidence of a hull fracture?"

"No," the ensign answered, "just the two burn-throughs. I wonder what went wrong?"

"A for-real China Syndrome. It finally happened to somebody." Ames shook his head. If there was anything the navy preached about reactors, it was safety. "Get the transducer against the hull. We'll see if anybody's alive in there."

"Aye." The electrician worked the waldo controls as Ames tried to keep the *Avalon* dead still. Neither task was easy. The DSRV was hovering, nearly resting on the sail. If there were survivors, they had to be in the control room or forward. There could be no life aft.

"Okay, I got contact."

All three men listened intently, hoping for something. Their job was search and rescue, and as submariners themselves they took it seriously.

"Maybe they're asleep." The ensign switched on the locater sonar. The high-frequency waves resonated through both vessels. It was a sound fit to wake the dead, but there was no response. The air supply in the *Politovskiy* had run out a day before.

"That's that," Ames said quietly. He maneuvered upward as the electrician rigged in the manipulator arm, looking for a spot to drop a sonar transponder. They would be back again when the topside weather was better. The navy would not pass up this chance to inspect an *Alfa,* and the *Glomar Explorer* was sitting unused somewhere on the West Coast. Would she be activated? Ames would not bet against that.

"*Avalon, Avalon,* this is *Scamp*—" the voice on the gertrude was distorted but readable, "—return at once. Acknowledge."

"*Scamp,* this is *Avalon.* On the way."

The *Scamp* had just received an ELF message and gone briefly to periscope depth for a FLASH operational order. "PROCEED AT BEST SPEED TO 33N 75W." The message didn't say why.

CIA Headquarters

"CARDINAL is still with is," Moore told Ritter.

"Thank God for that." Ritter sat down.

"There's a signal en route. This time he didn't try to kill himself getting it to us. Maybe being in the hospital scared him a little. I'm extending another offer to extract him."

"Again?"

"Bob, we have to make the offer."

"I know. I had one sent myself a few years back, you know. The old bastard just doesn't want to quit. You know how it goes, some people thrive on the action. Or maybe he hasn't worked out his rage yet . . . I just got a call from Senator Donaldson." Donaldson was the chairman of the Select Committee on Intelligence.

"Oh?"

"He wants to know what we know about what's going on. He doesn't buy the cover story about a rescue mission, and thinks we know something different."

Judge Moore leaned back. "I wonder who planted that idea in his head?"

"Yeah. I have a little idea we might try. I think it's time, and this is a dandy opportunity."

The two senior executives discussed this for an hour. Before Ritter left for the Hill, they cleared it with the president.

Washington, D.C.

Donaldson kept Ritter waiting in his outer office for fifteen minutes while he read the paper. He wanted Ritter to know his place. Some of the DDO's remarks about leaks from the Hill had touched a sore spot with the senator from Connecticut, and it was important for appointed and civil service officials to understand the difference between themselves and the elected representatives of the people.

"Sorry to keep you waiting, Mr. Ritter." Donaldson did not rise, nor did he offer to shake hands.

"Quite all right, sir. Took the chance to read a magazine. Don't get to do that much, what with the schedule I work." They fenced with each other from the first moment.

"So, what are the Soviets up to?"

"Senator, before I address that subject, I must say this: I had to clear this meeting with the president. This information is for you alone, no one else may hear it, sir. No one. That comes from the White House."

"There are other men on my committee, Mr. Ritter."

"Sir, if I do not have your word, as a gentleman," Ritter added with a smile, "I will not reveal this information. Those are my orders. I work for the executive branch, Senator. I take my orders from the president." Ritter hoped his recording device was getting all of this.

"Agreed," Donaldson said reluctantly. He was angry because of the foolish restrictions, but pleased that he was getting to hear this. "Go on."

"Frankly, sir, we're not sure exactly what's going on," Ritter said.

"Oh, so you've sworn me to secrecy so that I can't tell anyone that, again, the CIA doesn't know what the hell is going on?"

"I said we don't know exactly what's happening. We do know a few things. Our information comes mainly from the Israelis, and some from the French. From both channels we have learned that something has gone very wrong with the Soviet Navy."

"I gathered that. They've lost a sub."

"At least one, but that's not what's going on. Someone, we think, has played a trick on the operations directorate of the Soviet Northern Fleet. I can't say for sure, but I think it was the Poles."

"Why the Poles?"

"I don't know for sure that it is, but both the French and Israelis are well connected with the Poles, *and* the Poles have a long-standing beef with the Soviets. I do know—at least I think I know—that whatever this is did not come from a Western intelligence agency."

"So, what's happening?" Donaldson demanded.

"Our best guess is that someone has committed at least one forgery, possibly as many as three, all aimed at raising hell in the Soviet Navy—but whatever it was, it's gotten far out of hand. A lot of people are working hard to cover their asses, the Israelis say. As a guess, I think they managed to alter a submarine's operational orders, then forged a letter from her skipper threatening to fire his missiles. The amazing thing is that the Soviets went for it." Ritter frowned. "We may have it all backwards, though. All we really know for sure is that somebody, probably the Poles, has played a fantastic dirty trick on the Russians."

"Not us?" Donaldson asked pointedly.

"No, sir, absolutely not! If we tried something like that—even if we succeeded, which isn't likely—they might try the same thing with us. You could start a war that way, and you know the president would never authorize it."

"But someone at the CIA might not care what the president thinks."

"Not in my department! It would be my head. Do you really think we could run an operation like this and then successfully conceal it? Hell, Senator, I *wish* we could."

"Why the Poles, and why are they able to do it?"

"We've been hearing for some time about a dissident faction inside their intelligence community, one that does not especially love the Soviets. You can pick any number of reasons why. There's the fundamental historical enmity, and the Russians seem to forget that the Poles are Polish first, Communists second. My own guess is that it's this business with the pope, even more than the martial law thing. We know that our old friend Andropov initiated a replay of the Edward II/Becket business. The pope has given Poland a great deal of prestige, done things for the country that even Party members feel good about. Ivan went and spit on their whole country when he did that—you wonder that they're mad? As to their ability, people seem to overlook just what a class act their intelligence service always has been. They're the ones who made the Enigma breakthrough in 1939, not the Brits. They're damned effective, and for the same reason as the Israelis. They have enemies to the east and the west. That sort of thing breeds good agents. We know for certain that they have a lot of people inside Russia, guest workers paying Narmonov off for the economic supports given to their country. We also know that a lot of Polish engineers are working in Soviet shipyards. I admit it's funny, neither country has much of a maritime tradition, but the Poles build a lot of Soviet merchant hulls. Their yards are more efficient than the Russian ones, and lately they've been giving technical help, mainly in quality control, to the naval building yards."

"So, the Polish intelligence service has played a trick on

the Soviets," Donaldson summarized. "Gorshkov is one of the guys who took a hard line on intervention, wasn't he?"

"True, but he's probably just a target of opportunity. The real aim of this has to be to embarrass Moscow. The fact that this operation attacks the Soviet Navy has no significance in itself. The objective is to raise hell in their senior military channels, and they all come together in Moscow. God, I wish I knew what was really happening! From the five percent we do know, this operation has to be a real masterpiece, the sort of thing legends are made of. We're working on it, trying to find out. So are the Brits, and the French, and the Israelis—Benny Herzog of the Mossad is supposed to be going ape. The Israelis *do* pull this kind of trick on their neighbors, regularly. They say officially that they don't know anything beyond what they've told us. Maybe so. Or maybe they gave the Poles some technical help—hard to say. It's certain that the Soviet Navy is a strategic threat to Israel. But we need more time on that. The Israeli connection looks a little too pat at this point."

"But you don't know what's happening, just the how and why."

"Senator, it's not that easy. Give us some time. At the moment we may not even want to know. To summarize, somebody has laid a colossal piece of disinformation on the Soviet Navy. It was probably aimed at merely shaking them up, but it has clearly gotten out of hand. How or why it happened, we do not know. You can bet, however, that whoever initiated this operation is working very hard to cover his tracks." Ritter wanted the senator to get this right. "If the Soviets find out who did it, their reaction will be nasty—depend on it. In a few weeks we might know more. The Israelis owe us for a few things, and eventually they'll let us in on it."

"For a couple more F-15s and a company of tanks," Donaldson observed.

"Cheap at the price."

"But if we're not involved in this, why the secrecy?"

"You gave me your word, Senator," Ritter reminded him. "For one thing, if word leaked out, would the Soviets believe we're not involved? Not likely! We're trying to civilize the intelligence game. I mean, we're still enemies, but having the various intelligence services in conflict uses up too many assets, and it's dangerous to both sides. For another, well, if we ever do find out how all this happened, we just might want to make use of it ourselves."

"Those reasons are contradictory."

Ritter smiled. "The intelligence game is like that. If we find out who did this, we can use that information to our advantage. In any case, Senator, you gave me your word, and I will report that to the president on my return to Langley."

"Very well." Donaldson rose. The interview was at an end. "I trust you will keep us informed of future developments."

"That's what we have to do, sir." Ritter stood.

"Indeed. Thank you for coming down." They did not shake hands this time either.

Ritter walked into the hall without passing through the anteroom. He stopped to look down into the antrium of the Hart building. It reminded him of the local Hyatt. Uncharacteristically, he took the stairs instead of the elevator down to the first floor. With luck he had just settled a major score. His car was waiting for him outside, and he told the driver to head for the FBI building.

"Not a CIA operation?" Peter Henderson, the senator's chief aide, asked.

"No, I believe him," Donaldson said. "He's not smart enough to pull something like that."

"I don't know why the president doesn't get rid of him," Henderson commented. "Of course, the kind of person he is, maybe it's better that he's incompetent." The senator agreed.

When he returned to his office, Henderson adjusted the venetian blinds on his window, though the sun was on the other side of the building. An hour later the driver of a passing Black & White taxicab looked up at the window and made a mental note.

Henderson worked late that night. The Hart building was nearly empty with most of the senators out of town. Donaldson was there only because of personal business and to keep an eye on things. As chairman of the Select Committee on Intelligence, he had more duties than he would have liked at this time of year. Henderson took the elevator down to the main lobby, looking every inch the senior congressional aide—a three-piece gray suit, an expensive leather attaché case, his hair

just so, and his stride jaunty as he left the building. A Black
& White cab came around the corner and stopped to let out a
fare. Henderson got in.

"Watergate," he said. Not until the taxi had driven a few
blocks did he speak again.

Henderson had a modest one-bedroom condo in the Watergate complex, an irony that he himself had considered many
times. When he got to his destination he did not tip the driver.
A woman got in as he walked to the main entrance. Taxis in
Washington are very busy in the early evening.

"Georgetown University, please," she said, a pretty young
woman with auburn hair and an armload of books.

"Night school?" the driver asked, checking the mirror.

"Exams," the girl said, her voice a trace uneasy. "Psych."

"Best thing to do with exams is relax," the driver advised.

Special Agent Hazel Loomis fumbled with her books. Her
purse dropped to the floor. "Oh, damn." She bent over to pick
it up, and while doing so retrieved a miniature tape recorder
that another agent had left under the driver's seat.

It took fifteen minutes to get to the university. The fare was
$3.85. Loomis gave the driver a five and told him to keep the
change. She walked across the campus and entered a Ford
which drove straight to the J. Edgar Hoover Building. A lot
of work had gone into this—and it had been so easy!

"Always is, when the bear walks into your sight." The
inspector who had been running the case turned left onto Pennsylvania Avenue. "The problem is finding the damned bear in
the first place."

The Pentagon

"Gentlemen, you have been asked here because each of you is
a career intelligence officer with a working knowledge of submarines and Russian," Davenport said to the four officers seated
in his office. "I have need of officers with your qualifications.
This is a volunteer assignment. It could involve a considerable
element of danger—we cannot be sure at this point. The only
other thing I can say is that this will be a dream job for an
intelligence officer—but the sort of dream that you'll never be
able to tell anyone about. We're all used to that, aren't we?"

Davenport ventured a rare smile. "As they say in the movies, if you want in, fine; if not, you may leave at this point, and nothing will ever be said. It is asking a lot to expect men to walk into a potentially dangerous assignment blindfolded."

Of course nobody left; the men who had been called here were not quitters. Besides, something would be said, and Davenport had a good memory. These were professional officers. One of the compensations for wearing a uniform and earning less money than an equally talented man can make in the real world is the off chance of being killed.

"Thank you, gentlemen. I think you will find this worth your while." Davenport stood and handed each man a manila envelope. "You will soon have the chance to examine a Soviet missile submarine—from the inside." Four pairs of eyes blinked in unison.

33N 75W

The USS *Ethan Allen* had been on station now for more than thirty hours. She was cruising in a five-mile circle at a depth of two hundred feet. There was no hurry. The submarine was making just enough speed to maintain steerage way, her reactor producing only ten percent of rated power. The chief quartermaster was assisting in the galley.

"First time I've ever done this in a sub," one of the *Allen*'s officers who was acting as ship's cook noted, stirring an omelette.

The quartermaster sighed imperceptibly. They ought to have sailed with a proper cook, but theirs had been a kid, and every enlisted man aboard now had over twenty years of service. The chiefs were all technicians, except the quartermaster, who could handle a toaster on a good day.

"You cook much at home, sir?"

"Some. My parents used to have a restaurant down at Pass Christian. This is my mama's special Cajun omelette. Shame we don't have any bass. I can do some nice things with bass and a little lemon. You fish much, Chief?"

"No, sir." The small complement of officers and senior chiefs was working in an informal atmosphere, and the quartermaster was a man accustomed to discipline and status boundaries. "Commander, can I ask what the hell we're doing?"

"Wish I knew, Chief. Mostly we're waiting for something."

"But what, sir?"

"Damned if I know. You want to hand me those ham cubes? And could you check the bread in the oven? Ought to be about done."

The New Jersey

Commander Eaton was perplexed. His battle group was holding twenty miles south of the Russians. If it hadn't been dark he could have seen the *Kirov*'s towering superstructure on the horizon from his perch on the flat bridge. Her escorts were in a single broad line ahead of the battle cruiser, pinging away in the search for a submarine.

Since the air force had staged its mock attack the Soviets had been acting like sheep. This was out of character to say the least. The *New Jersey* and her escorts were keeping the Russian formation under constant observation, and a pair of Sentry aircraft were watching for good measure. The Russian redeployment had switched Eaton's responsibility to the *Kirov* group. This suited him. His main battery turrets were trained in, but the guns were loaded with eight-inch guided rounds and the fire control stations were fully manned. The *Tarawa* was thirty miles south, her armed strike force of Harriers sitting ready to move at five-minute notice. The Soviets had to know this, even though their ASW helicopters had not come within five miles of an American ship for two days. The Bear and Backfire bombers which were passing overhead in shuttle rounds to Cuba—only a few, and those returning to Russia as quickly as they could be turned around—could not fail to report what they saw. The American vessels were in extended attack formation, the missiles on the *New Jersey* and her escorts being fed continuous information from the ships' sensors. And the Russians were ignoring them. Their only electronic emissions were routine navigation radars. Strange.

The *Nimitz* was now within air range after a five-thousand-mile dash from the South Atlantic; the carrier and her nuclear-powered escorts, the *California, Bainbridge,* and *Truxton,* were now only four hundred miles to the south, with the *America* battle group half a day behind them. The *Kennedy* was five hundred miles to the east. The Soviets would have to consider the danger of three carrier air wings at their backs and hundreds of land-based air force birds gradually shifting south from one base to another. Perhaps this explained their docility.

The Backfire bombers were being escorted in relays all the way from Iceland, first by navy Tomcats from the *Saratoga*'s air wing, then by air force Phantoms operating in Maine, which handled the Soviet aircraft off to Eagles and Fighting Falcons as they worked down the coast almost as far south as Cuba. There was not much doubt how seriously the United States was taking this, though American units were no longer actively harassing the Russians. Eaton was glad they weren't. There was nothing more to be gained from harassment, and anyway, if it had to, his battle group could switch from a peace to a war footing in about two minutes.

The Watergate Apartments

"Excuse me. I just moved in down the hall, and my phone isn't hooked up yet. Would you mind if I made a call?"

Henderson arrived at that decision quickly enough. Five three or so, auburn hair, gray eyes, adequate figure, a dazzling smile, and fashionably dressed. "Sure, welcome to the Watergate. Come on in."

"Thank you. I'm Hazel Loomis. My friends call me Sissy." She held out her hand.

"Peter Henderson. The phone's in the kitchen. I'll show you." Things were looking up. He'd just ended a lengthy relationship with one of the senator's secretaries. It had been hard on both of them.

"I'm not disturbing anything, am I? You don't have anyone here, do you?"

"No, just me and the TV. Are you new to D.C.? The night life isn't all it's cracked up to be. At least, not when you have to go to work the next day. Who do you work for—I take it you're single?"

"That's right. I work for DARPA, as a computer programmer. I'm afraid I can't talk about it very much."

All sorts of good news, Henderson thought. "Here's the phone."

Loomis looked around quickly as though evaluating the job

the decorator had done. She reached into her purse and took out a dime, handing it to Henderson. He laughed.

"The first call is free, and believe me, you can use my phone whenever you want."

"I just knew," she said, punching the buttons, "that this would be nicer than living in Laurel. Hello, Kathy? Sissy. I just got moved in, haven't even got my phone hooked up yet ... Oh, a guy down the hall was kind enough to let me use his phone... Okay, see you tomorrow for lunch. Bye, Kathy."

Loomis looked around. "Who decorated for you?"

"Did it myself. I minored in art at Harvard, and I know some nice shops in Georgetown. You can find some good bargains if you know where to look."

"Oh, I'd just *love* to have my place look like this! Could you show me around?"

"Sure, the bedroom first?" Henderson laughed to show that he had no untoward intentions—which of course he did, though he was a patient man in such matters. The tour, which lasted several minutes, assured Loomis that the condo was indeed empty. A minute later there was a knock at the door. Henderson grumbled good-naturedly as he went to answer it.

"Pete Henderson?" The man asking the question was dressed in a business suit. Henderson had on jeans and a sport shirt.

"Yes?" Henderson backed up, knowing what this had to be. What came next, though, surprised him.

"You're under arrest, Mr. Henderson," Sissy Loomis said, holding up her ID card. "The charge is espionage. You have the right to remain silent, you have the right to speak with an attorney. If you give up the right to remain silent, everything you say will be recorded and may be used against you. If you do not have an attorney or cannot afford one, we will see to it that an attorney is appointed to represent you. Do you understand these rights, Mr. Henderson?" It was Sissy Loomis' first espionage case. For five years she had specialized in bank robbery stakeouts, often working as a teller with a .357 magnum revolver in her cash drawer. "Do you wish to waive these rights?"

"No, I do not." Henderson's voice was raspy.

"Oh, you will," the inspector observed. "You will." He turned to the three agents who accompanied him. "Take this place apart. Neatly, gentlemen, and quietly. We don't want to wake anyone. You, Mr. Henderson, will come with us. You can change first. We can do this the easy way or the hard way. If you promise to cooperate, no cuffs. But if you try to run— you don't want to do that, believe me." The inspector had been in the FBI for twenty years and had never even drawn his service revolver in anger, while Loomis had already shot and killed two men. He was old-time FBI, and couldn't help but wonder what Mr. Hoover would think of that, not to mention the new Jewish director.

The Red October

Ramius and Kamarov conferred over the chart for several minutes, tracing alternate course tracks before agreeing on one. The enlisted men ignored this. They had never been encouraged to know about charts. The captain walked to the aft bulkhead and lifted the phone.

"Comrade Melekhin," he ordered, waiting a few seconds. "Comrade, this is the captain. Any further difficulties with the reactor systems?"

"No, Comrade Captain."

"Excellent. Hold things together another two days." Ramius hung up. It was thirty minutes to the turn of the next watch.

Melekhin and Kirill Surzpoi, the assistant engineer, had the duty in the engine room. Melekhin monitored the turbines and Surzpoi handled the reactor systems. Each had a *michman* and three enlisted men in attendance. The engineers had had a very busy cruise. Every gauge and monitor in the engine spaces, it seemed, had been inspected, and many had been entirely rebuilt by the two senior officers, who had been helped by Valintin Bugayev, the electronics officer and on-board genius who was also handling the political awareness classes for the crewmen. The engine room crewmen were the most rattled on the vessel. The supposed contamination was common knowledge—there are no long-lived secrets on a submarine. To ease their loads ordinary seamen were supplementing the engine watches. The captain called this a good chance for the cross-training he believed in. The crew thought it was a good way to get poisoned. Discipline was being maintained, of course. This was owing partly to the trust the men had in their commanding officer, partly to their training, but mostly to their knowledge of what would happen if they failed to carry out their orders immediately and enthusiastically.

"Comrade Melekhin," Surzpoi called, "I am showing pressure fluctuation on the main loop, number six gauge."

"Coming." Melekhin hurried over and shoved the *michman* out of the way when he got to the master control panel. "More bad instruments! The others show normal. Nothing important," the chief engineer said blandly, making sure everyone could hear. The whole compartment watch saw the chief engineer whisper something to his assistant. The younger one shook his head slowly, while two sets of hands worked the controls.

A loud two-phase buzzer and a rotating red alarm light went off.

"SCRAM the pile!" Melekhin ordered.

"SCRAMing." Surzpoi stabbed his finger on the master shutdown button.

"You men, get forward!" Melekhin ordered next. There was no hesitation. "No, you, connect battery power to the caterpillar motors, quickly!"

The warrant officer raced back to throw the proper switches, cursing his change of orders. It took forty seconds.

"Done, Comrade!"

"*Go!*"

The warrant officer was the last man out of the compartment. He made certain that the hatches were dogged down tight before running to the control room.

"What is the problem?" Ramius asked calmly.

"Radiation alarm in the heat-exchange room!"

"Very well, go forward and shower with the rest of your watch. Get control of yourself." Ramius patted the *michman* on the arm. "We have had these problems before. You are a trained man. The crewmen look to you for leadership."

Ramius lifted the phone. It was a moment before the other end was picked up. "What has happened, Comrade?" The control room crew watched their captain listen to the answer. They could not help but admire his calm. Radiation alarms had sounded throughout the hull. "Very well. We do not have too many hours of battery power left, Comrade. We must go to snorkling depth. Stand by to activate the diesel. Yes." He hung up.

"Comrades, you will listen to me." Ramius' voice was under total control. "There has been a minor failure in the reactor control systems. The alarm you heard was not a major radiation leak, but rather a failure of the reactor rod control systems. Comrades Melekhin and Surzpoi successfully executed an emergency reactor shutdown, but we cannot operate the reactor properly without the primary controls. We will, therefore, complete our cruise on diesel power. To ensure against any *possible* radiation contamination, the reactor spaces have been isolated, and all compartments, engineering spaces first, will be vented with surface air when we snorkle. Kamarov, you will go aft to work the environmental controls. I will take the conn."

"Aye, Comrade Captain!" Kamarov went aft.

Ramius lifted the microphone to give this news to the crew. Everyone was waiting for something. Forward, some crewmen muttered among themselves that *minor* was a word suffering from overuse, that nuclear submarines did not run on diesel and ventilate with surface air for the hell of it.

Finished with his terse announcement, Ramius ordered the submarine to approach the surface.

The Dallas

"Beats me, Skipper." Jones shook his head. "Reactor noises have stopped, pumps are cut way back, but he's running at the same speed, just like before. On battery, I guess."

"Must be a hell of a battery system to drive something that big this fast," Mancuso observed.

"I did some computations on that a few hours ago." Jones held up his pad. "This is based on the *Typhoon* hull, with a nice slick hull coefficient, so it's probably conservative."

"Where did you learn to do this, Jonesy?"

"Mr. Thompson looked up the hydrodynamic stuff for me. The electrical end is fairly simple. He might have something exotic—fuel cells, maybe. If not, if he's running ordinary batteries, he has enough raw electrical power to crank every car in L.A."

Mancuso shook his head. "Can't last forever."

Jones held up his hand. "Hull creaking . . . Sounds like he's going up some."

The Red October

"Raise snorkle," Ramius said. Looking through the periscope he verified that the snorkle was up. "Well, no other ships in view. That is good news. I think we have lost our imperialist hunters. Raise the ESM antenna. Let's be sure no enemy aircraft are lurking about with their radars."

"Clear, Comrade Captain." Bugayev was manning the ESM board. "Nothing at all, not even airline sets."

"So, we have indeed lost our rat pack." Ramius lifted the phone again. "Melekhin, you may open the main induction and vent the engine spaces, then start the diesel." A minute later everyone aboard felt the vibration as the *October*'s massive diesel engine cranked on battery power. This sucked up all the air from the reactor spaces, replacing it with air drawn through the snorkle and ejecting the "contaminated" air into the sea.

The engine continued to crank two minutes, and throughout the hull men waited for the rumble that would mean the engine had caught and could generate power to run the electric motors. It didn't catch. After another thirty seconds the cranking stopped. The control room phone buzzed. Ramius lifted it.

"What is wrong with the diesel, Comrade Chief Engineer?" the captain asked sharply. "I see. I'll send men back—oh. Stand by." Ramius looked around, his mouth a thin, bloodless smile. The junior engineering officer, Svyadov, was standing at the back of the compartment. "I need a man who knows diesel engines to help Comrade Melekhin."

"I grew up on a State farm," Bugayev said. "I started playing with tractor engines as a boy."

"There is an additional problem . . ."

Bugayev nodded knowingly. "So I gather, Comrade Captain, but we need the diesel, do we not?"

"I will not forget this, Comrade," Ramius said quietly.

"Then you can buy me some rum in Cuba, Comrade." Bugayev smiled courageously. "I wish to meet a Cuban comrade, preferably one with long hair."

"May I accompany you, Comrade?" Svyadov asked anxiously. He had just been going on watch, approaching the reactor room hatch, when he'd been knocked aside by escaping crewmen.

"Let us assess the nature of the problem first," Bugayev said, looking at Ramius for confirmation.

"Yes, there is plenty of time. Bugayev, report to me yourself in ten minutes."

"Aye aye, Comrade Captain."

"Svyadov, take charge of the lieutenant's station." Ramius pointed to the ESM board. "Use the opportunity to learn some new skills."

The lieutenant did as he was ordered. The captain seemed very preoccupied. Svyadov had never seen him like this before.

THE FOURTEENTH DAY

THURSDAY, 16 DECEMBER

A Super Stallion

They were traveling at one hundred fifty knots, two thousand feet over the darkened sea. The Super Stallion helicopter was old. Built towards the end of the Vietnam War, she had first seen service clearing mines off Haiphong harbor. That had been her primary duty, pulling a sea sled and acting as a flying minesweeper. Now, the big Sikorski was used for other purposes, mainly long-range heavy-lift missions. The three turbine engines perched atop the fuselage packed a considerable amount of power and could carry a platoon of armed combat troops a great distance.

Tonight, in addition to her normal flight crew of three, she was carrying four passengers and a heavy load of fuel in the outrigger tanks. The passengers were clustered in the aft corner of the cargo area, chatting among themselves or trying to over the racket of the engines. Their conversation was animated. The intelligence officers had dismissed the danger implicit in their mission—no sense dwelling on that—and were speculating on what they might find aboard an honest-to-God Russian submarine. Each man considered the stories that would result, and decided it was a shame that they would never be able to tell them. None voiced this thought, however. At most a handful of people would ever know the entire story; the others would only see disjointed fragments that later might be thought parts of any number of other operations. Any Soviet agent trying to determine what this mission had been would find himself in a maze with dozens of blank walls.

The mission profile was a tight one. The helicopter was flying on a specific track to HMS *Invincible*, from which they would fly to the USS *Pigeon* aboard a Royal Navy Sea King. The Stallion's disappearance from Oceana Naval Air Station for only a few hours would be viewed merely as a matter of routine.

The helicopter's turboshaft engines, running at maximum cruising power, were gulping down fuel. The aircraft was now four hundred miles off the U.S. coast and had another eighty miles to go. Their flight to the *Invincible* was not direct; it was a dogleg course intended to fool whoever might have noticed their departure on radar. The pilots were tired. Four hours is a long time to sit in a cramped cockpit, and military aircraft are not known for their creature comforts. The flight instruments glowed a dull red. Both men were especially careful to watch their artificial horizon; a solid overcast denied them a fixed reference point aloft, and flying over water at night was mesmerizing. It was by no means an unusual mission, however. The pilots had done this many times, and their concern was not unlike that of an experienced driver on a slick road. The dangers were real, but routine.

"Juliet 6, your target is bearing zero-eight-zero, range seventy-five miles," the Sentry called in.

"Thinks we're lost?" Commander John Marcks wondered over the intercom.

"Air force," his copilot replied. "They don't know much about flying over water. They think you get lost without roads to follow."

"Uh-huh," Marcks chuckled. "Who do you like in the Eagles game tonight?"

"Oilers by three and a half."

"Six and a half. Philly's fullback is still hurt."

"Five."

"Okay, five bucks. I'll go easy on you." Marcks grinned. He loved to gamble. The day after Argentina had attacked the Falklands, he'd asked if anyone in the squadron wanted to take Argentina and seven points.

A few feet above their heads and a few feet aft, the engines were racing at thousands of RPM, turning gears to drive the seven-bladed main rotor. They had no way of knowing that a fracture was developing in the transmission casing, near the fluid test port.

"Juliet 6, your target has just launched a fighter to escort you in. Will rendezvous in eight minutes. Approaching you at eleven o'clock, angels three."

"Nice of them," Marcks said.

Harrier 2-0

Lieutenant Parker was flying the Harrier that would escort the Super Stallion. A sublieutenant sat in the back seat of the Royal Navy aircraft. Its purpose was not actually to escort the chopper to the *Invincible;* it was to make a last check for any Soviet submarines that might notice the Super Stallion in flight and wonder what it was doing.

"Any activity on the water?" Parker asked.

"Not a glimmer." The sublieutenant was working the FLIR package, which was sweeping left and right over their course track. Neither man knew what was going on, though both had speculated at length, incorrectly, on what it was that was chasing their carrier all over the bloody ocean.

"Try looking for the helicopter," Parker said.

"One moment . . . There. Just south of our track." The sublieutenant pressed a button and the display came up on the pilot's screen. The thermal image was mainly of the engines clustered atop the aircraft inside the fainter, dull-green glow of the hot rotor tips.

"Harrier 2-0, this is Sentry Echo. Your target is at your one o'clock, distance twenty miles, over."

"Roger, we have him on our IR box. Thank you, out,"

Parker said. "Bloody useful things, those Sentries."

"The Sikorski's running for all she's worth. Look at that engine signature."

The Super Stallion

At this moment the transmission casing fractured. Instantly the gallons of lubricating oil became a greasy cloud behind the rotor hub, and the delicate gears began to tear at one another. An alarm light flashed on the control panels. Marcks and the copilot instantly reached down to cut power to all three engines. There was not enough time. The transmission tried to freeze, but the power of the three engines tore it apart. What happened was the next thing to an explosion. Jagged pieces burst through the safety housing and ripped the forward part of the aircraft. The rotor's momentum twisted the Stallion savagely around, and it dropped rapidly. Two of the men in the back, who had loosened their seatbelts, jerked out of their seats and rolled forward.

"MAYDAY MAYDAY MAYDAY, this is Juliet 6," the co- pilot called. Commander Marcks' body slumped over the con- trols, a dark stain at the back of his neck. "We're goin' in, we're goin' in. MAYDAY MAYDAY MAYDAY."

The copilot was trying to do something. The main rotor was windmilling slowly—too slowly. The automatic decoupler that was supposed to allow it to autorotate and give him a vestige of control had failed. His controls were nearly useless, and he was riding the point of a blunt lance towards a black ocean. It was twenty seconds before they hit. He fought with his airfoil controls and tail rotor in order to jerk the aircraft around. He succeeded, but it was too late.

Harrier 2-0

It was not the first time Parker had seen men die. He had taken a life himself after sending a Sidewinder missile up the tailpipe of an Argentine Dagger fighter. That had not been pleasant. This was worse. As he watched, the Super Stallion's hump- backed engine cluster blew apart in a shower of sparks. There was no fire as such, for what good it did them. He watched and tried to will the nose to come up—and it did, but not enough. The Stallion hit the water hard. The fuselage snapped apart in the middle. The front end sank in an instant, but the after part wallowed for a few seconds like a bathtub before beginning to fill with water. According to the picture supplied by the FLIR package, no one got clear before it sank.

"Sentry, Sentry, did you see that, over?"

"Roger that, Harrier. We're calling a SAR mission right now. Can you orbit?"

"Roger, we can loiter here." Parker checked his fuel. "Nine-zero minutes. I—stand by." Parker nosed his fighter down and flicked on his landing lights. This lit up the low-light TV system. "Did you see that, Ian?" he asked his backseater.

"I think it moved."

"Sentry, Sentry, we have a possible survivor in the water. Tell *Invincible* to get a Sea King down here straightaway. I'm going down to investigate. Will advise."

"Roger that, Harrier 2-0. Your captain reports a helo spooling up right now. Out."

The Royal Navy Sea King was there in twenty-five minutes. A rubber-suited paramedic jumped in the water to get a collar on the one survivor. There were no others, and no wreckage, only a slick of jet fuel evaporating slowly into the cold air. A second helicopter continued the search as the first raced back to the carrier.

The Invincible

Ryan watched from the bridge as the medics carried the stretcher into the island. Another crewman appeared a moment later with a briefcase.

"He had this, sir. He's a lieutenant commander, name of Dwyer, one leg and several ribs broken. He's in a bad way, Admiral."

"Thank you." White took the case. "Any possibility of other survivors?"

The sailor shook his head. "Not a good one, sir. The Sikorski must have sunk like a stone." He looked at Ryan. "Sorry, sir."

Ryan nodded. "Thanks."

"Norfolk on the radio, Admiral," a communications officer said.

"Let's go, Jack." Admiral White handed him the briefcase and led him to the communications room.

"The chopper went in. We have one survivor being worked on right now," Ryan said over the radio. It was silent for a moment.

"Who is it?"

"Name's Dwyer. They took him right to sick bay, Admiral. He's out of action. Tell Washington. Whatever this operation is supposed to be, we have to rethink it."

"Roger. Out," Admiral Blackburn said.

"Whatever we decide to do," Admiral White observed, "it will have to be fast. We must get our helo off to the *Pigeon* in two hours to have her back before dawn."

Ryan knew exactly what that would mean. There were only four men at sea who both knew what was going on and were close enough to do anything. He was the only American among them. The *Kennedy* was too far away. The *Nimitz* was close enough, but using her would mean getting the data to her by radio, and Washington was not enthusiastic about that. The only other alternative was to assemble and dispatch another intelligence team. There just wasn't enough time.

"Let's get this case open, Admiral. I need to see what this plan is." They picked up a machinist's mate on the way to White's cabin. He proved to be an excellent locksmith.

"Dear God!" Ryan breathed, reading the contents of the case. "You better see this."

"Well," White said a few minutes later, "that is clever."

"It's cute, all right," Ryan said. "I wonder what genius thought it up. I know I'm going to be stuck with this. I'll ask Washington for permission to take a few officers along with me."

Ten minutes later they were back in communications. White had the compartment cleared. Then Jack spoke over the encrypted voice channel. Both hoped the scrambling device worked.

"I hear you fine, Mr. President. You know what happened to the helicopter."

"Yes, Jack, most unfortunate. I need you to pinch-hit for us."

"Yes, sir, I anticipated that."

"I can't order you, but you know what the stakes are. Will you do it?"

Ryan closed his eyes. "Affirmative."

"I appreciate it, Jack."

Sure you do. "Sir, I need your authorization to take some help with me, a few British officers."

"One," the president said.

"Sir, I need more than that."

"One."

"Understood, sir. We'll be moving in an hour."

"You know what's supposed to happen?"

"Yes, sir. The survivor had the ops orders with him. I've already read them over."

"Good luck, Jack."

"Thank you, sir. Out." Ryan flipped off the satellite channel and turned to Admiral White. "Volunteer once, just one time, and see what happens."

"Frightened?" White did not appear amused.

"Damned right I am. Can I borrow an officer? A guy who speaks Russian if possible. You know what this may involve."

"We'll see. Come on."

Five minutes later they were back in White's cabin awaiting the arrival of four officers. All turned out to be lieutenants, all under thirty.

"Gentlemen," the admiral began, "this is Commander Ryan. He needs an officer to accompany him on a voluntary basis for a mission of some importance. Its nature is secret and most unusual, and there may be some danger involved. You four have been asked here because of your knowledge of Russian. That is all I can say."

"Going to talk to a Sov submarine?" the oldest of them chirped up. "I'm your man. I have a degree in the language, and my first posting was aboard HMS *Dreadnought*."

Ryan weighed the ethics of accepting the man before telling him what was involved. He nodded, and White dismissed the others.

"I'm Jack Ryan." He extended his hand.

"Owen Williams. So, what are we up to?"

"The submarine is named *Red October*—"

"*Krazny Oktyabr*." Williams smiled.

"And she's attempting to defect to the United States."

"Indeed? So that's what we've been mucking about for. Jolly decent of her CO. Just how certain are we of this?"

Ryan took several minutes to detail the intelligence information. "We blinkered instructions to him, and he seems to have played along. But we won't know for sure until we get aboard. Defectors have been known to change their minds, it happens a lot more often than you might imagine. Still want to come along?"

"Miss a chance like this? Exactly how do we get aboard, Commander?"

"The name's Jack. I'm CIA, not navy." He went on to explain the plan.

"Excellent. Do I have time to pack some things?"

"Be back here in ten minutes," White said.

"Aye aye, sir." Williams drew to attention and left.

White was on the phone. "Send Lieutenant Sinclair to see me." The admiral explained that he was the commander of the *Invincible*'s marine detachment. "Perhaps you might need another friend along."

The other friend was an FN nine-millimeter automatic pistol with a spare clip and a shoulder holster that disappeared nicely under his jacket. The mission orders were shredded and burned before they left.

Admiral White accompanied Ryan and Williams to the flight deck. They stood at the hatch, looking at the Sea King as its engines screeched into life.

"Good luck, Owen." White shook hands with the youngster, who saluted and moved off.

"My regards to your wife, Admiral." Ryan took his hand.

"Five and a half days to England. You'll probably see her before I do. Be careful, Jack."

Ryan smiled crookedly. "It's my intelligence estimate, isn't it? If I'm right, it'll just be a pleasure cruise—assuming the helicopter doesn't crash on me."

"The uniform looks good on you, Jack."

Ryan hadn't expected that. He drew himself to attention and saluted as he'd been taught at Quantico. "Thank you, Admiral. Be seeing you."

White watched him enter the chopper. The crew chief slid the door shut, and a moment later the Sea King's engines increased power. The helicopter lifted unevenly for a few feet before its nose dipped to port and began a climbing turn to the south. Without flying lights the dark shape was lost to sight in less than a minute.

33N 75W

The *Scamp* rendezvoused with the *Ethan Allen* a few minutes after midnight. The attack sub took up station a thousand yards astern of the old missile boat, and both cruised in an easy circle as their sonar operators listened to the approach of a diesel-powered vessel, the USS *Pigeon*. Three of the pieces were now in place. Three more were to come.

The Red October

"There is no choice," Melekhin said. "I must continue to work on the diesel."

"Let us help you," Svyadov said.

"And what do you know of diesel fuel pumps?" Melekhin asked in a tired but kind voice. "No, Comrade. Surzpoi, Bugayev, and I can handle it alone. There is no reason to expose you also. I will report back in an hour."

"Thank you, Comrade." Ramius clicked the speaker off. "This cruise has been a troublesome one. Sabotage. Never in my career has something like this happened! If we cannot fix the diesel . . . We have only a few hours more of battery power, and the reactor requires a total overhaul and safety inspection. I swear to you, Comrades, if we find the bastard who did this to us . . ."

"Shouldn't we call for help?" Ivanov asked.

"This close to the American coast, and perhaps an imperialist submarine still on our tail? What sort of 'help' might we get, eh? Comrades, perhaps our problem is no accident, have you considered that? Perhaps we have become pawns in a murderous game." He shook his head. "No, we cannot risk this. The Americans must not get their hands on this submarine!"

CIA Headquarters

"Thank you for coming on such short notice, Senator. I apologize for getting you up so early." Judge Moore met Donaldson at the door and led him into his capacious office. "You know Director Jacobs, don't you?"

"Of course, and what brings the heads of the FBI and CIA together at dawn?" Donaldson asked with a smile. This had to be good. Heading the Select Committee was more than a job, it was fun, real fun to be one of the few people who were really in the know.

The third person in the room, Ritter, helped a fourth person out of a high-backed chair that had blocked him from view. It was Peter Henderson, Donaldson saw to his surprise. His aide's suit was rumpled as though he'd been up all night. Suddenly it wasn't fun anymore.

Judge Moore waxed solicitous. "You know Mr. Henderson, of course."

"What is the meaning of this?" Donaldson asked, his voice more subdued than anyone expected.

"You lied to me, Senator," Ritter said. "You promised that you would not reveal what I told you yesterday, knowing all the time you'd tell this man—"

"I did no such thing."

"—who then told a fellow KGB agent," Ritter went on. "Emil?"

Jacobs set his coffee down. "We've been onto Mr. Henderson for some time. It was his contact that had us stumped. Some things are just too obvious. A lot of people in D.C. have regular cab pickup. Henderson's contact was a cab driver. We finally got it right."

"The way we found out about Henderson was through you, Senator." Moore explained: "We had a very good agent in Moscow a few years ago, a colonel in their Strategic Rocket Forces. He'd been giving us good information for five years, and we were about to get him and his family out. We try to do that, you know; you can't run agents forever, and we really owed this man. But I made the mistake of revealing his name to your committee. One week later, he was gone—vanished.

He was eventually shot, of course. His wife and three daughters were sent to Siberia. Our information is that they live in a lumber settlement east of the Urals. Typical sort of place, no plumbing, lousy food, no medical facilities available, and since they're the family of a convicted traitor, you can probably imagine what sort of hell they must endure. A good man dead, and a family destroyed. Try thinking about that, Senator. This is a true story, and these are real people.

"We didn't know at first who had leaked it. It had to be you, or one of two others, so we began to leak information to individual committee members. It took six months, but your name came up three times. After that we had Director Jacobs check out all of your staffers. Emil?"

"When Henderson was an assistant editor of the Harvard *Crimson*, in 1970, he was sent to Kent State to do a piece on the shooting. You remember, the 'Days of Rage' thing after the Cambodian incursion and that awful screw-up with the national guard. I was in on that, too, as luck would have it. Evidently it turned Henderson's stomach. Understandable. But not his reaction. When he graduated and joined your staff he started talking with his old activist friends about his job. This led to a contract from the Russians, and they asked for some information. That was during the Christmas bombing—he really didn't like that. He delivered. It was low-level stuff at first, nothing they couldn't have gotten a few days later from the *Post*. That's how it works. They offered the hook, and he nibbled at it. A few years later, of course, they struck the hook nice and hard and he couldn't get away. We all know how the game works.

"Yesterday we planted a tape recorder in his taxi. You'd be amazed how easy it was. Agents get lazy, too, just like the rest of us. To make a long story short, we have you on tape promising not to reveal the information to anyone, and we have Henderson here spilling that data not three hours later to a known KGB agent, also on tape. You have violated no laws, Senator, but Mr. Henderson has. He was arrested at nine last night. The charge is espionage, and we have the evidence to make it stick."

"I had no knowledge whatever of this," Donaldson said.

"We hadn't the slightest thought that you might," Ritter said.

Donaldson faced his aide. "What do you have to say for yourself?"

Henderson didn't say anything. He thought about saying how sorry he was, but how to explain his emotions? The dirty feeling of being an agent for a foreign power, juxtaposed with the thrill of fooling a whole legion of government spooks. When he was caught these emotions changed to fear at what would happen to him, and relief that it was all over.

"Mr. Henderson has agreed to work for us," Jacobs said helpfully. "As soon as you leave the Senate, that is."

"What does that mean?" Donaldson asked.

"You've been in the Senate, what? Thirteen years, isn't it? You were originally appointed to fill out an unexpired term, if memory serves," Moore said.

"You might try asking my reaction to blackmail," the senator observed.

"Blackmail?" Moore held his hands out. "Good Lord, Senator, Director Jacobs has already told you that you have broken no laws, and you have my word that the CIA will not leak a word of this. Now, whether or not the Justice Department decides to prosecute Mr. Henderson is not in our hands. 'Senate Aide Convicted of Treason: Senator Donaldson Professes No Knowledge of Aide's Action.'"

Jacobs went on, "Senator, the University of Connecticut has offered you the chair in their school of government for some years now. Why not take it?"

"Or Henderson goes to prison. You put that on my conscience?"

"Obviously he cannot go on working for you, and it should be equally obvious that if he is fired after so many years of exemplary service in your office, it will be noticed. If, on the other hand, you decide to leave public life, it would not be too surprising if he were not able to get a job of equivalent stature with another senator. So, he will get a nice job in the General Accounting Office, where he will still have access to all sorts of secrets. Only from now on," Ritter said, "we decide which secrets he passes along."

"No statute of limitations on espionage," Jacobs pointed out.

"If the Soviets find out," Donaldson said, and stopped. He

didn't really care, did he? Not about Henderson, not about the fictitious Russian. He had an image to save, losses to cut.

"You win, Judge."

"I thought you'd see it our way. I'll tell the president. Thanks for coming in, Senator. Mr. Henderson will be a little late to the office this morning. Don't feel too badly about him, Senator. If he plays ball with us, in a few years we might let him off the hook. It's happened before, but he'll have to earn it. Good morning, sir."

Henderson would play along. His alternative was life in a maximum security penitentiary. After listening to the tape of his conversation in the cab, he'd made his confession in front of a court stenographer and a television camera.

The Pigeon

The ride to the *Pigeon* had been mercifully uneventful. The catamaran-hull rescue ship had a small helicopter platform aft, and the Royal Navy helicopter had hovered two feet above it, allowing Ryan and Williams to jump down. They were taken immediately to the bridge as the helicopter buzzed back northeast to her home.

"Welcome aboard, gentlemen," the captain said agreeably. "Washington says you have orders for me. Coffee?"

"Do you have tea?" Williams asked.

"We can probably find some."

"Let's go someplace we can talk in private," Ryan said.

The Dallas

The *Dallas* was now in on the plan. Alerted by another ELF transmission, Mancuso had brought her to antenna depth briefly during the night. The lengthy EYES ONLY message had been decrypted by hand in his cabin. Decryption was not Mancuso's strong point. It took him an hour as Chambers conned the *Dallas* back to trail her contact. A crewman passing the captain's cabin heard a muted *damn* through the door. When Mancuso reappeared, his mouth couldn't keep from twitching into a smile. He was not a good card player either.

The Pigeon

The *Pigeon* was one of the navy's two modern submarine rescue ships designed to locate and reach a sunken nuclear sub quickly enough to save her crew. She was outfitted with a variety of sophisticated equipment, chief among them the DSRV. This vessel, the *Mystic,* was hanging on its rack between the *Pigeon*'s twin catamaran hulls. There was also a 3-d sonar operating at low power, mainly as a beacon, while the *Pigeon* cruised in slow circles a few miles south of the *Scamp* and *Ethan Allen.* Two *Perry*-class frigates were twenty miles north, operating in conjunction with three Orions to sanitize the area.

"*Pigeon,* this is *Dallas,* radio check, over."

"*Dallas,* this is *Pigeon.* Read you loud and clear, over," the rescue ship's captain replied on the secure radio channel.

"The package is here. Out."

"Captain, on *Invincible* we had an officer send the message with a blinker light. Can you handle the blinker light?" Ryan asked.

"To be part of this? Are you kidding?"

The plan was simple enough, just a little too cute. It was clear that the *Red October* wanted to defect. It was even possible that everyone aboard wanted to come over—but hardly likely. They were going to get everyone off the *Red October* who might want to return to Russia, then pretend to blow up the ship with one of the powerful scuttling charges Russian ships are known to carry. The remaining crewmen would then take their boat northwest into Pamlico Sound to wait for the Soviet fleet to return home, sure that the *Red October* had been sunk and with the crew to prove it. What could possibly go wrong? A thousand things.

The Red October

Ramius looked through his periscope. The only ship in view was the USS *Pigeon,* though his ESM antenna reported surface radar activity to the north, a pair of frigates standing guard over the horizon. So, this was the plan. He watched the blinker light, translating the message in his mind.

Norfolk Naval Medical Center

"Thanks for coming down, Doc." The intelligence officer had taken over the office of assistant hospital administrator. "I understand our patient woke up."

"About an hour ago," Tait confirmed. "He was conscious for about twenty minutes. He's asleep now."

"Does that mean he'll make it?"

"It's a positive sign. He was reasonably coherent, so there's no evident brain damage. I was a little worried about that. I'd have to say the odds are in his favor now, but these hypothermia cases have a way of souring on you in a hurry. He's a sick kid, that hasn't changed." Tait paused. "I have a question for you, Commander: Why aren't the Russians happy?"

"What makes you think that?"

"Kind of hard to miss. Besides, Jamie found a doctor on staff who understands Russian, and we have him attending the case."

"Why didn't you let me know about that?"

"The Russians don't know either. That was a medical judgment, Commander. Having a physician around who speaks the patient's language is simply good medical practice." Tait smiled, pleased with himself for having thought up his own intelligence ploy while at the same time adhering to proper medical ethics and naval regulations. He took a file card from his pocket. "Anyway, the patient's name is Andre Katyskin. He's a cook, like we thought, from Leningrad. The name of his ship was the *Politovskiy*."

"My compliments, Doctor." The intelligence officer acknowledged Tait's maneuver, though he wondered why it was that amateurs had to be so damned clever when they butted into things that didn't concern them.

"So why are the Russians unhappy?" Tait did not get an answer. "And why don't *you* have a guy up there? You knew all along, didn't you? You knew what ship he escaped from, and you knew why she sank . . . So, if they wanted most of all to know what ship he came from, and if they don't like the news they got—does that mean they have *another* missing sub out there?"

CIA Headquarters

Moore lifted his phone. "James, you and Bob get in here right now!"

"What is it, Arthur?" Greer asked a minute later.

"The latest from CARDINAL." Moore handed xeroxed copies of a message to both men. "How quick can we get word out?"

"That far out? Means a helicopter, a couple of hours at least. We have to get this out quicker than that," Greer urged.

"We can't endanger CARDINAL, period. Draw up a message and get the navy or air force to relay it by hand." Moore didn't like it, but he had no choice.

"It'll take too long!" Greer objected loudly.

"I like the boy, too, James. Talking about it doesn't help. Get moving."

Greer left the room cursing like the fifty-year sailor he was.

The Red October

"Comrades. Officers and men of *Red October,* this is the captain speaking." Ramius' voice was subdued, the crewmen noticed. The incipient panic that had started a few hours earlier had driven them to the brittle edge of riot. "Efforts to repair our engines have failed. Our batteries are nearly flat. We are too far from Cuba for help, and we cannot expect help from the *Rodina.* We do not have enough electrical power even to operate our environmental control systems for more than a few hours. We have no choice, we must abandon ship.

"It is no accident that an American ship is now close to us, offering what they call assistance. I will tell you what has happened, comrades. An imperialist spy has sabotaged our ship, and somehow they knew what our orders were. They were waiting for us, comrades, waiting and hoping to get their dirty hands on our ship. They will not. The crew will be taken off. They will not get our *Red October!* The senior officers and I will remain behind to set off the scuttling charges. The water here is five thousand meters deep. They will not have our ship. All crewmen except those on duty will assemble in their quarters. That is all." Ramius looked around the control room. "We have lost, comrades. Bugayev, make the necessary signals to Moscow and to the American ship. We will then dive to a hundred meters. We will take no chance that they will seize our ship. I take full responsibility for this—disgrace! Mark this well, comrades. The fault is mine alone."

The Pigeon

"Signal received: 'SSS,'" the radioman reported.

"Ever been on a submarine before, Ryan?" Cook asked.

"Nope, I hope it's safer 'n flying." Ryan tried to make a joke of it. He was deeply frightened.

"Well, let's get you down to *Mystic*."

The Mystic

The DSRV was nothing more than three metal spheres welded together with a propeller on the back and some boiler plating all around to protect the pressure-bearing parts of the hull. Ryan was first through the hatch, then Williams. They found seats and waited. A crew of three was already at work.

The *Mystic* was ready for operation. On command, the *Pigeon*'s winches lowered her to the calm water below. She dived at once, her electric motors hardly making any noise. Her low-power sonar system immediately acquired the Russian submarine, half a mile away, at a depth of three hundred feet. The operating crew had been told that this was a straightforward rescue mission. They were experts. The *Mystic* was hovering over the missile sub's forward escape trunk within ten minutes.

The directional propellers worked them carefully into place and a petty officer made certain that the mating skirt was securely fastened. The water in the skirt between *Mystic* and *Red October* was explosively vented into a low-pressure chamber on the DSRV. This established a firm seal between the two vessels, and the residual water was pumped out.

"Your ball now, I guess." The lieutenant motioned Ryan to the hatch in the floor of the middle segment.

"I guess." Ryan knelt by the hatch and banged a few times with his hand. No response. Next he tried a wrench. A moment later three clangs echoed back, and Ryan turned the locking wheel in the center of the hatch. When he pulled the hatch up, he found another that had already been opened from below. The lower perpendicular hatch was shut. Ryan took a deep breath and climbed down the ladder of the white painted cylinder, followed by Williams. After reaching the bottom Ryan knocked on the lower hatch.

The Red October

It opened at once.

"Gentlemen, I am Commander Ryan, United States Navy. Can we be of assistance?"

The man he spoke to was shorter and heavier than himself. He wore three stars on his shoulder boards, an extensive set of ribbons on his breast, and a broad gold stripe on his sleeve. So, this was Marko Ramius...

"Do you speak Russian?"

"No sir, I do not. What is the nature of your emergency, sir?"

"We have a major leak in our reactor system. The ship is contaminated aft of the control room. We must evacuate."

At the words *leak* and *reactor* Ryan felt his skin crawl. He remembered how positive he had been that his scenario was correct. On land, nine hundred miles away, in a nice, warm office, surrounded by friends—well, not enemies. The looks he was getting from the twenty men in this compartment were lethal.

"Dear God! Okay, let's get moving then. We can take off twenty-five men at a time, sir."

"Not so fast, Commander Ryan. What will become of my men?" Ramius asked loudly.

"They will be treated as our guests, of course. If they need medical attention, they will get it. They will be returned to the Soviet Union as quickly as we can arrange it. Did you think we'd put them in prison?"

Ramius grunted and turned to speak with the others in Russian. On the flight from the *Invincible* Ryan and Williams had decided to keep the latter's knowledge of Russian secret for a while, and Williams was now dressed in an American uniform. Neither thought a Russian would notice the different accent.

"Dr. Petrov," Ramius said, "you will take the first group of twenty-five. Keep control of the men, Comrade Doctor! Do not let the Americans speak to them as individuals, and let no man wander off alone. You will behave correctly, no more, no less."

"Understood, Comrade Captain."

Ryan watched Petrov count the men off as they passed through the hatch and up the ladder. When they were finished, Williams secured first the *Mystic*'s hatch and then the one on the *October*'s escape truck. Ramius had a *michman* check it. They heard the DSRV disengage and motor off.

The silence that ensued was as long as it was awkward. Ryan and Williams stood in one corner of the compartment, Ramius and his men opposite them. It made Ryan think back to high school dances where boys and girls gathered in separate groups and there was a no-man's-land in the middle. When an officer fished out a cigarette, he tried breaking the ice.

"May I have a cigarette, sir?"

Borodin jerked the pack, and a cigarette came part way out. Ryan took it, and Borodin lit it with a paper match.

"Thanks. I gave it up, but underwater in a sub with a bad reactor, I don't think it's too dangerous, do you?" Ryan's first experience with a Russian cigarette was not a happy one. The black coarse tobacco made him dizzy, and it added an acrid smell to the air around them, which was already thick with the odor of sweat, machine oil, and cabbage.

"How did you come to be here?" Ramius asked.

"We were heading towards the coast of Virginia, Captain. A Soviet submarine sank there last week."

"Oh?" Ramius admired the cover story. "A Soviet submarine?"

"Yes, Captain. The boat was what we call an *Alfa*. That's all I know for sure. They picked up a survivor, and he's in the Norfolk naval hospital. May I ask your name, sir?"

"Marko Aleksandrovich Ramius."

"Jack Ryan."

"Owen Williams." They shook hands all around.

"You have a family, Commander Ryan?" Ramius asked.

"Yes, sir. A wife, a son, and a daughter. You, sir?"

"No, no family." He turned and addressed a junior officer in Russian. "Take the next group. You heard my instructions to the doctor?"

"Yes, Comrade Captain!" the young man said.

They heard the *Mystic*'s electric motors overhead. A moment later came the metallic clang of the mating collar gripping the escape trunk. It had taken forty minutes, but it had seemed like a week. God, what if the reactor really was bad? Ryan thought.

The Scamp

Two miles away, the *Scamp* had halted a few hundred yards from the *Ethan Allen*. Both submarines were exchanging messages on their gertrudes. The *Scamp* sonarmen had noted the passage of the three submarines an hour earlier. The *Pogy* and *Dallas* were now between the *Red October* and the other two American subs, their sonar operators listening intently for any interference, any vessel that might come their way. The transfer area was far enough offshore to miss the coastal traffic of commercial freighters and tankers, but that might not keep them from meeting a stray vessel from another port.

The Red October

When the third set of crewmen left under the control of Lieutenant Svyadov, a cook at the end of the line broke away, explaining that he wanted to retrieve his cassette tape machine, something he had saved months for. No one noticed when he didn't return, not even Ramius. His crewmen, even the experienced *michmanyy*, jostled one another to get out of their submarine. There was only one more group to go.

The Pigeon

On the *Pigeon*, the Soviet crewmen were taken to the crew's mess. The American sailors were observing their Russian counterparts closely, but no words passed. The Russians found the tables set with a meal of coffee, bacon, eggs, and toast. Petrov was happy for that. It was no problem keeping control of the men when they ate like wolves. With a junior officer acting as interpreter, they asked for and got plenty of additional bacon. The cooks had orders to stuff the Russians with all the food they could eat. It kept everyone busy as a helicopter landed from shore with twenty new men, one of whom raced to the bridge.

The Red October

"Last group," Ryan murmured to himself. The *Mystic* mated again. The last round trip had taken an hour. When the pair of hatches was opened, the lieutenant from the DSRV came down.

"Next trip will be delayed, gentlemen. Our batteries have about had it. It'll take ninety minutes to recharge. Any problem?"

"It will be as you say," Ramius replied. He translated for his men and then ordered Ivanov to take the next group. "The senior officers will stay behind. We have work to do." Ramius took the young officer's hand. "If something happens, tell them in Moscow that we have done our duty."

"I will do that, Comrade Captain." Ivanov nearly choked on his answer.

Ryan watched the sailors leave. The *Red October*'s escape trunk hatch was closed, then the *Mystic*'s. One minute later there was a clanging sound as the minisub lifted free. He heard the electric motors whirring off, fading rapidly away, and felt the green-painted bulkheads closing in on him. Being on an airplane was frightening, but at least the air didn't threaten to crush you. Here he was, underwater, three hundred miles from shore in the world's largest submarine, with only ten men aboard who knew how to run her.

"Commander Ryan," Ramius said, drawing himself to attention, "my officers and I request political asylum in the United States—and we bring you this small present." Ramius gestured toward the steel bulkheads.

Ryan had already framed his reply. "Captain, on behalf of the president of the United States, it is my honor to grant your request. Welcome to freedom, gentlemen."

No one knew that the intercom system in the compartment had been switched on. The indicator light had been unplugged hours before. Two compartments forward the cook listened, telling himself that he had been right to stay behind, wishing he had been wrong. Now what will I do? he wondered. His duty. That sounded easy enough—but would he remember how to carry it out?

"I don't know what to say about you guys." Ryan shook

everyone's hand again. "You pulled it off. You really pulled it off!"

"Excuse me, Commander," Kamarov said. "Do you speak Russian?"

"Sorry, Lieutenant Williams here does, but I do not. A group of Russian-speaking officers was supposed to be here in my place, but their helicopter crashed at sea last night." Williams translated this. Four of the officers had no knowledge of English.

"And what happens now?"

"In a few minutes, a missile submarine will explode two miles from here. One of ours, an old one. I presume that you told your men you were going to scuttle—Jesus, I hope you didn't say what you were really doing?"

"And have a war aboard my ship?" Ramius laughed. "No, Ryan. Then what?"

"When everybody thinks *Red October* has sunk, we'll head northwest to the Ocracoke Inlet and wait. USS *Dallas* and *Pogy* will be escorting us. Can these few men operate the ship?"

"These men can operate any ship in the world!" Ramius said it in Russian first. His men grinned. "So, you think that our men will not know what has become of us?"

"Correct. *Pigeon* will see an underwater explosion. They have no way of knowing it's in the wrong place, do they? You know that your navy has many ships operating off our coast right now? When they leave, well, then we'll figure out where to keep this present permanently. I don't know where that will be. You men, of course, will be our guests. A lot of our people will want to talk with you. For the moment, you can be sure that you will be treated very well—better than you can imagine." Ryan was sure that the CIA would give each a considerable sum of money. He didn't say so, not wanting to insult this kind of bravery. It had surprised him to learn that defectors rarely expect to receive money, almost never ask for any.

"What about political education?" Kamarov asked.

Ryan laughed. "Lieutenant, somewhere along the line somebody will take you aside to explain how our country works. That will take about two hours. After that you can immediately start telling us what we do wrong—everybody else in the world does, why shouldn't you? But I can't do that now. Believe this, you will love it, probably more than I do. I have never lived in a country that was not free, and maybe I don't appreciate my home as much as I should. For the moment, I suppose you have work to do."

"Correct," Ramius said. "Come, my new comrades, we will put you to work also."

Ramius led Ryan aft through a series of watertight doors. In a few minutes he was in the missile room, a vast compartment with twenty-six dark-green tubes towering through two decks. The business end of a boomer, with two-hundred-plus thermonuclear warheads. The menace in this room was enough to make hair bristle at the back of Ryan's neck. These were not academic abstractions, these were real. The upper deck he walked on was a grating. The lower deck, he could see, was solid. After passing through this and another compartment they were in the control room. The interior of the submarine was ghostly quiet; Ryan sensed why sailors are superstitious.

"You will sit here." Ramius pointed Ryan to the helmsman's station on the port side of the compartment. There was an aircraft-style wheel and a gang of instruments.

"What do I do?" Ryan asked, sitting.

"You will steer the ship, Commander. Have you never done this before?"

"No, sir. I've never been on a submarine before."

"But you are a naval officer."

Ryan shook his head. "No, captain. I work for the CIA."

"CIA?" Ramius hissed the acronym as if it were poisonous.

"I know, I know." Ryan dropped his head on the wheel. "They call us the Dark Forces. Captain, this is one Dark Force who's probably going to wet his pants before we're finished here. I work at a desk, and believe me on this if nothing else— there's nothing I'd like better than to be home with my wife and kids right now. If I had half a brain, I would have stayed in Annapolis and kept writing my books."

"Books? What do you mean?"

"I'm an historian, Captain. I was asked to join the CIA a few years ago as an analyst. Do you know what that is? Agents bring in their data, and I figure out what it means. I got into this mess by mistake—shit, you don't believe me, but it's true. Anyway, I used to write books on naval history."

"Tell me your books," Ramius ordered.

"Options and Decisions, Doomed Eagles, and a new one coming out next year, *Fighting Sailor,* a biography of Admiral Halsey. My first one was about the Battle of Leyte Gulf. It was reviewed in *Morskoi Sbornik,* I understand. It dealt with the nature of tactical decisions made under combat conditions. There's supposed to be a dozen copies at the Frunze library."

Ramius was quiet for a moment. "Ah, I know this book. Yes, I read parts of it. You were wrong, Ryan. Halsey acted stupidly."

"You will do well in my country, Captain Ramius. You are already a book critic. Captain Borodin, can I trouble you for a cigarette?" Borodin tossed him a full pack and matches. Ryan lit one. It was terrible.

The Avalon

The *Mystic's* fourth return was the signal for the *Ethan Allen* and *Scamp* to act. The *Avalon* lifted off her bed and motored the few hundred yards to the old missile boat. Her captain was already assembling his men in the torpedo room. Every hatch, door, manhole, and drawer had been opened all over the boat. One of the officers was coming forward to join the others. Behind him trailed a black wire that led to each of the bombs aboard. This he connected to a timing device.

"All ready, Captain."

The Red October

Ryan watched Ramius order his men to their posts. Most went aft to run the engines. Ramius had the good manners to speak in English, repeating himself in Russian for those who did not understand their new language.

"Kamarov and Williams, will you go forward and secure all hatches." Ramius explained for Ryan's benefit. "If something goes wrong—it won't, but if it does—we do not have enough men to make repairs. So, we seal the entire ship."

It made sense to Ryan. He set an empty cup on the control pedestal to serve as an ashtray. He and Ramius were alone in the control room.

"When are we to leave?" Ramius asked.

"Whenever you are ready, sir. We have to get to Ocracoke Inlet at high tide, about eight minutes after midnight. Can we make it?"

Ramius consulted his chart. "Easily."

Kamarov led Williams through the communications room forward of control. They left the watertight door there open, then went forward to the missile room. Here they climbed down a ladder and walked forward on the lower missile deck to the forward missile room bulkhead. They proceeded through the door into the stores compartments, checking each hatch as they went. Near the bow they went up another ladder into the torpedo room, dogging the hatch down behind them, and proceeded aft through the torpedo storage and crew spaces. Both men sensed how strange it was to be aboard a ship with no crew, and they took their time, Williams twisting his head to look at everything and asking Kamarov questions. The lieutenant was happy to answer them in his mother language. Both men were competent officers, sharing a romantic attachment to their profession. For his part, Williams was greatly impressed by the *Red October* and said as much several times. A great deal of attention had been paid to small details. The deck was tiled. The hatches were lined with thick rubber gaskets. They hardly made any noise at all as they moved about checking watertight integrity, and it was obvious that more than mere lip service had been paid to making this submarine a quiet one.

Williams was translating a favorite sea story into Russian as they opened the hatch to the missile room's upper deck. When he stepped through the hatch behind Kamarov, he remembered that the missile room's bright overhead lights had been left on. Hadn't they?

Ryan was trying to relax and failing at it. The seat was uncomfortable, and he recalled the Russian joke about how they were shaping the New Soviet Man—with airliner seats that contorted an individual into all kinds of impossible shapes. Aft, the engine room crew had begun powering up the reactor. Ramius was speaking over the intercom phone with his chief engineer, just before the sound of moving reactor coolant increased to generate steam for the turboalternators.

Ryan's head went up. It was as though he felt the sound before hearing it. A chill ran up the back of his neck before his brain told him what the sound had to be.

"What was that?" he said automatically, knowing already what it was.

"What?" Ramius was ten feet aft, and the caterpillar engines were now turning. A strange rumble reverberated through the hull.

"I heard a shot—no, several shots."

Ramius looked amused as he came a few steps forward. "I think you hear the sounds of the caterpillar engines, and I think it is your first time on a submarine boat, as you said. The first time is always difficult. It was so even for me."

Ryan stood up. "That may be, Captain, but I know a shot when I hear it." He unbottoned his jacket and pulled out the pistol.

"You will give me that." Ramius held out his hand. "You may not have a pistol on my submarine!"

"Where are Williams and Kamarov?" Ryan wavered.

Ramius shrugged. "They are late, yes, but this is a big ship."

"I'm going forward to check."

"You will stay at your post!" Ramius ordered. "You will do as I say!"

"Captain, I just heard something that sounded like gunshots, and I am going forward to check it out. Have you ever been shot at? I have. I have the scars on my shoulder to prove it. You'd better take the wheel, sir."

Ramius picked up a phone and punched a button. He spoke in Russian for a few seconds and hung up. "I will go to show you that my submarine has no souls—ghosts, yes? Ghosts, no ghosts." He gestured to the pistol. "And you are no spy, eh?"

"Captain, believe what you want to believe, okay? It's a long story, and I'll tell it to you someday." Ryan waited for the relief that Ramius had evidently called for. The rumble of the tunnel drive made the sub sound like the inside of a drum.

An officer whose name he did not remember came into the control room. Ramius said something that drew a laugh—which stopped when the officer saw Ryan's pistol. It was obvious that neither Russian was happy he had one.

"With your permission, Captain?" Ryan gestured forward.

"Go on, Ryan."

The watertight door between control and the next space had been left open. Ryan entered the radio room slowly, eyes tracing left and right. It was clear. He went forward to the missile room door, which was dogged tight. The door, four feet or so high and about two across, was locked in place with a central wheel. Ryan turned the wheel with one hand. It was well oiled. So were the hinges. He pulled the door open slowly and peered around the hatch coaming.

"Oh, shit," Ryan breathed, waving the captain forward. The missile compartment was a good two hundred feet long, lit only by six or eight small glow lights. Hadn't it been brightly lit before? At the far end was a splash of bright light, and the far hatch had two shapes sprawled on the gratings next to it. Neither moved. The light Ryan saw them by was flickering next to a missile tube.

"Ghosts, Captain?" he whispered.

"It is Kamarov." Ramius said something else under his breath in Russian.

Ryan pulled the slide back on his FN automatic to make sure a round was in the chamber. Then he stepped out of his shoes.

"Better let me handle this. Once upon a time I was a lieutenant in the marines." And my training at Quantico, he thought to himself, had damned little to do with this. Ryan entered the compartment.

The missile room was almost a third of the submarine's length and two decks high. The lower deck was solid metal. The upper one was made of metal grates. Sherwood Forest, this place was called on American missile boats. The term was apt enough. The missile tubes, a good nine feet in diameter and painted a darker green than the rest of the room, looked like the trunks of enormous trees. He pulled the hatch shut behind him and moved to his right.

The light seemed to be coming from the farthest missile tube on the starboard side of the upper missile deck. Ryan stopped to listen. Something was happening there. He could hear a low rustling sound, and the light was moving as though it came from a hand-held work lamp. The sound was traveling down the smooth sides of the interior hull plating.

"Why me?" he whispered to himself. He'd have to get past thirteen missile tubes to get to the source of that light, cross over two hundred feet of open deck.

He moved around the first one, pistol in his right hand at
waist level, his left hand tracing the cold metal of the tube.
Already he was sweating into the checkered hard-rubber pistol
grips. That, he told himself, is why they're checkered. He got
between the first and second tubes, looked to port to make sure
nobody was there, and got ready to move forward. Twelve to
go.

The deck grating was welded out of eighth-inch metal bars.
Already his feet hurt from walking on it. Moving slowly and
carefully around the next circular tube, he felt like an astronaut
orbiting the moon and crossing a continuous horizon. Except
on the moon there wasn't anybody waiting to shoot you.

A hand came down on his shoulder. Ryan jumped and whirled
around. Ramius. He had something to say, but Ryan put his
fingertips on the man's lips and shook his head. Ryan's heart
was beating so loudly that he could have used it for sending
Morse code, and he could hear his own breathing—so why
the hell hadn't he heard Ramius?

Ryan gestured his intention to go around the outboard side
of each missile. Ramius indicated that he would go around the
inboard sides. Ryan nodded. He decided to button his jacket
and turn the collar up. It would make him a harder target.
Better a dark shape than one with a white triangle on it. Next
tube.

Ryan saw that words were painted on the tubes, with other
inscriptions forged onto the metal itself. The letters were in
Cyrillic and probably said No Smoking or Lenin Lives or something similarly useless. He saw and heard everything with great
acuity, as though someone had taken sandpaper to all his senses
to make him fantastically alert. He edged around the next tube,
his fingers flexing nervously on the pistol grip, wanting to wipe
the sweat from his eyes. There was nothing here; the port side
was okay. Next one . . .

It took five minutes to get halfway down the compartment,
between the sixth and seventh tubes. The noise from the forward
end of the compartment was more pronounced now. The light
was definitely moving. Not by much, but the shadow of the
number one tube was jittering ever so slightly. It had to be a
work light plugged into a wall socket or whatever they called
that on a ship. What was he doing? Working on a missile? Was
there more than one man? Why didn't Ramius do a head count

getting his crew into the DSRV?

Why didn't *I*? Ryan swore to himself. Six more to go.

As he went around the next tube he indicated to Ramius that there was probably one man all the way at the far end. Ramius nodded curtly, having already reached that conclusion. For the first time he noticed that Ryan's shoes were off, and, thinking that was a good idea, he lifted his left foot to take off a shoe. His fingers, which felt awkward and stiff, fumbled with the shoe. It fell on a loose piece of grating with a clatter. Ryan was caught in the open. He froze. The light at the far end shifted, then went dead still. Ryan darted to his left and peered around the edge of the tube. Five more to go. He saw part of a face—and a flash.

He heard the shot and cringed as the bullet hit the after bulkhead with a *clang*. Then he drew back for cover.

"I will cross to the other side," Ramius whispered.

"Wait till I say." Ryan grabbed Ramius' upper arm and went back to the starboard side of the tube, pistol in front. He saw the face and this time he fired first, knowing he'd miss. At the same moment he pushed Ramius left. The captain raced to the other side and crouched behind a missile tube.

"We have you," Ryan said aloud.

"You have nothing." It was a young voice, young and very scared.

"What are you doing?" Ryan asked.

"What do you think, Yankee?" This time the taunt was more effective.

Probably figuring a way to set off a warhead, Ryan decided. A happy thought.

"Then you will die too," Ryan said. Didn't the police try to reason with barricaded suspects? Didn't a New York cop say on TV once, "We try to bore them to death?" But those were criminals. What was Ryan dealing with? A sailor who stayed behind? One of Ramius' own officers who'd had second thoughts? A KGB agent? A GRU agent covered as a crewman?

"Then I will die," the voice agreed. The light moved. Whatever he was doing, he was trying to get back to it.

Ryan fired twice as he went around the tube. Four to go. His bullets clanged uselessly as they hit the forward bulkhead. There was a remote chance that a carom shot—no . . . He looked left and saw that Ramius was still with him, shading to the port side of the tubes. He had no gun. Why hadn't he gotten himself one?

Ryan took a deep breath and leaped around the next tube. The guy was waiting for this. Ryan dove to the deck, and the bullet missed him.

"Who are you?" Ryan asked, raising himself on his knees and leaning against the tube to catch his breath.

"A Soviet patriot! You are the enemy of my country, and you shall not have this ship!"

He was talking too much, Ryan thought. Good. Probably. "You have a name?"

"My name is of no account."

"How about a family?" Ryan asked.

"My parents will be proud of me."

A GRU agent. Ryan was certain. Not the political officer. His English was too good. Probably some kind of backup for the political officer. He was up against a trained field officer. Wonderful. A trained agent, and just like he said, a patriot. Not a fanatic, a man trying to do his duty. He was scared, but he'd do it.

And blow this whole fucking ship up, with me on it.

Still, Ryan knew he had an edge. The other guy had something he had to do. Ryan only had to stop him or delay him long enough. He went to the starboard side of the tube and looked around the edge with just his right eye. There was no light at his end of the compartment—another edge. Ryan could see him more easily than he could see Ryan.

"You don't have to die, my friend. If you just set the gun down . . ." And *what?* End up in a federal prison? More likely just disappear. Moscow could not learn that the Americans had their sub.

"And CIA will not kill me, eh?" the voice sneered, quavering. "I am no fool. If I am to die, it will be to my purpose, my friend!"

Then the light clicked off. Ryan had wondered how long that would take. Did it mean that he was finished whatever the hell he was doing? If so, in an instant they'd be all gone. Or maybe the guy just realized how vulnerable the light made him. Trained field officer or not, he was a kid, a frightened kid, and probably had as much to lose as Ryan had. Like hell, Ryan thought, I have a wife and two kids, and if I don't get to him fast, I'll sure as hell lose them.

Merry Christmas, kids, your daddy just got blown up. Sorry there's no body to bury, but you see . . . It occurred to Ryan to pray briefly—but for what? For help in killing another man? *It's like this, Lord . . .*

"Still with me, Captain?" he called out.

"Da."

That would give the GRU agent something to worry about. Ryan hoped the captain's presence would force the man to shade more to the port side of his tube. Ryan ducked and rushed around the port side of his. Three to go. Ramius followed suit on his side. He drew a shot, but Ryan heard it miss.

He had to stop, to rest. He was hyperventilating. It was the wrong time for that. He had been a marine lieutenant—for three whole months before the chopper crashed—and he was supposed to know what to do! He had *led* men. But it was a whole lot easier to lead forty men with rifles than it was to fight all by himself.

Think!

"Maybe we can make a deal," Ryan suggested.

"Ah, yes, we can decide which ear the shot comes in."

"Maybe you'd like being an American."

"And my parents, Yankee, what of them?"

"Maybe we can get them out," Ryan said from the starboard side of his tube, moving left as he waited for a reply. He jumped again. Now there were two missile tubes separating him from his friend in the GRU, who was probably trying to crosswire the warheads and make half a cubic mile of ocean turn to plasma.

"Come, Yankee, we will die together. Now only one *puskatel* separates us."

Ryan thought quickly. He couldn't remember how many times he'd fired, but the pistol held thirteen rounds. He'd have enough. The extra clip was useless. He could toss it one way and move the other, creating a diversion. Would it work? Shit! It worked in the movies. It was for damned sure that doing nothing wasn't going to work.

Ryan took the gun in his left hand and fished in his coat pocket for the spare clip with his right. He put the clip in his

mouth while he switched the gun back. A poor highwayman's
shift . . . He took the clip in his left hand. Okay. He had to toss
the clip right and move left. Would it work? Right or wrong,
he didn't have a hell of a lot of time.

At Quantico he was taught to read maps, evaluate terrain,
call in air and artillery strikes, maneuver his squads and fire
teams with skill—and here he was, stuck in a goddamned steel
pipe three hundred feet under water, shooting it out with pistols
in a room with two hundred hydrogen bombs!

It was time to do something. He knew what that had to
be—but Ramius moved first. Out the corner of his eye he
caught the shape of the captain running toward the forward
bulkhead. Ramius leaped at the bulkhead and flicked a light
switch on as the enemy fired at him. Ryan tossed the clip to
the right and ran forward. The agent turned to his left to see
what the noise was, sure that a cooperative move had been
planned.

As Ryan covered the distance between the last two missile
tubes he saw Ramius go down. Ryan dove past the number
one missile tube. He landed on his left side, ignoring the pain
that set his arm on fire as he rolled to line up his target. The
man was turning as Ryan jerked off six shots. Ryan didn't hear
himself screaming. Two rounds connected. The agent was lifted
off the deck and twisted halfway around from the impact. His
pistol dropped from his hand as he fell limp to the deck.

Ryan was shaking too badly to get up at once. The pistol,
still tight in his hand, was aimed at his victim's chest. He was
breathing hard and his heart was racing. Ryan closed his mouth
and tried to swallow a few times; his mouth was as dry as
cotton. He got slowly to his knees. The agent was still alive,
lying on his back, eyes open and still breathing. Ryan had to
use his hand to stand up.

He'd been hit twice, Ryan saw, once in the upper left chest
and once lower down, about where the liver and spleen are.
The lower wound was a wet red circle which the man's hands
clutched. He was in his early twenties, if that, and his clear
blue eyes were staring at the overhead while he tried to say
something. His face was rigid with pain as he mouthed words,
but all that came out was an unintelligible gurgle.

"Captain," Ryan called, "you okay?"

"I am wounded, but I think I shall live, Ryan. Who is it?"

"How the hell should I know?"

The blue eyes fixed on Jack's face. Whoever he was, he knew death was coming to him. The pain on the face was replaced by something else. Sadness, an infinite sadness... He was still trying to speak. A pink froth gathered at the corners of his mouth. Lung shot. Ryan moved closer, kicking the gun clear and kneeling down beside him.

"We could have made a deal," he said quietly.

The agent tried to say something, but Ryan couldn't understand it. A curse, a call for his mother, something heroic? Jack would never know. The eyes went wide with pain one last time. The last breath hissed out through the bubbles and the hands on the belly went limp. Ryan checked for a pulse at the neck. There was none.

"I'm sorry." Ryan reached down to close his victim's eyes. He was sorry—why? Tiny beads of sweat broke out all over his forehead, and the strength he had drawn up in the shootout deserted him. A sudden wave of nausea overpowered him. "Oh, Jesus, I'm—" He dropped to all fours and threw up violently, his vomit spilling through the grates onto the lower deck ten feet below. For a whole minute his stomach heaved, well past the time he was dry. He had to spit several times to get the worst of the taste from his mouth before standing.

Dizzy from the stress and the quart of adrenalin that had been pumped into his system, he shook his head a few times, still looking at the dead man at his feet. It was time to come back to reality.

Ramius had been hit in the upper leg. It was bleeding. Both his hands, covered with blood, were placed on the wound, but it didn't look that bad. If the femoral artery had been cut, the captain would already have been dead.

Lieutenant Williams had been hit in the head and chest. He was still breathing but unconscious. The head wound was only a crease. The chest wound, close to the heart, made a sucking noise. Kamarov was not so lucky. A single shot had gone straight through the top of his nose, and the back of his head was a bloody wreckage.

"Jesus, why didn't somebody come and help us!" Ryan said when the thought hit him.

"The bulkhead doors are closed, Ryan. There is the—how do you say it?"

Ryan looked where the captain pointed. It was the intercom system. "Which button?" The captain held up two fingers. "Control room, this is Ryan. I need help here, your captain has been shot."

The reply came in excited Russian, and Ramius responded loudly to make himself heard. Ryan looked at the missile tube. The agent had been using a work light, just like an American one, a lightbulb in a metal holder with wire across the front. A door into the missile tube was open. Beyond it a smaller hatch, evidently leading into the missile itself, was also open.

"What was he doing, trying to explode the warheads?"

"Impossible," Ramius said, in obvious pain. "The rocket warheads—we call this special safe. The warheads cannot— not fire."

"So what was he doing?" Ryan went over to the missile tube. A sort of rubber bladder was lying on the deck. "What's this?" He hefted the gadget in his hand. It was made of rubber or rubberized fabric with a metal or plastic frame inside, a metal nipple on one corner, and a mouthpiece.

"He was doing something to the missile, but he had an escape device to get off the sub," Ryan said. "Oh, Christ! A timing device." He bent down to pick up the work light and switched it on, then stood back and peered into the missile compartment. "Captain, what's in here?"

"That is—the guidance compartment. It has a computer that tells the rocket how to fly. The door—," Ramius' breaths were coming hard, "—is a hatch for the officer."

Ryan peered into the hatch. He found a mass of multicolored wires and circuit boards connected in a way he'd never seen before. He poked through the wires half expecting to find a ticking alarm clock wired to some dynamite sticks. He didn't.

Now what should he do? The agent had been up to something—but what? Did he finish? How could Ryan tell? He couldn't. One part of his brain screamed at him to do something, the other part said that he'd be crazy to try.

Ryan put the rubber-coated handle to the light between his teeth and reached into the compartment with both hands. He grabbed a double handful of wires and yanked back. Only a few broke loose. He released one bunch and concentrated on the other. A clump of plastic and copper spaghetti came loose. He did it again for the other bunch. "Aaah!" he gasped, receiving an electric shock. An eternal moment followed while he waited to be blown up. It passed. There were more wires to pull. In under a minute he'd ripped out every wire he could see along with a half-dozen small breadboards. Next he smashed the light against everything he thought might break until the compartment looked like his son's toybox—full of useless fragments.

He heard people running into the compartment. Borodin was in front. Ramius motioned him over to Ryan and the dead agent.

"Sudets?" Borodin said. "Sudets?" He looked at Ryan. "This is cook."

Ryan took the pistol from the deck. "Here's his recipe file. I think he was a GRU agent. He was trying to blow us up. Captain Ramius, how about we launch this missile—just jettison the goddamned thing, okay?"

"A good idea, I think." Ramius' voice had become a hoarse whisper. "First close the inspection hatch, then we—can fire from the control room."

Ryan used his hand to sweep the fragments away from the missile hatch, and the door slid neatly back into place. The tube hatch was different. It was a pressure-bearing one and much heavier, held in place by two spring-loaded latches. Ryan slammed it three times. Twice it rebounded, but the third time it stuck.

Borodin and another officer were already carrying Williams aft. Someone had set a belt on Ramius' leg wound. Ryan got him to his feet and helped him walk. Ramius grunted in pain every time he had to move his left leg.

"You took a foolish chance, Captain," Ryan observed.

"This is my ship—and I do not like the dark. It was my fault! We should have made a careful counting as the crew left."

They arrived at the watertight door. "Okay, I'll go through first." Ryan stepped through and helped Ramius through backward. The belt had loosened, and the wound was bleeding again.

"Close the hatch and lock it," Ramius ordered.

It closed easily. Ryan turned the wheel three times, then got under the captain's arm again. Another twenty feet and they were in the control room. The lieutenant at the wheel was ashen.

Ryan sat the captain in a chair on the port side. "You have a knife, sir?"

Ramius reached in his pocket and came out with a folding knife and something else. "Here, take this. It's the key for the rocket warheads. They cannot fire unless this is used. You keep it." He tried to laugh. It had been Putin's, after all.

Ryan flipped it around his neck, opened the knife, and cut the captain's pants all the way up. The bullet had gone clean through the meaty part of the thigh. He took a clean handkerchief from his pocket and held it against the entrance wound. Ramius handed him another handkerchief. Ryan placed this against the half-inch exit wound. Next he set the belt across both, drawing it as tight as he could.

"My wife might not approve, but that will have to do."

"Your wife?" Ramius asked.

"She's a doc, an eye surgeon to be exact. The day I got shot she did this for me." Ramius' lower leg was growing pale. The belt was too tight, but Ryan didn't want to loosen it just yet. "Now, what about the missile?"

Ramius gave an order to the lieutenant at the wheel, who relayed it through the intercom. Two minutes later three officers entered the control room. Speed was cut to five knots, which took several minutes. Ryan worried about the missile and whether or not he had destroyed whatever boobytrap the agent had installed. Each of the three newly arrived officers took a key from around his neck. Ramius did the same, giving his second key to Ryan. He pointed to the starboard side of the compartment.

"Rocket control."

Ryan should have guessed as much. Arrayed throughout the control room were five panels, each with three rows of twenty-six lights and a key slot under each set.

"Put your key in number one, Ryan." Jack did, and the others inserted their keys. The red light came on and a buzzer sounded.

The missile officer's panel was the most elaborate. He turned a switch to flood the missile tube and open the number one hatch. The red panel lights began to blink.

"Turn your key, Ryan," Ramius said.

"Does this fire the missile?" Christ, what if that happens? Ryan wondered.

"No no. The rocket must be armed by the rocket officer. This key explodes the gas charge."

Could Ryan believe him? Sure he was a good guy and all that, but how could Ryan know he was telling the truth?

"Now!" Ramius ordered. Ryan turned his key at the same instant as the others. The amber light over the red light blinked on. The one under the green cover stayed off.

The *Red October* shuddered as the number one SS-N-20 was ejected upward by the gas charge. The sound was like a truck's air brake. The three officers withdrew their keys. Immediately the missile officer shut the tube hatch.

The Dallas

"What?" Jones said. "Conn, sonar, the target just flooded a tube—a missile tube? God almighty!" On his own, Jones powered up the under-ice sonar and began high-frequency pinging.

"What the hell are you doing?" Thompson demanded. Mancuso was there a second later.

"What's going on?" the captain snapped. Jones pointed at his display.

"The sub just launched a missile, sir. Look, Cap'n, two targets. But it's just hangin' there, no missile ignition. God!"

The Red October

Will it float? Ryan wondered.

It didn't. The Seahawk missile was pushed upward and to starboard by the gas charge. It stopped fifty feet over her deck as the *October* cruised past. The guidance hatch that Ryan had closed was not fully sealed. Water filled the compartment and flooded the warhead bus. The missile in any case had a sizable negative bouyancy, and the added mass in the nose tipped it over. The nose-heavy trim gave it an eccentric path, and it spiraled down like a seedpod from a tree. At ten thousand feet water pressure crushed the seal over the missile blast cones, but the Seahawk, otherwise undamaged, retained its shape all the way to the bottom.

The Ethan Allen

The only thing still operating was the timer. It had been set for thirty minutes, which had allowed the crew plenty of time to board the *Scamp,* now leaving the area at ten knots. The old reactor had been completely shut down. It was stone cold. Only a few emergency lights remained on from residual battery power. The timer had three redundant firing circuits, and all went off within a millisecond of one another, sending a signal down the detonator wires.

They had put four Pave Pat Blue bombs on the *Ethan Allen.* The Pave Pat Blue was a FAE (fuel-air explosive) bomb. Its blast efficiency was roughly five times that of an ordinary chemical explosive. Each bomb had a pair of gas-release valves, and only one of the eight valves failed. When they burst open, the pressurized propane in the bomb casings expanded violently outward. In an instant the atmospheric pressure in the old submarine tripled as her every part was saturated with an explosive air-gas mixture. The four bombs filled the *Ethan Allen* with the equivalent of twenty-five tons of TNT evenly distributed throughout the hull.

The squibs fired almost simultaneously, and the results were catastrophic: the *Ethan Allen*'s strong steel hull burst as if it were a balloon. The only item not totally destroyed was the reactor vessel, which fell free of the shredded wreckage and dropped rapidly to the ocean floor. The hull itself was blasted into a dozen pieces, all bent into surreal shapes by the explosion. Interior equipment formed a metallic cloud within the shattered hull, and everything fluttered downward, expanding over a wide area during the three-mile descent to the hard sand bottom.

The Dallas

"Holy shit!" Jones slapped the headphones off and yawned to clear his ears. Automatic relays within the sonar system protected his ears from the full force of the explosion, but what had been transmitted was enough to make him feel as though his head had been hammered flat. The explosion was heard through the hull by everyone aboard.

"Attention all hands, this is the captain speaking. What you just heard is nothing to worry about. That's all I can say."

"Gawd, Skipper!" Mannion said.

"Yeah, let's get back on the contact."

"Aye, Cap'n." Mannion gave his commander a curious look.

The White House

"Did you get the word to him in time?" the president asked.

"No, sir." Moore slumped into his chair. "The helicopter arrived a few minutes too late. It may be nothing to worry about. You'd expect that the captain would know enough to get everyone off except for his own people. We're concerned, of course, but there isn't anything we can do."

"I asked him personally to do this, Judge. Me."

Welcome to the real world, Mr. President, Moore thought. The chief executive had been lucky—he'd never had to send men to their deaths. Moore reflected that it was something easy to consider beforehand, less easy to get used to. He had affirmed death sentences from his seat on an appellate bench, and that had not been easy—even for men who had richly deserved their fates.

"Well, we'll just have to wait and see, Mr. President. The source this data comes from is more important than any one operation."

"Very well. What about Senator Donaldson?"

"He agreed to our suggestion. This aspect of the operation has worked out very well indeed."

"Do you really expect the Russians to buy it?" Pelt asked.

"We've left some nice bait, and we'll jerk the line a little to get their attention. In a day or two we'll see if they nibble at it. Henderson is one of their all-stars—his code name is Cassius—and their reaction to this will tell us just what sort of disinformation we can pass through him. He could turn out to be very useful, but we'll have to watch out for him. Our KGB colleagues have a very direct method for dealing with doubles."

"We don't let him off the hook unless he earns it," the president said coldly.

Moore smiled. "Oh, he'll earn it. We own Mr. Henderson."

THE FIFTEENTH DAY

FRIDAY, 17 DECEMBER

Ocracoke Inlet

There was no moon. The three-ship procession entered the inlet at five knots, just after midnight to take advantage of the extra-high spring tide. The *Pogy* led the formation since she had the shallowest draft, and the *Dallas* trailed the *Red October*. The coast guard stations on either side of the inlet were occupied by naval officers who had relieved the "coasties."

Ryan had been allowed atop the sail, a humanitarian gesture from Ramius that he much appreciated. After eighteen hours inside the *Red October* Jack had felt confined, and it was good to see the world—even if it was nothing but dark empty space. The *Pogy* showed only a dim red light that disappeared if it was looked at for more than a few seconds. He could see the water's feathery wisps of foam and the stars playing hide-and-seek through the clouds. The west wind was a harsh twenty knots coming off the water.

Borodin was giving terse, monosyllabic orders as he conned

the submarine up a channel that had to be dredged every few months despite the enormous jetty which had been built to the north. The ride was an easy one, the two or three feet of chop not mattering a whit to the missile sub's 30,000-ton bulk. Ryan was thankful for this. The black water calmed, and when they entered sheltered waters a Zodiac-type rubber boat zoomed towards them.

"Ahoy *Red October!*" a voice called in the darkness. Ryan could barely make out the gray lozenge shape of the Zodiac. It was ahead of a tiny patch of foam formed by the sputtering outboard motor.

"May I answer, Captain Borodin?" Ryan asked, getting a nod. "This is Ryan. We have two casualties aboard. One's in bad shape. We need a doctor and a surgical team right away! Do you understand?"

"Two casualties, and you need a doc, right." Ryan thought he saw a man holding something to his face, and thought he heard the faint crackle of a radio. It was hard to tell in the wind. "Okay. We'll have a doc flown down right away, *October*. *Dallas* and *Pogy* both have medical corpsmen aboard. You want 'em?"

"Damn straight!" Ryan replied at once.

"Okay. Follow *Pogy* two more miles and stand by." The Zodiac sped forward, reversed course, and disappeared in the darkness.

"Thank God for that," Ryan breathed.

"You are be—believer?" Borodin asked.

"Yeah, sure." Ryan should not have been surprised by the question. "Hell, you gotta believe in something."

"And why is that, Commander Ryan?" Borodin was examining the *Pogy* through oversized night glasses.

Ryan wondered how to answer. "Well, because if you don't, what's the point of life? That would mean Sartre and Camus and all those characters were right—all is chaos, life has no meaning. I refuse to believe that. If you want a better answer, I know a couple priests who'd be glad to talk to you."

Borodin did not respond. He spoke an order into the bridge microphone, and they altered course a few degrees to starboard.

The Dallas

A half mile aft, Mancuso was holding a light-amplifying night scope to his eyes. Mannion was at his shoulder, struggling to see.

"Jesus Christ," Mancuso whispered.

"You got that one right, Skipper," Mannion said, shivering in his jacket. "I'm not sure I believe it either. Here comes the Zodiac." Mannion handed his commander the portable radio used for docking.

"Do you read?"

"This is Mancuso."

"When our friend stops, I want you to transfer ten men to her, including your corpsman. They report two casualties who need medical attention. Pick good men, Commander, they'll need help running the boat—just make damned sure they're men who don't talk."

"Acknowledged. Ten men including the medic. Out." Mancuso watched the raft speed off to the *Pogy*. "Want to come along, Pat?"

"Bet your ass, uh, sir. You planning to go?" Mannion asked.

Mancuso was judicious. "I think Chambers is up to handling *Dallas* for a day or so, don't you?"

On shore, a naval officer was on the phone to Norfolk. The coast guard station was crowded, almost entirely with officers. A fiberglass box sat next to the phone so that they could communicate with CINCLANT in secrecy. They had been here only two hours and would soon leave. Nothing could appear out of the ordinary. Outside, an admiral and a pair of captains watched the dark shapes through starlight scopes. They were as solemn as men in a church.

Cherry Point, North Carolina

Commander Ed Noyes was resting in the doctor's lounge of the naval hospital at the U.S. Marine Corps Air Station, Cherry Point, North Carolina. A qualified flight surgeon, he had the duty for the next three nights so that he'd have four days off over Christmas. It had been a quiet night. This was about to change.

"Doc?"

Noyes looked up to see a marine captain in MP livery. The doctor knew him. Military police delivered a lot of accident cases. He set down his *New England Journal of Medicine*.

"Hi, Jerry. Something coming in?"

"Doc, I got orders to tell you to pack everything you need for emergency surgery. You got two minutes, then I take you to the airfield."

"What for? What kind of surgery?" Noyes stood.

"They didn't say, sir, just that you fly out somewheres, alone. The orders come from topside, that's all I know."

"Damn it, Jerry, I have to know what sort of surgery it is so I know what to take!"

"So take everything, sir. I gotta get you to the chopper."

Noyes swore and went into the trauma receiving room. Two more marines were waiting there. He handed them four sterile sets, prepackaged instrument trays. He wondered if he'd need some drugs and decided to grab an armful, along with two units of plasma. The captain helped him on with his coat, and they moved out the door to a waiting jeep. Five minutes later they pulled up to a Sea Stallion whose engines were already screaming.

"What gives?" Noyes asked the colonel of intelligence inside, wondering where the crew chief was.

"We're heading out over the sound," the colonel explained. "We have to let you down on a sub that has some casualties aboard. There's a pair of corpsmen to assist you, and that's all I know, okay?" It had to be okay. There was no choice in the matter.

The Stallion lifted off at once. Noyes had flown in them often enough. He had two hundred hours piloting helicopters, another three hundred in fixed-wing aircraft. Noyes was the kind of doctor who'd discovered too late that flying was as attractive a calling as medicine. He went up at every opportunity, often giving pilots special medical care for their dependents to get backseat time in an F-4 Phantom. The Sea Stallion, he noted, was not cruising. It was running flat out.

Pamlico Sound

The *Pogy* came to a halt about the time the helicopter left Cherry Point. The *October* altered course to starboard again and halted even with her to the north. The *Dallas* followed suit. A minute after that the Zodiac reappeared at the *Dallas'* side, then approached the *Red October* slowly, almost wallowing with her cargo of men.

"Ahoy *Red October!*"

This time Borodin answered. He had an accent but his English was understandable. "Identify."

"This is Bart Mancuso, commanding officer of USS *Dallas*. I have our ship's medical representative aboard and some other men. Request permission to come aboard, sir."

Ryan saw the *starpom* grimace. For the first time Borodin really had to face up to what was happening, and he would have been less than human to accept it without some kind of struggle.

"Permission is—yes."

The Zodiac edged right up to the curve of the hull. A man leaped aboard with a line to secure the raft. Ten men clambered off, one breaking away to climb up the submarine's sail.

"Captain? I'm Bart Mancuso. I understand you have some hurt men aboard."

"Yes," Borodin nodded, "the captain and a British officer, both shot."

"Shot?" Mancuso was surprised.

"Worry about that later," Ryan said sharply. "Let's get your doc working on them, okay?"

"Sure, where's the hatch?"

Borodin spoke into the bridge mike, and a few seconds later a circle of light appeared on deck at the foot of the sail.

"We haven't got a physician, we have an independent duty corpsman. He's pretty good, and *Pogy*'s man will be here in another couple minutes. Who are you, by the way?"

"He is a spy," Borodin said with palpable irony.

"Jack Ryan."

"And you, sir?"

"Captain Second Rank Vasily Borodin. I am—first officer, yes? Come over into the station, Commander. Please excuse me, we are all very tired."

"You're not the only ones." There wasn't that much room. Mancuso perched himself on the coaming. "Captain, I want you to know we had a bastard of a time tracking you. You are to be complimented for your professional skill."

The compliment did not elicit the anticipated response from Borodin. "You were able to track us. How?"

"I brought him along, you can meet him."

"And what are we to do?"

"Orders from shore are to wait for the doc to arrive and dive. Then we sit tight until we get orders to move. Maybe a day, maybe two. I think we could all use the rest. After that, we get you to a nice safe place, and I will personally buy you the best damned Italian dinner you ever had." Mancuso grinned. "You get Italian food in Russia?"

"No, and if you are accustomed to good food, you may find *Krazny Oktyabr* not to your liking."

"Maybe I can fix that. How many men aboard?"

"Twelve. Ten Soviet, the Englishman, and the spy." Borodin glanced at Ryan with a thin smile.

"Okay." Mancuso reached into his coat and came out with a radio. "This is Mancuso."

"We're here, Skipper," Chambers replied.

"Get some food together for our friends. Six meals for twenty-five men. Send a cook over with it. Wally, I want to show these men some good chow. Got it?"

"Aye aye, Skipper. Out."

"I got some good cooks, Captain. Shame this wasn't last week. We had lasagna, just like momma used to make. All that was missing was the Chianti."

"They have vodka," Ryan observed.

"Only for spies," Borodin said. Two hours after the shootout Ryan had had the shakes badly, and Borodin had sent him a drink from the medical stores. "We are told that your submarine men are greatly pampered."

"Maybe so," Mancuso nodded. "But we stay out sixty or seventy days at a time. That's hard enough, don't you think?"

"How about we go below?" Ryan suggested. Everyone agreed. It was getting cold.

Borodin, Ryan and Mancuso went below to find the Americans on one side of the control room and the Soviets on the other, just like before. The American captain broke the ice.

"Captain Borodin, this is the man who found you. Come here, Jonesy."

"It wasn't very easy, sir," Jones said. "Can I get to work?

Can I see your sonar room?"

"Bugayev." Borodin waved the ship's electronics officer over. The captain-lieutenant led the sonarman aft.

Jones took one look at the equipment and muttered, "Kludge." The face plates all had louvers on them to let out the heat. God, did they use vacuum tubes? Jones wondered. He pulled a screwdriver from his pocket to find out.

"You speak English, sir?"

"Yes, a little."

"Can I see the circuit diagrams for these, please?"

Bugayev blinked. No enlisted man, and only one of his *michmanyy*, had ever asked for it. Then he took the binder of schematics from its shelf on the forward bulkhead.

Jones matched the code number of the set he was checking with the right section of the binder. Unfolding the diagram, he noted with relief that ohms were ohms, all over the world. He began tracing his finger along the page, then pulled the cover panel off to look inside the set.

"Kludge, megakludge to the max!" Jones was shocked enough to lapse into Valspeak.

"Excuse me, what is this 'kludge'?"

"Oh, pardon me, sir. That's an expression we use in the navy. I don't know how to say it in Russian. Sorry." Jones stifled a grin as he went back to the schematic. "Sir, this one here's a low-powered high-frequency set, right? You use this for mines and stuff?"

It was Bugayev's turn to be shocked. "You have been trained in Soviet equipment?"

"No, sir, but I've sure heard a lot of it." Wasn't this obvious? Jones wondered. "Sir, this is a high-frequency set, but it doesn't draw a lot of power. What else is it good for? A low-power FM set you use for mines, for work under ice, and for docking, right?"

"Correct."

"You have a gertrude, sir?"

"Gertrude?"

"Underwater telephone, sir, for talking to other subs." Didn't this guy know anything?

"Ah, yes, but it is located in control, and it is broken."

"Uh-huh." Jones looked over the diagram again. "I think I

can rig a modulator on this baby, then, and make it into a gertrude for ya. Might be useful. You think your skipper would want that, sir?"

"I will ask." He expected Jones to stay put, but the young sonarman was right behind him when he went to control. Bugayev explained the suggestion to Borodin while Jones talked to Mancuso.

"They got a little FM set that looks just like the old gertrudes in sonar school. We have a spare modulator in stores, and I can probably rig it up in thirty minutes, no sweat," the sonarman said.

"Captain Borodin, do you agree?" Mancuso asked.

Borodin felt as if he were being pushed too fast, even though the suggestion made perfectly good sense. "Yes, have your man do it."

"Skipper, how long we gonna be here?" Jones asked.

"A day or two, why?"

"Sir, this boat looks kinda thin on creature comforts, you know? How 'bout I grab a TV and a tape machine? Give 'em something to look at, you know, sort of give 'em a quick look at the USA?"

Mancuso laughed. They wanted to learn everything they could about this boat, but they had plenty of time for that, and Jones' idea looked like a good way to ease the tension. On the other hand, he didn't want to incite a mutiny on his own sub. "Okay, take the one from the wardroom."

"Right, Skipper."

The Zodiac delivered the *Pogy*'s corpsman a few minutes later, and Jones took the boat back to the *Dallas*. Gradually the officers were beginning to engage in conversation. Two Russians were trying to talk to Mannion and were looking at his hair. They had never met a black man before.

"Captain Borodin, I have orders to take something out of the control room that will identify—I mean, something that comes from this boat." Mancuso pointed. "Can I take that depth gauge? I can have one of my men rig a substitute." The gauge, he saw, had a number.

"For what reason?"

"Beats me, but those are my orders."

"Yes," Borodin replied.

Mancuso ordered one of his chiefs to perform the job. The

chief pulled a crescent wrench from his pocket and removed the nut holding the needle and dial in place.

"This is a little bigger than ours, Skipper, but not by much. I think we have a spare. I can flip it backwards and scribe in the markings, okay?"

Mancuso handed his radio over. "Call it in and have Jonesy bring the spare back with him."

"Aye, Cap'n." The chief put the needle back in place after setting the dial on the deck.

The Sea Stallion did not attempt to land, though the pilot was tempted. The deck was almost large enough to try. As it was, the helicopter hovered a few feet over the missile deck, and the doctor leaped into the arms of two seamen. His supplies were tossed down a moment later. The colonel remained in the back of the chopper and slid the door shut. The bird turned slowly to move back southwest, its massive rotor raising spray from the waters of Pamlico Sound.

"Was that what I think it was?" the pilot asked over the intercom.

"Wasn't it backwards? I thought missile subs had the missiles aft of the sail. Those were in front of the sail, weren't they? I mean, wasn't that the rudder sticking up behind the sail?" the copilot responded quizzically.

"It was a Russian sub!" the pilot said.

"What?" It was too late to see, they were already two miles away. "Those were our guys on the deck. They weren't Russians."

"Son of a bitch!" the major swore wonderingly. And he couldn't say a thing. The colonel of division intelligence had been damned specific about that: "You don't see nothin', you don't hear nothin', you don't think nothin', and you goddamned well don't ever say nothin'."

"I'm Doctor Noyes," the commander said to Mancuso in the control room. He had never been on a submarine before, and when he looked around he saw a compartment full of instruments all in a foreign language. "What ship is this?"

"Krazny Oktyabr," Borodin said, coming over. In the centerpiece of his cap there was a gleaming red star.

"What the hell is going on here?" Noyes demanded.

"Doc," Ryan took him by the arm, "you have two patients aft. Why not let's worry about them?"

Noyes followed him aft to sick bay. "What's going on here?" he persisted more quietly.

"The Russians just lost a submarine," Ryan explained, "and now she belongs to us. And if you tell anybody—"

"I read you, but I don't believe you."

"You don't have to believe me. What kind of cutter are you?"

"Thoracic."

"Good," Ryan turned into sick bay, "you have a gunshot wound victim who needs you bad."

Williams was lying naked on the table. A sailor came in with an armful of medical supplies and set them on Petrov's desk. The *October*'s medical locker had a supply of frozen plasma, and the two corpsmen already had two units running into the lieutenant. A chest tube was in, draining into a vacuum bottle.

"We got a nine-millimeter in this man's chest," one of the corpsmen said after introducing himself and his partner. "He's had a chest tube in the last ten hours, they tell me. The head looks worse than it is. Right pupil is a little blown, but no big deal. The chest is bad, sir. You'd better take a listen."

"Vitals?" Noyes fished in his bag for a stethoscope.

"Heart is 110 and thready. Blood pressure's eighty over forty."

Noyes moved his stethoscope around Williams' chest, frowning. "Heart's in the wrong place. We have a left tension pneumothorax. There must be a quart of fluid in there, and it sounds like he's heading for congestive failure." Noyes turned to Ryan. "You get out of here. I've got a chest to crack."

"Take care of him, Doc. He's a good man."

"Aren't they all," Noyes observed, stripping off his jacket. "Let's get scrubbed, people."

Ryan wondered if a prayer would help. Noyes looked and talked like a surgeon. Ryan hoped he was. He went aft to the captain's cabin, where Ramius was sleeping with the drugs he'd been given. The leg had stopped bleeding, and evidently one of the corpsmen had checked on it. Noyes could work on him next. Ryan went forward.

Borodin felt he had lost control and didn't like it, though it was something of a relief. Two weeks of constant tension plus the nerve-wrenching change in plans had shaken the officer more than he would have believed. The situation now was unpleasant—the Americans were trying to be kind, but they were so damned overpowering! At least the *Red October*'s officers were not in danger.

Twenty minutes later the Zodiac was back again. Two sailors went topside to unload a few hundred pounds of frozen food, then helped Jones with his electronic gear. It took several minutes to get everything squared away, and the seamen who took the food forward came back shaken after finding two stiff bodies and a third frozen solid. There had not been time to move the two recent casualties.

"Got everything, Skipper," Jones reported. He handed the depth gauge dial to the chief.

"What is all of this?" Borodin asked.

"Captain, I got the modulator to make the gertrude." Jones held up a small box. "This other stuff is a little color TV, a video cassette recorder, and some movie tapes. The skipper thought you gentlemen might want something to relax with, to get to know us a little, you know?"

"Movies?" Borodin shook his head. "Cinema movies?"

"Sure," Mancuso chuckled. "What did you bring, Jonesy?"

"Well, sir, I got *E.T.*, *Star Wars*, *Big Jake*, and *Hondo*." Clearly Jones wanted to be careful what parts of America he introduced the Russians to.

"My apologies, Captain. My crewman has limited taste in movies."

At the moment Borodin would have settled for *The Battleship Potemkin*. The fatigue was really hitting him hard.

The cook bustled aft with an armload of groceries. "I'll have coffee in a few minutes, sir," he said to Borodin on his way to the galley.

"I would like something to eat. None of us has eaten in a day," Borodin said.

"Food!" Mancuso called aft.

"Aye, Skipper. Let me figure this galley out."

Mannion checked his watch. "Twenty minutes, sir."

"We have everything we need aboard?"

"Yes, sir."

Jones bypassed the pulse control on the sonar amplifier and wired in the modulator. It was even easier than he'd expected. He had taken a radio microphone from the *Dallas* along with everything else and now connected it to the sonar set before powering the system up. He had to wait for the set to warm up. Jones hadn't seen this many tubes since he'd gone out on TV repair jobs with his father, and that had been a long time ago.

"*Dallas,* this is Jonesy, do you copy?"

"Aye." The reply was scratchy, like a taxicab radio.

"Thanks. Out." He switched off. "It works. That was pretty easy, wasn't it?"

Enlisted man, hell! And not even trained on Soviet equipment! the *October's* electronics officer thought. It never occurred to him that this piece of equipment was a near copy of an obsolete American FM system. "How long have you been a sonarman?"

"Three and a half years, sir. Since I dropped out of college."

"You learn all this in three years?" the officer asked sharply.

Jones shrugged. "What's the big deal, sir? I've been foolin' with radios and stuff since I was a kid. You mind if I play some music, sir?"

Jones had decided to be especially nice. He had only one tape of a Russian composer, the Nutcracker Suite, and had brought that along with four Bachs. Jones liked to hear music while he prayed over circuit diagrams. The young sonarman was in Hog Heaven. All the Russian sets he had listened to for three years—now he had their schematics, their hardware, and the time to figure them all out. Bugayev continued to watch in amazement as Jones' fingers did their ballet through the manual pages to the music of Tchaikovsky.

"Time to dive, sir," Mannion said in control.

"Very well. With your permission, Captain Borodin, I will assist with the vents. All hatches and openings are . . . shut." The diving board used the same light-array system as American boats, Mancuso noticed.

Mancuso took stock of the situation one last time. Butler and his four most senior petty officers were already tending to the nuclear tea kettle aft. The situation looked pretty good, considering. The only thing that could really go badly wrong would be for the *October's* officers to change their minds. The

Dallas would be keeping the missile sub under constant sonar observation. If she moved, the *Dallas* had a ten-knot speed advantage with which to block the channel.

"The way I see it, Captain, we are rigged for dive," Mancuso said.

Borodin nodded and sounded the diving alarm. It was a buzzer, just like on American boats. Mancuso, Mannion, and the Russian officer worked the complex vent controls. The *Red October* began her slow descent. In five minutes she was resting on the bottom, with seventy feet of water over the top of her sail.

The White House

Pelt was on the phone to the Soviet embassy at three in the morning. "Alex, this is Jeffrey Pelt."

"How are you, Dr. Pelt? I must offer my thanks and that of the Soviet people for your action to save our sailor. I was informed a few minutes ago that he is now conscious, and that he is expected to recover fully."

"Yes, I just learned that myself. What's his name, by the way?" Pelt wondered if he had awakened Arbatov. It didn't sound like it.

"Andre Katyskin, a cook petty officer from Leningrad."

"Good, Alex, I am informed that USS *Pigeon* has rescued nearly the entire crew of another Soviet submarine off the Carolinas. Her name, evidently, was *Red October*. That's the good news, Alex. The bad news is that the vessel exploded and sank before we could get them all off. Most of the officers, and two of our officers, were lost."

"When was this?"

"Very early yesterday morning. Sorry about the delay, but *Pigeon* had trouble with the radio, as a result of the underwater explosion, they say. You know how that sort of thing can happen."

"Indeed." Pelt had to admire the response, not a trace of irony. "Where are they now?"

"The *Pigeon* is sailing to Charleston, South Carolina. We'll have your crewmen flown directly to Washington from there."

"And this submarine exploded? You are sure?"

"Yeah, one of the crewmen said they had a major reactor

accident. It was just good luck that *Pigeon* was there. She was heading to the Virginia coast to look at the other one you lost. I think your navy needs a little work, Alex," Pelt observed.

"I will pass that along to Moscow, Doctor," Arbatov responded dryly. "Can you tell us where this happened?"

"I can do better than that. We have a ship taking a deep-diving research sub down to look for the wreckage. If you want, you can have your navy fly a man to Norfolk, and we'll fly him out to check it for you. Fair enough?"

"You say you lost two officers?" Arbatov played for time, surprised at the offer.

"Yes, both rescue people. We did get a hundred men off, Alex," Pelt said defensively. "That's something."

"Indeed it is, Dr. Pelt. I must cable Moscow for instructions. I will be back to you. You are at your office?"

"Correct. Bye, Alex." He hung up and looked at the president. "Do I pass, boss?"

"Work a little bit on the sincerity, Jeff." The president was sprawled in a leather chair, a robe over his pajamas. "They'll bite?"

"They'll bite. They sure as hell want to confirm the destruction of the sub. Question is, can we fool 'em?"

"Foster seems to think so. It sounds plausible enough."

"Hmph. Well, we have her, don't we?" Pelt observed.

"Yep, I guess that story about the GRU agent was wrong, or else they kicked him off with everybody else. I want to see that Captain Ramius. Jeez! Pulling a reactor scare, no wonder he got everybody off the ship!"

The Pentagon

Skip Tyler was in the CNO's office trying to relax in a chair. The coast guard station on the inlet had had a low-light television, the tape from which had been flown by helicopter to Cherry Point and from there by Phantom jet fighter to Andrews. Now it was in the hands of a courier whose automobile was just pulling up at the Pentagon's main entrance.

"I have a package to hand deliver to Admiral Foster," an ensign announced a few minutes later. Foster's flag secretary pointed him to the door.

"Good morning, sir! This is for you, sir." The ensign handed Foster the wrapped cassette.

"Thank you. Dismissed."

Foster inserted the cassette in the tape player atop his office television. The set was already on, and the picture appeared in several seconds.

Tyler was standing beside the CNO as it focused. "Yep."

"Yep," Foster agreed.

The picture was lousy—no other word for it. The low-light television system did not give a very sharp picture since it amplified all of the ambient light equally. This tended to wash out many details. But what they saw was enough: a very large missile submarine whose sail was much farther aft than the sails on anything a Western country made. She dwarfed the *Dallas* and *Pogy*. They watched the screen without a word for the next fifteen minutes. Except for the wobbly camera, the picture was about as lively as a test pattern.

"Well," Foster said as the tape ended, "we got us a Russian boomer."

"How 'bout that?" Tyler grinned.

"Skip, you were up for command of *Los Angeles*, right?"

"Yes, sir."

"We owe you for this, Commander, we owe you a lot. I did some checking the other day. An officer injured in the line of duty does not necessarily have to retire unless he is demonstrably unfit for duty. An accident while returning from working on your boat is line of duty, I think, and we've had a few ship commanders who were short a leg. I'll go to the president myself on this, son. It will mean a year's work getting back in the groove, but if you still want your command, by God, I'll get it for you."

Tyler sat down for that. It would mean being fitted for a new leg, something he'd been considering for months, and a few weeks getting used to it. Then a year—a good year—relearning everything he needed to know before he could go to sea . . . He shook his head. "Thank you, Admiral. You don't know what that means to me—but, no. I'm past that now. I have a different life, and different responsibilities now, and I'd just be taking someone else's slot. Tell you what, you let me get a look at that boomer, and we're even."

"That I can guarantee." Foster had hoped he'd respond that way, had been nearly sure of it. It was too bad, though. Tyler, he thought, would have been a good candidate for his own flag except for the leg. Well, nobody ever said the world was fair.

The Red October

"You guys seem to have things under control," Ryan observed. "Does anybody mind if I flake out somewhere?"

"Flake out?" Borodin asked.

"Sleep."

"Ah, take Dr. Petrov's cabin, across from the medical office."

On his way aft Ryan looked in Borodin's cabin and found the vodka bottle that had been liberated. It didn't have much taste, but it was smooth enough. Petrov's bunk was not very wide or very soft. Ryan was past caring. He took a long swallow and lay down in his uniform, which was already so greasy and dirty as to be beyond hope. He was asleep in five minutes.

The Sea Cliff

The air-purifier system was not working properly, Lieutenant Sven Johnsen thought. If his sinus cold had lasted a few more days he might not have noticed. The *Sea Cliff* was just passing ten thousand feet, and they couldn't tinker with the system until they surfaced. It was not dangerous—the environmental control systems had as many built-in redundancies as the Space Shuttle—just a nuisance.

"I've never been so deep," Captain Igor Kaganovich said conversationally. Getting him here had been complicated. It had required a Helix helicopter from the *Kiev* to the *Tarawa*, then a U.S. Navy Sea King to Norfolk. Another helicopter had taken him to the USS *Austin*, which was heading for 33N 75W at twenty knots. The *Austin* was a landing ship dock, a large vessel whose aft end was a covered well. She was usually used for landing craft, but today she carried the *Sea Cliff*, a three-man submarine that had been flown down from Woods Hole, Massachusetts.

"Does take some getting used to," Johnsen agreed, "but when you get down to it, five hundred feet, ten thousand feet, doesn't make much difference. A hull fracture would kill you just as fast, just down here there'd be less residue for the next boat to try and recover."

"Keep thinking those happy thoughts, sir," Machinist's Mate First Class Jesse Overton said. "Still clear on sonar?"

"Right, Jess." Johnsen had been working with the machinist's mate for two years. The *Sea Cliff* was their baby, a small, rugged research submarine used mainly for oceanographic tasks, including the emplacement or repair of SOSUS sensors. On the three-man sub there was little place for bridge discipline. Overton was not well educated or very articulate—at least not politely articulate. His skill at maneuvering the minisub was unsurpassed, however, and Johnsen was just as happy to leave that job to him. It was the lieutenant's task to manage the mission at hand.

"Air system needs some work," Johnsen observed.

"Yeah, the filters are about due for replacement. I was going to do that next week. Coulda' done it this morning, but I figured the backup control wiring was more important."

"Guess I have to go along with you on that. Handling okay?"

"Like a virgin." Overton's smile was reflected in the thick Lexan view port in front of the control seat. The *Sea Cliff*'s awkward design made her clumsy to maneuver. It was as though she knew what she wanted to do, just not quite how she wanted to do it. "How wide's the target area?"

"Pretty wide. *Pigeon* says after the explosion the pieces spread from hell to breakfast."

"I believe it. Three miles down, and a current to spread it around."

"The boat's name is *Red October*, Captain? A *Victor*-class attack submarine, you said?"

"That is your name for the class," Kaganovich said.

"What do you call them?" Johnsen asked. He got no reply. What was the big deal? he wondered. What did the name of the class matter to anybody?

"Switching on locater sonar." Johnsen activated several systems, and the *Sea Cliff* pulsed with the sound of the high-frequency sonar mounted on her belly. "There's the bottom." The yellow screen showed bottom contours in white.

"Anything sticking up, sir?" Overton asked.

"Not today, Jess."

A year before they had been operating a few miles from this spot and nearly been impaled on a Liberty ship, sunk around 1942 by a German U-boat. The hulk had been sitting up at an angle, propped up by a massive boulder. That near collision would surely have been fatal, and it had taught both men caution.

"Okay, I'm starting to get some hard returns. Directly ahead, spread out like a fan. Another five hundred feet to the bottom."

"Right."

"Hmph. There's one big piece, 'bout thirty feet long, maybe nine or ten across, eleven o'clock, three hundred yards. We'll go for that one first."

"Coming left, lights coming on now."

A half-dozen high-intensity floodlights came on, at once surrounding the submersible in a globe of light. It did not penetrate more than ten yards in the water, which ate up the light energy.

"There's the bottom, just where you said, Mr. Johnsen," Overton said. He halted the powered descent and checked for buoyancy. Almost exactly neutral, good. "This current's going to be tough on battery power."

"How strong is it?"

"Knot an' a half, maybe more like two, depending on bottom contours. Same as last year. I figure we can maneuver an hour, hour an' a half, tops."

Johnsen agreed. Oceanographers were still puzzling over this deep current, which seemed to change direction from time to time in no particular pattern. Odd. There were a lot of odd things in the ocean. That's why Johnsen got his oceanography degree, to figure some of the buggers out. It sure beat working for a living. Being three miles down wasn't work, not to Johnsen.

"I see somethin', a flash off the bottom right in front of us. Want I should grab it?"

"If you can."

They couldn't see it yet on any of the *Sea Cliff*'s three TV monitors, which looked straight ahead, forty-five degrees left and right of the bow.

"Okay." Overton put his right hand on the waldo control. This was what he was really best at.

"Can you see what it is?" Johnsen asked, fiddling with the TV.

"Some kinda instrument. Can you kill the number one flood, sir? It's dazzlin' me."

"Wait one." Johnsen leaned forward to kill the proper switch. The number one floodlight provided illumination for the bow camera, which went immediately blank.

"Okay, baby, now let's just hold steady . . ." The machinist's mate's left hand worked the directional propeller controls; his right was poised in the waldo glove. Now he was the only one who could see the target. Overton's reflection was grinning at itself. His right hand moved rapidly.

"Gotcha!" he said. The waldo took the depth-gauge dial a diver had magnetically affixed to the *Sea Cliff's* bow prior to setting out from the *Austin's* dock bay. "You can hit the light again, sir."

Johnsen flicked it on, and Overton maneuvered his catch in front of the bow camera. "Can ya see what it is?"

"Looks like a depth gauge. Not one of ours, though," Johnsen observed. "Can you make it out, Captain?"

"*Da,*" Kaganovich said at once. He let out a long breath, trying to sound unhappy. "It is one of ours. I cannot read the number, but it is Soviet."

"Put it in the basket, Jess," Johnsen said.

"Right." He maneuvered the waldo, placing the dial in a basket welded on the bow, then getting the manipulator arm back to its rest position. "Getting some silt. Let's pick up a little."

As the *Sea Cliff* got too close to the bottom the wash from her propellers stirred up the fine alluvial silt. Overton increased power to get back to a twenty-foot height.

"That's better. See what the current is doin', Mr. Johnsen? Good two knots. Gonna cut our bottom time." The current was wafting the cloud to port, rather quickly. "Where's the big target?"

"Dead ahead, hundred yards. Let's make sure we see what that is."

"Right. Going forward . . . There's something, looks like a butcher knife. We want it?"

"No, let's keep going."

"Okay, range?"

"Sixty yards. Ought to be seeing it soon."

The two officers saw it on TV the same time Overton did. Just a spectral image at first, it faded like an afterimage in one's eye. Then it came back.

Overton was the first to react. "Damn!"

It was more than thirty feet long and appeared perfectly round. They approached from its rear and saw the main circle and within it four smaller cones that stuck out a foot or so.

"That's a missile, Skipper, a whole fuckin' Russkie nuclear missile!"

"Hold position, Jess."

"Aye aye." He backed off on the power controls.

"You said she was a *Victor*," Johnsen said to the Soviet.

"I was mistaken." Kaganovich's mouth twitched.

"Let's take a closer look, Jess."

The *Sea Cliff* moved forward, up the side of the rocket body. The Cyrillic lettering was unmistakable, though they were too far off to make out the serial numbers. There was a new treasure for Davey Jones, an SS-N-20 Seahawk, with its eight five-hundred-kiloton MIRVs.

Kaganovich was careful to note the markings on the missile body. He'd been briefed on the Seahawk immediately before flying from the *Kiev*. As an intelligence officer, he ordinarily knew more about American weapons than their Soviet counterparts.

How convenient, he thought. The Americans had allowed him to ride in one of their most advanced research vessels whose internal arrangements he had already memorized, and they had accomplished his mission for him. The *Red October* was dead. All he had to do was get that information to Admiral Stralbo on the *Kirov* and the fleet could leave the American coast. Let them come to the Norwegian Sea to play their nasty games! See who would win them up there!

"Position check, Jess. Mark the sucker."

"Aye." Overton pressed a button to deploy a sonar transponder that would respond only to a coded American sonar signal. This would guide them back to the missile. They would return later with their heavy-lift rig to put a line on the missile and haul it to the surface.

"That is the property of the Soviet Union," Kaganovich pointed out. "It is in—under international waters. It belongs to my country."

"Then you can fuckin' come and get it!" snapped the American seaman. He must be an officer in disguise, Kaganovich thought. "Beg pardon, Mr. Johnsen."

"We'll be back for it," Johnsen said.

"You'll never lift it. It is too heavy," Kaganovich objected.

"I suppose you're right." Johnsen smiled.

Kaganovich allowed the Americans their small victory. It

could have been worse. Much worse. "Shall we continue to search for more wreckage?"

"No, I think we'll go back up," Johnsen decided.

"But your orders—"

"My orders, Captain Kaganovich, were to search for the remains of a *Victor*-class attack submarine. We found the grave of a boomer. You lied to us, Captain, and our courtesy to you ends at this point. You got what you wanted, I guess. Later we'll be back for what we want." Johnsen reached up and pulled the release handle for the iron ballast. The metal slab dropped free. This gave the *Sea Cliff* a thousand pounds of positive buoyancy. There was no way to stay down now, even if they wanted to.

"Home, Jess."

"Aye aye, Skipper."

The ride back to the surface was a silent one.

The USS Austin

An hour later, Kaganovich climbed to the *Austin*'s bridge and requested permission to send a message to the *Kirov*. This had been agreed upon beforehand, else the *Austin*'s commanding officer would have refused. Word on the dead sub's identity had spread fast. The Soviet officer broadcast a series of code words, accompanied by the serial number from the depth-gauge dial. These were acknowledged at once.

Overton and Johnsen watched the Russian board the helicopter, carrying the depth-gauge dial.

"I didn't like him much, Mr. Johnsen. *Keptin Kaganobitch*. The name sounds like a terminal studder. We snookered him, didn't we?"

"Remind me never to play cards with you, Jess."

The Red October

Ryan woke up after six hours to music that seemed dreamily familiar. He lay in his bunk for a minute trying to place it, then slipped his feet into his shoes and went forward to the wardroom.

It was *E.T.* Ryan arrived just in time to see the credits scrolling up the thirteen-inch TV set sitting on the forward end of the wardroom table. Most of the Russian officers and three

Americans had been watching it. The Russians were all dabbing their eyes. Jack got a cup of coffee and sat at the end of the table.

"You liked it?"

"It was magnificent!" Borodin proclaimed.

Lieutenant Mannion chuckled. "Second time we ran it."

One of the Russians started speaking rapidly in his native language. Borodin translated for him. "He asks if all American children act with such—Bugayev, *svobodno?*"

"Free," Bugayev translated, incorrectly but close enough.

Ryan laughed. "I never did, but the movie was set in California—people out there are a little crazy. The truth is, no, kids don't act like that—at least I've never seen it, and I have two. At the same time, we do raise our kids to be a lot more independent than Soviet parents do."

Borodin translated, and then gave the Russian response. "So, all American children are not such hooligans?"

"Some are. America is not perfect, gentlemen. We make lots of mistakes." Ryan had decided to tell the truth insofar as he could.

Borodin translated again. The reactions around the table were a little dubious.

"I have told them this movie is a child's story and should not be taken too seriously. This is so?"

"Yes, sir," Mancuso, who had just come in, said. "It's a kid's story, but I've seen it five times. Welcome back, Ryan."

"Thank you, Commander. I take it you have things under control."

"Yep. I guess we all needed the chance to unwind. I'll have to write Jonesy another commendation letter. This really was a good idea." He waved at the television. "We have lots of time to be serious."

Noyes came in. "How's Williams?" Ryan asked.

"He'll make it." Noyes filled his cup. "I had him open for three and a half hours. The head wound was superficial— bloody as hell, but head wounds are like that. The chest was a close one, though. The bullet missed the pericardium by a whisker. Captain Borodin, who gave that man first aid?"

The *starpom* pointed to a lieutenant. "He does not speak English."

"Tell him that Williams owes him his life. Putting that chest tube in was the difference. He would have died without it."

"You're sure he'll make it?" Ryan persisted.

"Of course he'll make it, Ryan. That's what I do for a living. He'll be a sick boy for a while, and I'd feel better if we had him in a real hospital, but everything's under control."

"And Captain Ramius?" Borodin asked.

"No problem. He's still sleeping. I took my time sewing it up. Ask him where he got his first aid training."

Borodin did. "He said he likes to read medical books."

"How old is he?"

"Twenty-four."

"Tell him if he ever wants to study medicine, I'll tell him how to get started. If he knows how to do the right thing at the right time, he might just be good enough to do it for a living."

The young officer was pleased by this comment and asked how much money a doctor could make in America.

"I'm in the service, so I don't make very much. Forty-eight thousand a year, counting flight pay. I could do a lot better on the outside."

"In the Soviet Union," Borodin pointed out, "doctors are paid about the same as factory workers."

"Maybe that explains why your docs are no good," Noyes observed.

"When will the captain be able to resume command?" Borodin asked.

"I'm going to keep him down all day," Noyes said. "I don't want him to start bleeding again. He can start moving around tomorrow. Carefully. I don't want him on that leg too much. He'll be fine, gentlemen. A little weak from the blood loss, but he'll recover fully." Noyes made his pronouncements as though he were quoting physical laws.

"We thank you, Doctor," Borodin said.

Noyes shrugged. "It's what they pay me for. Now can I ask a question? What the hell is going on here?"

Borodin laughed, translating the question for his comrades. "We will all become American citizens."

"And you're bringing a sub along with you, eh? Son of a gun. For a while there I thought this was some sort of—I don't know, something. This is quite a story. Guess I can't tell it to anybody, though."

"Correct, Doctor." Ryan smiled.

"Too bad," Noyes muttered as he headed back to sick bay.

Moscow

"So, Comrade Admiral, you report success to us?" Narmonov asked.

"Yes, Comrade General Secretary," Gorshkov nodded, surveying the conference table in the underground command center. All of the inner circle were here, along with the military chiefs and the head of the KGB. "Admiral Stralbo's fleet intelligence officer, Captain Kaganovich, was permitted by the Americans to view the wreckage from aboard one of their deep-submergence research vessels. The craft recovered a fragment of wreckage, a depth-gauge dial. These objects are numbered, and the number was immediately relayed to Moscow. It was positively from *Red October*. Kaganovich also inspected a missile blasted loose from the submarine. It was definitely a Seahawk. *Red October* is dead. Our mission is accomplished."

"By chance, Comrade Admiral, not by design," Mikhail Alexandrov pointed out. "Your fleet failed in its mission to *locate* and destroy the submarine. I think Comrade Gerasimov has some information for us."

Nikolay Gerasimov was the new KGB chief. He had already given his report to the political members of this group and was eager to release it to these strutting peacocks in uniform. He wanted to see their reactions. The KGB had scores to settle with these men. Gerasimov summarized the report he had from agent Cassius.

"Impossible!" Gorshkov snapped.

"Perhaps," Gerasimov conceded politely. "There is a strong probability that this is a very clever piece of disinformation. It is now being investigated by our agents in the field. There are, however, some interesting details which support this hypothesis. Permit me to review them, Comrade Admiral.

"First, why did the Americans allow our man aboard one of their most sophisticated research submarines? Second, why did they cooperate with us at all, saving our sailor from the *Politovskiy* and *telling* us about it? They let us see our man immediately. Why? Why not keep our man, use him, and dispose of him? Sentimentality? I think not. Third, at the same time they picked this man up their air and fleet units were harassing our fleet in the most blatant and aggressive manner. This suddenly stopped, and a day later they were tripping over their own feet in their efforts to assist in our 'search and rescue.'"

"Because Stralbo wisely and courageously decided to refrain from reacting to their provocations," Gorshkov replied.

Gerasimov nodded politely again. "Perhaps so. That was an intelligent decision on the admiral's part. It cannot be easy for a uniformed officer to swallow his pride so. On the other hand, I speculate that it is also possible that about this time the Americans received this information which Cassius passed on to us. I further speculate that the Americans were fearful of our reaction were we to suspect that they had perpetrated this entire affair as a CIA operation. We know now that several imperialist intelligence services are inquiring as to the reason for this fleet operation.

"Over the past two days we have been doing some fast checking of our own. We find," Gerasimov consulted his notes, "that there are twenty-nine Polish engineers at the Polyarnyy submarine yard, mainly in quality control and inspection posts, that mail and message-handling procedures are very lax, and the Captain Ramius did not, as he supposedly threatened in his letter to Comrade Padorin, sail his submarine into New York harbor, but was rather in a position a thousand kilometers south when the submarine was destroyed."

"That was an obvious piece of disinformation on Ramius' part," Gorshkov objected. "Ramius was both baiting us and deliberately misleading us. For that reason we deployed our fleet at all of the American ports."

"And never did find him," Alexandrov noted quietly. "Go on, Comrade."

Gerasimov continued. "Whatever port he was supposedly heading for, he was over five hundred kilometers from any of them, and we are certain that he could have reached any of them on a direct course. In fact, Comrade Admiral, as you reported in your initial briefing, he could have reached the American coast within seven days of leaving port."

"To do that, as I explained at length last week, would have meant traveling at maximum speed. Missile submarine commanders prefer not to do this," Gorshkov said.

"I can understand it," Alexandrov observed, "in view of the fate of the *Politovskiy*. But you would expect a traitor to the *Rodina* to run like a thief."

"Into the trap we set," Gorshkov replied.

"Which failed," Narmonov commented.

"I do not claim that this story is true, nor do I claim it is even a likely one at this point," Gerasimov said, keeping his voice detached and clinical, "but there is sufficient circumstantial evidence supporting it that I must recommend an indepth investigation by the Committee for State Security touching on all aspects of this affair."

"Security in my yards is a naval and GRU matter," Gorshkov said.

"No longer." Narmonov announced the decision reached two hours earlier. "The KGB will investigate this shameful business along two lines. One group will investigate the information from our agent in Washington. The other will proceed on the assumption that the letter from—allegedly from—Captain Ramius was genuine. If this was a traitorous conspiracy, it could only have been possible because Ramius was able under current regulations and practices to choose his own officers. The Committee for State Security will report to us on the desirability of continuing this practice, on the current degree of control ship captains have over the careers of their officers, and over Party control of the fleet. I think we will begin our reforms by allowing officers to transfer from one ship to another with greater frequency. If officers stay in one place too long, obviously they may develop confusion in their loyalties."

"What you suggest will destroy the efficiency of my fleet!" Gorshkov pounded on the table. It was a mistake.

"The People's fleet, Comrade Admiral," Alexandrov corrected. "The Party's fleet." Gorshkov knew where that idea came from. Narmonov still had Alexandrov's support. That made the comrade general secretary's position secure, and that meant the positions of other men around this table were not. Which men?

Padorin's mind revolted at the suggestion from the KGB. What did those bastard spies know about the navy? Or the Party? They were all corrupt opportunists. Andropov had proven that, and the Politburo was now letting this whelp Gerasimov attack the armed services, which safeguarded the nation against the imperialists, had saved it from Andropov's clique, and had never been anything but the stalwart servants of the Party. But it does all fit, doesn't it? he thought. Just as Khrushchev had deposed Zhukov, the man who made his succession possible when Beria was done away with, so these bastards would now play the KGB against the uniformed men who had made their positions safe in the first place . . .

"As for you, Comrade Padorin," Alexandrov went on.

"Yes, Comrade Academician." For Padorin there was no apparent escape. The Main Political Administration had passed final approval on Ramius' appointment. If Ramius were indeed a traitor, then Padorin stood condemned for gross misjudgment, but if Ramius had been an unknowing pawn, then Padorin along with Gorshkov had been duped into precipitous action.

Narmonov took his cue from Alexandrov. "Comrade Admiral, we find that your secret provisions to safeguard the security of the submarine *Red October* were successfully implemented—unless, that is, Captain Ramius was blameless and scuttled the ship himself along with his officers and the Americans who were doubtless trying to steal it. In either case, pending the KGB's inspection of the parts recovered from the wreck, it would appear that the submarine did not fall into enemy hands."

Padorin blinked several times. His heart was beating fast, and he could feel a twinge of pain in his left chest. Was he being let off? Why? It took him a second to understand. He was the political officer, after all. If the Party was seeking to reestablish political control over the fleet—no, to reassert what never had been lost—then the Politburo could not afford to depose the Party's representative in high command. This would make him the vassal of these men, Alexandrov especially. Padorin decided that he could live with that.

And it made Gorshkov's position extremely vulnerable. Though it would take some months, Padorin was sure that the Russian fleet would have a new chief, one whose personal power would not be sufficient to make policy without Politburo approval. Gorshkov had become too big, too powerful, and the Party chieftains did not wish to have a man with so much personal prestige in high command.

I have my head, Padorin thought to himself, amazed at his good fortune.

"Comrade Gerasimov," Narmonov went on, "will be working with the political security section of your office to review your procedures and to offer suggestions for improvements."

So, now he became the KGB's spy in high command? Well, he had his head, his office, his dacha, and his pension in two years. It was a small price to pay. Padorin was more than content.

THE SIXTEENTH DAY

SATURDAY, 17 DECEMBER

The East Coast

The USS *Pigeon* arrived at her dock in Charleston at four in the morning. The Soviet crewmen, quartered in the crew's mess, had become a handful for everyone. As much as the Russian officers had worked to limit contact between their charges and their American rescuers, this had never really been possible. To state it simply, they had been unable to block the call of nature. The *Pigeon* had stuffed her visitors with good navy chow, and the nearest head was a few yards aft. On the way to and from the facilities, the *Red October*'s crewmen met with American sailors, some of whom were Russian-speaking officers disguised as enlisted men, others of whom were Russian language specialists in the enlisted rates flown out just as the last load of Soviets had arrived aboard. The fact that they were aboard a putatively hostile vessel and had found friendly Russian-speaking men had been overpowering for many of the young conscripts. Their remarks had been recorded on hidden tape machines for later examination in Washington. Petrov and the three junior officers had been slow to catch on, but when they did they took to escorting the men to the toilet in relays, like protective parents. What they were not able to prevent was an intelligence officer in a bosun's uniform making an offer of asylum: anyone who wished to remain in the United States would be permitted to do so. It took ten minutes for the information to spread throughout the crew.

When it came time for the American crewmen to eat, the Russian officers could hardly prohibit contact, and it turned out that the officers themselves got very little to eat, so busy were they patrolling the mess tables. To the bemused surprise of their American counterparts, they were forced to decline repeated invitations to the *Pigeon*'s wardroom.

The *Pigeon* docked carefully. There was no hurry. As the gangway was set in place, the band on the dock played a selection of Soviet and American airs to mark the cooperative nature of the rescue mission. The Soviets had expected that their arrival would be a quiet one given the time of day. They were mistaken in this. When the first Soviet officer was halfway down the gangway, he was dazzled by fifty high-intensity television lights and the shouted questions of television reporters routed out of bed to meet the rescue ship and so have a bright piece of Christmas season news for the morning network broadcasts. The Russians had never encountered anything like Western newsmen before, and the resulting cultural collision was total chaos. Reporters singled out the officers, blocking their paths to the consternation of marines trying to keep control of things. To a man the officers pretended not to know a word of English, only to find that an enterprising reporter had brought along a Russian language professor from the University of South Carolina in Columbia. Petrov found himself stumbling through politically acceptable platitudes in front of a half-dozen cameras and wishing the entire affair were the bad dream it seemed to be. It took an hour to get every Russian sailor aboard the three buses chartered for the purpose and off to the airport. Along the way cars and vans filled with news crews raced alongside the buses, continuing to annoy the Russians with camera lights and further shouted questions that no one could understand. The scene at the airport was not much different. The air force had sent down a VC-135 transport, but before the Russians could board it they again had to jostle their way through a sea of reporters. Ivanov found himself confronted with a Slavic language expert whose Russian was marred by a horrendous accent. Boarding took another half hour.

A dozen air force officers got everyone seated and passed out cigarettes and liquor miniatures. By the time the VIP transport reached twenty thousand feet, it was a very happy flight. An officer spoke to them over the intercom system, explaining what was to happen. Medical checks would be made of everyone. The Soviet Union would be sending a plane for them the next day, but everyone hoped their stay might be extended a day or two so that they might experience American hospitality in full. The flight crew outdid itself, telling their passengers the history of every landmark, town, village, interstate highway, and truck stop on the flight route, proclaiming through the interpreter the wish of all Americans for peaceful, friendly relations with the Soviet Union, expressing the professional admiration of the U.S. Air Force for the courage of the Soviet seamen, and mourning the deaths of the officers who had courageously lingered behind, allowing their men to go first. The whole affair was a masterpiece of duplicity aimed at overwhelming them, and it began to succeed.

The aircraft flew low over the Washington suburbs while approaching Andrews Air Force Base. The interpreter explained that they were flying over middle-class homes that belonged to ordinary workers in government and local industry. Three more buses awaited them on the ground, and instead of driving on the beltway around Washington, D.C., the buses drove directly through town. American officers on each bus apologized for the traffic jams, telling the passengers that nearly every American family has one car, many two or more, and that people only use public transportation to avoid the nuisance of driving. The *nuisance* of driving one's own car, the Soviet seaman thought in amazement. Their political officers might later tell them that this was a total lie, but who could deny the thousands of cars on the road? Surely this could not all be a sham staged for the benefit of a few sailors on an hour's notice? Driving through southeast D.C. they noted that black people owned cars—scarcely had room to park them all! The bus continued down the Mall, with the interpreters voicing the hope that they would be allowed to see the many museums open to everyone. The Air and Space Museum, it was mentioned, had a moon rock brought back by the Apollo astronauts ... The Soviets saw the joggers in the Mall and the thousands of people casually strolling around. They jabbered among themselves as the buses turned north to Bethesda through the nicer sections of northwest Washington.

At Bethesda they were met by television crews broadcasting live over all three networks and by friendly, smiling U.S. Navy doctors and corpsmen who led them into the hospital for medical checks.

Ten embassy officials were there, wondering how to control the group but politically unable to protest the attention given their men in the spirit of détente. Doctors had been brought in from Walter Reed and other government hospitals to give each man a quick and thorough medical examination, particularly to check for radiation poisoning. Along the way each man found himself alone with a U.S. Navy officer who asked politely if that individual might wish to stay in the United States, pointing out that each man making this decision would be required to make his intentions known in person to a representative of the Soviet embassy—but that if he wished to do so, he would be permitted to stay. To the fury of the embassy officials, four men made this decision, one recanting after a confrontation with the naval attaché. The Americans had been careful to have each meeting videotaped so that later accusations of intimidation could be refuted at once.

When the medical checks were completed—thankfully, radiation exposure levels had been slight—the men were again fed and bedded down.

Washington, D.C.

"Good morning, Mr. Ambassador," the president said. Arbatov noted that again Dr. Pelt was standing at his master's side behind the large antique desk. He had not expected this meeting to be a pleasant one.

"Mr. President, I am here to protest the attempted kidnapping of our seamen by the United States government."

"Mr. Ambassador," the president responded sharply, "in the eyes of a former district attorney, kidnapping is a vile and loathsome crime, and the government of the United States of

America will not be accused of such a thing—certainly not in this office! We have not, do not, and never will kidnap people. Is that clear to you, sir?"

"Besides which, Alex," Pelt said less forcefully, "the men to whom you refer would not be alive were it not for us. We lost two good men rescuing your servicemen. You might at least express some appreciation for our efforts to save your crew, and perhaps make a gesture of sympathy for the Americans who lost their lives in the process."

"My government notes the heroic effort of your two officers, and does wish to express its appreciation and that of the Soviet people for the rescue. Even so, gentlemen, deliberate efforts have been made to entice some of those men to betray their country."

"Mr. Ambassador, when your trawler rescued the crew of our patrol plane last year, officers of the Soviet armed forces offered money, women, and other enticements to our crewmen if they would give out information or agree to stay behind in Vladivostok, correct? Don't tell me that you have no knowledge of this. You know that's how the game is played. At the time we did not object to this, did we? No, we were sufficiently grateful that those six men were still alive, and now, of course, all of them are back at work. We remain grateful for your country's humanitarian concern for the lives of ordinary American citizens. In this case, each officer and enlisted man was told that he could stay if he wished to do so. No force of any kind was used. Each man wishing to remain here was required by us to meet with an official of your embassy so as to give you a fair chance to explain to him the error of his ways. Surely this is fair, Mr. Ambassador. We made no offers of money or women. We do not buy people, and we damned well do not—ever—kidnap people. Kidnappers are people I put in jail. I even managed to have one executed. Don't you ever accuse me of that again," the president concluded righteously.

"My government insists that all of our men be returned to their homeland," Arbatov persisted.

"Mr. Ambassador, any person in the United States, regardless of his nationality or the manner of his arrival, is entitled to the full protection of our law. Our courts have ruled on this many times, and under our law no man or woman may be compelled to do something against his will without due process.

The subject is closed. Now, I have a question for you. What was a ballistic missile submarine doing three hundred miles from the American coast?"

"A missile submarine, Mr. President?"

Pelt lifted a photograph from the president's desk and handed it to Arbatov. Taken from the tape recorder on the *Sea Cliff*, it showed the SS-N-20 sea-launched ballistic missile.

"The name of the submarine is—was *Red October*," Pelt said. "It exploded and sank three hundred miles from the coast of South Carolina. Alex, we have an agreement between our two countries that no such vessel will approach either country to within five hundred miles—eight hundred kilometers. We want to know what that submarine was doing there. Don't try to tell us that this missile is some kind of fabrication—even if we had wanted to do such a foolish thing, we wouldn't have had the time. That's one of your missiles, Mr. Ambassador, and the submarine carried nineteen more just like it." Pelt deliberately misstated the number. "And the government of the United States asks the government of the Soviet Union how it came to be there, in violation of our agreement, while so many other of your ships are so close to our Atlantic coast."

"That must be the lost submarine," Arbatov offered.

"Mr. Ambassador," the president said softly, "the submarine was not lost until Thursday, seven days after you told us about it. In short, Mr. Ambassador, your explanation of last Friday does not coincide with the facts we have physically established."

"What accusation are you making?" Arbatov bristled.

"Why, none, Alex," the president said. "If that agreement is no longer operative, then it is no longer operative. I believe we discussed that possibility last week also. The American people will know later today what the facts are. You are sufficiently familiar with our country to imagine their reaction. I will have an explanation. For the moment, I see no further reason for your fleet to be off our coast. The 'rescue' has been successfully concluded, and the further presence of the Soviet fleet can only be a provocation. I want you and your government to consider what my military commanders are telling me right now—or if you prefer, what your commanders would be telling General Secretary Narmonov if the situation were reversed. I will have an explanation. Without one I can reach one of only a few conclusions—and those are conclusions I would prefer not to choose from. Send that message to your government, and tell them that since some of your men have opted to stay here, we'll probably find out what was really happening in short order. Good day."

Arbatov left the office, turning left to leave by the west entrance. A marine guard held the door open, a polite gesture that stopped short of his eyes. The ambassador's driver, waiting outside in a Cadillac limousine, held the door open for him. The driver was chief of the KGB's political intelligence section at that organization's Washington station.

"So," he said, checking traffic on Pennsylvania Avenue before making a left turn.

"So, the meeting went exactly as I had predicted, and now we can be absolutely certain why they are kidnapping our men," Arbatov replied.

"And that is, Comrade Ambassador?" the driver prompted. He did not let his irritation show. Only a few years before this Party hack would not have dared temporize with a senior KGB officer. It was a disgrace, what had happened to the Committee for State Security since the death of Comrade Andropov. But things would be set right again. He was certain of that.

"The president all but accused us of sending the submarine deliberately to their shore in violation of our secret 1979 protocol. They are holding our men to interrogate them, to take their heads apart so that they can learn what the submarine's orders were. How long will that take the CIA? A day? Two?" Arbatov shook his head angrily. "They may know already—a few drugs, a woman, perhaps, to loosen their tongues. The president also invited Moscow to imagine what the Pentagon hotheads are telling him to think! And telling him to do. No mystery there, is there? They will say we were rehearsing a surprise nuclear attack—perhaps even executing one! As if we were not working harder than they to achieve peaceful coexistence! Suspicious fools, they are fearful about what has happened, and even more angry."

"Can you blame them, Comrade?" the driver asked, taking all of this in, filing, analyzing, composing his independent report to Moscow Center.

"And he said that there was no further reason for our fleet to be off their coast."

"How did he say this? Was it a demand?"

"His words were soft. Softer than I expected. This concerns me. They are planning something, I think. Rattling a saber makes noise, drawing it does not. He demands an explanation for this entire affair. What do I tell him? What *was* happening?"

"I suspect that we will never know." The senior agent did know—the original story, that is, incredible as it was. That the navy and the GRU could allow such a fantastic error to take place had amazed him. The story from agent Cassius was scarcely less mad. The driver had passed it on to Moscow himself. Was it possible that the United States and the Soviet Union were both victims of a third party? An operation gone awry, and the Americans trying to find out who was responsible and how it was done so that they might try to do it themselves? That part of the story made sense, but did the rest? He frowned at the traffic. He had orders from Moscow Center: if this was a CIA operation, he was supposed to find out immediately. He didn't believe it was. If so the CIA was being unusually effective in covering it. Was it possible to cover such a complex operation? He didn't think so. Regardless, he and his colleagues would be working for several weeks to penetrate any cover there was, to find out what was being said in Langley and in the field, while other KGB sections did the same throughout the world. If the CIA had penetrated the Northern Fleet's high command he'd find out. Of that he was confident. He could almost wish they had done so. The GRU would be responsible for the disaster, and would be disgraced after profiting from the KGB's loss of prestige a few years back. If he was reading the situation correctly, the Politburo was turning the KGB loose on the GRU and the military, allowing Moscow Center to initiate its own independent investigation of the affair. Regardless of what was found, the KGB would come out ahead and deflate the armed services. One way or another, his organization would discover what had taken place, and if it was damaging to his rivals, so much the better . . .

When the door closed behind the Soviet ambassador, Dr. Pelt opened a side door to the Oval Office. Judge Moore came in.

"Mr. President, it's been a while since I've had to do things like hide in closets."

"You really expect this to work?" Pelt said.

"Yes, I do now," Moore settled comfortably into a leather chair.

"Isn't this a little shaky, Judge?" Pelt asked. "I mean, running an operation this complex?"

"That's the beauty of it, Doctor, we're not running anything. The Soviets will be doing that for us. Oh, sure, we'll have a lot of our people prowling around Eastern Europe asking a lot of questions. So will Sir Basil's fellows. The French and the Israelis already are, because we've asked them if they know what's happening with the stray missile sub. The KGB will find out quickly enough and wonder why the four main Western intelligence agencies are all asking the same questions—instead of pulling into their shells like they'd expect them to if this were our operation.

"You have to appreciate the dilemma the Soviets face, a choice between two equally unattractive scenarios. On the one hand, they can choose to believe that one of their most trusted professional officers has committed high treason on an unprecedented scale. You've seen our file on Captain Ramius. He's the Communist version of an eagle scout, a genuine New Soviet Man. Add to that the fact that a defection conspiracy necessarily involves a number of equally trusted officers. The Soviets have a mind block against believing that individuals of this type will ever leave the Workers' Paradise. That seems paradoxical, I admit, given the strenuous efforts they expend to keep people from leaving their country, but it's true. Losing a ballet dancer or a KGB agent is one thing—losing the son of a Politburo member, an officer with nearly thirty years of unblemished service, is quite another. Moreover, a naval captain has a lot of privileges; you might call his defection the equivalent of a self-made millionaire leaving New York to live in Moscow. They simply will not believe it.

"On the other hand, they can believe the story we planted through Henderson, which is also unattractive but is supported by a good deal of circumstantial evidence, especially our efforts to entice their crewmen to defect. You saw how furious they are about that. The way they think, this is a gross violation of the rules of civilized behavior. The president's forceful reaction to our discovery that this was a missile submarine is also evidence that favors Henderson's story."

"So what side will they come down on?" the president asked

"That, sir, is a question of psychology more than anything else, and Soviet psychology is very hard for us to read. Given the choice between the collective treason of ten men and an outside conspiracy, my opinion is that they will prefer the latter For them to believe that this really was defection—well, i would force them to reexamine their own beliefs. Who likes to do that?" Moore gestured grandly. "The latter alternative means that their security has been violated by outsiders, bu being a victim is more palatable than having to recognize the intrinsic contradictions of their own governing philosophy. O top of that we have the fact that the KGB will be running the investigation."

"Why?" Pelt asked, caught up in the judge's plot.

"In either case, a defection or a penetration of naval oper ational security, the GRU would have been responsible. Se curity of the naval and military forces is their bailiwick, the more so with the damage done to the KGB after the departure of our friend Andropov. The Soviets can't have an organization investigating itself—not in their intelligence community! So the KGB will be looking to take its rival service apart. From the KGB's perspective, outside instigation is the far more at tractive alternative; it makes for a bigger operation. If they confirm Henderson's story and convince everyone that it's true— and they will, of course—it makes them look all that much better for having uncovered it."

"They will confirm the story?"

"Of course they will! In the intelligence business if you look hard enough for something, you find it, whether it's really there or not. Lord, we owe this Ramius fellow more than he wil ever know. An opportunity like this doesn't come along once in a generation. We simply can't lose."

"But the KGB will emerge stronger," Pelt observed. "Is tha a good thing?"

Moore shrugged. "Bound to happen eventually. Unseating and possibly killing Andropov gave the military services too much prestige, just like with Beria back in the fifties. The Soviets depend on political control of their military as much as we do—more. Having the KGB take their high comman apart gets the dirty work done for them. It had to happen anyway, so it's just as well that we can profit by it. There's only a few more things we have to do."

"Such as?" the president asked.

"Our friend Henderson will leak information in a month or so saying that we had a submarine tracking *Red October* all the way from Iceland."

"But why?" Pelt objected. "Then they'll know that we were lying, that all the excitement over the missile sub was a lie."

"Not exactly, Doctor," Moore said. "Having a missile sub this close to our coast remains a violation of the agreement, and from their point of view we have no way of knowing why she was there—until we interrogate the crewmen remaining behind, who will probably tell us little of value. The Soviets will expect that we have not been completely truthful with them on this affair. The fact that we were trailing their sub and were ready to destroy it at any time gives them the evidence of our duplicity that they'll be looking for. We'll also say that *Dallas* monitored the reactor incident on sonar, and that will explain the proximity of our rescue ship. They know, well, they certainly suspect, that we have concealed something. This will mislead them about what it was we really concealed. The Russians have a saying for this. They call it wolf meat. And they will launch an extensive operation to penetrate our operation, whatever it is. But they will find nothing. The only people in the CIA who know what is really going on are Greer, Ritter, and myself. Our operations people have orders to *find out* what was going on, and that's all that can leak out."

"What about Henderson, and how many of our people know about the submarine?" the president asked.

"If Henderson spills anything to them he'll be signing his own death warrant. The KGB deals severely with double agents, and would not believe that we tricked him into delivering false information. He knows it, and we'll be keeping a close eye on him in any case. How many of our people know about the sub? A hundred perhaps, and the number will increase somewhat— but remember that they think we now have two dead Soviet subs off our coast, and they have every reason to believe that whatever Soviet sub equipment turns up in our labs has been recovered from the ocean floor. We will, of course, be reactivating the *Glomar Explorer* for just that purpose. They'd be suspicious if we didn't. Why disappoint them? Sooner or late they just might figure the whole story out, but by that time the stripped hulk will be at the bottom of the sea."

"So, we can't keep this a secret forever?" Pelt asked.

"Forever's a long time. We have a plan for the possibility For the immediate future the secret should be fairly safe, wha with only a hundred people in on it. In a year, minimum, more likely two or three, they may have accumulated enough data to suspect what has happened, but by that time there won't be much physical evidence to point to. Moreover, if the KGE discovers the truth, will they *want* to report it? Were the GRU to find out, they certainly would, and the resulting chaos withir their intelligence community would also work to our benefit." Moore took a cigar from a leather holder. "As I said, Ramiu: has given us a fantastic opportunity on several levels. And the beauty of it is that we don't have to do much of anything. The Russians will be doing all the legwork, looking for something that isn't there."

"What about the defectors, Judge?" the president asked.

"They, Mr. President, will be taken care of. We know how to do this, and we rarely have a complaint about the CIA': hospitality. We'll take some months to debrief them, and at the same time we'll be preparing them for life in America. They'll get new identities, reeducation, cosmetic surgery if necessary and they'll never have to work another day as long as the live—but they will want to work. Almost all of them do. expect the navy will find places for them, paid consultants fo their submarine warfare department, that sort of thing."

"I want to meet them," the president said impulsively.

"That can be arranged, sir, but it will have to be discrete," Moore cautioned.

"Camp David, that ought to be secure enough. And Ryan Judge, I want him taken care of."

"Understood, sir. We're bringing him along rather quickly already. He has a big future with us."

Tyuratam, USSR

The reason *Red October* had been ordered to dive long before dawn was orbiting the earth at a height of eight hundred kil ometers. The size of a Greyhound bus, Albatross 8 had been sent aloft eleven months earlier by a heavy-lift booster from the Cosmodrome at Tyuratam. The massive satellite, called a RORSAT, for radar ocean reconnaissance satellite, was specifically designed for maritime surveillance.

Albatross 8 passed over Pamlico Sound at 1131 local time. Its on-board programming was designed to trace thermal receptors over the entire visible horizon, interrogating everything in sight and locking on any signature that fit its acquisition parameters. As it continued on its orbit and passed over elements of the U.S. fleet, the *New Jersey*'s jammers were aimed upward to scramble its signal. The satellite's tape systems dutifully recorded this. The jamming would tell the operators something about American electronic warfare systems. As Albatross 8 crossed the pole, the parabolic dish on its front tracked in on the carrier signal of another bird, the *Iskra* communications satellite.

When the reconnaissance satellite located its higher flying cousin, a laser side-link transmitted the contents of the Albatross' tape bank. The *Iskra* immediately relayed this to the ground station at Tyuratam. The signal was also received by a fifteen-meter dish located in western China which was operated by the U.S. National Security Agency in cooperation with the Chinese, who used the data received for their own purposes. The Americans transmitted it via their own communications satellite to NSA headquarters at Fort Meade, Maryland. At almost the same time the digital signal was examined by two teams of experts five thousand miles apart.

"Clear weather," a technician moaned. "*Now* we get clear weather!"

"Enjoy it while you can, Comrade." His neighbor at the next console was watching data from a geosynchronous weather satellite that monitored the Western Hemisphere. Knowing the weather over a hostile country can have great strategic value. "There's another cold front approaching their coast. Their winter has been like ours. I hope they are enjoying it."

"Our men at sea will not." The technician mentally shuddered at the thought of being at sea in a major storm. He'd taken a Black Sea cruise the previous summer and become hopelessly seasick. "Aha! What is this? Colonel!"

"Yes, Comrade?" The colonel supervising the watch came over quickly.

"See here, Comrade Colonel." The technician traced a finger on the TV screen. "This is Pamlico Sound, on the central coast of the United States. Look here, Comrade." The thermal image of the water on the screen was black, but as the technician adjusted the display it changed to green with two white patches, one larger than the other. Twice the large one split into two segments. The image was of the surface of the water, and some of the water was half a degree warmer than it should have been. The differential was not constant, but it did return enough to prove that something was adding heat to the water.

"Sunlight, perhaps?" the colonel asked.

"No, Comrade, the clear sky gives even sunlight to the entire area," the technician said quietly. He was always quiet when he thought he was on to something. "Two submarines, perhaps three, thirty meters under the water."

"You are certain?"

The technician flipped on a switch to display the radar picture, which showed only the corduroy pattern of small waves.

"There is nothing *on* the water to generate this heat, Comrade Colonel. Therefore it must be something *under* the water. The time of year is wrong for mating whales. It can only be nuclear submarines, probably two, perhaps three. I speculate, Colonel, that the Americans have been sufficiently frightened by the deployment of our fleet to seek shelter for their missile submarines. Their missile sub base is only a few hundred kilometers south. Perhaps one of their *Ohio*-class boats have taken shelter here and is being protected by a hunter sub, as ours are."

"Then he will soon move out. Our fleet is being recalled."

"Too bad, it would be good to track him. This is a rare opportunity, Comrade Colonel."

"Indeed. Well done, Comrade Academician." Ten minutes later the data had been transmitted to Moscow.

Soviet Naval High Command, Moscow

"We will make use of this opportunity, Comrade," Gorshkov said. "We are now recalling our fleet, and we will allow several submarines to remain behind to gather electronic intelligence. The Americans will probably lose several in the shuffle."

"Quite likely," the chief of fleet operations said.

"The *Ohio* will go south, probably to their submarine base at Charleston or Kings Bay. Or north to Norfolk. We have *Konovalov* at Norfolk, and *Shabilikov* off Charleston. Both will stay in place for several days, I think. We must do something right to show the politicians that we have a real navy. Being able to track on an *Ohio* would be a beginning."

"I'll have the orders out in fifteen minutes, Comrade." The chief of operations thought this was a good idea. He had not liked the report of the Politburo meeting that he'd gotten from Gorshkov—though if Sergey were on his way out, he would be in a good place to take over the job . . .

The New Jersey

The RED ROCKET message had arrived in Eaton's hand only moments before: Moscow had just transmitted a lengthy operational letter via satellite to the Soviet fleet. Now the Russians were in a real fix, the commodore thought. Around them were three carrier battle groups—the *Kennedy, America,* and *Nimitz*—all under Josh Painter's command. Eaton had them in sight, and had operational control of the *Tarawa* to augment his own surface action group. The commodore turned his binoculars on the *Kirov.*

"Commander, bring the group to battle stations."

"Aye." The group operations officer lifted the tactical radio mike. "Blue Boys, this is Blue King. Amber Light, Amber Light, execute. Out."

Eaton waited four seconds for the *New Jersey*'s general quarters alarm to sound. The crew raced to their guns.

"Range to *Kirov?*"

"Thirty-seven thousand six hundred yards, sir. We've been sneaking in a laser range every few minutes. We're dialed in, sir," the group operations officer reported. "Main battery turrets are still loaded with sabots, and gunnery's been updating the solution every thirty seconds."

A phone buzzed next to Eaton's command chair on the flag bridge.

"Eaton."

"All stations manned and ready, Commodore," the battleship's captain reported. Eaton looked at his stopwatch.

"Well done, Captain. We've got the men drilled very well indeed."

In the *New Jersey*'s combat information center the numerical displays showed the exact range to the *Kirov*'s mainmast. The logical first target is always the enemy flagship. The only question was how much punishment the *Kirov* could absorb—and what would kill her first, the gun rounds or the Tomahawk missiles. The important part, the gunnery officer had been saying for days, was to kill the *Kirov* before any aircraft could interfere. The *New Jersey* had never sunk a ship all on her own. Forty years was a long time to wait.

"They're turning," the group operations officer said.

"Yep, let's see how far."

The *Kirov*'s formation had been on a westerly course when the signal arrived. Every ship in the circular array turned to starboard, all together. Their turns stopped when they reached a heading of zero-four-zero.

Eaton set his glasses down in the holder. "They're going home. Let's inform Washington and keep the men at stations for a while."

Dulles International Airport

The Soviets outdid themselves getting their men away from the United States. An Aeroflot Illyushin IL-62 was taken out of regular international service and sent directly from Moscow to Dulles. It landed at sunset. A near copy of the British VC-10, the four-engine aircraft taxied to the remotest service area for refueling. Along with some other passengers who did not deplane to stretch their legs, a spare flight crew was brought along so that the plane could immediately return home. A pair of mobile lounges drove from the terminal building two miles to the waiting aircraft. Inside them the crewmen of the *Red October* looked out at the snow-dusted countryside, knowing this was their final look at America. They were quiet, having been roused from bed in Bethesda and taken by bus to Dulles only an hour earlier. This time no reporters harassed them.

The four officers, nine *michmanyy*, and the remaining enlisted crew were split into distinct groups as they boarded. Each group was taken to a separate part of the aircraft. Each officer and *michman* had his own KGB interrogator, and the debriefing began as the aircraft started its takeoff roll. By the time the Illyushin reached cruising altitude most of the crewmen were asking themselves why they had not opted to remain behind with their traitorous countrymen. These interviews were decidedly unpleasant.

"Did Captain Ramius act strangely?" a KGB major asked Petrov.

"Certainly not!" Petrov answered quickly, defensively. "Didn't you know our submarine was sabotaged? We were lucky to escape with our lives!"

"Sabotaged? How?"

"The reactor systems. I am the wrong one to ask on this, I am not an engineer, but it was I who detected the leaks. You see, the radiation film badges showed contamination, but the engine room instruments did not. Not only was the reactor tampered with, but all of the radiation-sensing instruments were disabled. I saw this myself. Chief Engineer Melekhin had to rebuild several to locate the leaking reactor piping. Svyadov can tell this better. He saw it himself."

The KGB officer was scribbling notes. "And what was your submarine doing so close to the American coast?"

"What do you mean? Don't you know what our orders were?"

"What were your orders, Comrade Doctor?" The KGB officer stared hard into Petrov's eyes.

The doctor explained, concluding, "I saw the orders. They were posted for all to see, as is normal."

"Signed by whom?"

"Admiral Korov. Who else?"

"Did you not find those orders a little strange?" the major asked angrily.

"Do you question your orders, Comrade Major?" Petrov summoned up some spine. "*I* do not."

"What happened to your political officer?"

In another space Ivanov was explaining how the *Red October* had been detected by American and British ships. "But Captain Ramius evaded them brilliantly! We would have made it except for that damned reactor accident. You must find who did that to us, Comrade Captain. I wish to see him die myself!"

The KGB officer was unmoved. "And what was the last thing the captain said to you?"

"He ordered me to keep control of my men, not to let them speak with Americans any more than necessary, and he said that the Americans would never get their hands on our ship." Ivanov's eyes teared at the thought of his captain and his ship, both lost. He was a proud and privileged young Soviet man, the son of a Party academician. "Comrade, you and your people must find the bastards who did this to us."

"It was very clever," Svyadov was recounting a few feet away. "Even Comrade Melekhin only found it on his third attempt, and he swore vengeance on the men who did it. I saw it myself," the lieutenant said, forgetting that he never had, really. He explained in detail, to the point of drawing a diagram of how it had been done. "I don't know about the final accident. I was just coming on duty then. Melekhin, Surzpoi, and Bugayev worked for hours attempting to engage our auxiliary power systems." He shook his head. "I tried to join them, but Captain Ramius forbade it. I tried again, against orders, but Comrade Petrov prevented me."

Two hours over the Atlantic the senior KGB interrogators met aft to compare notes.

"So, if this captain was acting, he was devilishly good at it," the colonel in charge of the initial interrogations summarized. "His orders to his men were impeccable. The mission orders were announced and posted as is normal—"

"But who among these men knows Korov's signature? And we can't very well ask Korov, can we?" a major said. The commander of the Northern Fleet had died of a cerebral hemorrhage two hours into his first interrogation in the Lubyanka, much to everyone's disappointment. "It could have been forged in any case. Do we have a secret submarine base in Cuba? And what of the death of the *zampolit?*"

"The doctor is sure it was an accident," another major answered. "The captain thought he had struck his head, but he had actually broken his neck. I feel they should have radioed for instructions, though."

"A radio silence order," the colonel said. "I checked. This is entirely normal for missile submarines. Was this Captain Ramius skilled in unarmed combat? Might he have murdered the *zampolit?*"

"A possibility," mused the major who had questioned Petrov. "He was not trained in such things, but it is not hard to do."

The colonel did not know whether to agree. "Do we have any evidence that the crew thought a defection was being attempted?" All heads shook negatively. "Was the submarine's operational routine otherwise normal?"

"Yes, Comrade Colonel," a young captain said. "The surviving navigation officer, Ivanov, says that the evasion of imperialist surface and sub forces was effected perfectly—exactly in accordance with established procedures, but executed brilliantly by this Ramius fellow over a period of twelve hours. I have not even suggested that treason might be involved. Yet." Everyone knew that these sailors would be spending time in the Lubyanka until each head had been picked clean.

"Very well," the colonel said, "up to this point we have no indication of treason by the officers of the submarine? I thought not. Comrades, you will continue your interrogations in a gentler fashion until we arrive in Moscow. Allow your charges to relax."

The atmosphere on the aircraft gradually became more pleasant. Snacks were served, and vodka to loosen the tongues and encourage comradely good fellowship with the KGB officers, who were drinking water. The men all knew that they would be imprisoned for some time, and this fate was accepted with what to a Westerner would be surprising fatalism. The KGB would be working for weeks to reconstruct every event on the submarine from the time the last line was cast off at Polyarnyy to the moment the last man entered the *Mystic*. Other teams of agents were already working worldwide to learn if what happened to the *Red October* was a CIA plot or the plot of some other intelligence service. The KGB would find its answer, but the colonel in charge of the case was beginning to think the answer did not lie with these seamen.

The Red October

Noyes allowed Ramius to walk the fifteen feet from sick bay to the wardroom under supervision. The patient did not look very good, but this was largely because he needed a wash and a shave, like everyone else aboard. Borodin and Mancuso assisted him into his seat at the head of the table.

"So, Ryan, how are you today?"

"Good, thank you, Captain Ramius." Ryan smiled over his

coffee. In fact he was hugely relieved, having for the past several hours been able to leave the question of running the sub to the men who actually knew something about it. Though he was counting the hours until he could get out of the *Red October*, for the first time in two weeks he was neither seasick nor terrified. "How is your leg, sir?"

"Painful. I must learn not to be shot again. I do not remember saying to you that I owe you my life, as all of us do."

"It was my life, too," Ryan replied, a little embarrassed.

"Good morning, sir!" It was the cook. "May I fix you some breakfast, Captain Ramius?"

"Yes, I am very hungry."

"Good! One U.S. Navy breakfast. Let me get some fresh coffee, too." He disappeared into the passageway. Thirty seconds later he was back with fresh coffee and a place setting for Ramius. "Ten minutes on the breakfast, sir."

Ramius poured a cup of coffee. There was a small envelope in the saucer. "What is this?"

"Coffee Mate," Mancuso chuckled. "Cream for your coffee, Captain."

Ramius tore open the packet, staring suspiciously inside before dumping the contents into the cup and stirring.

"When do we leave?"

"Sometime tomorrow," Mancuso answered. The *Dallas* was going to periscope depth periodically to receive operational orders and relaying them to the *October* by gertrude. "We learned a few hours ago that the Soviet fleet is heading back northeast. We'll know for sure by sundown. Our guys are keeping a close eye on them."

"Where do we go?" Ramius asked.

"Where did you tell them you were going?" Ryan wanted to know. "What exactly did your letter say?"

"You know about the letter—how?"

"We know—that is, I know about the letter, but that's all I can say, sir."

"I told Uncle Yuri that we were sailing to New York to make a present of this ship to the president of the United States."

"But you didn't head for New York," Mancuso objected.

"Certainly not. I wished to enter Norfolk. Why go to a civilian port when a naval base is so close? You say I should tell Padorin the truth?" Ramius shook his head. "Why? Your coast is so large."

Dear Admiral Padorin, I'm sailing for New York ... No wonder they went ape! Ryan thought.

"We go to Norfolk or Charleston?" Ramius asked.

"Norfolk, I think," Mancuso said.

"Didn't you know they'd send the whole fleet after you?" Ryan snapped. "Why send the letter at all?"

"So they will know," Ramius answered. "So they will know. I did not expect that anyone would locate us. There you surprised us."

The American skipper tried to smile. "We detected you off the coast of Iceland. You were luckier than you imagine. If we'd sailed from England on schedule, we'd have been fifteen miles closer in shore, and we would have had you cold. Sorry, Captain, but our sonars and sonar operators are very good. You can meet the man who first tracked you later. He's working with your man Bugayev at the moment."

"Starshina," Borodin said.

"Not an officer?" Ramius asked.

"No, just a very good operator," Mancuso said, surprised. Why would anyone want an officer to stand watch on sonar gear?

The cook came back in. His idea of the standard U.S. Navy breakfast was a large platter with a slab of ham, two eggs over easy, a pile of hash browns, and four slices of toast, with a container of apple jelly.

"Let me know if you want more, sir," the cook said.

"This is a normal breakfast?" Ramius asked Mancuso.

"Nothing unusual about it. I prefer waffles myself. Americans eat big breakfasts." Ramius was already attacking his. After two days without a normal meal and all the blood loss from his leg wound, his body was screaming for food.

"Tell me, Ryan," Borodin was lighting a cigarette, "what is it in America that we will find most amazing?"

Jack motioned to the captain's plate. "Food stores."

"Food stores?" Mancuso asked.

"While I was sitting on *Invincible* I read over a CIA report on people who come over to our side." Ryan didn't want to say *defectors.* Somehow the word sounded demeaning. "Supposedly the first thing that surprises people, people from your part of the world, is going through a supermarket."

"Tell me about them," Borodin ordered.

"A building about the size of a football field—well, maybe a little smaller than that. You go in the front door and get a shopping cart. The fresh fruits and vegetables are on the right, and you gradually work your way left through the other departments. I've been doing that since I was a kid."

"You say fresh fruits and vegetables? What about now, in winter?"

"What about winter?" Mancuso said. "Maybe they cost a little more, but you can always get fresh produce. That's the one thing we miss on the boats. Our supply of fresh produce and milk only lasts us about a week."

"And meat?" Ramius asked.

"Anything you want," Ryan answered. "Beef, pork, lamb, turkey, chicken. American farmers are very efficient. The United States feeds itself and has plenty left over. You know that, the Soviet Union buys our grain. Hell, we pay farmers not to grow things, just to keep the surplus under control." The four Russians were doubtful.

"What else?" Borodin asked.

"What else will surprise you? Nearly everyone has a car. Most people own their own homes. If you have money, you can buy nearly anything you want. The average family in America makes something like twenty thousand dollars a year, I guess. These officers all make more than that. The fact of the matter is that in our country if you have some brains—and all of you men do—and you are willing to work—and all of you men are—you will live a comfortable life even without any help. Besides, you can be sure that the CIA will take good care of you. We wouldn't want anybody to complain about our hospitality."

"And what will become of my men?" Ramius asked.

"I can't say exactly, sir, since I've never been involved in this sort of thing myself. I would guess that you will be taken to a safe place to relax and unwind. People from the CIA and the navy will want to talk to you at length. That's no surprise, right? I told you this before. A year from now you will be doing whatever you choose to do."

"And anybody who wants to take a cruise with us is welcome o," Mancuso added.

Ryan wondered how true this was. The navy would not want to let any of these men on a 688-class boat. It might give one of them information valuable enough to enable him to return home and keep his head.

"How does a friendly man become a CIA spy?" Borodin asked.

"I am not a spy, sir," Ryan said again. He couldn't blame them for not believing him. "Going through graduate school I got to know a guy who mentioned my name to a friend of his in the CIA, Admiral James Greer. Back a few years ago I was asked to join a team of academics that was called in to check up on some of the CIA's intelligence estimates. At the time I was happily engaged writing books on naval history. At Langley—I was there for two months during the summer—I did a paper on international terrorism. Greer liked it, and two years ago he asked me to go to work there full time. I accepted. It was a mistake," Ryan said, not really meaning it. Or did he? "A year ago I was transferred to London to work on a joint intelligence evaluation team with the British Secret Service. My normal job is to sit at a desk and figure out the stuff that field agents send in. I got myself roped into this because I figured out what you were up to, Captain Ramius."

"Was your father a spy?" Borodin asked.

"No, my dad was a police officer in Baltimore. He and my mother were killed in a plane crash ten years ago."

Borodin expressed his sympathy. "And you, Captain Mancuso, what made you a sailor?"

"I wanted to be a sailor since I was a kid. My dad's a barber. I decided on submarines at Annapolis because I thought it looked interesting."

Ryan was watching something he had never seen before, men from two different places and two very different cultures trying to find common ground. Both sides were reaching out, seeking similarities of character and experience, building a foundation for understanding. This was more than interesting. It was touching. Ryan wondered how difficult it was for the Soviets. Probably harder than anything he had ever done—their bridges were burned. They had cast themselves away from everything they had known, trusting that what they found would be better. Ryan hoped they would succeed and make their transition from Communism to freedom. In the past two days he had come to realize what courage it took for men to defect. Facing a gun in a missile room was a small matter compared with walking away from one's whole life. It was strange how easily Americans put on their freedoms. How difficult would it be for these men who had risked their lives to adapt to something that men like Ryan so rarely appreciated? It was people like these who had built the American Dream, and people like these who were needed to maintain it. It was odd that such men should come from the Soviet Union. Or perhaps not so odd, Ryan thought, listening to the conversation going back and forth in front of him.

THE SEVENTEENTH DAY

SUNDAY, 19 DECEMBER

The Red October

"Eight more hours," Ryan whispered to himself. That's what they had told him. An eight-hour run to Norfolk. He was back at the rudder diving-plane controls by his own request. Operating them was the only thing he knew how to do, and he had to do something. The *October* was still badly shorthanded. Nearly all of the Americans were helping out in the reactor and engine spaces aft. Only Mancuso, Ramius, and himself were in control. Bugayev, with the help of Jones, was monitoring the sonar equipment a few feet away, and the medical people were still worrying over Williams in sick bay. The cook was shuttling back and forth with sandwiches and coffee, which Ryan found disappointing, probably because he had been spoiled by Greer's.

Ramius was half sitting on the rail that surrounded the periscope pedestal. The leg wound was not bleeding, but it had to be hurting more than the man admitted since he was letting Mancuso check the instruments and handle the navigation.

"Rudder amidships," Mancuso ordered.

"Midships," Ryan turned the wheel back to the right to center it, checking his rudder angle indicator. "Rudder is amidships, steady on course one-two-zero."

Mancuso frowned at his chart, nervous at being forced to pilot the massive submarine in so cavalier a manner. "You have to be careful around here. The sandbar keeps building up from the southerly littoral drift, and they have to dredge it every few months. The storms this area's been having can't have helped much." Mancuso went back to look through the periscope.

"I am told this is a dangerous area," Ramius said.

"The graveyard of the Atlantic," Mancuso confirmed. "A lot of ships have died along the Outer Banks. Weather and current conditions are bad enough. The Germans are supposed to have had a hell of a time here during the war. Your charts don't show it, but there's hundreds of wrecks spotted on the bottom." He went back to the chart table. "Anyway, we give this place a nice wide berth, and we don't turn north till about here." He traced a line on the chart.

"These are your waters," Ramius agreed.

They were in a loose three-boat formation. The *Dallas* was leading them out to sea, the *Pogy* was trailing. All three boats were traveling flooded-down, their decks nearly awash, with no one on their bridge stations. All visual navigation was being done by periscope. No radar sets were operating. None of the three boats was making any electronic noise. Ryan glanced casually at the chart table. They were beyond the inlet proper, but the chart was marked with sandbars for several more miles.

Nor were they using the *Red October*'s caterpillar drive system. It had turned out to be almost exactly what Skip Tyler had predicted. There were two sets of tunnel impellers, a pair about a third of the way back from the bow and three more just aft of midships. Mancuso and his engineers had examined the plans with great interest, then commented at length on the quality of the caterpillar design.

For his part, Ramius had not wanted to believe that he had been detected so early on. Mancuso had ultimately produced Jones with his personal map to show the *October*'s estimated course off Iceland. Though a few miles off the ship's log, it was too close to have been a coincidence.

"Your sonar must be better than we expected," Ramius

grumbled a few feet from Ryan's control station.

"It is pretty good," Mancuso allowed. "Better yet, there's Jonesy—he's the best sonarman I've ever had."

"So young, and so smart."

"We get a lot of them that way," Mancuso smiled. "Never as many as we'd like, of course, but our kids are all volunteers. They know what they're getting into. We're picky about who we take, and then we train the hell out of 'em."

"Conn, sonar." It was Jones' voice. "*Dallas* is diving, sir."

"Very well." Mancuso lit a cigarette as he went to the intercom phone. He punched the button for engineering. "Tell Mannion we need him forward. We'll be diving in a few minutes. Yeah." He hung up and went back to the chart.

"You have them for more than three years, then?" Ramius asked.

"Oh, yeah. Hell, otherwise we'd be letting them go right after they're fully trained, right?"

Why couldn't the Soviet Navy get and retain people like this? Ramius thought. He knew the answer all too well. The Americans fed their men decently, gave them a proper mess room, paid them decently, gave them trust—all the things he had fought twenty years for.

"You need me to work the vents?" Mannion said, coming in.

"Yeah, Pat, we'll dive in another two or three minutes."

Mannion gave the chart a quick look on his way to the vent manifold.

Ramius hobbled to the chart. "They tell us that your officers are chosen from the bourgeois classes to control ordinary sailors from the working class."

Mannion ran his hands over the vent controls. There sure were enough of them. He'd spent two hours the previous day figuring the complex system out. "That's true, sir. Our officers do come from the ruling class. Just look at me," he said deadpan. Mannion's skin was about the color of coffee grounds, his accent pure South Bronx.

"But you are a black man," Ramius objected, missing the jibe.

"Sure, we're a real ethnic boat." Mancuso looked through the periscope again. "A Guinea skipper, a black navigator, and a crazy sonarman."

"I heard that, sir!" Jones called out rather than use the intercom speaker. "Gertrude message from *Dallas*. Everything looks okay. They're waiting for us. Last gertrude message for a while."

"Conn, aye. We're clear, finally. We can dive whenever you wish, Captain Ramius," Mancuso said.

"Comrade Mannion, vent the ballast tanks," Ramius said. The *October* had never actually surfaced and was still rigged for dive.

"Aye aye, sir." The lieutenant turned the topmost rank of master switches on the hydraulic controls.

Ryan winced. The sound made him think of a million toilets being flushed at once.

"Five degrees down on the planes, Ryan," Ramius said.

"Five degrees down, aye." Ryan pushed forward on the yoke. "Planes five degrees down."

"She's slow going down," Mannion observed, watching the handpainted depth-gauge replacement. "So durn big."

"Yeah," Mancuso said. The needle passed twenty meters.

"Planes to zero," Ramius said.

"Planes to zero angle, aye." Ryan pulled back on the control. It took thirty seconds for the submarine to settle. She seemed very slow to respond to the controls. Ryan had thought that submarines were as responsive as aircraft.

"Make her a little light, Pat. Enough that it takes a degree of down to hold her level," Mancuso said.

"Uh-huh." Mannion frowned, checking the depth gauge. The ballast tanks were now fully flooded, and the balancing act would have to be done with the much smaller trim tanks. It took him five minutes to get the balance exactly right.

"Sorry, gentlemen. I'm afraid she's too big to dial in quick," he said, embarrassed with himself.

Ramius was impressed but too annoyed to show it. He had expected the American captain to take longer than this to do it himself. Trimming a strange sub so expertly on his first try . . .

"Okay, now we can come around north," Mancuso said. They were two miles past the last charted bar. "Recommend new course zero-zero-eight, Captain."

"Ryan, rudder left ten degrees," Ramius ordered. "Come to zero-zero-eight."

"Okay, rudder left ten degrees," Ryan responded, keeping

one eye on the rudder indicator, the other on the gyro compass repeater. "Come to oh-oh-eight."

"Caution, Ryan. He turns slowly, but once turning you must use much backward—"

"Opposite," Mancuso corrected politely.

"Yes, opposite rudder to stop him on proper course."

"Right."

"Captain, do you have rudder problems?" Mancuso asked. "From tracking you it seemed that your turning circle was rather large."

"With the caterpillar it is. The flow from the tunnels strikes the rudder very hard, and it flutters if you use too much rudder. On our first sea trials, we had damage from this. It comes from—how do you say—the come-together of the two caterpillar tunnels."

"Does this affect operations with the propellers?" Mannion asked.

"No, only with the caterpillar."

Mancuso didn't like that. It didn't really matter. The plan was a simple, direct one. The three boats would make a straight dash to Norfolk. The two American attack boats would leapfrog forward at thirty knots to sniff out the areas ahead while the *October* plodded along at a constant twenty.

Ryan began to ease his rudder as the bow came around. He waited too long. Despite five degrees of right rudder, the bow swung right past the intended course, and the gyro repeater clicked accusingly on every third degree until it stopped at zero-zero-one. It took another two minutes to get back on the proper course.

"Sorry about that. Steady on zero-zero-eight," he finally reported.

Ramius was forgiving. "You learn fast, Ryan. Perhaps one day you will be a true sailor."

"No thanks! The one thing I've learned on this trip is that you guys earn every nickel you get."

"Don't like subs?" Mannion chuckled.

"No place to jog."

"True. Unless you still need me, Captain, I'm ready to go aft. The engine room's awful shorthanded," Mannion said.

Ramius nodded. Was he from the ruling class? the captain wondered.

The V. K. Konovalov

Tupolev was heading back west. The fleet order had instructed
everyone but his *Alfa* and one other to return home at twenty
knots. Tupolev was to move west for two and half hours. Now
he was on a reciprocal heading at five knots, about the top
speed the *Alfa* could travel without making much noise. The
idea was that his sub would be lost in the shuffle. So, an *Ohio*
was heading for Norfolk—or Charleston more probably. In any
case, Tupolev would circle quietly and observe. The *Red October* was destroyed. That much he knew from the ops order.
Tupolev shook his head. How could Marko have done such a
thing? Whatever the answer, he had paid for his treason with
his life.

The Pentagon

"I'd feel better if we had some more air cover," Admiral Foster
said, leaning against the wall.

"Agreed, sir, but we can't be so obvious, can we?" General
Harris asked.

A pair of P-3Bs was now sweeping the track from Hatteras
to the Virginia Capes as though on a routine training mission.
Most of the other Orions were far out at sea. The Soviet fleet
was already four hundred miles offshore. The three surface
groups had rejoined and were now ringed by their submarines.
The *Kennedy, America,* and *Nimitz* were five hundred miles to
their east, and the *New Jersey* was dropping back. The Russians
would be watched all the way home. The carrier battle groups
would be following them all the way to Iceland, keeping a
discrete distance and maintaining air groups at the fringe of
their radar coverage continuously, just to let them know that
the United States still cared. Aircraft based in Iceland would
track them the rest of the way home.

HMS *Invincible* was now out of operation and about halfway
home. American attack subs were returning to normal patrol
patterns, and all Soviet subs were reported to be off the coast,
though this data was sketchy. They were traveling in loose
packs and the noise generated made tracking difficult for the
patrolling Orions, which were short of sonobuoys. Still and

all, the operation was about over, the J-3 judged.

"You heading for Norfolk, Admiral?" Harris asked.

"Thought I might get together with CINCLANT, a post-action conference, you understand," Foster said.

"Aye aye, sir," Harris said.

The New Jersey

She was traveling at twelve knots, with a destroyer fueling on either beam. Commodore Eaton was in the flag plot. It was all over and nothing had happened, thank God. The Soviets were now a hundred miles ahead, within Tomahawk range but well beyond everything else. All in all, he was satisfied. His force had operated successfully with the *Tarawa*, which was now headed south to Mayport, Florida. He hoped they'd be able to do this again soon. It had been a long time since a flag officer on a battleship had had a carrier respond to his command. They had kept the *Kirov* force under continuous surveillance. If there had been a battle, Eaton was convinced that they'd have handled Ivan. More importantly, he was certain that Ivan knew it. All they awaited now was the order to return to Norfolk. It would be nice to be back home for Christmas. He figured his men had earned it. Many of the battleship's men were oldtimers, and nearly everyone had a family.

The Red October

Ping. Jones noted the time on his pad and called out, "Captain, just got a ping from *Pogy*."

The *Pogy* was now ten miles ahead of the *October* and *Dallas*. The idea was that after she got ahead and listened for ten minutes, a single ping from her active sonar would signal that the ten miles to the *Pogy* and the twenty or more miles beyond her were clear. The *Pogy* would drift slowly to confirm this, and a mile to the *October*'s east the *Dallas* went to full speed to leapfrog ten miles beyond the other attack sub.

Jones was experimenting with the Russian sonar. The active gear, he'd found, was not too bad. The passive systems he didn't want to think about. When the *Red October* had been lying still in Pamlico Sound, he'd been unable to track in on the American subs. They had also been still, with their reactors only turning generators, but they had been no more than a mile away. He was disappointed that he'd not been able to locate them.

The officer with him, Bugayev, was a friendly enough guy. At first he'd been a little standoffish—as if he were a lord and I were a serf, Jones thought—until he'd seen how the skipper treated him. This surprised Jones. From what little he knew of Communism, he had expected everyone to be fairly equal. Well, he decided, that's what I get from reading *Das Kapital* in a freshman poli-sci course. It made a lot more sense to look at what Communism built. Garbage, mostly. The enlisted men didn't even have their own mess room. Wasn't that some crap! Eating your meals in your bunk rooms!

Jones had taken an hour—when he was supposed to be sleeping—to explore the submarine. Mr. Mannion had joined him. They started in the bunkroom. The individual footlockers didn't lock—probably so that officers could rifle through them. Jones and Mannion did just that. There was nothing of interest. Even the sailor porn was junk. The poses were just plain dumb, and the women—well, Jones had grown up in California. Garbage. It was not at all hard for him to understand why the Russians wanted to defect.

The missile had been interesting. He and Mannion opened an inspection hatch to examine the inside of the missile. Not too shabby, they thought. There was a little too much loose wiring, but that probably made testing easier. The missile seemed awfully big. So, he thought, that's what the bastards have been aiming at us. He wondered if the navy would hold onto a few. If it was ever necessary to flip some at old Ivan, might as well include a couple of his own. *Dumb* idea, Jonesy, he said to himself. He didn't ever want those goddamned things to fly. One thing was for sure: everything on this bucket would be stripped off, tested, taken apart, tested again—and he was the navy's number one expert on Russian sonar. Maybe he'd be present during the analysis . . . It might be worth staying in the navy a few extra months for.

Jones lit a cigarette. "Want one of mine, Mr. Bugayev?" He held his pack out to the electronics officer.

"Thank you, Jones. You were in university?" The lieutenant took the American cigarette that he'd wanted but been too proud to ask for. It was dawning on him slowly that this enlisted man was his technical equal. Though not a qualified watch officer, Jones could operate and maintain sonar gear as well as anyone he'd known.

"Yes, sir." It never hurt to call officers sir, Jones knew. Especially the dumb ones. "California Institute of Technology. Five semesters completed. A average. I didn't finish."

"Why did you leave?"

Jones smiled. "Well, sir, you gotta understand that Cal Tech is, well, kinda a funny place. I played a little trick on one of my professors. He was working with strobe lights for high-speed photography, and I rigged a little switch to work the room lights off the strobe. Unfortunately there was a short in the switch, and it started this little electrical fire." Which had burned out a lab, destroying three months of data and fifteen thousand dollars of equipment. "That broke the rules."

"What did you study?"

"I was headin' for a degree in electrical engineering, with a strong minor in cybernetics. Three semesters to go. I'll get it, then my masters, then my doctorate, and then I'll go back to work for the navy as a civilian."

"Why are you a sonar operator?" Bugayev sat down. He had never spoken like this with an enlisted man.

"Hell, sir, it's fun! When something's going on—you know, a war game, tracking another sub, like that—*I* am the skipper. All the captain does is react to the data I give him."

"And you like your commander?"

"Sure thing! He's the best I've had—I've had three. My skipper's a good guy. You do your job okay, and he doesn't hassle you. You got something to say to him, and he listens."

"You say you will go back to college. How do you pay for it? They tell us that only the ruling class sons go to university."

"That's crap, sir. In California if you're smart enough to go, you go. In my case, I've been saving my money—you don't spend much on a sub, right?—and the navy pitches in, too. I got enough to see me all the way through my masters. What's your degree in?"

"I attended a higher naval school. Like your Annapolis. I would like to get a proper degree in electronics," Bugayev said, voicing his own dream.

"No sweat. I can help you out. If you're good enough for Cal Tech, I can tell you who to talk to. You'd like California. That is the place to live."

"And I wish to work on a real computer," Bugayev went on, wishful.

Jones laughed quietly. "So, buy yourself one."

"Buy a computer?"

"Sure, we got a couple of little ones, Apples, on *Dallas*. Cost you about, oh, two thousand for a nice system. That's a lot less than what a car goes for."

"A computer for two thousand dollars?" Bugayev went from wishful to suspicious, certain that Jones was leading him on.

"Or less. For three grand you can get a really nice rig. Hell, you tell Apple who you are, and they'll probably give it to you for free, or the navy will. If you don't want an Apple, there's the Commodore, TRS-80, Atari. All kinds. Depends on what you want to use it for. Look, just one company, Apple, has sold over a million of 'em. They're little, sure, but they're real computers."

"I have never heard of this—Apple?"

"Yeah, Apple. Two guys started the company back when I was in junior high. Since then they've sold a million or so, like I said—and they are some kinda rich! I don't have one myself—no room on a sub—but my brother has his own computer, an IBM-PC. You still don't believe me, do you?"

"A working man with his own computer? It is hard to believe." He stabbed out the cigarette. American tobacco was a little bland, he thought.

"Well, sir, then you can ask somebody else. Like I said, *Dallas* has a couple of Apples, just for the crew to use. There's other stuff for fire control, navigation, and sonar, of course. We use the Apples for games—you'll *love* computer games, for sure. You've never had fun till you've tried Choplifter— and other things, education programs, stuff like that. Honest, Mr. Bugayev, you can walk into most any shopping center and find a place to buy a computer. You'll see."

"How do you use a computer with your sonar?"

"That would take a while to explain, sir, and I'd probably have to get permission from the skipper." Jones reminded himself that this guy was still the enemy, sort of.

The V. K. Konovalov

The *Alfa* drifted slowly at the edge of the continental shelf, about fifty miles southeast of Norfolk. Tupolev ordered the reactor plant chopped back to about five percent of total output, enough to operate the electrical systems and little else. It also made his submarine almost totally quiet. Orders were passed by word of mouth. The *Konovalov* was on a strict silent ship routine. Even ordinary cooking was forbidden. Cooking meant moving metal pots on metal grates. Until further notice, the crew was on a diet of cheese sandwiches. They spoke in whispers when they spoke at all. Anyone who made noise would attract the attention of the captain, and everyone aboard knew what that meant.

SOSUS Control

Quentin was reviewing data sent by digital link from the two Orions. A crippled missile boat, the USS *Georgia*, was heading into Norfolk after a partial turbine failure, escorted by a pair of attack boats. They had been keeping her out, the admiral had said, because of all the Russian activity on the coast, and the idea now was to get her in, fixed, and out as quickly as possible. The *Georgia* carried twenty-four Trident missiles, a noteworthy fraction of the country's total deterrent force. Repairing her would be a high priority item now that the Russians were gone. It was safe to bring her in, but they wanted the Orions first to check and see if any Soviet submarines had lingered behind in the general confusion.

A P-3B was cruising at nine hundred feet about fifty miles southeast of Norfolk. The FLIR showed nothing, no heat signature on the surface, and the MAD gear detected no measurable disturbance in the earth's magnetic field, though one aircraft's flight path took her within a hundred yards of the *Alfa*'s position. The *Konovalov*'s hull was made of non-magnetic titanium. A sonobuoy dropped seven miles to the south of her position also failed to pick up the sound of her reactor plant. Data was being transmitted continuously to Norfolk, where Quentin's operations staff entered it into his computer. The problem was, not all of the Soviet subs had been accounted for.

Well, the commander thought, that figures. Some of the boats had taken the opportunity to creep away from their charted loci. There was the odd chance, he had reported, that one or two strays were still out there, but there was no evidence of this. He wondered what CINCLANT had working. Certainly he had seemed awfully pleased with something, almost euphoric. The operation against the Soviet fleet had been handled pretty well, what he'd seen of it, and there was that dead *Alfa* out there. How long until the *Glomar Explorer* came out of mothballs to go and get that? He wondered if he'd get a chance to look the wreck over. What an opportunity!

Nobody was taking the current operation all that seriously. It made sense. If the *Georgia* were indeed coming in with a sick engine she'd be coming slow, and a slow *Ohio* made about as much noise as a virgin whale determined to retain her status. And if CINCLANTFLT were all that concerned about it, he would not have detailed the delousing operation to a pair of P-3s piloted by reservists. Quentin lifted the phone and dialed CINCLANTFLT Operations to tell them again that there was no indication of hostile activity.

The Red October

Ryan checked his watch. It had been five hours already. A long time to sit in one chair, and from a quick glance at the chart it appeared that the eight-hour estimate had been optimistic — or he'd misunderstood them. The *Red October* was tracing up the shelf line and would soon begin to angle west for the Virginia Capes. Maybe it would take another four hours. It couldn't be too soon. Ramius and Mancuso looked pretty tired. Everybody was tired. Probably the engine room people most of all — no, the cook. He was ferrying coffee and sandwiches to everyone. The Russians seemed especially hungry.

The Dallas/The Pogy

The Dallas passed the *Pogy* at thirty-two knots, leapfrogging again, with the *October* a few miles aft. Lieutenant Commander Wally Chambers, who had the conn, did not like being blind on the speed run of thirty-five minutes despite word from the *Pogy* that everything was clear.

The *Pogy* noted her passage and turned to allow her lateral array to track on the *Red October*.

"Noisy enough at twenty knots," the *Pogy*'s sonar chief said to his companions. *"Dallas* doesn't make that much at thirty."

The V. K. Konovalov

"Some noise to the south," the *michman* said.

"What, exactly?" Tupolev had been hovering at the door for hours, making life unpleasant for the sonarmen.

"Too soon to say, Comrade Captain. Bearing is not changing, however. It is heading this way."

Tupolev went back to the control room. He ordered power reduced further in the reactor systems. He considered killing the plant entirely, but reactors took time to start up and there was no telling yet how distant the contact might be. The captain smoked three cigarettes before going back to sonar. It would not do at all to make the *michman* nervous. The man was his best operator.

"One propeller, Comrade Captain, an American, probably a *Los Angeles,* doing thirty-five knots. Bearing has changed only two degrees in fifteen minutes. He will pass close aboard, and—wait . . . His engines have stopped." The forty-year-old warrant officer pressed the headphones against his ears. He could hear the cavitation sounds diminish, then stop entirely as the contact faded away to nothing. "He has stopped to listen, Comrade Captain."

Tupolev smiled. "He will not hear us, Comrade. Racing and stopping. Can you hear anything else? Might he be escorting something?"

The *michman* listened to the headphones again and made some adjustments on his panel. "Perhaps . . . there is a good deal of surface noise, Comrade, and I—wait. There seems to be some noise. Our last target bearing was one-seven-one, and this new noise is . . . one-seven-five. Very faint, Comrade Captain—a ping, a single ping on active sonar."

"So." Tupolev leaned against the bulkhead. "Good work, Comrade. Now we must be patient."

The Dallas

Chief Laval pronounced the area clear. The BQQ-5's sensitive receptors revealed nothing, even after the SAPS system had been used. Chambers maneuvered the bow around so that the single ping would go out to the *Pogy,* which in turn fired off her own ping to the *Red October* to make sure the signal was received. It was clear for another ten miles. The *Pogy* moved out at thirty knots, followed by the U.S. Navy's newest boomer.

The V. K. Konovalov

"Two more submarines. One single screw, the other twin screw, I think. Still faint. The single-screw submarine is turning much more rapidly. Do the Americans have twin-screw submarines, Comrade Captain?"

"Yes, I believe so." Tupolev wondered about this. The difference in signature characteristics was not all that pronounced. They'd see in any case. The *Konovalov* was creeping along at two knots, one hundred fifty meters beneath the surface. Whatever was coming seemed to be coming right for them. Well, he'd teach the imperialists something after all.

The Red October

"Can anybody spell me at the wheel?" Ryan asked.

"Need a stretch?" Mancuso asked, coming over.

"Yeah. I could stand a trip to the head, too. The coffee's about to bust my kidneys."

"I relieve you, sir." The American captain moved into Ryan's seat. Jack headed aft to the nearest head. Two minutes later he was feeling much better. Back in the control room, he did some knee bends to get circulation back in his legs, then looked briefly at the chart. It seemed strange, almost sinister, to see the U.S. coast marked in Russian.

"Thank you, Commander."

"Sure." Mancuso stood.

"It is certain that you are no sailor, Ryan." Ramius had been watching him without a word.

"I have never claimed to be one, Captain," Ryan said agreeably. "How long to Norfolk?"

"Oh, another four hours, tops," Mancuso said. "The idea's to arrive after dark. They have something to get us in unseen, but I don't know what."

"We left the sound in daylight. What if somebody saw us then?" Ryan asked.

"I didn't see anything, but if anybody was there, all he'd have seen was three sub conning towers with no numbers on them." They had left in daylight to take advantage of a "window" in Soviet satellite coverage.

Ryan lit another cigarette. His wife would give him hell for this, but he was tense from being on the submarine. Sitting at the helmsman's station left him with nothing to do but stare at the handful of instruments. The sub was easier to hold level than he had expected, and the only radical turn he had attempted showed how eager the sub was to change course in any direction. Thirty-some-thousand tons of steel, he thought—no wonder.

The Pogy/The Red October

The *Pogy* stormed past the *Dallas* at thirty knots and continued for twenty minutes, stopping eleven miles beyond her—and three miles from the *Konovalov*, whose crew was scarcely breathing now. The *Pogy*'s sonar, though lacking the new BC-10/SAPS signal-processing system, was otherwise state of the art, but it was impossible to hear something that made no noise at all, and the *Konovalov* was silent.

The *Red October* passed the *Dallas* at 1500 hours after receiving the latest all-clear signal. Her crew was tired and looking forward to arriving at Norfolk two hours after sundown. Ryan wondered how quickly he could fly back to London. He was afraid that the CIA would want to debrief him at length. Mancuso and the crewmen of the *Dallas* wondered if they'd get to see their families. They weren't counting on it.

The V. K. Konovalov

"Whatever it is, it is big, very big, I think. His course will take him within five kilometers of us."

"An *Ohio*, as Moscow said," Tupolev commented.

"It sounds like a twin-screw submarine, Comrade Captain," the *michman* said.

"The *Ohio* has one propeller. You know that."

"Yes, Comrade. In any case, he will be with us in twenty minutes. The other attack submarine is moving at thirty-plus knots. If the pattern holds, he will proceed fifteen kilometers beyond us."

"And the other American?"

"A few kilometers seaward, drifting slowly, like us. I do not have an exact range. I could raise him on active sonar, but that—"

"I am aware of the consequences," Tupolev snapped. He went back to the control room.

"Tell the engineers to be ready to answer bells. All men at battle stations?"

"Yes, Comrade Captain," the *starpom* replied. "We have an excellent firing solution on the American hunter sub—the one moving, that is. The way he runs at full speed makes it easy for us. The other we can localize in seconds."

"Good, for a change," Tupolev smiled. "You see what we can do when circumstances favor us?"

"And what shall we do?"

"When the big one passes us, we will close and ream his asshole. They have played their games. Now we shall play ours. Have the engineers increase power. We will need full power shortly.

"It will make noise, Comrade," the *starpom* cautioned.

"True, but we have no choice. Ten percent power. The *Ohio* cannot possibly hear that, and perhaps the near hunter sub won't either."

The Pogy

"Where did that come from?" The sonar chief made some adjustments on his board. "Conn, sonar, I got a contact, bearing two-three-zero."

"Conn, aye," Commander Wood answered at once. "Can you classify?"

"No, sir. It just came up. Reactor plant and steam noises, real faint, sir. I can't quite read the plant signature . . ." He flipped the gain controls to maximum. "Not one of ours. Skipper, I think maybe we got us an *Alfa* here."

"Oh, great! Signal *Dallas* right now!"

The chief tried, but the *Dallas,* running at thirty-two knots, missed the five rapid pings. The *Red October* was now eight miles away.

The Red October

Jones' eyes suddenly screwed shut. "Mr. Bugayev, tell the skipper I just heard a couple of pings."

"Couple?"

"More 'n one, but I didn't get a count."

The Pogy

Commander Wood made his decision. The idea had been to send the sonar signals on a highly directional, low-power basis so as to minimize the chance of revealing his own position. But the *Dallas* hadn't picked that up.

"Max power, Chief. Hit *Dallas* with everything."

"Aye aye." The chief flipped his power controls to full. It took several seconds until the system was ready to send a hundred-kilowatt blast of energy.

Ping ping ping ping ping!

The Dallas

"Wow!" Chief Laval exclaimed. "Conn, sonar, danger signal from *Pogy!*"

"All stop!" Chambers ordered. "Quiet ship."

"All stop." Lieutenant Goodman relayed the orders a second later. Aft, the reactor watch reduced steam demand, increasing the temperature in the reactor. This allowed neutrons to escape out of the pile, rapidly slowing the fission reaction.

"When speed gets to four knots, go to one-third speed," Chambers told the officer of the deck as he went aft to the sonar room. "Frenchie, I need data in a hurry."

"Still going too fast, sir," Laval said.

The Red October

"Captain Ramius, I think we should slow down," Mancuso said judiciously.

"The signal was not repeated," Ramius disagreed. The second directional signal had missed them, and the *Dallas* had not relayed the danger signal yet because she was still traveling too fast to locate the *October* and pass it along.

The *Pogy*

"Okay, sir, *Dallas* has killed power."

Wood chewed on his lower lip. "All right, let's find the bastard. Yankee search, Chief, max power." He went back to control. "Man battle stations." An alarm went off two seconds later. The *Pogy* had already been at increased readiness, and within forty seconds all stations were manned, with the executive officer, Lieutenant Commander Tom Reynolds, as fire control coordinator. His team of officers and technicians were waiting for data to feed into the Mark 117 fire control computer.

The sonar dome in the *Pogy's* bow was blasting sound energy into the water. Fifteen seconds after it started the first return signal appeared on Chief Palmer's screen.

"Conn, sonar, we have a positive contact, bearing two-three-four, range six thousand yards. Classify probable *Alfa* class from his plant signature," Palmer said.

"Get me a solution!" Wood said urgently.

"Aye." Reynolds watched the data input as another team of officers was making a paper and pencil plot on the chart table. Computer or not, there had to be a backup. The data paraded across the screen. The *Pogy's* four torpedo tubes contained a pair of Harpoon antiship missiles and two Mark 48 torpedoes. Only the torpedoes were useful at the moment. The Mark 48 was the most powerful torpedo in the inventory; wire-guided— and able to home in with its own active sonar—it ran at over fifty knots and carried a half-ton warhead. "Skipper, we got a solution for both fish. Running time four minutes, thirty-five seconds."

"Sonar, secure pinging," Wood said.

"Aye aye. Pinging secured, sir." Palmer killed power to the active systems. "Target elevation-depression angle is near zero, sir. He's about at our depth.

"Very well, sonar. Keep on him." Wood now had his target's position. Further pinging would only give it a better idea of his own.

The Dallas

"*Pogy* was pinging something. They got a return, bearing one-nine-one, about," Chief Laval said. "There's another sub out there. I don't know what. I can read some plant and steam noises, but not enough for a signature."

The Pogy

"The boomer's still movin', sir," Chief Palmer reported.

"Skipper," Reynolds looked up from the paper tracks, "her course takes her between us and the target."

"Terrific. All ahead one-third, left twenty degrees rudder." Wood moved to the sonar room while his orders were carried out. "Chief, power up and stand by to ping the boomer hard."

"Aye aye, sir." Palmer worked his controls. "Ready, sir."

"Hit him straight on. I don't want him to miss this time."

Wood watched the heading indicator on the sonar plot swing. The *Pogy* was turning rapidly, but not rapidly enough to suit him. The *Red October*—only he and Reynolds knew that she was Russian, though the crew was speculating like mad—was coming in too fast.

"Ready, sir."

"Hit it."

Palmer punched the impulse control.

Ping ping ping ping ping!

The Red October

"Skipper," Jones yelled. "Danger signal!"

Mancuso jumped to the annunciator without waiting for Ramius to react. He twisted the dial to All Stop. When this was done he looked at Ramius. "Sorry, sir."

"All right." Ramius scowled at the chart. The phone buzzed a moment later. He took it and spoke in Russian for several seconds before hanging up. "I told them that we have a problem but we do not know what it is."

"True enough." Mancuso joined Ramius at the chart. Engine noises were diminishing, though not quickly enough to suit the American. The *October* was quiet for a Russian sub, but this was still too noisy for him.

"See if your sonarman can locate anything," Ramius suggested.

"Right." Mancuso took a few steps aft. "Jonesy, find what's out there."

"Aye, Skipper, but it won't be easy on this gear." He already had the sensor arrays working in the direction of the two escorting attack subs. Jones adjusted the fit of his headphones and started working on the amplifier controls. No signal processors, no SAPS, and the transducers weren't worth a damn! But this wasn't the time to get excited. The Soviet systems had to be manipulated electromechanically, unlike the computer-controlled ones he was used to. Slowly and carefully, he altered the directional receptor gangs in the sonar dome forward, his right hand twirling a cigarette pack, his eyes shut tight. He didn't notice Bugayev sitting next to him, listening to the same input.

The Dallas

"What do we know, Chief?" Chambers asked.

"I got a bearing and nothing else. *Pogy*'s got him all dialed in, but our friend powered back his engine right after he got lashed, and he faded out on me. *Pogy* got a big return off him. He's probably pretty close, sir."

Chambers had only moved up to his executive officer's posting four months earlier. He was a bright, experienced officer and a likely candidate for his own command, but he was only thirty-three years old and had only been back in submarines for those four months. The year and a half prior to that he'd been a reactor instructor in Idaho. The gruffness that was part of his job as Mancuso's principal on-board disciplinarian also shielded more insecurity than he would have cared to admit. Now his career was on the line. He knew exactly how important this mission was. His future would ride on the decisions he was about to make.

"Can you localize with one ping?"

The sonar chief considered this for a second. "Not enough for a shooting solution, but it'll give us something."

"One ping, do it."

"Aye." Laval worked on his board briefly, triggering the active elements.

The V. K. Konovalov

Tupolev winced. He had acted too soon. He should have waited until they were past—but then if he had waited that long, he would have had to move, and now he had all three of them hovering nearby, almost still.

The four submarines were moving only fast enough for depth control. The Russian *Alfa* was pointed southeast, and all four were arrayed in a roughly trapezoidal fashion, open end seaward. The *Pogy* and the *Dallas* were to the north of the *Konovalov*, the *Red October* was southeast of her.

The Red October

"Somebody just pinged her," Jones said quietly. "Bearing is roughly northwest, but she isn't making enough noise for us to read her. Sir, if I had to make a bet, I'd say she was pretty close."

"How do you know that?" Mancuso asked.

"I heard the pulse direct—just one ping to get a range, I think. It was from a BQQ-5. Then we heard the echo off the target. The math works out a couple of different ways, but smart money is he's between us and our guys, and a little west. I know it's shaky, sir, but it's the best we got."

"Range ten kilometers, perhaps less," Bugayev commented.

"That's kinda shaky, too, but it's as good a starting place as any. Not a whole lot of data. Sorry, Skipper. Best we can do," Jones said.

Mancuso nodded and returned to control.

"What gives?" Ryan asked. The plane controls were pushed all the way forward to maintain depth. He had not grasped the significance of what was going on.

"There's a hostile submarine out there."

"What information do we have?" Ramius asked.

"Not much. There's a contact northwest, range unknown, but probably not very far. I know for sure it's not one of ours. Norfolk said this area was cleared. That leaves one possibility. We drift?"

"We drift," Ramius echoed, lifting the phone. He spoke a few orders.

The *October*'s engines were providing the power to move

the submarine at a fraction over two knots, barely enough to maintain steerage way and not enough to maintain depth. With her slight positive buoyancy, the *October* was drifting upward a few feet per minute despite the plane setting.

The Dallas

"Let's move back south. I don't like the idea of having that *Alfa* closer to our friend than we are. Come right to one-eight-five, two-thirds," Chambers said finally.

"Aye aye," Goodman said. "Helm, right fifteen degrees rudder, come to new course one-eight-five. All ahead two thirds."

"Right fifteen degrees rudder, aye." The helmsman turned the wheel. "Sir, my rudder is right fifteen degrees, coming to new course one-eight-five."

The *Dallas'* four torpedo tubes were loaded with three Mark 48s and a decoy, an expensive MOSS (mobile submarine simulator). One of her torpedoes was targeted on the *Alfa,* but the firing solution was vague. The "fish" would have to do some of the tracking by itself. The *Pogy's* two torpedoes were almost perfectly dialed in.

The problem was that neither boat had authority to shoot. Both attack submarines were operating under the normal rules of engagement. They could fire in self-defense only and defend the *Red October* only by bluff and guile. The question was whether the *Alfa* knew what the *Red October* was.

The V. K. Konovalov

"Steer for the *Ohio,*" Tupolev ordered. "Bring speed to three knots. We must be patient, comrades. Now that the Americans know where we are they will not ping us again. We will move from our place quietly."

The *Konovalov's* bronze propeller turned more quickly. By shutting down some nonessential electrical systems, the engineers were able to increase speed without increasing reactor output.

The Pogy

On the *Pogy,* the nearest attack boat, the contact faded, degrading the directional bearing somewhat. Commander Wood debated whether or not to get another bearing with active sonar but decided against it. If he used active sonar his position would be like that of a policeman looking for a burglar in a dark building with a flashlight. Sonar pings could well tell his target more than they told him. Using passive sonar was the normal routine in such a case.

Chief Palmer reported the passage of the *Dallas* down their port side. Both Wood and Chambers decided not to use their underwater telephones to communicate. They could not afford to make any noise now.

The Red October

They had been creeping along for a half hour now. Ryan was chain-smoking at his station, and his palms were sweating as he struggled to maintain his composure. This was not the sort of combat he had been trained for, being trapped inside a steel pipe, unable to see or hear anything. He knew that there was a Soviet submarine out there, and he knew what her orders were. If her captain realized who they were—then what? The two captains, he thought, were amazingly cool.

"Can your submarines protect us?" Ramius asked.

"Shoot at a Russian sub?" Mancuso shook his head. "Only if he shoots first—at them. Under the normal rules, we don't count."

"*What?*" Ryan was stunned.

"You want to start a war?" Mancuso smiled, as though he found this situation amusing. "That's what happens when warships from two countries start exchanging shots. We have to smart our way out of this."

"Be calm, Ryan," Ramius said. "This is our usual game. The hunter submarine tries to find us, and we try not to be found. Tell me, Captain Mancuso, at what range did you hear us off Iceland?"

"I haven't examined your chart closely, Captain," Mancuso mused. "Maybe twenty miles, thirty or so kilometers."

"And then we were traveling at thirteen knots—noise increases faster than speed. I think we can move east, slowly, without being detected. We use the caterpillar, move at six knots. As you know, Soviet sonar is not so efficient as American. Do you agree, Captain?"

Mancuso nodded. "She's your boat, sir. May I suggest northeast? That ought to put us behind our attack boats inside an hour, maybe less."

"Yes." Ramius hobbled over to the control board to open the tunnel hatches, then went back to the phone. He gave the necessary orders. In a minute the caterpillar motors were engaged and speed was increasing slowly.

"Rudder right ten, Ryan," Ramius said. "And ease the plane controls."

"Rudder right ten, sir, easing the planes, sir." Ryan carried the orders out, glad that they were doing something.

"Your course is zero-four-zero, Ryan," Mancuso said from the chart table.

"Zero-four-zero, coming right through three-five-zero." From the helmsman's seat he could hear the water swishing down the portside tunnel. Every minute or so there was an odd rumble that lasted three or four seconds. The speed gauge in front of him passed through four knots.

"You are frightened, Ryan?" Ramius chuckled.

Jack swore to himself. His voice had wavered. "I'm a little tired, too."

"I know it is difficult for you. You do well for a new man with no training. We will be late to Norfolk, but we shall get there, you will see. Have you been on a missile boat, Mancuso?"

"Oh, sure. Relax, Ryan. This is what boomers do. Somebody comes lookin' for us, we just disappear." The American commander looked up from the chart. He had set coins at the estimated positions of the three other subs. He considered marking it up more but decided not to. There were some very interesting notations on this coastal chart—like programmed missile-firing positions. Fleet intelligence would go ape over this sort of information.

The *Red October* was moving northeast at six knots now. The *Konovalov* was coming southeast at three. The *Pogy* was heading south at two, and the *Dallas* south at fifteen. All four submarines were now within a six-mile-diameter circle, all converging on about the same point.

The V. K. Konovalov

Tupolev was enjoying himself. For whatever reason, the Americans had chosen to play a conservative game that he had not expected. The smart thing, he thought, would have been for one of the attack boats to close in and harrass him, allowing the missile sub to pass clear with the other escort. Well, at sea nothing was ever quite the same twice. He sipped at a cup of tea as he selected a sandwich.

His sonar *michman* noted an odd sound in his sonar set. It only lasted a few seconds, then was gone. Some far-off seismic rumble, he thought at first.

The Red October

They had risen because of the *Red October*'s positive trim, and now Ryan had five degrees of down-angle on the diving planes to get back down to a hundred meters. He heard the captains discussing the absence of a thermocline. Mancuso explained that it was not unusual for the area, particularly after violent storms. They agreed that it was unfortunate. A thermal layer would have helped their evasion.

Jones was at the aft entrance of the control room, rubbing his ears. The Russian phones were not very comfortable. "Skipper, I'm getting something to the north, comes and goes. I haven't gotten a bearing lock on it."

"Whose?" Mancuso asked.

"Can't say, sir. The active sonar isn't too bad, but the passive stuff just isn't up to the drill, Skipper. We're not blind, but close to it."

"Okay, if you hear something, sing out."

"Aye aye, Captain. You got some coffee out here? Mr. Bugayev sent me for some."

"I'll have a pot sent in."

"Right." Jones went back to work.

The V. K. Konovalov

"Comrade Captain, I have a contact, but I do not know what it is," the *michman* said over the phone.

Tupolev came back, munching on his sandwich. *Ohio*s had

been acquired so rarely by the Russians—three times to be
exact, and in each case the quarry had been lost within minutes—that no one had a feel for the characteristics of the class.

The *michman* handed the captain a spare set of phones. "It
may take a few minutes, Comrade. It comes and goes."

The water off the American coast, though nearly isothermal,
was not entirely perfect for sonar systems. Minor currents and
eddies set up moving walls that reflected and channeled sound
energy on a nearly random basis. Tupolev sat down and listened
patiently. It took five minutes for the signal to come back.

The *michman*'s hand waved. "Now, Comrade Captain."

His commanding officer looked pale.

"Bearing?"

"Too faint, and too short to lock in—but three degrees on
either bow, one-three-six to one-four-two."

Tupolev tossed the headphones on the table and went forward. He grabbed the political officer by the arm and led him
quickly to the wardroom.

"It's *Red October!*"

"Impossible. Fleet Command said that his destruction was
confirmed by visual inspection of the wreckage." The *zampolit*
shook his head emphatically.

"We have been tricked. The caterpillar acoustical signature
is unique, Comrade. The Americans have him, and he is out
there. We must destroy him!"

"No. We must contact Moscow and ask for instructions."

The *zampolit* was a good Communist, but he was a surface
ship officer who didn't belong on submarines, Tupolev thought.

"Comrade Zampolit, it will take several minutes to approach
the surface, perhaps ten or fifteen to get a message to Moscow,
thirty more for Moscow to respond at all—and then they will
request *confirmation!* An hour in all, two, three? By that time
Red October will be gone. Our original orders are operative,
and there is no time to contact Moscow."

"But what if you are wrong?"

"I am not wrong, Comrade!" the captain hissed. "I will
enter my contact report in the log, and my recommendations.
If you forbid this, I will log that also! I am right, Comrade. It
will be your head, not mine. Decide!"

"You are certain?"

"*Certain!*"

"Very well." The *zampolit* seemed to deflate. "How will you do this?"

"As quickly as possible, before the Americans have a chance to destroy us. Go to your station, Comrade." The two men went back to the control room. The *Konovalov*'s six bow torpedo tubes were loaded with Mark C 533-millimeter wire-guided torpedoes. All they needed was to be told where to go.

"Sonar, search forward on all active systems!" the captain ordered.

The *michman* pushed the button.

The Red October

"Ouch." Jones' head jerked around. "Skipper, we're being pinged. Port side, midships, maybe a little forward. Not one of ours, sir."

The Pogy

"Conn, sonar, the *Alfa*'s got the boomer! The *Alfa* bearing is one-nine-two."

"All ahead two-thirds," Wood ordered immediately.

"All ahead two-thirds, aye."

The *Pogy*'s engines exploded into life, and soon her propeller was thrashing the black water.

The V. K. Konovalov

"Range seven thousand, six hundred meters. Elevation angle zero," the *michman* reported. So, this was the submarine they had been sent to hunt, he thought. He had just donned a headset that allowed him to report directly to the captain and fire control officer.

The *starpom* was the chief fire control supervisor. He quickly entered the data into the computer. It was a simple problem of target geometry. "We have a solution for torpedoes one and two."

"Prepare to fire."

"Flooding tubes." The *starpom* flipped the switches himself, reaching past the petty officer. "Outer torpedo tube doors are open."

"Recheck firing solution!" Tupolev said.

The Pogy

The *Pogy*'s sonar chief was the only man to hear the transient noise.

"Conn, sonar, *Alfa* contact—she just flooded tubes, sir! Target bearing is one-seven-nine."

The V. K. Konovalov

"Solution confirmed, Comrade Captain," the *starpom* said.

"Fire one and two," Tupolev ordered.

"Firing one . . . Firing two." The *Konovalov* shuddered twice as compressed air charges ejected the electrically powered torpedoes.

The Red October

Jones heard it first. "High-speed screws port side!" he said loudly and clearly. "Torpedoes in the water port side!"

"Ryl nalyeva!" Ramius ordered automatically.

"What?" Ryan asked.

"Left, rudder left!" Ramius pounded his fist on the rail.

"Left full, do it!" Mancuso said.

"Left full rudder, aye." Ryan turned the wheel all the way and held it down. Ramius was spinning the annunciator to flank speed.

The Pogy

"Two fish running," Palmer said. "Bearing is changing right to left. I say again, torpedo bearing changing right to left rapidly on both fish. They're targeted on the boomer."

The Dallas

The *Dallas* heard them, too. Chambers ordered flank speed and a turn to port. With torpedoes running his options were limited, and he was doing what American practice taught, heading someplace else—very fast.

The Red October

"I need a course!" Ryan said.

"Jonesy, give me a bearing!" Mancuso shouted.

"Three-two-zero, sir. Two fish heading in," Jones responded at once, working his controls to nail the bearing down. This was no time to screw up.

"Steer three-two-zero, Ryan," Ramius ordered, "if we can turn so fast."

Thanks a lot, Ryan thought angrily, watching the gyrocompass click through three-five-seven. The rudder was hard over, and with the sudden increase in power from the caterpillar motors, he could feel feedback flutter through the wheel.

"Two fish heading in, bearing is three-two-zero, I say again bearing is constant," Jones reported, much cooler than he felt. "Here we go, guys..."

The Pogy

Her tactical plot showed the *October,* the *Alfa,* and the two torpedoes. The *Pogy* was four miles north of the action.

"Can we shoot?" the exec asked.

"At the *Alfa?*" Wood shook his head emphatically. "No, dammit. It wouldn't make a difference anyway."

The V. K. Konovalov

The two Mark C torpedoes were charging at forty-one knots, a slow speed for this range, so that they could be more easily guided by the *Konovalov*'s sonar system. They had a projected six-minute run, with one minute already completed.

The Red October

"Okay, coming through three-four-five, easing the rudder off," Ryan said.

Mancuso kept quiet now. Ramius was using a tactic that he didn't particularly agree with, turning into the fish. It offered a minimum target profile, but it gave them a simpler geometric intercept solution. Presumably Ramius knew what Russian fish could do. Mancuso hoped so.

"Steady on three-two-zero, Captain," Ryan said, eyes locked

on the gyro repeater as though it mattered. A small voice in his brain congratulated him for going to the head an hour earlier.

"Ryan, down, maximum down on the diving planes."

"All the way down." Ryan pushed the yoke to the stops. He was terrified, but even more frightened of fouling up. He had to assume that both commanders knew what they were about. There was no choice for him. Well, he thought, he did know one thing. Guided torpedoes can be tricked. Like radar signals that are aimed at the ground, sonar pulses can be obscured, especially when the sub they are trying to locate is near the bottom or the surface, areas where the pulses tend to be reflected. If the *October* dove she could lose herself in an opaque field—presuming she got there fast enough.

The V. K. Konovalov

"Target aspect has changed, Comrade Captain. Target is now smaller," the *michman* said.

Tupolev considered this. He knew everything there was on Soviet combat doctrine—and knew that Ramius had written a good deal of it. Marko would do what he taught all of us to do, Tupolev thought. Turn into the oncoming weapons to minimize target cross-section and dive for the bottom to become lost in the confused echoes. "Target will be attempting to dive into the bottom-capture field. Be alert."

"Aye, Comrade. Can he reach the bottom quickly enough?" the *starpom* asked.

Tupolev racked his brain for the *October*'s handling characteristics. "No, he cannot dive that deep in so short a time. We have him." Sorry, my old friend, but I have no choice, he thought.

The Red October

Ryan cringed each time the sonar lash echoed through the double hull. "Can't you jam that or something?" he demanded.

"Patience, Ryan," Ramius said. He had never faced live warheads before but had exercised this problem a hundred times in his career. "Let him know he has us first."

"Do you carry decoys?" Mancuso asked.

"Four of them, in the torpedo room, forward—but we have no torpedomen."

Both captains were playing the cool game, Ryan noted bitterly from inside his terrified little world. Neither was willing to show fright before his peer. But they were both trained for this.

"Skipper," Jones called, "two fish, bearing constant at three-two-zero—they just went active. I say again, the fish are now active—shit! they sound just like 48s. Skipper, they sound like Mark 48 fish."

Ramius had been waiting for this. "Yes, we stole the torpedo sonar from you five years ago, but not your torpedo engines. *Bugayev!*"

In the sonar room, Bugayev had powered up the acoustical jamming gear as soon as the fish were launched. Now he carefully timed his jamming pulses to coincide with those from the approaching torpedoes. The pulses were dialed into the same carrier frequency and pulse repetition rate. The timing had to be precise. By sending out slightly distorted return echoes, he could create ghost targets. Not too many, nor too far away. Just a few, close by, and he might be able to confuse the fire control operators on the attacking *Alfa*. He thumbed the trigger switch carefully, chewing on an American cigarette.

The V. K. Konovalov

"Damn! He's jamming us." The *michman*, noting a pair of new pips, showed his first trace of emotion. The fading pip from the true contact was now bordered with two new ones, one north and closer, the other south and farther away. "Captain, the target is using Soviet jamming equipment."

"You see?" Tupolev said to the *zampolit.* "Use caution now," he ordered his *starpom.*

The Red October

"Ryan, all up on planes!" Ramius shouted.

"All the way up." Ryan yanked back, pulling the yoke hard against his belly and hoping that Ramius knew what the hell he was doing.

"Jones, give us time and range."

"Aye." The jamming gave them a sonar picture plotted on the main scopes. "Two fish, bearing three-two-zero. Range to number one is 2,000 yards, to number two is 2,300—I got a depression angle on number one! Number one fish is heading down a little, sir." Maybe Bugayev wasn't so dumb after all, Jones thought. But they had two fish to sweat . . .

The Pogy

The *Pogy*'s skipper was enraged. The goddamned rules of engagement prevented him from doing a goddamned thing, except, maybe—

"Sonar, ping the sonuvabitch! Max power, blast the sucker!"

The *Pogy*'s BQQ-5 sent timed wave fronts of energy lashing at the *Alfa*. The *Pogy* couldn't shoot, but maybe the Russian didn't know that, and maybe this lashing would interfere with their targeting sonar.

The Red October

"Any time now—one of the fish has capture, sir. I don't know which." Jones moved the phones off one ear, his hand poised to slap the other off. The homing sonar on one torpedo was now tracking them. Bad news. If these were like Mark 48s . . . Jones knew all too well that those things didn't miss much. He heard the change in the Doppler shift of the propellers as they passed beneath the *Red October*. "One missed, sir. Number one missed under us. Number two is heading in, ping interval is shortening." He reached over and patted Bugayev on the shoulder. Maybe he really was the on-board genius that the Russians said he was.

The V. K. Konovalov

The second Mark C torpedo was cutting through the water at forty-one knots. This made the torpedo-target closing speed about fifty-five. The guidance and decision loop was a complex one. Unable to mimic the computer homing system on the American Mark 48, the Soviets had the torpedo's targeting sonar report back to the launching vessel through an insulated wire. The *starpom* had a choice of sonar data with which to guide the torpedoes, that from the sub-mounted sonar or that from the torpedoes themselves. The first fish had been duped by the ghost images that the jamming had duplicated on the torpedo sonar frequency. For the second, the *starpom* was using the lower-frequency bow sonar. The first one had missed low, he knew now. That meant that the target was the middle pip. A quick frequency change by the *michman* cleared the sonar picture for few seconds before the jamming mode was altered. Coolly and expertly, the *starpom* commanded the second torpedo to select the center target. It ran straight and true.

The five-hundred-pound warhead struck the target a glancing blow aft of midships, just forward of the control room. It exploded a millisecond later.

The Red October

The force of the explosion hurled Ryan from his chair, and his head hit the deck. He came to from a moment's unconsciousness with his ears ringing in the dark. The shock of the explosion had shorted out a dozen electrical switchboards, and it was several seconds before the red battle lights clicked on. Aft, Jones had flipped his headphones off just in time, but Bugayev, trying to the last second to spoof the incoming torpedo, had not. He was rolling in agony on the deck, one eardrum ruptured, totally deafened. In the engine spaces men were scrambling back to their feet. Here the lights had stayed on, and Melekhin's first action was to look at the damage-control status board.

The explosion had occurred on the outer hull, a skin of light steel. Inside it was a water-filled ballast tank, a beehive of cellular baffles seven feet across. Located beyond the tank were high-pressure air flasks. Then came the *October*'s battery and the inner pressure hull. The torpedo had impacted in the center of a steel plate on the outer hull, several feet from any weld joints. The force of the explosion had torn a hole twelve feet across, shredded the interior ballast tank baffles, and ruptured a half-dozen air flasks, but already much of its force had been dissipated. The final damage was done to thirty of the large nickle-cadmium battery cells. Soviet engineers had placed these here deliberately. They had known that such a placement would make them difficult to service, difficult to recharge, and worst of all expose them to seawater contamination. All this had been accepted in light of their secondary purpose as additional armor for the hull. The *October*'s batteries saved her. Had it not been for them, the force of the explosion would have been spent on the pressure hull. Instead it was greatly reduced by the layered defensive system which had no Western counterpart. A crack had developed at the weld joint on the inner hull, and water was spraying into the radio room as though from a high-pressure hose, but the hull was otherwise secure.

In control, Ryan was soon back in his seat trying to determine if his instruments still worked. He could hear water splashing into the next compartment forward. He didn't know what to do. He did know it would be a bad time to panic, much as his brain screamed for the release.

"What do I do?"

"Still with us?" Mancuso's face looked satanic in the red lights.

"No goddammit, I'm dead—what do I do?"

"Ramius?" Mancuso saw the captain holding a flashlight taken from a bracket on the aft bulkhead.

"Down, dive for bottom." Ramius took the phone and called engineering to order the engines stopped. Melekhin had already given the order.

Ryan pushed his controls forward. In a goddamned submarine that's got a goddamned hole punched in it, they tell you to go *down!* he thought.

The V. K. Konovalov

"A solid hit, Comrade Captain," the *michman* reported. "His engines stopped. I hear hull creaking noises, his depth is changing." He tried some additional pings but got nothing. The explosion had greatly disturbed the water. There were rumbling echoes of the initial explosion reverberating through the sea. Trillions of bubbles had formed, creating an "ensonified zone" around the target that rapidly obscured it. His active pings were reflected back by the cloud of bubbles, and his passive listing ability was greatly reduced by the recurring rumbles. All he knew for sure was that one torpedo had hit, probably the second. He was an experienced man trying to decide what was noise and what was signal, and he had reconstructed most of the events correctly.

The Dallas

"Score one for the bad guys," the sonar chief said. The *Dallas* was running too fast to make proper use of her sonar, but the explosion was impossible to miss. The whole crew heard it through the hull.

In the attack center Chambers plotted their position two miles from where the *October* had been. The others in the compartment looked at their instruments without emotion. Ten of their shipmates had just been hit, and the enemy was on the other side of the wall of noise.

"Slow to one-third," Chambers ordered.

"All ahead one-third," the officer of the deck repeated.

"Sonar, get me some data," Chambers said.

"Working on it, sir." Chief Laval strained to make sense of what he heard. It took a few minutes as the *Dallas* slowed to under ten knots. "Conn, sonar, the boomer took one hit. I don't hear her engines . . . but there ain't no breakup noises. I say again, sir, no breakup noises."

"Can you hear the *Alfa?*"

"No, sir, too much crud in the water."

Chamber's face screwed into a grimace. You're an officer, he told himself, they pay you to think. First, what's happening? Second, what do you do about it? Think it through, then act.

"Estimated distance to target?"

"Something like nine thousand yards, sir," Lieutenant Goodman said, reading the last solution off the fire control computer. "She'll be on the far side of the ensonified zone."

"Make your depth six hundred feet." The diving officer passed this on to the helmsman. Chambers considered the situation and decided on his course of action. He wished Mancuso and Mannion were here. The captain and navigator were the other two members of what passed for the *Dallas'* tactical management committee. He needed to exchange some ideas with other experienced officers—but there weren't any.

"Listen up. We're going down. The disturbance from the explosion will stay fairly steady. If it moves at all, it'll go up. Okay, we'll go under it. First we want to locate the boomer. If she isn't there, then she's on the bottom. It's only nine hundred feet here, so she could be on the bottom with a live crew. Whether or not she's on the bottom, we gotta get between her and the *Alfa.*" And, he thought on, if the *Alfa* shoots then, I kill the fucker, and rules of engagement be damned. They had to trick this guy. But how? And where was the *Red October?*

The Red October

She was diving more quickly than expected. The explosion had also ruptured a trim tank, causing more negative buoyancy than they had at first allowed for.

The leak in the radio room was bad, but Melekhin had noted the flooding on his damage control board and reacted immediately. Each compartment had its own electrically powered pump. The radio room pump, supplemented by a master-zone pump that he had also activated, was managing, barely, to keep up with the flooding. The radios were already destroyed, but no one was planning to send any messages.

"Ryan, all the way up, and come right full rudder," Ramius said.

"Right full rudder, all the way up on the planes," Ryan said. "We going to hit the bottom?"

"Try not to," Mancuso said. "It might spring the leak worse."

"Great," Ryan growled back.

The *October* slowed her descent, arcing east below the ensonified zone. Ramius wanted it between himself and the *Alfa*. Mancuso thought that they might just survive after all. In that case he'd have to give this boat's plans a closer look.

The Dallas

"Sonar, give me two low-powered pings for the boomer. I don't want anybody else to hear this, Chief."

"Aye." Chief Laval made the proper adjustments and sent the signals out. "All right! Conn, sonar, I got her! Bearing two-zero-three, range two thousand yards. She is not, repeat *not,* on the bottom, sir."

"Left fifteen degrees rudder, come to two-zero-three," Chambers ordered.

"Left fifteen degrees rudder, aye!" the helmsman sang out. "New course two-zero-three. Sir, my rudder is left fifteen degrees."

"Frenchie, tell me about the boomer!"

"Sir, I got . . . pump noises, I think . . . and she's moving a little, bearing is now two-zero-one. I can track her on passive, sir."

"Thompson, plot the boomer's course. Mr. Goodman, we

still have that MOSS ready for launch?"

"Aye aye," responded the torpedo officer.

The V. K. Konovalov

"Did we kill him?" the *zampolit* asked.

"Probably," Tupolev answered, wondering if he had or not. "We must close to be certain. Ahead slow."

"Ahead slow."

The Pogy

The *Pogy* was now within two thousand yards of the *Konovalov*, still pinging her mercilessly.

"He's moving, sir. Enough that I can read passive," Sonar Chief Palmer said.

"Very well, secure pinging," Wood said.

"Aye, pinging secured."

"We got a solution?"

"Locked in tight," Reynolds answered. "Running time is one minute eighteen seconds. Both fish are ready."

"All ahead one-third."

"All ahead one-third, aye." The *Pogy* slowed. Her commanding officer wondered what excuse he might find for shooting.

The Red October

"Skipper, that was one of our sonars that pinged us, off north-north-east. Low-power ping, sir, must be close."

"Think you can raise her on gertrude?"

"Yes sir!"

"Captain?" Mancuso asked. "Permission to communicate with my ship?"

"Yes."

"Jones, raise her right now."

"Aye. This is Jonesy calling Frenchie, do you copy?" The sonarman frowned at the speaker. "Frenchie, answer me."

The Dallas

"Conn, sonar, I got Jonesy on the gertrude."

Chambers lifted the control room gertrude phone. "Jones,

this is Chambers. What is your condition?"

Mancuso took the mike away from his man. "Wally, this is Bart," he said. "We took one midships, but she's holding together. Can you run interference for us?"

"Aye aye! Starting right now, out." Chambers replaced the phone. "Goodman, flood the MOSS tube. Okay, we'll go in behind the MOSS. If the *Alfa* shoots at it, we take her out. Set it to run straight for two thousand yards, then turn south."

"Done. Outer door open, sir."

"Launch."

"MOSS away, sir."

The decoy ran forward at twenty knots for two minutes to clear the *Dallas*, then slowed. It had a torpedo body whose forward portion carried a powerful sonar transducer that ran off a tape recorder and broadcast the recorded sounds of a 688-class submarine. Every four minutes it changed over from loud operation to silent. The *Dallas* trailed a thousand yards behind the decoy, dropping several hundred feet below its course track.

The *Konovalov* approached the wall of bubbles carefully, with the *Pogy* trailing to the north.

"Shoot at the decoy, you son of a bitch," Chambers said quietly. The attack center crew heard him and nodded grim agreement.

The Red October

Ramius judged that the ensonified zone was now between him and the *Alfa*. He ordered the engines turned back on, and the *Red October* proceeded on a north-easterly course.

The V. K. Konovalov

"Left ten degrees rudder," Tupolev ordered quietly. "We'll come around the dead zone to the north and see if he is still alive when we turn back. First we must clear the noise."

"Still nothing," the *michman* reported. "No bottom impact, no collapse noises . . . New contact, bearing one-seven-zero . . . Different sound, Comrade Captain, one propeller . . . Sounds like an American."

"What heading?"

"South, I think. Yes, south . . . The sound's changing. It is American."

"An American sub is decoying. We ignore it."

"Ignore it?" the *zampolit* said.

"Comrade, if you were heading north and were torpedoed, would you then head south? Yes, you would—but not Marko. It is too obvious. This American is decoying to try to take us away from him. Not too clever, this one. Marko would do better. And he would go north. I know him, I know how he thinks. He is now heading north, perhaps northeast. They would not decoy if he was dead. Now we know that he is alive but crippled. We will find him, and finish him," Tupolev said calmly, fully caught up in the hunt for *Red October,* remembering all he had been taught. He would prove now that he was the new master. His conscience was still. Tupolev was fulfilling his destiny.

"But the Americans—"

"Will not shoot, Comrade," the captain said with a thin smile. "If they could shoot, we would already be dead from the one to the north. They cannot shoot without permission. They must *ask* for permission, as we must—but we already have the permission, and the advantage. We are now where the torpedo struck him, and when we clear the disturbance we will find him again. Then we will have him."

The Red October

They couldn't use the caterpillar. One side was smashed by the torpedo hit. The *October* was moving at six knots, driven by her propellers, which made more noise than the other system. This was much like the normal drill of protecting a boomer. But the exercise always presupposed that the escorting attack boats could shoot to make the bad guy go away . . .

"Left rudder, reverse course," Ramius ordered.

"What?" Mancuso was astounded.

"Think, Mancuso," Ramius said, looking to be sure that Ryan carried out the order. Ryan did, not knowing why.

"Think, Commander Mancuso," Ramius repeated. "What has happened? Moskva ordered a hunter sub to remain behind, probably a *Politovskiy*-class boat, the *Alfa* you call him. I know all their captains. All young, all, ah, aggressive? Yes, aggressive. He must know we are not dead. If he knows this, he will pursue us. So, we go back like a fox and let him pass."

Mancuso didn't like this. Ryan could tell without looking.

"We cannot shoot. Your men cannot shoot. We cannot run from him—he is faster. We cannot hide—his sonar is better. He will move east, use his speed to contain us and his sonar to locate us. By moving west, we have the best chance to escape. This he will not expect."

Mancuso still didn't like it, but he had to admit it was clever. Too damned clever. He looked back down at the chart. It wasn't his boat.

The Dallas

"The bastard went right past. Either ignored the decoy or flat didn't hear it. He's abeam of us, we'll be in his baffles soon," Chief Laval reported.

Chambers swore quietly. "So much for that idea. Right fifteen degrees rudder." At least the *Dallas* had not been heard. The submarine responded rapidly to the controls. "Let's get behind him."

The Pogy

The *Pogy* was now a mile off the *Alfa*'s port quarter. She had the *Dallas* on sonar and noted her change of course. Commander Wood simply did not know what to do next. The easiest solution was to shoot, but he couldn't. He contemplated shooting on his own. His every instinct told him to do just this. The *Alfa* was hunting Americans... But he couldn't give in to his instinct. Duty came first.

There was nothing worse than overconfidence, he reflected bitterly. The assumption behind this operation had been that there wouldn't be anybody around, and even if there were the attack subs would be able to warn the boomer off well in advance. There was a lesson in this, but Wood didn't care to think about it just now.

The V. K. Konovalov

"Contact," the *michman* said into the microphone. "Ahead, almost dead ahead. Using propellers and going at slow speed. Bearing zero-four-four, range unknown."

"Is it *Red October?*" Tupolev asked.

"I cannot say, Comrade Captain. It could be an American. He's coming this way, I think."

"Damn!" Tupolev looked around the control room. Could they have passed the *Red October?* Might they already have killed him?

The Dallas

"Does he know we're here, Frenchie?" Chambers asked, back in sonar.

"No way, sir." Laval shook his head. "We're directly behind him. Wait a minute . . ." The chief frowned. "Another contact, far side of the *Alfa*. That's gotta be our friend, sir. Jesus! I think he's heading this way. Using his wheels, not that funny thing."

"Range to the *Alfa?*"

"Under three thousand yards, sir."

"All ahead two thirds! Come left ten degrees!" Chambers ordered. "Frenchie, ping, but use the under-ice sonar. He may not know what that is. Make him think we're the boomer."

"Aye aye, sir!"

The V. K. Konovalov

"High-frequency pinging aft!" the *michman* called out. "Does not sound like an American sonar, Comrade."

Tupolev was suddenly puzzled. Was it an American to seaward? The other one on his port quarter was certainly American. It had to be the *October*. Marko was still the fox. He had lain still, letting them go past, so that he could shoot at them!

"All ahead full, left full rudder!"

The Red October

"Contact!" Jones sang out. "Dead ahead. Wait . . . It's an *Alfa!* She's close! Seems to be turning. Somebody pinging her on the other side. Christ, she's *real* close. Skipper, the *Alfa* is not a point source. I got signal separation between the engine and the screw."

"Captain," Mancuso said. The two commanders looked at one another and communicated a single thought as if by telepathy. Ramius nodded.

"Get us range."

"Jonesy, ping the sucker!" Mancuso ran aft.

"Aye." The systems were fully powered. Jones loosed a single ranging ping. "Range fifteen hundred yards. Zero elevation angle, sir. We're level with her."

"Mancuso, have your man give us range and bearing!" Ramius twisted the annunciator handle savagely.

"Okay, Jonesy, you're our fire control. Track the mother."

The V. K. Konovalov

"One active sonar ping to starboard, distance unknown, bearing zero-four-zero. The seaward target just ranged on us," the *michman* said.

"Give me a range," Tupolev ordered.

"Too far aft of the beam, Comrade. I am losing him aft."

One of them was the *October*—but which? Could he risk shooting at an American sub? No!

"Solution to the forward target?"

"Not a good one," the *starpom* replied. "He's maneuvering and increasing speed."

The *michman* concentrated on the western target. "Captain, contact forward is not, repeat not Soviet. Forward contact is American."

"Which one?" Tupolev screamed.

"West and northwest are both American. East target unknown."

"Keep the rudder at full."

"Rudder is full," the helmsman responded, holding the wheel over.

"The target is behind us. We must lock on and shoot as we turn. Damn, we are going too fast. Slow to one-third speed."

The *Konovalov* was normally quick to turn, but the power reduction made her propeller act like a brake, slowing the maneuver. Still, Tupolev was doing the right thing. He had to point his torpedo tubes near the bearing of the target, and he had to slow rapidly enough for his sonar to give him accurate firing information.

The Red October

"Okay, the *Alfa* is continuing her turn, now heading right to left ... Propulsion sounds are down some. She just chopped power," Jones said, watching the screen. His mind was working furiously computing course, speed, and distance. "Range is now twelve hundred yards. She's still turning. We doin' what I think?"

"Looks that way."

Jones set the active sonar on automatic pinging. "Have to see what this turn does, sir. If she's smart she'll burn off south and get clear first."

"Then pray she ain't smart," Mancuso said from the passageway. "Steady as she goes!"

"Steady as she goes," Ryan said, wondering if the next torpedo would kill them.

"Her turn is continuing. We're on her port beam now, maybe her port bow." Jones looked up. "She's going to get around first. Here come the pings."

The *Red October* accelerated to eighteen knots.

The V. K. Konovalov

"I have him," the *michman* said. "Range one thousand meters, bearing zero-four-five. Angle zero."

"Set it up," Tupolev ordered his exec.

"It will have to be a zero-angle shot. We're swinging too rapidly," the *starpom* said. He set it up as quickly as he could. The submarines were now closing at over forty knots. "Ready for tube five only! Tube flooded, door—open. Ready!"

"Shoot!"

"Fire five!" The *starpom*'s finger stabbed the button.

The Red October

"Range down to nine hundred—high-speed screws dead ahead! We have one torpedo in the water dead ahead. One fish, heading right in!"

"Forget it, track the *Alfa!*"

"Aye, okay, the *Alfa*'s bearing two-two-five, steadying down. We need to come left a little, sir."

"Ryan, come left five degrees, your course is two-two-five."

"Left five rudder, coming to two-two-five."

"The fish is closing rapidly, sir," Jones said.

"Screw it! Track the *Alfa.*"

"Aye. Bearing is still two-two-five. Same as the fish."

The combined speed ate up the distance between the submarines rapidly. The torpedo was closing the *October* faster still, but it had a safety device built in. To prevent them from blowing up their own launch platform, torpedoes could not arm until they were five hundred to a thousand yards from the boat that launched them. If the *October* closed the *Alfa* fast enough, she could not be hurt.

The *October* was now passing twenty knots.

"Range to the *Alfa* is seven hundred fifty yards, bearing two-two-five. The torpedo is close, sir, a few more seconds." Jones cringed, staring at the screen.

Klonk!

The torpedo struck the *Red October* dead center in her hemispherical bow. The safety lock still had another hundred meters to run. The impact broke it into three pieces, which were batted aside by the accelerating missile submarine.

"A dud!" Jones laughed. "Thank you, God! Target still bearing two-two-five, range is seven hundred yards."

The V. K. Konovalov

"No explosion?" Tupolev wondered.

"The safety locks!" The *starpom* swore. He'd had to set it up too fast.

"Where is the target?"

"Bearing zero-four-five, Comrade. Bearing is constant," the *michman* replied, "closing rapidly."

Tupolev blanched. "Left full rudder, all ahead flank!"

The Red October

"Turning, turning left to right," Jones said. "Bearing is now two-three-zero, spreading out a little. Need a little right rudder, sir."

"Ryan, come right five degrees."

"Rudder is right five," Jack answered.

"No, rudder ten right!" Ramius countermanded his order. He had been keeping a track with pencil and paper. And he knew the *Alfa*.

"Right ten degrees," Ryan said.

"Near-field effect, range down to four hundred yards, bearing is two-two-five to the center of the target. Target is spreading out left and right, mostly left," Jones said rapidly. "Range . . . three hundred yards. Elevation angle is zero, we are level with the target. Range two hundred fifty, bearing two-two-five to target center. We can't miss, Skipper."

"We're gonna hit!" Mancuso called out.

Tupolev should have changed depth. As it was he depended on the *Alfa*'s acceleration and maneuverability, forgetting that Ramius knew exactly what these were.

"Contact spread way the hell out—instantaneous return, sir!"

"Brace for impact!"

Ramius had forgotten the collision alarm. He yanked at it only seconds before impact.

The *Red October* rammed the *Konovalov* just aft of midships at a thirty-degree angle. The force of the collision ruptured the *Konovalov*'s titanium pressure hull and crumpled the *October*'s bow as if it were a beer can.

Ryan had not braced hard enough. He was thrown forward, and his face struck the instrument panel. Aft, Williams was catapulted from his bed and caught by Noyes before his head hit the deck. Jones' sonar systems were wiped out. The missile submarine bounded up and over the top of the *Alfa*, her keel grating across the upper deck of the smaller vessel as the momentum carried her forward and upward.

The V. K. Konovalov

The *Konovalov* had had full watertight integrity set. It did not make a difference. Two compartments were instantly vented to the sea, and the bulkhead between the control room and the after compartments failed a moment later from hull deformation. The last thing that Tupolev saw was a curtain of white foam coming from the starboard side. The *Alfa* rolled to port, turned by the friction of the *October*'s keel. In a few seconds the submarine was upside down. Throughout her length men and gear tumbled about like dice. Half the crew were already drowning. Contact with the *October* ended at this point, when the *Konovalov*'s flooded compartments made her drop stern first toward the bottom. The political officer's last conscious act was to yank at the disaster beacon handle, but it was to no avail: the sub was inverted, and the cable fouled on the sail. The only marker on the *Konovalov*'s grave was a mass of bubbles.

The Red October

"We still alive?" Ryan's face was bleeding profusely.

"Up, up on the planes!" Ramius shouted.

"All the way up." Ryan pulled back with his left hand, holding his right over the cuts.

"Damage report," Ramius said in Russian.

"Reactor system is intact," Melekhin answered at once. "The damage control board shows flooding in the torpedo room—I think. I have vented high-pressure air into it, and the pump is activated. Recommend we surface to assess damage."

"Da!" Ramius hobbled to the air manifold and blew all tanks.

The Dallas

"Jesus," the sonar chief said, "somebody hit somebody. I got breakup noises going down and hull-popping noises going up. Can't tell which is which, sir. Both engines are dead."

"Get us up to periscope depth quick!" Chambers ordered.

The Red October

It was 1654 local time when the *Red October* broke the surface of the Atlantic Ocean for the first time, forty-seven miles southeast of Norfolk. There was no other ship in sight.

"Sonar is wiped out, Skipper." Jones was switching off his boxes. "Gone, crunched. We got some piddly-ass lateral hydrophones. No active stuff, not even the gertrude."

"Go forward, Jonesy. Nice work."

Jones took the last cigarette from his pack. "Any time, sir—but I'm gettin' out next summer, depend on it."

Bugayev followed him forward, still deafened and stunned from the torpedo hit.

The *October* was sitting still on the surface, down by the bow and listing twenty degrees to port from the vented ballast tanks.

The Dallas

"How about that," Chambers said. He lifted the microphone.
"This is Commander Chambers. They killed the *Alfa!* Our guys
are safe. Surfacing the boat now. Stand by the fire and rescue
party!"

The Red October

"You okay, Commander Ryan?" Jones turned his head carefully.
"Looks like you broke some glass the hard way, sir."

"You don't worry till it stops bleeding," Ryan said drunk-
nly.

"Guess so." Jones held his handkerchief over the cuts. "But
sure hope you don't always drive this bad, sir."

"Captain Ramius, permission to lay to the bridge and communicate with my ship?" Mancuso asked.

"Go, we may need help with the damage."

Mancuso got into his jacket, checking to make sure his small
locking radio was still in the pocket where he had left it. Thirty
seconds later he was atop the sail. The *Dallas* was surfacing
as he made his first check of the horizon. The sky had never
looked so good.

He couldn't recognize the face four hundred yards away,
but it had to be Chambers.

"Dallas, this is Mancuso."

"Skipper, this is Chambers. You guys okay?"

"Yes! But we may need some hands. The bow's all stove
in and we took a torpedo midships."

"I can see it, Bart. Look down."

"Jesus!" The jagged hole was awash, half out of the water,
and the submarine was heavily down by the bow. Mancuso
wondered how she could float at all, but it wasn't the time to
question why.

"Come over here, Wally, and get the raft out."

"On the way. Fire and rescue is standing by, I—there's our
other friend," Chambers said.

The *Pogy* surfaced three hundred yards directly ahead of
the *October*.

"Pogy says the area's clear. Nobody here but us. Heard that

one before?" Chambers laughed mirthlessly. "How about we radio in?"

"No, let's see if we can handle it first." The *Dallas* approached the *October*. Within minutes Mancuso's command submarine was seventy yards to port, and ten men on a raft were struggling across the chop. Up to this time only a handful of men aboard the *Dallas* had known what was going on. Now everyone knew. He could see his men pointing and talking. What a story they had.

Damage was not as bad as they had feared. The torpedo room had not flooded—a sensor damaged by the impact had given a false reading. The forward ballast tanks were permanently vented to the sea, but the submarine was so big and her ballast tanks so subdivided that she was only eight feet down at the bow. The list to port was only a nuisance. In two hours the radio room leak had been plugged, and after a lengthy discussion among Ramius, Melekhin, and Mancuso it was decided that they could dive again if they kept their speed down and did not go below thirty meters. They'd be late getting to Norfolk.

THE EIGHTEENTH DAY

MONDAY, 20 DECEMBER

The Red October

Ryan again found himself atop the sail thanks to Ramius, who said that he had earned it. In return for the favor, Jack had helped the captain up the ladder to the bridge station. Mancuso was with them. There was now an American crew below in the control room, and the engine room complement had been supplemented so that there was something approaching a normal steaming watch. The leak in the radio room had not been fully contained, but it was above the waterline. The compartment had been pumped out, and the *October*'s list had eased to fifteen degrees. She was still down by the bow, which was partially compensated for when the intact ballast tanks were blown dry. The crumpled bow gave the submarine a decidedly asymmetrical wake, barely visible in the moonless, cloud-laden sky. The *Dallas* and the *Pogy* were still submerged, somewhere aft, sniffing for additional interference as they neared Capes Henry and Charles.

Somewhere farther aft an LNG (liquified natural gas) carrier was approaching the passage, which the coast guard had closed to all normal traffic in order to allow the floating bomb to travel without interference all the way to the LNG terminal at Cove Point, Maryland—or so the story went. Ryan wondered how the navy had persuaded the ship's skipper to fake engine trouble or somehow delay his arrival. They were six hours late. The navy must have been nervous as all hell until they had finally surfaced forty minutes earlier and been spotted immediately by a circling Orion.

The red and green buoy lights winked at them, dancing on the chop. Forward he could see the lights of the Chesapeake Bay Bridge-Tunnel, but there were no moving automobile lights. The CIA had probably staged a messy wreck to shut it down, maybe a tractor-trailer or two full of eggs or gasoline. Something creative.

"You've never been to America before," Ryan said, just to make conversation.

"No, never to a Western country. Cuba once, many years ago."

Ryan looked north and south. He figured they were inside the capes now. "Well, welcome home, Captain Ramius. Speaking for myself, sir, I'm damned glad you're here."

"And happier that you are here," Ramius observed.

Ryan laughed out loud. "You can bet your ass on that. Thanks again for letting me up here."

"You have earned it, Ryan."

"The name's Jack, sir."

"Short for John, is it?" Ramius asked. "John is the same as Ivan, no?"

"Yes, sir, I believe it is." Ryan didn't understand why Ramius' face broke into a smile.

"Tug approaching." Mancuso pointed.

The American captain had superb eyesight. Ryan didn't see the boat through his binoculars for another minute. It was a shadow, darker that the night, perhaps a mile away.

"Sceptre, this is tug *Paducah.* Do you read? Over."

Mancuso took the docking radio from his pocket. *"Paducah,* this is *Sceptre.* Good morning, sir." He was speaking in an English accent.

"Please form up on me, Captain, and follow us in."

"Jolly good, *Paducah*. Will do. Out."

HMS *Sceptre* was the name of an English attack submarine. he must be somewhere remote, Ryan thought, patrolling the alklands or some other faraway location so that her arrival at Iorfolk would be just another routine occurrence, not unusual nd difficult to disprove. Evidently they were thinking about ome agent's being suspicious of a strange sub's arrival.

The tug approached to within a few hundred yards, then arned to lead them in at five knots. A single red tuck light howed.

"I hope we don't run into any civilian traffic," Mancuso aid.

"But you said the harbor entrance was closed," Ramius said.

"Might be some guy in a little sailboat out there. The public as free passage through the yard to the Dismal Swamp Canal, nd they're damned near invisible on radar. They slip through ll the time."

"This is crazy."

"It's a free country, Captain," Ryan said softly. "It will take ou some time to understand what free really means. The word s often misused, but in time you will see just how wise your ecision was."

"Do you live here, Captain Mancuso?" Ramius asked.

"Yes, my squadron is based in Norfolk. My home is in 'irginia Beach, down that way. I probably won't get there nytime soon. They're going to send us right back out. Only hing they can do. So, I miss another Christmas at home. Part f the job."

"You have a family?"

"Yes, Captain. A wife and two sons. Michael, eight, and)ominic, four. They're used to having daddy away."

"And you, Ryan?"

"Boy and a girl. Guess I will be home for Christmas. Sorry, Commander. You see, for a while there I had my doubts. After hings get settled down some I'd like to get this whole bunch >gether for something special."

"Big dinner bill," Mancuso chuckled.

"I'll charge it to the CIA."

"And what will the CIA do with us?" Ramius asked.

"As I told you, Captain, a year from now you will be livin
your own lives, wherever you wish to live, doing whateve
you wish to do."

"Just so?"

"Just so. We take pride in our hospitality, sir, and if I eve
get transferred back from London, you and your men are we
come in my home at any time."

"Tug's turning to port." Mancuso pointed. The conversatio
was taking too maudlin a turn for him.

"Give the order, Captain," Ramius said. It was, after al
Mancuso's harbor.

"Left five degrees rudder," Mancuso said into the micro
phone.

"Left five degrees rudder, aye," the helmsman responded
"Sir, my rudder is left five degrees."

"Very well."

The *Paducah* turned into the main channel, past the *Sara
toga,* which was sitting under a massive crane, and heade
towards a mile-long line of piers in the Norfolk Naval Shipyard
The channel was totally empty, just the *October* and the tug
Ryan wondered if the *Paducah* had a normal complement o
enlisted men or a crew made entirely of admirals. He woul
not have given odds either way.

Norfolk, Virginia

Twenty minutes later they were at their destination. The Eigh
Ten Dock was a new dry dock built to service the *Ohio*-clas
fleet ballistic missile submarines, a huge concrete box ove
eight hundred feet long, larger than it had to be, covered wit
a steel roof so that spy satellites could not see if it were occupie
or not. It was in the maximum security section of the base
and one had to pass several security barriers of armed guards—
marines, not the usual civilian guards—to get near the dock
much less into it.

"All stop," Mancuso ordered.

"All stop, aye."

The *Red October* had been slowing for several minutes, an
it was another two hundred yards before she came to a comple
halt. The *Paducah* curved around to starboard to push her bo
round. Both captains would have preferred to power their ow

way in, but the damaged bow made maneuvering tricky. The diesel-powered tug took five minutes to line the bow up properly, headed directly into the water-filled box. Ramius gave the engine command himself, the last for this submarine. She eased forward through the black water, passing slowly under the wide roof. Mancuso ordered his men topside to handle the lines tossed them by a handful of sailors on the rim of the lock, and the submarine came to a halt exactly in its center. Already the gate they had passed through was closing, and a canvas cover the size of a clipper's mainsail was being drawn across it. Only when cover was securely in place were the overhead lights switched on. Suddenly a group of thirty or so officers began screaming like fans at a ballgame. The only thing left out was the band.

"Finished with the engines," Ramius said in Russian to the crew in the maneuvering room, then switched to English with a trace of sadness in his voice. "So. We are here."

The overhead traveling crane moved down toward them and stopped to pick up the brow, which it brought around and laid carefully on the missile deck forward of the sail. The brow was hardly in place when a pair of officers with gold braid nearly to their elbows walked—ran—across it. Ryan recognized the one in front. It was Dan Foster.

The chief of naval operations saluted the quarterdeck as he got to the edge of the gangway, then looked up at the sail. "Request permission to come aboard, sir."

"Permission is—"

"Granted," Mancuso prompted.

"Permission is granted," Ramius said loudly.

Foster jumped aboard and hurried up the exterior ladder on the sail. It wasn't easy, since the ship still had a sizable list to port. Foster was puffing as he reached the control station.

"Captain Ramius, I'm Dan Foster." Mancuso helped the CNO over the bridge coaming. The control station was suddenly crowded. The American admiral and the Russian captain shook hands, then Foster shook Mancuso's. Jack came last.

"Looks like the uniform needs a little work, Ryan. So does the face."

"Yeah, well, we ran into some trouble."

"So I see. What happened?"

Ryan didn't wait for the explanation. He went below without

excusing himself. It wasn't his fraternity. In the control room the men were standing around exchanging grins, but they were quiet, as if they feared the magic of the moment would evaporate all too quickly. For Ryan it already had. He looked for the deck hatch and climbed up through it, taking with him everything he'd brought aboard. He walked up the gangway against traffic. No one seemed to notice him. Two hospital corpsmen were carrying a stretcher, and Ryan decided to wait on the dock for Williams to be brought out. The British officer had missed everything, having only been fully conscious for the past three hours. As Ryan waited he smoked his last Russian cigarette. The stretcher, with Williams tied onto it, was man-handled out. Noyes and the medical corpsmen from the sub tagged along.

"How are you feeling?" Ryan walked alongside the stretcher toward the ambulance.

"Alive," Williams said, looking pale and thin. "And you?"

"What I feel under my feet is solid concrete. Thank God for that!"

"And what he's going to feel is a hospital bed. Nice meeting you, Ryan," the doctor said briskly. "Let's move it, people." The corpsmen loaded the stretcher into an ambulance parked just inside the oversized doors. A minute later it was gone.

"You Commander Ryan, sir?" a marine sergeant asked after saluting.

Ryan returned the salute. "Yes."

"I have a car waiting for you, sir. Will you follow me please?"

"Lead on, Sergeant."

The car was a gray navy Chevy that took him directly to the Norfolk Naval Air Station. Here Ryan boarded a helicopter. By now he was too tired to care if it were a sleigh with reindeer attached. During the thirty-five-minute trip to Andrews Air Force Base Ryan sat alone in the back, staring into space. He was met by another car at the base and driven straight to Langley.

CIA Headquarters

It was four in the morning when Ryan finally entered Greer's office. The admiral was there, along with Moore and Ritter

he admiral handed him something to drink. Not coffee, Wild
urkey bourbon whiskey. All three senior executives took his
and.

"Sit down, boy," Moore said.

"Damned well done." Greer smiled.

"Thank you." Ryan took a long pull on the drink. "Now
hat?"

"Now we debrief you," Greer answered.

"No, sir. Now I fly the hell home."

Greer's eyes twinkled as he pulled a folder from a coat
ocket and tossed it in Ryan's lap. "You're booked out of Dulles
7:05 A.M. First flight to London. And you really should wash
o, change your clothes, and collect your Skiing Barbie."

Ryan tossed the rest of the drink off. The sudden slug of
hiskey made his eyes water, but he was able to refrain from
oughing.

"Looks like that uniform got some hard use," Ritter ob-
erved.

"So did the rest of me." Jack reached inside the jacket and
ulled out the automatic pistol. "This got some use, too."

"The GRU agent? He wasn't taken off with the rest of the
ew?" Moore asked.

"You *knew* about him? You knew and you didn't get word
me, for Christ's sake!"

"Settle down, son," Moore said. "We missed connections
y half an hour. Bad luck, but you made it. That's what counts."

Ryan was too tired to scream, too tired to do much of
nything. Greer took out a tape recorder and a yellow pad full
f questions.

"Williams, the British officer, is in a bad way," Ryan said,
vo hours later. "The doc says he'll make it, though. The sub
n't going anywhere. Bow's all crunched in, and there's a
retty nice hole where the torpedo got us. They were right
oout the *Typhoon*, Admiral, the Russians built that baby strong,
ank God. You know, there may be people left alive on that
lfa..."

"Too bad," Moore said.

Ryan nodded slowly. "I figured that. I don't know that I
ke it, sir, leaving men to die like that."

"Nor do we," Judge Moore said, "nor do we, but if we were
) rescue someone from her, well, then everything we've—"

everything you've been through would be for nothing. Wou
you want that?"

"It's a chance in a thousand anyway," Greer said.

"I don't know," Ryan said, finishing off his third drink ar
feeling it. He had expected Moore to be uninterested in chec
ing the *Alfa* for signs of life. Greer had surprised him. So, th
old seaman had been corrupted by this affair—or just by beir
at the CIA—into forgetting the seaman's code. And what d
this say about Ryan? "I just don't know."

"It's a war, Jack," Ritter said, more kindly than usual, "
real war. You did well, boy."

"In a war you do well to come home alive," Ryan stoo
"and that, gentlemen, is what I plan to do, right now."

"Your things are in the head." Greer checked his watcl
"You have time to shave if you want."

"Oh, almost forgot." Ryan reached inside his collar to pu
out the key. He handed it to Greer. "Doesn't look like mucl
does it? You can kill fifty million people with that. 'My nan
is Ozymandias, king of kings! Look on my works, ye might
and despair!'" Ryan headed for the washroom, knowing l
had to be drunk to quote Shelley.

They watched him disappear. Greer switched off the tar
machine, looking at the key in his hand. "Still want to tal
him to see the president?"

"No, not a good idea," Moore said. "Boy's half smashe
not that I blame him a bit. Get him on the plane, James. We'
send a team to London tomorrow or the next day to finish tl
debriefing."

"Good." Greer looked into his empty glass. "Kind of ear
in the day for this, isn't it?"

Moore finished off his third. "I suppose. But then it's bee
a fairly good day, and the sun's not even up yet. Let's go, Bol
We have an operation of sorts to run."

Norfolk Naval Shipyard

Mancuso and his men boarded the *Paducah* before dawn ar
were ferried back to the *Dallas*. The 688-class attack submari
sailed immediately and was back underwater before the su
rose. The *Pogy*, which had never entered port, would comple
her deployment without her corpsman aboard. Both submarin

had orders to stay out thirty more days, during which their crewmen would be encouraged to forget everything they had seen, heard, or wondered about.

The *Red October* sat alone with the dry dock draining around her, guarded by twenty armed marines. This was not unusual in the Eight-Ten Dock. Already a select group of engineers and technicians was inspecting her. The first items taken off were her cipher books and machines. They would be in National Security Agency headquarters at Fort Meade before noon.

Ramius, his officers, and their personal gear were taken by bus to the same airfield Ryan had used. An hour later they were in a CIA safe house in the rolling hills south of Charlottesville, Virginia. They went immediately to bed except for two men, who stayed awake watching cable television, already amazed at what they saw of life in the United States.

Dulles International Airport

Ryan missed the dawn. He boarded a TWA 747 that left Dulles on time, at 7:05 A.M. The sky was overcast, and when the aircraft burst through the cloud layer into sunlight, Ryan did something he had never done before. For the first time in his life, Jack Ryan fell asleep on an airplane.

ABOUT THE AUTHOR

He has had a private chat with the President of the United States who proclaimed himself to be an avid fan of *The Hunt for Red October*. He has lunched with the White House staff. His novel has been a top seller at the Pentagon. Yet the author in question is neither a former intelligence nor naval officer. Rather, Tom Clancy is an insurance broker from a small town in Maryland whose only previously published writing was a letter to the editor and a three-page article about the MX missile. Clancy always wanted to write a suspense novel, and a newspaper article about a mutiny on a Soviet frigate gave him the initial idea for *Red October*. He did extensive research about Soviet–American naval strategies and submarine technology. Then, in the time he could spare from his insurance business, Clancy sat down at his typewriter and wrote. The rest is history ... and now Clancy is at work on a major new novel.